RAMSEY CAMPBELL

SOMEBODY'S VOICE

This is a **FLAME TREE PRESS** book

Text copyright © 2021 Ramsey Campbell

FLAME TREE PRESS
6 Melbray Mews, London, SW6 3NS, UK
flametreepress.com

US sales, distribution and warehouse:
Simon & Schuster
simonandschuster.biz

UK distribution and warehouse:
Marston Book Services Ltd
marston.co.uk

Publisher's Note: This is a work of fiction. Names, characters, places, and incidents are a product of the author's imagination. Locales and public names are sometimes used for atmospheric purposes. Any resemblance to actual people, living or dead, or to businesses, companies, events, institutions, or locales is completely coincidental.

Thanks to the Flame Tree Press team, including:
Taylor Bentley, Frances Bodiam, Federica Ciaravella, Don D'Auria,
Chris Herbert, Josie Karani, Molly Rosevear, Mike Spender,
Cat Taylor, Maria Tissot, Nick Wells, Gillian Whitaker.

The cover is created by Flame Tree Studio with
thanks to Nik Keevil and Shutterstock.com.
The font families used are Avenir and Bembo.

Flame Tree Press is an imprint of Flame Tree Publishing Ltd
flametreepublishing.com

A copy of the CIP data for this book is available from the British Library
and the Library of Congress.

HB ISBN: 978-1-78758-608-6
US PB ISBN: 978-1-78758-606-2
UK PB ISBN: 978-1-78758-607-9
ebook ISBN: 978-1-78758-609-3

Printed and bound in Great Britain by Clays Ltd, Elcograf S.p.A.

RAMSEY CAMPBELL

SOMEBODY'S VOICE

FLAME TREE PRESS
London & New York

For Priya and Mark –
at least you can believe the dedication!

CARLA

My stepfather nearly killed my mother, and I used to wish he'd killed me. Now I'm glad I'm here to tell the truth, but first I want to tell some about my father.

"My queen and my princess, your carriage awaits." They're the first words I remember. My father meant his taxi, and every Sunday he drove us to St Brendan's and took us for a treat after mass. I think I was three when I learned the priest's name – Father Brendan. I was amazed to think he owned the church, which was so much bigger than our little house that I couldn't fit my mind around the idea. I dabbed at my eyes with my Sunday handkerchief, which was perfumed with Persil, and whispered "Mummy, he's sad."

"Hush, child. You know you mustn't talk in church," she said, and then "Who is?"

"The man at the front. Does he live here all by himself?"

"He doesn't live here," my mother said and aimed an embarrassed laugh at the people next to her in the pew. "It's God's house."

"Won't God let him stay in it? That's mean."

"You talk to her, Bertie," my mother said across me. "You've got the patience."

"Shush now," my father said, "and I'll tell you after we've thanked God we can go."

"Bertie," my mother said as if she was tired of being shocked by him.

Once everyone had thanked God that the mass was ended, we found the priest waiting outside. My father shook his hand while Father Brendan patted my head with the other one, which felt as soft and light as an empty glove. "Our Carla was having a weep about you," my father said.

The priest fondled me under my chin. "Why was that, now?"

"Isn't it your house? It's got your name on."

"I'm not the saint, young lady. I'm just a man."

"And he's got a house of his own, princess."

I still needed to find out "Who do you live with, then?"

"Say father, Carla," my mother said. "She's still learning, father."

I didn't want to call him that when he wasn't mine. "She's growing up like they all do," he said. "My child, I live with God."

This sounded like living alone, since I'd been told God was everywhere. "No," I persisted, "I mean people."

"I live with all my flock, and that means you, Carla. When you're older you'll come to me for guidance."

I might have asked more questions, but my mother was growing restless with embarrassment. As we headed for the taxi my father said "He doesn't mind living on his own, princess. Priests aren't like us, some of them."

Even then I didn't know how much of that to believe, but my mother shook her head to warn me not to argue. "Mum for mum," my father used to say if I didn't comply. She didn't even come up to his shoulder, but her size seemed to condense her fierceness. She was so angular that I once made a figure of her out of building blocks, and my father laughed at how much it looked like her till she gave him that shake of the head. As well as tall, he was broad enough for two of me to hide behind, and his features were so generous there was barely room for them. "When God was handing faces out," he told me once, "he gave me extra for good luck," but my mother shook her head at the joke.

I don't know where he drove us to after I'd talked to Father Brendan – maybe Speke Hall in Liverpool, where he told me a guide in a Victorian costume was a ghost, and I ran out into the sunlight because the corridor was so dark, though I was never afraid of the dark at home. Or perhaps we ended up in Chester, where he walked around the city walls talking what some people thought was Latin till my mother hushed him: "Dinus restaurantum fulltum plumpbum...." Or it could have been Freshfield, where red squirrels leapt from tree to tree and I saw one blaze up as the sunlight caught it. "Watch out or they'll be setting the forest on fire," my father said. At the end of these outings we'd drive home for my mother's Sunday dinner, which made the house smell of cauliflower no matter what the meat was. As soon as my father finished mopping his lips with his square of Sunday linen, which my mother insisted only common people called a napkin rather than a serviette, he would head for the taxi office. "Forgive me, your majesty," he would say while my mother sighed at hearing it again, "the people have need of your coachman."

He often made her laugh or frown or comment fiercely when he told us over dinner about his day at Reliablest Cars, a name he often turned into Really Not So Blessed. "You'll know which words are real when you're at university, Carly," he used to say, though I was only a toddler. He'd tell us about searching for an address on a new estate where the streets all looked alike and the street names weren't much better, or how he'd turned up for a fare to find twice as many passengers as the taxi would take and the ones who had to wait for a second car blamed him. Once he came home late because he'd driven twenty miles to return a purse with several hundred pounds in it a lady had left on the seat. "I hope she gave you a decent reward," my mother said.

"She offered but I wouldn't let her. She'd already given me a good tip, and now here's one for you, Carly. Never take from somebody when you can give, because that'll make you happier."

"You could have given it to us, Bertie," my mother objected. "She sounds better off than we are."

"We're happy, though, aren't we? You don't want me turning into Limo Man."

"Of course I don't want him," my mother said as if he'd suggested she might be unfaithful, though she could just have been telling him not to perform his impression of Malcolm Randal.

Mr Randal owned the taxi firm and drove the only limousine, and behaved as though this made him better than all the other drivers put together. My father used to imitate him by squeezing his face small and strangling his voice like air leaking out of a balloon. "Curtsy costs nothing," he would say, and for years I thought his boss bowed at the knees as my father pretended he did, but it was how Mr Randal said a different word. "But rudeness costs us rides," he would remind the drivers, it seemed like at least once a day. "Waste is a sin," he would squeak as well, and my father said the receptionists gobbled their sandwiches for fear that the boss would think they'd had enough and finish off their lunch, as he apparently once had. He only picked up customers he thought were superior, leaving the lesser drivers to deal with calls he felt weren't worthy of him. According to my father, he'd been known to turn down passengers if he disapproved of how they dressed. "Knees oughtn't to be seen by anyone except your husband," my father made him whinny. "They're a sin."

My mother used to laugh at the show he put on, but I could tell she was being dutiful. That seemed to drive him to carry on till she protested "You're giving me a headache." I wondered how often his jokes did, if that was even what they were. When he found her vacuuming his taxi one Sunday morning before church, he cried "The queen mustn't lower herself. That's the coachman's job." I thought she would be pleased, but she said "No need to let the whole street know. You take everything too far."

I thought she felt like that about the presents he brought home. "What have I got for my ladies today?" he wanted us to wonder, and then he'd produce the answer from behind his back − a box of chocolates or some earrings for my mother and one of the metal puzzles I used to like, where you had to find the secret way to separate the twisted bits of metal. I would hug him for the present and hug my mother too in case she felt left out, but also I was trying to make sure they didn't argue. When they did it was nearly always about money − the way he spent it when he didn't have to and didn't care enough how much he made − which left me feeling our life wasn't as secure as they wanted me to think.

I was four when I heard him talking about starting his own taxi firm. My mother thought he shouldn't try to compete with Mr Randal's, which only made him more determined. I wondered if he made fun of his boss because he felt he could do better than Mr Randal. When he went to the bank for a loan they said he didn't earn enough and hadn't saved enough. "They only lend to people who've already got it," he told my mother. "I'll show them I can make it or my name's not Bertie Batchelor."

I didn't realise how serious he was till he started cutting our Sunday outings short so he could spend extra hours on the road. Before long he went to Reliablest as soon as he'd driven us home from church. Some weeks he was on call every day and still didn't get in before midnight, because I heard my mother say so. She was worried working all those hours might affect his driving, which made me anxious too. I started lying awake and praying he would be safe, and sometimes I woke when he came in. Once I heard my mother greet him by protesting "Aren't you ever going to be home?"

"I'm doing this for us, Elaine. I promise you'll like what it brings."

"Come and have your dinner," she said like a penance she was giving both of them.

On my first day at school I could tell his driving made her nervous. I couldn't see anything wrong with it, and starting school didn't worry me either. The school opposite our house wasn't Catholic, and the one my parents chose for me was most of a mile away. I would be walking to it with my mother, but since this was a special occasion my father drove us. "You show them what you're made of, princess," he said and gave me a hug that felt as if he meant it to last all day. "You'll have lots to tell us when we pick you up."

My mother's hug felt more like urging me to do well. My parents stood at the railings while I found Bridie Shea, my friend from next door. They had their arms round each other, and my father was offering a handkerchief my mother waved away so nobody would notice her rubbing her eyes with her knuckles. "She won't be our little girl much longer," I heard her say. Bridie wanted to show me the glittery bag she was wearing on her back, and when I looked for my parents again, they'd gone.

The day wasn't much of an adventure. We all sat on the floor to be told what school was going to be like, and then we had to sort things by their colours to show the teachers if we could. We did get taken to the dining hall before everybody else came in for lunch, and the dinner ladies served us what they thought we should eat, to let us know how to ask next time. I made them laugh by asking why they were called dinner ladies when they were serving lunch. One of them said I was the first person who'd asked, but I didn't know whether any of them were laughing at me. In the afternoon we were allowed to choose what to do, and I drew my father driving a limousine with *Batchelor Taxis* written on the side. Miss O'Hagan, the teacher, said it was lovely and I should take it to show him, and she'd make sure she asked for him next time she phoned for a taxi. When we'd all finished our activities she read us a book called *The Little Red Car*, about a car that took its driver safely home when they got lost in a fog, and that was the end of my first day at school.

I ran out to show my parents the Batchelor Taxis picture. All along the railings grownups were waving to their children, but I couldn't see my parents. I knew my father never liked to be late picking someone up, but that meant he had been sometimes, and I told myself he was making money from a fare that would help him own a business, though I wouldn't have put it in those words. I saw Bridie's father beckoning to her, and then I realised he wanted me as well. His face looked as if it couldn't quite get rid of a smile because it didn't know how else to look. "Carla, you're coming home with us," he said.

"My dad's coming in a minute. He's taking me home."

"He isn't, love. You can play with Bridie at ours."

The way his face seemed to be struggling to keep hold of its expression made me uneasy. "I will when he's brought me home," I said.

"I told you that's not happening. Don't make a scene, now. You like playing with Bridie. You like coming to our house."

His voice had begun to sound as false as I thought his face looked, and I backed away from the railings in case he made a grab for me. A mother frowned at me and then at him. "What's the trouble?"

"He wants me to go with him," I said. "I'm supposed to wait for my dad."

"Your dad's Bertie from the taxis, isn't he? I saw him bring you this morning." I thought I could tell my father he was famous till she said "He carried my mam's shopping all the way up to her flat and wouldn't take a tip."

As I decided I wouldn't relay her comments to my father while my mother could hear, the lady frowned at Mr Shea again. "He's a nice man, your dad," she told me. "You wait for him and I'll wait with you, chick."

Mr Shea let out a sigh that came close to breathing in her face. "Please excuse me, but you don't know the situation."

"I hope it isn't what it looks like. You come here to me, chick."

"Just wait there, Carla. Bridie, stay with her," Mr Shea said and reached for the lady's shoulder. "Please just come with me and listen."

"Don't you think you can handle me," she said and fended off his hand with a shrug that looked disgusted. She turned her back as they began a conversation too low for me to hear over the babble of the other children. Soon she swung round, and I saw her looking for her own child, and wondered why she didn't want to look at me. When she did she put on a smile her tight lips fixed before she said "Better do what he says, chick. They'll explain to you at home."

"But I don't want to go with him," I protested so loud that several parents turned to stare.

"You do as grownups tell you." She grabbed her daughter and ushered her away at speed. "This gentleman is only looking after you," she called without looking back.

"Trust me, Carla," Mr Shea said, "that's the gospel truth."

Perhaps the mention of the Bible convinced me I should, because I didn't think anybody who invoked it could be lying. I was anxious to be home, where at least I was promised an explanation. When I ventured out of the gates Mr Shea led Bridie and me to his car. As soon as we climbed in he said "Put your seat belts on."

"Dad, you never tell me to."

"I'm telling you now. See, Carla has."

I only had so we'd be home faster. I would have put Bridie's on for her if she hadn't heeded the warning in his voice, though I saw it puzzled her. "What did you do at school today?" Mr Shea said as he started the car, but I didn't like how bright he was making his voice sound and besides, I wanted to save the answer for my parents. I let Bridie tell her tale, but she'd only got as far as lunchtime when we reached home. A police car was parked outside the Sheas' house, and so Mr Shea had to park outside ours. The instant he stopped the car I released my safety belt, because it made me feel held back from learning what was going on. As soon as I climbed out of the car I saw my mother in the front room.

Mrs Shea was with her, and they were sitting as still as the waxworks my father took us to see one Sunday in a museum. Their faces looked as if they couldn't move or didn't want to, but their eyes were glinting like the ones the waxworks had. When I ran into our tiny stone-flagged garden I saw their eyes were wet, and heard a man's low voice. What was my father telling them to make them cry? I was afraid he might have lost his job or crashed the taxi, since I couldn't see it anywhere. I thought of showing them my picture to cheer them up, but I'd left it in the car. "Come away, Carla," Mr Shea called, which made my mother glance towards the window. As she caught sight of me her face wavered and then tried to be more like a waxwork. "Go away, child," she said, and louder "Go away for now."

She sounded like nobody I knew, which dismayed and frightened me. "Mummy, I want to come in."

"You can't at the moment. Go and play with Bridie. Mrs Shea's giving you your tea."

This might have sounded like a treat if her voice hadn't grown harsh. "Daddy, let me in," I pleaded, sidling alongside the window to find him. The man sitting forward on the chair the curtain had hidden from me was a policeman. "Where's my dad?" I cried. "I want to see him."

"You're never going to." I didn't think my mother meant me to hear this, but then she raised her voice. "For God's sake go away, child, till I come and get you."

I knew taking the Lord's name in vain was a sin, and hearing her do it disconcerted me so much that I fled. Mr Shea had unlocked his front door, and I followed Bridie in. He was about to close the door when I heard my mother come out of our house. "I'm going to see him," she said, holding her voice stiff.

Mr Shea tried to catch me, but I dodged past the door and ran to her. "You're going to my dad. Please, I want to."

"You can't, Carla." My mother's face seemed to clench around her eyes, squeezing trickles out of them. "Just remember him the way he was."

"But what is he now?"

"He's in heaven, child. You say a prayer so he will be."

I couldn't say a prayer or even speak. I clung to her and pressed my face against her stomach, which smelled of cigarette ash that she'd spilled on herself. As much as anything, this departure from her usual fastidiousness upset me. I pulled my head back and managed to ask "Mummy, what happened to him?"

"They've killed him," my mother said, glaring at the officer who had followed Mrs Shea out of our house. "The police killed your father."

ALEX

"In three hundred yards turn left into Manly Lane." But when the rush-hour traffic in the unfamiliar town lets Alex reach the junction, it's blocked by a diversion. Since Manly Lane is a one-way street, he can't enter by the far end. The next road on the left brandishes a No Entry sign, and the phone urges him to backtrack. When the car manages to crawl to the next junction, he's able to turn left into a tangle of back streets where most of the pedestrians appear to think traffic shouldn't be allowed or isn't even there, to judge by how they amble across his path. The route confuses the phone even more than it bewilders him, and he silences the robot voice before dropping the mobile into his breast pocket. At last he escapes onto a main road, and is heading for Manly Lane once more when the phone announces an unknown caller. Lee slips a hand like a caress into his pocket to retrieve the phone and says "Hello?"

"Sorry, have I typed you wrong? That isn't Alex."

"Not unless we've switched identities," he says. "It's my partner Lee."

"This is Janet at the bookshop. Sorry to ask, but could you use the back door? We've got people at the front protesting about your book."

"You don't want me to thank them for the advertising."

"Best not antagonise them if you don't mind. Whereabouts are you?"

"Just coming to the wrong end of your road."

"Go past." This sounds like a warning until Janet adds "Then take the first right and you're bound to find some parking."

As Alex coasts past Manly Lane he sees pickets poling slogans, some of which Lee reads aloud. "Tell Truth without a comma Not Tales," she says and corrects the others too. "Our Lives Aren't with no apostrophe Fiction, Tell Your Own Story Not Ours with an apostrophe...." Her long face framed by straight red hair cut short across her high brows makes it plain that she's amused, a state her large dark eyes and wide lips seem constantly to hope for. The right turn leads to a multistorey car park, where Alex finds space on the second level. On the way past Manly Lane he slows down to read the placards, and Lee takes his arm to propel him onwards before anyone recognises him. A sign she didn't read to him takes his fancy: WE ARE NOT MATERIAL. "Maybe some of my critics on Twitter are showing their faces at last," he says. "They don't look immaterial to me."

"Depends how much you feel they ought to be."

"They can't realise they're publicity. That's they're with an apostrophe in case you were wondering."

"Their with an i would work as well."

They've performed this sort of routine ever since Lee began copyediting his books among the many her job brings. As they find an alley that leads behind Texts they hear demonstrators chanting on the far side of the bookshop. "No semicolon no," Alex punctuates the chorus, "semicolon no."

"Writers don't need those. Colonisation isn't good."

"I can think of a few who'd give you an argument, except they wouldn't dare."

"So long as you do when you think you should."

"That's a collectible event," Alex says and rings the bell beside a wordless door. "No colon no colon no."

"Here's the girl who'll leave you with no colon."

"Just keep your hands off my brackets." He gives her time to anticipate his saying "Except in bed."

A young woman in trousers and a Texts T-shirt opens the door as Lee wrinkles her long elegant nose at him. "Is everything all right?" the bookseller says, not without alarm.

"We'd say so, wouldn't we? Alex and Lee, who helped me find my voice."

"Janet," Janet says, shaking hands with both of them at once as if to demonstrate efficiency. "We can wait in the office."

In the room to which she ushers them a desk is strewn with stacks of books, while the walls are patched with posters and sketches of mountain ranges – performance charts, on one of which a lonely member of staff is stranded in the foothills. Janet hangs their coats on a single prong protruding from a laden board and offers them wine from a box in a dwarfish refrigerator. "Don't drink too much before you read," Lee says.

"I never do." When she lowers her delicate brows to emphasise the look she gives him, Alex admits "Not for years."

"Never's longer," Lee says and tells Janet "Sometimes I can't stop editing."

Alex sips his drink and restrains himself to doing so several unhurried times before he glances at his watch. He ought to be performing by now, and abruptly Janet appears to agree, though he hopes she's more enthusiastic than her words. "We may as well go through."

Of the several dozen unfolded chairs that face a podium between shelves marked Fantasy and Crime, more than half are occupied. To the left of the central aisle the front row is empty apart from a tall man sprawling with his legs thrust out and wide. His stubbly face looks hammered broad and almost flat, spreading all the features, and his scalp resembles a translucent cover for a greyish hint of hair. Most of the rest of him is encased in black: polo-neck, jeans, socks, shoes. He sees Janet escort Lee to a reserved seat in the other half of the front row and then watches Alex take the solitary chair on the low podium, where a squat table bearing a bottle of water and a copy of his latest novel scrapes his calves when he tries to stretch his legs. As he opens the bottle, which is so full that a liberated trickle runs under his shirt cuff, Janet stands in front of him. "We're delighted to welcome Alex Grand, bestselling author of the Palgrave Patten series," she says. "He's going to talk about his work and read from his new book *Nobody Sees* and then take questions."

She leads the applause as she makes for a seat next to Lee. The bald sprawler donates just a pair of sluggish claps. Perhaps he's withholding enthusiasm until he feels impressed, which makes him a challenge to be tackled. Alex eyes him while explaining that in *Nobody Sees* Palgrave Patten's sidekick Dyann is away on a sabbatical from teaching film noir, and so he's helped by his latest client, who wants Patten to find a girl who was abused as a child. The search leads deep into the world of paedophiles, with Andrew the client posing as one, and Patten feels soiled by the experience despite arranging numerous arrests. None of this appears to gratify the bald spectator, who may be distracted by the chanting in the street. As Alex wonders if this will impair his reading it fades away, and he sees the placards sink beyond the window on the far side of the shop as the demonstrators disperse. He reads from the chapter where Andrew talks to Sandy, the victim he hired Patten to track down, only to leave her unidentified and hidden. "His reason's on the last page," Alex says and shuts the book.

Janet steps in front of him to ask for questions, and the bald man speaks at once. "He's talking to himself."

"He's been talking to everyone," Lee objects.

"I don't mean Mr Grand." The man gives her no more favourable a look than he did when she sat down. "You're with him."

"I shouldn't think I'm the only one."

"Clever as him too." This is plainly not intended as a compliment. "You came with Mr Grand."

Lee reacts to the way he makes it sound like a gibe. "Yes, that's his name."

"Just Alex is the rest, is it? Hiding his gender to go with his book."

"I've used it ever since I was published," Alex retorts. "Lee cut it down for me."

"Lee." The man makes this sound suspect too, having glanced at her. "What are you saying the rest of you is?" he challenges Alex.

"Alexander Evelyn Grand. We decided shorter was better, us and the publishers."

The man greets the expanded name with an aborted laugh, which provokes Lee to demand "Since you're so interested in names, what's yours?"

"I'm ToM."

He pronounces it not just with pride but with considerable emphasis on the last letter. "Tom," Lee says with none.

"ToM with a capital M." More fiercely still he says "M for man and TM for TransMission."

"You were outside picketing before." Lee clearly feels she should have realised sooner. "You had the sign about material."

In front of the podium Janet turns her head so vigorously that Alex sees the action ridge her neck. "I'm afraid we'll have to ask you to leave," she tells ToM.

"Don't send him out on my account," Alex says. "I'm happy to have a debate."

"That's very generous of you," Janet says but appeals to the audience. "Who has the next question?"

A woman on the back row calls out "I didn't understand the business about talking to himself."

"Andrew in the book, he's Sandy," ToM says at once. "She's supposed to have transitioned because she was abused, and all that conversation he read you is really just one person."

Alex regrets having encouraged him. "Well, thank you so much for giving my twist away."

"Think nothing of it, because we don't. It's not just a twist for all of us who've lived it."

"Alex, your book is about a lot more than that," Lee says and assures the audience "In some ways it's better second time around."

With all the pride he showed in his name ToM declares "I've read it less than once myself."

"Then how can you criticise," Lee protests, "if that's what you think you're doing?"

ToM aims his response at Alex. "Have you changed your gender?"

"I won't pretend I have."

"Then you're pretending when you try and write about it. I have and everybody in TransMission has, so don't you dare claim you know what it's like."

"I've never been burgled, I've never known anyone who was murdered, and nobody's objected to my writing about those."

"Then they should, because your sort of book trivialises crime, but I'm talking about something people live through their whole lives. It doesn't just happen to us, it's what we are."

"You seem to be missing a point," a man says behind Lee. "His book's fiction."

"That's exactly what it shouldn't be," ToM says and turns on Alex again. "Were you abused as a child?"

"I'm glad to say I never was."

"More lies." As Alex opens his mouth to deny it ToM says "That's all your book can be."

"I think fiction can be a way of telling truths."

"Yours can't," ToM says and grabs his widely outstretched knees. "Have you had enough of a debate?"

"Delighted to continue so long as we let other people in."

"I doubt they know any more about it than you do," ToM says, levering himself lankily to his feet. "If I've saved a few people from buying your book I've achieved something worth doing."

Alex picks up the bottle of water to take a nonchalant swallow, only for the plastic to creak in his fist, so loudly it sounds close to splintering. While ToM stalks towards the exit, members of the audience mime support for Alex, grimacing wryly or casting their upturned hands apart or scratching their heads, and Lee tilts hers like a depiction of unbalance. As the gestures subside Janet says "Any more questions?" and Alex is the first to laugh.

CARLA

"He was a good man, your Bertie. I was proud to have him on my team. I could always rely on him to do the job, not like some of them, and he'd go the extra mile for anyone. It saddens me to say it, Mrs Batchelor, but that's how he came to leave us. Another driver let a fare down and your Bertie was on his way to pick them up. I'm not saying he was speeding, but I understand the police were, and you'd think they should have had their siren on. There's still a dispute about who had the right of way at the crossroads, but I don't think it can make any difference now, do you? We mustn't blame our friends the police for what happened to your daddy, Carla. They were only trying to catch a bad man. Just so you know, Mrs Batchelor, I gave the driver who let me down his walking papers, though that won't bring your Bertie back. At least we know he's with the Saviour."

"We pray he is, Mr Randal. Tell Mr Randal what you do before you go to bed."

I felt awkward telling him, and I was afraid that if I opened my mouth a giggle would escape. Just now his visits to our house were the only thing that stopped my mother crying, but I kept remembering how my father had made fun of him. I thought he had at least twice as big a head as its features needed – his small eyes were set close together, and he didn't have much of a nose or mouth. I had the idea that the size of his mouth was the reason his voice was so high, and that his face had squeezed his shock of curly blond hair out of the top of his head like froth. At least he wasn't using any of the phrases my father used to say he did. I couldn't stay quiet while he and my mother expected an answer, and so I said "Pray daddy's gone to heaven."

"It's no laughing matter, Carla," Mr Randal said, because I hadn't managed to hold my voice quite steady. "Remember God sees everything you do."

"I expect the child's nervous, Mr Randal," my mother said, though

I thought that was truer of her. "And she's bound to be upset for a while."

"Shall I tell you what you ought to think, Carla?"

I was old enough to know I wasn't meant to take this as a question. "If you like."

"Please excuse her, Mr Randal. Of course she wants you to."

"Carla, everything that happens is what God wants to happen." He glanced at my mother as if she'd objected, and said "Everything that's not a sin."

I was wondering what I needed to be excused for, and found out as soon as he'd gone. "Don't ever let me down like that again," my mother said so furiously it seemed to dry her tears up. "Mr Randal's a kind man and you'd no reason on God's earth to laugh at him."

This felt disloyal to my father's memory. "Daddy did."

"He just needed to be cheerful when he was doing so much for us, God rest his soul." I thought my mother was trying to convince herself, and then she turned on me again. "Never you mind what grownups do," she said. "Your poor father's been taken from us, so just you be grateful his boss is being such a saviour."

Soon there were more reasons I was meant to be appreciative. Mr Randal brought me sweets whenever he came to visit, and gave my mother cuts of meat from a butcher, the brother of one of his drivers. I felt as if he was trying to improve on the presents my father used to bring home, and one day I overheard him lending money to my mother while the payment of my father's life insurance was delayed. I managed not to laugh at him any more except when I was in bed and nobody could hear, though I hoped my father might be hearing. Laughing at Mr Randal felt like keeping my father alive somewhere closer than heaven.

When my mother walked me home the day before the funeral she behaved as though she'd brought me a surprise. "Mr Randal is taking us in his limousine," she said.

She was making it sound like a treat for me, but I thought he was trying to outdo my father again. "Keep your feet off Mr Randal's seats," she said when he drove us in the car that smelled laundered, though I hadn't put them anywhere near. At the church he went in Father Brendan's pulpit to talk about my father. He repeated all the things he'd told my mother about him, which made me feel he'd rehearsed a performance. When he joined in the hymns we had to sing he kept trying to deepen his voice, but every time it sprang up high. My mother couldn't hold hers steady, and so as not to laugh at Mr Randal I pretended I was crying like her, only soon I didn't have to pretend.

After the mass he came with us to the grave, holding most of his umbrella over my mother while I huddled against her. It was raining so hard that the ropes the undertaker's men were using to lower the coffin nearly slipped through their hands, and when it landed in the grave it made a noise like squashing rotten fruit. My mother seemed not to know what to do, and so Mr Randal dropped soil on the coffin, which upset me more than the rest of the day had. "He's throwing mud at my daddy," I cried.

"I hope nobody thinks I'd do any such thing. You should never do that to anyone, Carla."

While I felt he was accusing me of more than I could grasp, I thought he was warning me not to denounce him. My mother threw some earth as if she had to copy him. "You as well, Carla," she whispered, but I fled out of Mr Randal's shelter and kept away from the grave, even though I was instantly drenched. He followed me with the umbrella and ushered us to the limousine, but I saw people throwing earth into the grave and thought they meant to cover up my father so he'd be forgotten. At the wake my mother sent me to take sandwiches around to everyone, but I could tell she had more to say to me. Once the mourners and Mr Randal had gone, she told me off for running away from the grave. "I can't imagine what Mr Randal must think of you," she said.

I tried not to care, even though he seemed to want to treat me like a daughter. He had no children of his own and wasn't married. He kept bringing me bags of sweets, till my mother said "You'll be turning her into a little pig, Mr Randal."

"Plump's attractive too," he said and touched my mother's arm. "Call me Malcolm."

I thought these sounded like the sayings my father joked about, but my mother simpered at them as if she'd forgotten she was a grownup. "Then you'll have to call me Elaine," she said.

He started bringing her flowers as well as meat, and every time she said he shouldn't, except the way she said it meant the opposite. They made the house smell like a graveyard, reminding me of the wreath he'd collected money from his drivers for. He'd put a notice on it saying *In memory of Bertie, our reliable friend who lived up to our name, from all at Reliablest Cars*. I'd thought it looked more like an advertisement for his firm than a tribute to my father, and now I felt the flowers he brought my mother were an advertisement for himself.

I don't know how many weeks it was after my father died that he first took her out for dinner. At first I didn't mind, because it meant I slept next door in Bridie's room and we could talk when we were supposed to be asleep. Then I started feeling as if my mother had some news for me. One day as I came out of school I saw she was ready to speak, though I couldn't tell if she was eager or determined. She made sure we'd left everyone else behind, and then she said "I hope you realise how much Mr Randal has done for us."

I thought she meant I was failing to appreciate him as much as she did. "I always say thank you."

"You like it when he comes to see us, don't you?"

"Yes," I said, partly because I saw her urging me to.

"Well, soon he will for good."

"What do you mean, mummy?"

"For the good of both of us. He'll be looking after us the way your father tried."

I was dismayed to think I understood. "He can't be my daddy," I protested.

"Of course he'll never take his place, but just be glad we'll be a family again." As if she was pretending I couldn't hear, my mother added "And he won't be such a worry as your father."

I resented this on my father's behalf. The next time Mr Randal gave me sweets my mother had to prompt "What do you say?"

My thanks must have sounded as forced as I felt, because Mr Randal took the bag out of my hand. "No treats for sullen little girls, are there, mother? I think someone ought to go to bed."

"You heard Mr Randal. Off you go and stay there till you learn to be polite."

"And don't forget to say your prayers," Mr Randal called after me.

As far as I was concerned I'd been polite to him. I hated him for rustling the bag of sweets as an extra punishment as I trudged out of the room. I crawled into bed without getting undressed, because my mother hadn't said I should. I prayed that my father was happy in heaven, and as I wondered what to pray about Mr Randal I heard the stairs creak. I thought my mother was coming to lecture me, but Mr Randal opened the door. "You aren't supposed to come in my room," I cried.

"Your mother has no problem with it. Don't upset her more than you already have." He shut the door and sat on the end of my bed. His weight tugged at the bedclothes as if he meant to strip them off me, and I was glad I hadn't undressed. "Do you want to make her ill?" he said.

I took this for one of the questions grownups asked that didn't invite any answer, but he frowned at me so hard that his face seemed to shrink further. "No," I pleaded.

"Then try and be a good girl. Your mother says you used to be one. Don't you know how ill it makes her when she has to worry about you?"

I'd begun to feel he wouldn't let me say anything except "No."

"That's because she does her best to hide it from you. You don't need to know how much she's had to worry about money, because that's over now. You'd like that, wouldn't you? You want your mother to be happy, don't you?"

He seemed to have left me no answer but "Yes."

"Then let's talk about something nicer. I know what little girls like." I thought he was going to offer me a sweet, but he said "You like dressing up, don't you? You'll be a bridesmaid when I marry your mother."

I felt as if I was agreeing to more than I might welcome by saying "Yes," but I thought at least I'd placated him till he said "No need for that. What do you think you're doing?"

I was keeping hold of the bedclothes with both hands, because he'd sat towards me, pulling harder at them. "Come downstairs if you think you're going to be able to behave yourself," he said and stood up so quickly he might have been trying to pretend he hadn't sat on my bed. "Just promise me you won't upset your mother."

I didn't mean to distress her, and I wanted to be with her. "I promise."

When I followed him downstairs my mother said "I hope you've made your peace."

I thought she should be talking to him too or even might be, but he said "We've got ourselves a little maid. Now where's a sweet for a good girl?"

I wanted to enjoy the wedding for my mother's sake, even if it felt like sending my father away. Bridie and I were all in white like Mr Randal and my mother, and a fat white flower stuck out of his lapel. I was expecting my mother's dress to have a train for me and Bridie to carry – it would have made her seem like a queen – but I was glad she didn't have one, since it would have brought back the name my father couldn't call her any more.

That afternoon the sun was so fierce it looked like one of those lights police in films shine in people's eyes to find out what they've done wrong. It woke up the scents of flowers in our house, making it smell even more like a funeral. When we went out to the limousine our clothes turned so bright I almost couldn't look at them. I had to slit my eyes, but Mr Randal said I shouldn't or I'd end up working in a Chinese takeaway, which made my mother laugh and tell him he was terrible. I expected him to drive the limousine, but he sat facing me and Bridie and my mother. All the way to St Brendan's he told the driver what to do – "Easy on my gears, Dave" and "No call to brake so hard" and "About time you were signalling." He kept his hands clasped in his lap, and I nearly asked if he was praying, but now I wonder what they hid.

"Little angels," I heard someone say when Bridie and I followed Mr Randal up the aisle, and I thought how our dresses were the colour Father Brendan said our souls had been when we were born. All the outfits were Mr Randal's idea, and my mother had seemed flattered, though back then I didn't understand why. When Father Brendan asked her such a long question that I'd forgotten how it had started by the time he finished, she said "I do" as if she was daring anyone to contradict her. When he asked Mr Randal something like the same, Mr Randal said "I do" as though he couldn't believe anyone might doubt it. A lady in the front row dabbed at her eyes, and her face was squashed so small for the size of her head that I knew she was his mother. Across the aisle my grandmother hid a sniff in her lace handkerchief, and her husband cleared his throat as though she'd given him a cold.

After the wedding Mr Randal drove us to a local hotel, just my mother and me while Bridie went in the family car. There was a buffet I would have enjoyed more if Mr Randal hadn't made me nervous, telling me to keep my dress clean "like the good girl you are." I managed not to spill my plateful, but I was impatient to see where we were going to live. When he took us back where we'd always lived I couldn't muffle my disappointment. "Aren't we going to the big house?"

"She means Speke Hall, Malcolm. I expect he'll take us one day soon, Carla."

"Not there. Where Mr Randal lives."

"You think I deserve a mansion, do you? That's a thoughtful little girl. I've never needed one of those, and I've got your house now. We wouldn't have had room in my apartment. And no more of the Mr Randal. You just call me dad."

I was so unhappy to be robbed of the fairy-tale dwelling I'd imagined was a compensation for his presence that I blurted "You aren't."

"Would you like your poor mother to bring you up all by herself with nobody to help?"

I didn't see how he could assume I'd meant that, but I had to say "No."

"Then just you remember what we agreed, and that includes calling me dad."

He was reminding me not to upset my mother, and now I saw I couldn't even explain that to her. I could only mumble "Dad."

"That's the spirit. Keep it up till it's natural. And speaking of helping, I hope you do around the house. You should be glad it's not a mansion."

He stared at me without a blink till I said "Yes, dad."

I told myself I would never call him daddy, which belonged to my father and nobody else. That night I prayed he would look after my mother as much as he made out he meant to, and me as well. I was still awake when I heard them come upstairs to what used to be my parents' room, and Mr Randal murmured "Let's just be certain she's asleep." I huddled under the bedclothes as he opened my door, and I stayed there once he shut it, because I was afraid to learn the secret they were anxious for me not to know. When I heard my mother cry out I thought she was yearning for my father. I hoped she was, but the sound disturbed me so much that I pressed my hand against the ear that wasn't buried in the pillow, and soon fell asleep.

When my father came home and went to my mother Mr Randal pushed him out of the bed, telling him "It's all mine now." I woke up feeling the dream was stuck to my mind, which dismayed me so much I ran across the landing to the other bedroom. I'd only just opened the door when Mr Randal sat up in the bed. I could barely see his face in the dark, but it looked the way he'd met my father in the dream. "What do you mean by coming in like that?" he whispered. "You've no idea what your mother and I might have been doing. At least, I pray you've none."

My mother rolled over to peer at me. "You listen to him, Carla. Some things are private. In future just you knock and wait to be told."

"But you and daddy used to let me come in when I was lonely in the night."

I suppose I should have understood why this didn't please my mother. "Well, you can't any more without making sure you're welcome."

"Nobody's saying you have to be lonely," Mr Randal added. "Remember that now and go back to your bed."

"Just you do as he tells you, Carla."

I felt as if they were united against me in a way she and my father never had been. As my mother walked me to school next day she said "It's about time you started appreciating your new father. He's a blessing and I thank God for him." I had no idea what I'd done to deserve the rebuke, and I wondered what she and Mr Randal might have said about me while I wasn't there. "He cares so much about us he's gone straight back to work," she wanted me to know. "He hasn't even had a honeymoon."

I thought she wished she'd had one, which made me feel left out, because where would I have been? I felt the one she'd had with my real father should have been enough, but she seemed to think Mr Randal was suffering for us, though I'd been led to believe only Jesus had. She had nothing but sympathy for him whenever he told us about his day – how one of the receptionists had got an address wrong again, or yet another driver had shown up late or called in sick, whereas Mr Randal had never taken a day off in his life "except to marry my pet." Apparently she didn't wonder how much time he spent sitting around the taxi office or waiting for his employees to do something else wrong, since he took the limousine out so seldom. When he did we were treated to more tributes to his passengers than Mr Randal had given my father at the funeral, though they sounded just like footballers and stage performers and owners of companies I'd never heard of.

My mother let him know she was impressed, as if she thought he was the only man who could have done the job. Maybe she had to think that, and it bothered me less than how he made her feel she needed help around the house, as though he meant to leave her helpless. Before long, if I didn't show enough enthusiasm for my household tasks when I came home from school, I felt I'd let her down, though she'd never expected so much of me while my father was alive. "Don't tire me out, child," she would say more like my grandmother than herself, but I blamed Mr Randal for exhausting her or persuading her she deserved to be fatigued.

Did he mean to do that on our Sunday outings? "Open the door for your mother, Carla," he would say when we were getting into the limousine and out of it as well. Soon she made me feel I'd let her down if I didn't do it readily enough. The first time he took us out a neighbour admired the car and said "Gone up in the world, Mrs Randal." I thought the idea was as disloyal to my father as her new name, and when my mother asked me what was wrong I couldn't speak. "Keep your secret and see if I care," she complained, but I'd grown wary of provoking Mr Randal.

He drove us into the countryside for walks, though not too much of them. "Don't go scurrying off," he warned me as the two of them strolled a little way through a wood. "Have a thought for your mother." Soon he just took us for drives, and I remember him saying "You sit and rest and enjoy the view. You've earned it, Elaine." I'd have liked to stop at some of the places we passed – at least, I would have while I was with my mother.

One day we stopped at a petrol station for Mr Randal to check the tyre pressures and fill up the tank. "Come and feel this, Carla," he said as he pumped the tyres up. I held the hose and felt it throb with each surge of air. "If you think that's exciting try this one," he said when he'd finished, and let me hold part of the tube while he filled the petrol tank. As I felt the liquid surging through my grasp I saw my mother frown at us through the window. "What's wrong, mummy?" I said once I was back in the car.

"Nothing I know about and nothing you should either. I'm sure I don't know what you mean, child."

Her reaction confused me as much as it hurt me. As Mr Randal returned to the car he said "Has someone been upsetting somebody again?"

"Just a misunderstanding," my mother said, staring hard at me to see I knew it was, which didn't help me understand. "Let's leave it behind, Malcolm."

I felt blamed for something I hadn't done and didn't even know had happened, and I thought it was my fault that next Sunday she stayed home. "You look worn out, my pet," Mr Randal told her. "You try and have a snooze and I'll look after our child."

He started taking me out for hours once he'd brought us all home from mass. He would find somewhere in the countryside to park and then stride off as if leaving my mother behind set him free. "You need tiring out," he told me. "It's only fair to your mother." Though he brought the binoculars he'd used to show her birds, he wouldn't let me look through them. "Some things are too big for you to handle just yet," he said with a smile that seemed to be meant purely for himself. Instead he'd lift me up to see birds and their nests, and once his hands slipped under my dress. I started wriggling because his fingers felt like cold fat worms, but at first he didn't put me down. "No need to kick," he said after a while, and let me down. "Nothing's the matter, is there?"

I couldn't find words to express my doubts, unless I was afraid to. "Don't suppose," I mumbled.

"That's right, don't do that. I hope you're enjoying your walk after you made such a fuss about wanting them."

I didn't think I had, but felt I was only allowed to say "Yes."

"Then please see you tell your mother you've enjoyed it. We don't want her worrying about it and making herself ill. A good girl is a healthy girl."

Though this reminded me of the things my father used to say Mr Randal said, I no longer felt like laughing. I told my mother I'd had a good walk, but after that I made sure to change into my jeans after church. I didn't want to feel Mr Randal's wormy fingers under my skirt again, and at least my mother agreed jeans were more suitable for the sort of walks we took. I didn't like him lifting me with a hand on my bottom either. I mightn't have minded if he'd put me on his shoulders the way my father used to, telling me that when I grew as tall as him I'd go high in the world. Once I tried pretending I felt too ill for a Sunday outing, and doing my best to convince my mother did give me a headache, but she acted as if I simply wanted to be ill like her. "Get some fresh air and you'll feel better," she said. "Go with your dad and get to know each other."

I thought I knew him as well as I wanted to. He would never be my dad – he was more like a parody of one, but not the joke my father used to make of him. Now my mother only walked me and Bridie to school on some days, and Mrs Shea did on most of them. Once when my mother brought us home I went to fetch my new doll to show Bridie, and found Mr Randal with his binoculars at my bedroom window. Girls in their sports kits were practicing in the schoolyard across the road, but he said he'd been watching a bird that had just flown away. I was more concerned about his intrusion. "You said I couldn't come in mummy's room if I didn't ask."

"That's completely different. This is my house now," he said, which reminded me of dreaming that my father had come home and found him in the bed. I wasn't to know that the nightmare had hardly begun.

ALEX

The tower of offices on Euston Road is so full of windows that it resembles a concrete lattice embedded in a block of glass. The upper storeys are an incandescent mass of sunlight, but nobody apart from Alex seems to notice. Many of the pedestrians are intent on phones, while the rest of the crowd hurry past without meeting anybody's eyes, as if they're anxious to avoid facing any threat – a terrorist, perhaps, or someone with a knife. On the ground floor Alex displays Kirsty Palmer's email to a guard behind a desk, and without having said a word the man releases the waist-high hurdle of a barrier.

As the scenic lift elevates Alex, pedestrians shrink into their bodies until they're no more than a swarm of toys in the shape of heads sprouting mechanically active limbs. Halfway up the shaft the sunlight blazes in, and he turns his back to be confronted by a version of himself surrounded by his shadow. At the thirteenth floor, which is numbered fourteen, his reflection splits in two, vanishing as the glass doors admit him to the lobby of Tiresias Press. Rod is at the reception desk, which is made of glass so black it's opaque, and gives him a flawless polished smile that enlivens Rod's immaculately made-up face. "I'll tell Kirsty you're here," Rod says and, with the switchboard, does. "She'll be with you in a pair of shakes."

Alex takes a seat beside an equally low table scattered with recent Tiresias books. As he leafs through a copy of *Nobody Sees*, someone emerges from Men, where the faceless sketchy emblem of a man flares with light as the door next to Rod's desk shuts. The newcomer's extravagantly wide face looks as though he doesn't own a razor or is resolved to live without one. He plants himself on the seat opposite Alex, and Rod seems about to speak, but returns to reading his phone instead. Now that Alex is observed he feels more self-regarding than he wants to be, and lays his book down. The man scowls at it, provoking Alex to ask "Not your taste?"

The man's voice sounds resolutely gruff. "Don't like that kind of thing."

"We all have our preferences." Having tried to leave it at that, Alex says "What kind would that be?"

"Books about how awful someone's childhood was."

"I ought to say this is a novel, and it isn't just about that."

"If they made it up when they haven't been through it, that's worse."

This feels like the argument Alex had with ToM, and he's about to pursue it when Kirsty appears. Her ankle-length black and white pinstriped dress makes her look taller and slimmer than ever. Her high blond eyebrows lend her smooth oval face a perpetually surprised expression or at any rate the air of expecting to be. The grin of welcome she starts to give Alex snags on an obstruction, and she turns to his neighbour. "With you shortly, Carl," she says, and to Alex "Come through for a minute."

He thought they were going for lunch. Has the stubbly man taken some sort of precedence? Alex feels vulnerable in a way he hasn't felt since he sent his first novel to his agent Linder. In Kirsty's office, where slatted blinds blot out the world, the sight of a copy of *Nobody Sees* doesn't help – it's singled out from heaps of books on her desk as if it needs to be discussed. Perching on an undernourished leather chair while Kirsty sinks into its plump relative behind the desk, Alex says "How are we doing?"

"I'm pretty fair." As he hopes this will be true in every sense, she says "You?"

"Fine as far as I know." His wary query has left him having to explain "I meant our book."

"Not as well as it started out. Not as well as your others."

"Oh, hasn't it?" Alex detests questions that have been answered in advance, and now himself for asking one. "Too much of a departure," he wonders aloud, "do we think?"

"That could be part of the problem."

"I'm guessing you're wanting me to return to my old ways. I'm sure I can."

The guess is closer to a hope, and stays that way while Kirsty blinks at him. "I don't know if that will fix it, Alex."

He's by no means certain of wanting to learn "Fix what?"

She looks saddened, perhaps only by his lack of comprehension. "The response."

"Our sales, you mean."

"I wish it were only those. Haven't you seen all the comments on Twitter?"

"They're publicity for us, don't you think?"

"No publicity is bad publicity." He's about to agree when Kirsty says "That isn't how it works these days, if it ever did. We're glad you didn't answer them."

"Too busy working on my next book for you." This appears to revive her unhappiness, which leaves him afraid to speak, but he makes himself say "Can't we turn the controversy to our advantage?"

"You don't seem to have when you were talking at Texts."

He's angry now. "What am I meant to have done?"

"Didn't you read what people said about it on Twitter?"

"People." When Kirsty looks offended by his gibe he says "Just one person who was actually there, and they brought their agenda."

"Are you saying what they wrote about you wasn't true?"

"I am, and so would Lee."

"I'm sure she would be on your side. So you didn't try to get this man ejected from the shop."

"Tommm, you mean."

"I hope you didn't make fun of him like that either."

"That's how he pronounces himself. ToM with two capitals, just like TransMission. It's their joke, not mine."

"If you think it's a joke."

"And it was Janet from the shop who wanted him to leave. I kept him."

Kirsty consults her computer screen. "Did you encourage somebody to bully him?"

"I most certainly did not, and he wasn't bullied. He had a disagreement with Lee."

"Would he have known you were together?"

"We don't hide anything, not like him."

"What are you saying he hid?"

"How he picketed the shop and then sneaked in to disrupt the show, but Lee recognised him."

"Then I suppose he might say he didn't try to hide it. Here he's saying you acted as if the twist in your story was more important than what people like him have to go through."

"I should think it would have been to the rest of the audience." When she doesn't respond Alex says "And you good folk at Tiresias."

"We need to be sensitive when other people are. Did you try to silence him when he gave away your ending?"

"No, Janet tried to involve the rest of the audience."

"Maybe that's what made him feel bullied."

"Maybe he should act more like the man he wants to be." Reining in his anger, Alex says "Sorry, that was sexist."

"That's some of what it was. I shouldn't like to think you'd say that kind of thing in public."

"I don't like being lied about, that's all. I told him I'd never been abused and never changed my gender. Honestly, I don't see how anything I said to him can do us any harm."

"It isn't only what he posted. It's the replies as well."

Alex hasn't bothered looking. His phone shows him that since he last visited Twitter, hundreds of people have responded to ToM, most of them attacking Alex. Some of the comments are so vicious, wishing abuse or emasculation if not both on him, that he has to laugh. "In case you're worried," he tells Kirsty, "I won't be provoked."

"Our director thought you should apologise."

"I've done nothing to apologise for. I hope you don't think I have."

"Sometimes we should even if we don't think there's a reason, if it can resolve a problem."

"I'd rather make amends for things I've actually done." Her regretful expression drives him to enquire "Just what would you expect me to say?"

"That's what she thought at first, but she's decided an apology won't be enough."

"What more can I do?" His plea infuriates him, and he demands "What am I doing it for? How much of a threat are these people really?"

"Maybe more than you know. They aren't just picketing bookshops, they're boycotting them."

"Not many, surely."

"More shops every day and more people doing it, and it isn't just the shops. They're boycotting all our books."

"So what are you saying we can do?"

"It's funny you should put it that way, Alex."

He can't see how, and then he's afraid he can. He was including her and Tiresias Press, but suppose she means he won't be involved any longer? Before he can bring himself to ask, she turns her attention to the glass door at his back. "Samira," she calls, "can you tell my guest in reception I'll be with them in just a few minutes?"

Alex feels more vulnerable than ever – about to be sent away for good, perhaps. "You'd better tell me whatever you need to," he says but can't bring it out too loud.

Her eyebrows mime bemusement. "I'm looking for a way to rescue your career."

He does his best not to sound as anxious as he feels. "Any luck?"

"Let me ask you this first. You and Lee work pretty closely on your books before you send them to Linder, don't you?"

"Lee's my other set of eyes."

This seems not to be the answer Kirsty wants. "Wouldn't you say you collaborate? And you've been happy to work on suggestions I've sent you. I've enjoyed working with you as well."

"I hope we still can."

"Would you consider working with somebody else?"

"Why, who would I have to lose?"

"Nobody at all if we can make this happen. I'm suggesting the next book could be ghostwritten."

The relief he began to feel at her first remark turns into dismay on the brink of rage. "I'd rather stay myself."

"Our director thinks it's the only answer, and I don't mind telling you I had to fight for it."

"I'm sorry you had to, but shouldn't you have asked me first? I'm certain I can come up with a story she'd approve, and I don't need anybody else to write it for me."

"Alex, I'm sorry." Kirsty's laugh seems grotesquely at odds with this. "I wasn't clear, was I?" she says. "I meant you could write one for somebody else."

He experiences relief again and then immediately less of it. "What sort of book?"

"We've been approached by an abuse survivor. They want their story to be told."

"I'm sure it ought to be, but why should I come to mind?"

"You came to mine, Alex. I think it could be the solution for us all, and it might help you grow as a writer."

"I thought I'd been doing that."

"I didn't say otherwise." Just the same, Kirsty looks disappointed by his response. "You don't have to decide here and now," she says. "I expect you'll want to discuss it with Linder and maybe Lee as well."

"More like definitely Lee."

"So would you like to meet your subject?"

"I'd say that would be a good idea."

"Wait here," Kirsty says and heads for the corridor so fast he could think she's eager to leave him. Beyond the open door he hears a gruff complaint: "Thought you'd gone home." In a moment Kirsty reappears with the stubbled man. "Alex, let me introduce Carl Batchelor," she says. "Carl, Alex Grand."

Alex stands up, though not entirely, and thrusts out a hand. Batchelor's handshake is aggressively firm but terse. "We've met," Alex says. "Mr Batchelor let me know what he thinks of my novel."

Kirsty resumes her seat while Batchelor sprawls in the one beside Alex. "It brought you to us, didn't it, Carl?"

"How did it do that?" Alex needs to hear.

"You put out a story," Batchelor says, not necessarily to him. "Time you put out some truth."

"That's how Carl pitched it to our director."

"And whose idea was it for me to help him write it?"

"I told you, Alex, mine."

He senses how she's urging him to accept, but that's just half the situation. "Are you comfortable with that, Mr Batchelor?"

"Name's Carl," Batchelor says more forcefully than Alex finds applicable.

"I honestly believe Alex is your man. I don't know any writers who are more professional."

"I think I'm demonstrating that." Not without an effort, Alex tells

Batchelor "I can see how you might think my book can't live up to your experience."

"Nowhere near."

"I take it you're prepared to talk about that."

"I'll have to," Batchelor says but looks at Kirsty. "To whoever's going to write my book."

"Kirsty was saying you were abused."

"More ways than you could make up."

"I won't be making any." As Batchelor gazes at him while withholding his expression Alex says "May I ask how old you were when it began?"

"Not much more than six."

"I'm truly sorry to hear that." Although Alex imagined in *Nobody Sees* how victims might grow up, the dull haunted look that fills Batchelor's eyes suggests he failed to do the consequences justice. "Who was responsible?" he says.

"Hope you're not saying I was."

"Of course not, not at all. I meant who was the perpetrator."

"My mother's second husband."

"That wouldn't have been your father."

"Wish it had been." As Alex searches for an apt reply, if there is one, Batchelor lets out an unamused laugh. "I mean," he says, "I wish my dad hadn't gone and died."

"I hope you'll let me offer you my sympathies for everything. Any abuse of a child is appalling, but I wonder if in some ways it could be worse for a boy of your age to be abused by a man."

Kirsty looks anxious to intervene, but it's Batchelor who speaks. "I wasn't."

"Sorry, I thought you said—" Alex feels not much less bewildered by suggesting "You mean he, how should I put it, made the change."

"No." Batchelor gives him time to suffer his mistake and then says "I have."

"Oh, of course." At once Alex hears how this sounds like a comment on the man's appearance. Apologising won't help, and so he says "Are you with TransMission?"

"Don't even know what that is."

"It's a pressure group for people who've taken your route." Alex barely hesitates before settling on the last phrase. "They've been picketing shops that sell my book," he confines himself to adding.

"Don't need anyone like them."

Batchelor looks close to insulted, though surely not by Alex. Is he implying he needs him? Kirsty seems to think so, and Alex sees that both their jobs may be in jeopardy. All of this feels like enough, and he says "I'll be happy to talk more if you are, Carl."

"In that case I do believe it's time for lunch." Kirsty stands up as though Alex has released her from detention. "Let's go and celebrate the birth of a team," she says, and Alex vows to make it work.

CARLA

I was nearly six when my mother started being ill every day before she took me to school. Sometimes I heard her throwing up in the toilet while I was having my breakfast, and that made me feel ill too. She would come downstairs pretending she was fine so as not to bother Mr Randal. I was afraid she might ask him to walk me or drive me to school and let him take over more of my life, but she said "I'm all right walking, Malcolm. You've got enough on your plate."

I had the impression that she wanted me to appreciate how brave she was being at the same time she convinced herself she was keeping it from him. It made me feel her illness was my fault, because he'd given me the notion that anything wrong with her could be. One morning on the way to school I blurted out "Mummy, why are you sick?"

"It's God's way, Carla. It's only natural. You made me like that, child."

This confirmed my fears and Mr Randal's opinion of me. "I'm sorry, mummy."

"I don't mean now," she said, tousling my hair the way my father used to. "When you were inside me."

If it wasn't my fault any longer I could only think Mr Randal was to blame. "Who's doing it now?"

"Someone who's coming to see you. Wait till next year and you'll get a lovely surprise."

"Do you mean a baby, mummy?"

"That's right," she said as if I'd spoiled her treat. "I was more innocent at your age. You're growing up too fast, child."

I didn't understand the accusation. It was just one more of the ways I'd felt blamed ever since Mr Randal had entered our lives. Perhaps my mother saw how she'd affected me, because she said "Your father and I have made you a little friend."

So it was Mr Randal's fault, and yet another way he was trying to take over from my actual father. I nearly said he wasn't mine, but instead I asked "How long are you going to be sick?"

"Maybe you'll have a little brother or a sister by your birthday. That would be a special present, wouldn't it? Which would you like?"

"Can't we have both?"

"One's enough for me to go through, Carla. You don't know what ladies have to put up with. You gave me more pain than I thought I could stand. I felt as if you'd never come." I saw she wished she hadn't said so much, and she added "You'll learn for yourself when you grow up. There's no need for you to know about it now." Even this made me feel it was somehow my fault, particularly when she said "You look a fright, child. What will they think of me, sending you to school like that. Let's get a comb through your hair."

Before long her state was plain to everyone. I thought she looked like a walking egg. The neighbour ladies cooed like birds at it, and some of them offered to help with her shopping as the egg got bigger, but Mr Randal didn't seem to want her friends in the house. "You've got a little helper," he told her, meaning me. He kept telling her to take it easy and watching to make sure I did my household tasks, but he still made her cry out in bed. I had a confused idea that he wasn't meant to do that to her in her condition, and some nights I couldn't sleep for hearing her. When I tried blocking my ears with the pillow and the bedclothes I felt as if I was hiding from Mr Randal. I couldn't help hoping that when his child arrived it would divert his attention from me.

It hadn't come by my birthday, even though my mother's dress looked like a tent someone was hiding under. Sometimes she made me put my hand on it, but if I felt a kick I imagined Mr Randal's child trying to push me away from her. Mr Randal took us out for my birthday dinner, which I thought he meant more as a treat for her, though she showed her gratitude by saying "You've never had a birthday like this, have you, Carla?" I wished I were spending it at home with my mother and my real father as we always used to, and I felt Mr Randal was waiting for me to behave some way you weren't supposed to in a restaurant, even though he kept telling me "There's a good girl" and "You're growing up fast, Carla." At the end the waiter brought a birthday cake, and I didn't realise I was meant to thank Mr

Randal till my mother urged me to and shook her head at him about me. I'd only just blown out the candles when she jumped up and ran to the toilet. "That was a lovely meal, Malcolm," she wanted him to know as soon as she came back. "The child blew her smoke in my face, that was all."

This wasn't the only stain on the day. I was disappointed that the baby hadn't come. I thought it would have stopped my mother being sick, but then I felt guilty because that should have been my first concern instead of wanting it to be an extra present. I'd been given books, because I was one of the top readers in my school class, but Mr Randal had bought them to save my mother shopping, and they seemed too young for me. I didn't understand why he'd chosen these when he kept saying how big I'd grown. It didn't strike me that he might want my body to grow up but not my mind.

We didn't have a party for me at our house, though when my father was alive we always had, with Bridie and our playmates from the street. I'd been looking forward to inviting friends from school, but I didn't need Mr Randal to tell me that my mother wasn't up to it, though he did. I made myself anticipate next year, when I could have a party like that and there'd be one for the baby too. I fancied the baby would bring nothing except good till the day my mother told me that when I came home from school she would be in hospital, and I realised I'd be left alone with Mr Randal. "Can I stay at Bridie's?" I pleaded.

"Why would you want to do that?" Mr Randal's look across the breakfast table seemed to say he didn't know the answer any more than I should. "No need to trouble them," he said.

"I stayed with them when daddy died. You wouldn't have to make my dinner."

Saving him the trouble of me might have meant more to my mother than imposing on our neighbours, because she said "I'll have a word with them, Malcolm."

"I wouldn't like anyone to think I'm not up to looking after her, Elaine."

"I'm certain everybody knows how much you do for her." I was afraid he'd changed my mother's mind till she said "But you've got your own job. You shouldn't have to do mine as well."

"It's up to both of us to care for her."

"You get some rest while you can, like you're always telling me I should. You'll have plenty to do when I come home from hospital, so don't take on anything you don't need to now."

I didn't mind this meaning me so long as it protected me from being left alone with Mr Randal. I was while my mother went next door, and he watched me as if he was about to speak. His silence seemed to threaten worse than words even though a smile kept his mouth zipped shut. He'd said nothing by the time my mother came back. "They're fine with her, Malcolm."

"Just tell them if she gives them any problems they can send her back," Mr Randal said and left me a warning look.

Did he mean to leave me afraid to misbehave without realising, the way I'd felt at my birthday treat? Now if I did anything wrong, Bridie's parents might return me to him. At the dinner Mrs Shea made me and Bridie, I was so nervous that I dropped a fork and spilled a glass of orange juice. Bridie's mother wiped the fork and mopped the table and refilled my glass. "She'll be anxious for her mam, James," she told her husband, who didn't seem to welcome me as much as she wanted me to feel. "You take it easy, Carly. She was fine when she had you, wasn't she?"

This only reminded me how much my mother said she'd suffered. While Bridie and I watched cartoons before bed I saw the limousine draw up outside. You couldn't hear it, which made me feel Mr Randal was creeping home to deliver a surprise. I hoped this would be my mother with the baby, but he got out by himself. Mr Shea answered the doorbell, and I heard Mr Randal ask "How's my little girl been?"

"Just a bit fidgety. We're used to it with ours."

"Don't be afraid to say if you've had enough of her."

"We said we'd take her, so we will. You and Elaine have enough to cope with."

"Let me look in on her at any rate," Mr Randal said and came into the front room. "I hope you aren't being troublesome, Carla."

"She's not a bit of trouble," Mrs Shea declared. "We like having a pair of them in the house, and I'm sure you will."

"How's Elaine getting on?" Mr Shea said as if someone should already have asked.

"There may be complications. Say a prayer for them both."

"We will," Mrs Shea said, "and tell her she's in everybody's thoughts."

"I will once I've had my dinner. The slop they serve you at the hospital would leave you needing treatment. It's a good job Elaine's off her food."

"You should have let us know," Mrs Shea cried. "You could have eaten with us."

"We've imposed on you enough," Mr Randal said and looked at me. "I hope you appreciate the kindness, Carla."

I did, more than I wanted him to know, but I was eager to ask "Can I go and see mummy in hospital?"

"Your mother's not an exhibition. Didn't you hear what I told Mr Shea? She needs rest and quiet so she'll be ready for the task God has given her."

"Never mind, Carly," Mrs Shea said. "You'll see her and the new babbie soon."

"Excuse me, Mrs Shea, but I wish you wouldn't call the child that. It's the name the swarthies call one of their evil gods." As though Bridie's mother had rebuked him for denying me a visit to the hospital, Mr Randal said "For everybody's information, Elaine doesn't want the child there making a fuss."

"I wouldn't," I protested.

"You do as Mr Randal says," Mrs Shea said. "He knows what's best for you and your mother."

I felt as if she'd turned against me, and my mother had. I was just an inconvenience, even to Bridie, who complained that night I was taking up too much room in her bed. I went to sleep praying that the baby wouldn't hurt my mother or make her even sicker and that they'd both be home soon. Bridie kept elbowing me in the ribs, maybe more often than woke me, and the last time she did it was time to get up.

We were in the kitchen, having a breakfast cereal like a rainbow broken into crisps, when the phone rang in the hall. "Don't say there's another problem with the plastering," Mr Shea said, because he was a builder, and sounded as if he'd like to add some words we shouldn't hear. He tramped to the phone, and I heard him say "Yes" and "Oh Lord" and "Yes" again a few times, and then he hung up with a note of the bell, which sounded too loud and shrill. "Maddy, can you come here for a minute?"

When she joined him he muttered "Shut the door," and I couldn't hear what they said till their voices grew a little louder. "Does he expect you to tell her?" Mrs Shea said, and her husband grumbled "Seems like we're always bringing her bad news." Bridie looked at me as if she couldn't help wanting to learn the worst, and as soon as her parents came into the kitchen I pleaded "What's happened to my mummy?"

"She's going to be all right, Carly," Mrs Shea said. "Carla, I should say. And you'll have a little angel to watch over you, one of your very own."

I assumed she hadn't reached the bad news yet. "When are they coming home?"

"Your mother," Mr Shea said, "in a few days, Mr Randal thinks. But I'm sorry, lovey, the baby didn't manage to be born."

"God must have other plans for her," Mrs Shea said, dabbing at her eyes with a paper towel. "That's why I told you there's a new angel."

She tore a towel off the roll for me and then saw I wasn't crying. Though I missed the little sister I would have had, I was mostly relieved my mother hadn't died and left me alone with her husband. "At least you're taking it well, Carla," Mrs Shea said, but it didn't sound like admiration. "Maybe she needs to let it catch up with her," Mr Shea said.

That made me think he wanted me to be caught, and who would do that except Mr Randal? I felt sad when I prayed for the baby who would have been my little sister, but I thought she should have been praying for me, since I'd been told they prayed for us in heaven. I prayed hardest that my mother would come home, but when she did I felt as if I'd made her leave the hospital too soon. She was thinner than she'd been before she started to swell up, and her colour seemed to have faded. I had a feeling she'd been emptied of more than just the baby, as if the hospital had sent back a hollow imitation of her, which tried to act and sound like my mother but kept running out of the energy it took. I expected her at least to take me to school and bring me home, but Mrs Shea did.

I thought Mr Randal was encouraging my mother to stay sick

instead of trying to help her get better. "You just sit," he said whenever she went to do housework. I didn't mind helping if she needed it, but I was afraid it might leave her even weaker, because exercise was meant to make you strong. That was one reason I asked Mrs Shea "Isn't mummy ever going to walk me to school again?"

"She's tired out, poppet. We have to help her get over what she's been through."

"I think Mr Randal is making her tired."

"You do have some strange notions, child. He's doing just the opposite." Before I had a chance to argue Mrs Shea said "I shouldn't say this but I will. If anyone exhausted her it was your father, never helping round the house, but she didn't dare to complain."

I thought she was slandering my father's memory. "Mummy wasn't scared of him."

"I mean she didn't want to because she thought he had enough to do. But of course she wasn't frightened of him, any more than anyone could be of your new daddy."

I didn't know why she had to add that, and I wasn't sure it was true. Last night I'd heard him help my mother climb the stairs, so slowly she sounded reluctant. It made me anxious to hear what happened next, and I strained my ears. In her room that Mr Randal had turned into his, my mother said "I don't know if we should yet, Malcolm."

"It isn't our decision, my pet. It's God's commandment to us. Just make sure you don't disturb the child."

His words did that and made me scared of worse. Soon I heard my mother do her best not to cry out, and blocked my ears so hard they ached. Even her cry wasn't the one I remembered. Maybe that had expressed some kind of pleasure, but now it sounded distressed if not painful. It left me afraid of going up to bed at night, fearful of hearing, and I tried to fall asleep before Mr Randal brought my mother upstairs, which often meant I couldn't. I never heard them talking in her room any more, and I imagined them performing a duty in silence, because God said they should. I wondered if my mother could be praying so as not to cry out. I was learning the commandments from the catechism at school, but I didn't remember any like that. I thought perhaps there were extra ones that weren't meant for children to read.

I had to learn the catechism before I made my first confession and communion. Anticipating those gave my mother back some life, but it was Mr Randal who tested me on the catechism every evening. "We'll see you're a good girl," he said, and my mother said "Just you heed your father." She tutted if I forgot an answer or stumbled over any, and said "Try harder, Carla." I don't know if she noticed how Mr Randal seemed to find some answers particularly meaningful. "Are we bound to assist our parents in their wants?" The answer could only be yes, but you had to say "We are bound to assist our parents in their wants." Of course my mother endorsed this, and being commanded to obey priests and the authorities. The same commandment forbade 'all contempt, stubbornness, and disobedience to our parents and lawful superiors', which meant that even if I didn't think of Mr Randal as my father, God said I had to obey him. His smile at my answer screwed his eyes even smaller, but I expect my mother thought he was just pleased I was doing well.

He took us in the limousine to choose a communion dress. "You look just like an angel," my mother told me, and Mr Randal said "That's our little innocent for us." I would have liked the white dress better if it hadn't reminded me of their wedding. "Thank your father for buying you such a lovely dress," my mother urged. "Just you show him how grateful you are," and I felt as if she'd delegated me to act out her enthusiasm or even take her place.

My first communion fell on Guy Fawkes Day. To begin with the fireworks felt like a celebration. I heard some going off in daylight as Mr Randal drove me and my mother to St Brendan's. Bridie's dress was longer than mine, but I tried not to be jealous, because that was a sin I'd have to tell the priest in his box another day, and it would mean I couldn't take communion. I'd made my first confession the day before, and I'd just been able to make out Father Brendan's face through the mesh between the halves of the box, hiding from me and yet watching me, the way I was led to believe God behaved. Supposedly both of them were listening, and I told them how I sometimes didn't want to do things Mr Randal said I had to. "What must you do with your father, child?" the priest said, and I had to mumble "Honour him." Resenting his orders turned out to be worth three Hail Marys and a good act of contrition, which was more than I thought he deserved. Saying how I tried to hear him and my mother in her room would have made me too uncomfortable, and I told myself it wasn't a sin, particularly since I always ended up doing my best not to hear.

When Bridie and I and the other children went in a procession to the altar rail I saw Mr Randal and my mother watching nobody but me. Her smile looked determined to pretend her eyes weren't sad, and his lips were so straight I couldn't tell what he expected to happen, unless he thought I was going to let him and my mother down. I did my utmost not to fidget while I waited for my turn at the rail, and clasped my hands together so hard my fingers ached. I must have looked as though I was praying, but really I didn't know what else to do with them and was afraid everyone would notice. When I reached the rail at last I nearly hitched my dress up too high as I knelt down, which left me feeling I'd almost been wicked. As Father Brendan approached along the kneeling line of us he made the sign of the cross over each child and then planted a wafer on their tongue, which gave me far too much time to worry about ruining the moment, biting the wafer though you weren't allowed to, or choking on it, or starting to cough when he put it in my mouth and spitting it out. You were meant to shut your eyes when the priest came to you, but I couldn't quite, for fear that the arrival of an object in my mouth would be too much of a shock. I closed my eyes to slits and saw Father Brendan wave his hand up and down and back and forth in front of me, and then reach in his silver goblet while an altar boy stood close to him with a napkin. As the priest produced a wafer I threw my head back and opened my mouth as far as I could, bruising my tongue against the back of my bottom teeth. Father Brendan murmured some Latin, which reminded me of the words my father had made up on the walls in Chester, and I was afraid I might cry or laugh or both. Then the priest said "Amen" and I nearly did too, but he stopped my mouth with a wafer. I was expecting it to taste like meat, since it was Christ's body, but it tasted of nothing at all and seemed hardly to be there. It was easy enough to swallow without spluttering, and I managed to stand up with my hands still clasped and walk not too fast to my mother and Mr Randal. "Now you're a proper girl," he said as I had to sidle past him, and my mother said "You did us proud."

I'd only wanted to make her proud, not him. By the time we went to the firework display in the park she'd run out of enthusiasm.

It started late as usual, and some children were howling because they had to wait or because their parents were taking them home. I didn't even fidget, which I hoped would keep my mother proud of me. At last we saw men in safety jackets taking flames across the field. "Look, he's touching it off," Mr Randal said as one man poked a flame at the nearest tube stuck upright in the ground. "It's starting inside now. It'll shoot up in a minute. Wait, it's getting ready, it can't stop now, it can't control itself, it's going to explode...." Some of the parents around us stared at him, but I thought he fell silent because he was watching the firework send its dazzling stream into the sky. "Did you like that, Carla?" he said over the next explosion, and when I said I had my mother urged "Then thank your father for bringing us."

He hadn't even driven us. As we walked home after the display, fireworks died like fiery willows in the sky. When I went to bed I could still hear them, and didn't want to stop. I didn't need to block my ears even once Mr Randal and my mother came upstairs, because my mother said "I'm worn out, Malcolm" and he told her "You've had a long day, my pet. You go to sleep." That was all I heard from her room, and I was listening to fireworks when I fell asleep.

After that she very rarely cried out that way I didn't like. More often I heard her telling Mr Randal she was tired and a grudging mumble from him. I thought her state was his fault, not least for making her sick in hospital and all the months before. When Mrs Shea brought me and Bridie home I sometimes found my mother asleep in her chair. She often dozed off in it while I was washing up the dinner things, and once I found Mr Randal standing over her with a smile. Some people might have thought he looked affectionate, but he glanced at me as if I'd caught him out. "Don't disturb your mother," he said.

She was snoring in the chair the first time he took me upstairs. Though she hadn't said good night to me, he wouldn't let me waken her. "Brush your teeth," he said and stayed in the bathroom while I did, and when I used the toilet as well. "Nothing wrong, is there, Carla?" he said, looking at me in the mirror. "Say your prayers and you can go to sleep." I might have imagined he was telling me to pray on the toilet, but I didn't start till he followed me into my room. He didn't speak while he watched me kneel, but when I said "God bless the baby" he waved a hand almost in my face, like a sloppy version of the sign Father Brendan made. "Her name is Hilary," he said. "That's my mother's name."

His parents lived in Devon, which was why I'd only met them at the wedding. I said "God bless Hilary" and "God bless daddy" and wondered why he kept on smiling. Maybe he thought that meant him, unless he had something else on his mind. When I said "Amen" he joined in, and I was making to stand up when he waved at me. "Stay there for a minute," he said, and I wondered if he was going to give me more prayers to say. "Do you like secrets, Carla?"

"Expect so." When he fixed me with a look that made his eyes bulge I said "Yes."

"Then this will be ours, all right? A secret just for us to share," he said and lowered his hand to his trousers. "Remember how you liked the fireworks? I've got something just like one of them for you." The sound of his zipper wasn't nearly as loud as my mother's snores, and he glanced towards the door he'd shut tight. "You'll be helping mummy get her strength back," he said.

ALEX AND ALEXANDER

"Let's start at the beginning. What's the first thing you remember?"

"I want to start with Randal."

"What would you like to say about him?"

"How he nearly killed my mother." With a grimace that wriggles stubble on his cheeks Carl says "How I used to wish he'd killed me."

"Perhaps we could begin by saying that and then go back."

They're in the office of Carl's Cars. Carl is seated in an off-white plastic bucket chair behind the desk while Alex perches on its double. His phone lies between them on the desk, recording the conversation. Before he can prompt Carl again, the receptionist looks in. Her crimson lipstick and augmented eyelashes seem determined to proclaim that she's the woman it's already plain she is. "Mrs Balakrishnan wants to know if you can pick her up today instead of Friday, Carl," she says.

"Never a problem. What time?"

"A bit earlier than usual. She says half five and I said I didn't think you'd mind."

"Tell her I'll be there." As the receptionist closes the door Carl says "One of our disabled fares. All the lads and lasses are reliable, but I like to deal with those."

"You're making sure you're better than your stepfather."

"No." Carl's stare adds weight to the word. "Trying to be as good as my dad."

"We'll come to him, but shall we try for your earliest memory first?"

Alex always plots his novels by starting with the earliest scene, but he's wondering whether interviewing a biographee requires a different approach when Carl says "It's thinking the priest lived in the church."

He grimaces more fiercely than Alex thinks the memory of childishness should call for. "What can you tell me about that?" Alex says.

"I thought he did because they had the same name. Father Brendan and St Brendan's."

"Did you think he was a saint?"

"I was never that stupid."

Alex doesn't feel deserving of the stare this brings. "All right," he says in the hope of placating Carl, "you tell me how it was."

"I thought something when I should've known it wasn't true."

"How old would you have been?"

Carl frowns at the solitary photograph that stands on his desk, of himself as a toddler between a man and woman who partially resemble him. The back of the mount is so fingermarked that patches have been worn away. Eventually Carl says "Must have been three or so."

"No shame in getting things wrong at that age or older for that matter. My first time at school, I thought we'd have to wait all day to eat because they called the servers dinner ladies."

"I'm not ashamed of anything I thought. Randal tried to make me but he's got no chance."

"I hope our book will help. Did you mention your idea about the church to anyone?"

"My parents. My real ones. And him."

"That's your stepfather."

"Not Randal." Carl appears to have no time to leave his disgust behind as he adds "Father Brendan."

"Might you remember what you said?"

"Told my parents I was sad because he lived there all alone."

Presumably his lingering disgust is aimed at the mistake. "I expect they said he lived with God, did they?"

"He did." As if he's furious with any ambiguity Carl says "He said."

"As you say, you told him your idea."

"They did when he was waiting for us."

"Do you remember why he wanted you?"

"Not just us." Carl appears to dislike the suggestion. "Everyone who'd been at mass."

Alex searches for another way to bring the scene alive. "What did your parents call you?"

"She called me Carla. My dad mostly called me princess, and she was his queen."

Alex makes an effort not to find any of this disconcerting. "Is your mother still alive? Perhaps I should meet her."

"She's gone as well."

"In that case I think you've given me enough for now to work up."

"What do you mean," Carl demands, "work up?"

"Flesh it out for our first scene. I'll show you everything I do before it goes anywhere near the publisher."

"Are you going to write it now?"

"I don't think my phone's quite up to that. I'm not, at any rate." Alex tries not to feel amused but has to keep that failure to himself. "Let's talk until you've had enough," he says, "and I'll work on it at the hotel."

With some prompting Carl reminisces mostly chronologically until it's time for him to pick up Mrs Balakrishnan. "We'll get to Randal tomorrow," he says like a curse.

Alex drives through the Manchester rush hour, where every halt sees drivers take the chance to consult their phones, to a hotel overlooking a suburban park. Cyclists are circling the park while pedestrians with dogs parade counterclockwise as if they're all components of an obscure mechanism. Alex dines at the nearest restaurant, the Nifty Bistro – beetroot and lentil soup, duck with scallops – and then returns to the Look Out hotel.

It's inexpensive compared to accommodation in the city centre, and not too far from Carl's firm. His room feels obsessively feminine, the chair and dressing-table draped with lace, the bedspread dangling elongated tassels, the flowered wallpaper against which desiccated blossoms are trapped under framed glass. He sits at the dressing-table, where the gap between two stacks of drawers leaves him no space to part his legs, and uploads the interview with Carl onto his laptop, into the folder containing Malcolm Randal's death certificate that Carl emailed him. He's deleting the interview from his phone when the mobile rings, a sound that recalls the landlines of his childhood. "Dad," he says, much as the phone just did.

"Alexander." With enough of a pause to be prompting a reply his father says "Should I ask how you are?"

"We're fine, thanks."

"Ah, you and your collaborator. You'll be hard at it, no doubt." As if it's too late now for Alex to ask, his father says "Your mother and I are still enjoying our retirement."

"Maybe that's because you aren't completely retired."

"Retired from lecturing. We like to think we're helping maintain standards at the magazine. Perhaps in time you may submit another essay for appraisal."

The essay Alex sent in – printed, since *Continuity* won't accept electronic submissions – came back so wounded with red ink it looked flayed. He'd already taken months to analyse the revival of the English detective story, but even once he made all the revisions the essay was rejected. Apparently the editors prefer material more like his father's article identifying vintage slang as a hidden subtext in novels such as Mrs Gaskell's *North and South*. "I'm working on a book just now," Alex says.

"More of the same, I take it. We gather you're achieving your ambition."

This sounds no more approving than Alex knows it is. "I hope I'm on my way there," he retorts.

"Lord forbid you should go any further. We see how you've descended to offending people as a means to sell your wares."

"I just tried to make it true." When the answer is a silence that feels like a denial too indisputable to need words, Alex says "I assume we're talking about my new novel, but can I ask whether you've read it?"

"We paid good money for a copy."

"I would have given you one. I thought neither of you had time for my work."

"There are so many things we no longer seem to have the time for," his mother says at a little distance. "At our age that isn't something you can make."

As though he finds this too placatory his father says "We wouldn't have wanted to feel obliged by your gift."

"Well, thanks for shelling out for it. If anybody gets around to reading it— "

"I've done so."

Though his father's tone discourages any response, Alex says "I hope I didn't disappoint you too much."

"I suppose it's something that you hope it. I'm afraid you exceeded expectations."

"I'm guessing you didn't care much for the book."

"No more than it appears to care for us."

Alex wonders if his father's mind is giving way to age. "What does it have to do with you and mother?"

"Exactly." As Alex fears his diagnosis was correct his father says "We knew you wrote popular trash, but we could never have imagined that kind. I believe we were entitled to expect better from your years at university."

"They do teach courses on popular fiction, Gordon," Alex's mother says.

"Small cause for celebration. In fact, none at all."

Alex struggles not to be provoked but says "Can I ask why you object to my book so much?"

"Obscenity is one reason. Obscene material that's aimed at a market, whatever you'd like us to think."

"The subject is obscene, if you want to use that word, and I don't think I show any more than I have to."

"I'm sure there are books that are more obscene than Alexander's, Gordon."

"That's even feebler than his excuse, Amy. You may be careless of your reputation, Alexander, but perhaps you might consider ours."

Alex feels his father has by no means retired from lecturing. With more bitterness than he's able to contain he says "You'd rather not be associated with a popular novelist."

"We've become inured to that after fifteen years. I'm referring to the image of us your book presents."

"Which image?"

"The book is full of abusive parents. Who do you suppose your readers will take them to be based on?"

"I'm sure they'll assume I made them up."

"You've more faith in people's critical abilities than your mother and I have. We saw how many students lack it, never mind your class of readership. In any case you claimed just now that your book was the truth, and presumably that's how you sell it to the public."

"The truth about the characters and their kind of experience, as near as I can imagine. Not about real people." When this earns no audible reaction Alex says "If you both like I'll post some kind of disclaimer online about you."

"Please don't attempt to drive a wedge between us. You used to play that game as a child. And please refrain from publishing anything about us. We'll content ourselves with hoping the attention dies down sooner than later. I'm sure the public has more important issues to concern it than your books."

As though to atone for at least some of this Alex's mother says "What are you working on now, Alexander?"

"A bit of a departure, but the publishers suggested it. It's still about abuse, only this time it isn't fiction."

After a silence long enough to let his parents exchange more than a glance, his father says "And how do you propose to achieve that?"

"They've linked me up with someone who wants their story told."

"Whose name will be on the book?"

"Both of ours, the publishers are saying."

"You'll make it clear whose story it is," his mother says, "won't you, Alexander?"

"I'm sure that will be obvious. I'll see it is."

"Perhaps the best course," his father says, "will be to let us have sight of the book before it sees print."

"I don't really think I can do that when it isn't my story."

"I assume your lady friend will have a preview of the book."

"She always does. It's her job, as you know."

"But you're determined to withhold it from your own family." His father pauses, no doubt giving Alex a chance to change his mind. "One might think," his father says, "you're anxious to keep something hidden."

This is untypically imprecise, and Alex has a sense of talking to someone he doesn't altogether know. Before he can reply, the line is dead. He would like to speak to Lee, but he has already called her once today, and she doesn't need to hear about his unsatisfactory conversation with his parents. Instead he lingers in the bath and dons a robe as plump and white as the bath towel and its baby sibling. Now he's too relaxed to work, and goes to bed.

Ideas waken him well before dawn. He recalls how his childhood mistake about dinner ladies prompted Carl to recall a similar incident. This brings Carl's account of his first day at school alive in his mind, and he shrugs the bathrobe on before heading for his laptop. Beyond the window orange streetlamps on the park road illuminate a few trees like expansive flares arrested in the gloom. As he types, his thoughts grow almost too rapid for his fingers to keep pace, and he feels he's not just engaging with Carl's memories but inhabiting them. He types until his fingertips ache, and continues typing. The sun has put the streetlamps out by the time he finishes, and once he returns from breakfast he reads through the chapter before driving to Carl's office. *My stepfather nearly killed my mother, and I used to wish he'd killed me....*

CARLA

It wasn't long after my tenth birthday that Mr Randal threw my mother down the stairs. By now he was putting me to bed every night while she stayed in her chair. Her goodnight hug and kiss felt like a duty she was having to perform. Maybe sending me upstairs with him made them feel that way, and at first I tried pleading with her. "Won't you come and tuck me in like you and daddy used to?"

"You've still got your father. You let him see to you like a good girl."

I couldn't believe she'd misunderstood who I meant. Did she still hope I might call him by the name I'd saved for my real father? "I want you as well," I begged.

"Don't make my head hurt, child. I'm in enough pain without that. I'm up and down those stairs half the time as it is."

"Let your mother rest now, Carla. Her life's hard enough."

Sometimes he only kissed me on the mouth after I'd said my prayers and retreated under the sheets, but it threatened worse. Whenever I had to watch his face descend towards me it blotted out the rest of the world, yet at the same time his features seemed to bunch smaller as I shrank inside myself. Sometimes I'd hear sirens racing away from the police station up the road. I used to hate the sound, because it reminded me of the car that had killed my father, but now I wished they were coming to rescue me from Mr Randal. Maybe he guessed my wish, because he said "They're off to catch bad people. Nobody like that in my house, is there? You're the good girl your mother wants and I do."

By now he wasn't just showing me what he called a firework, he was having me hold it to make it explode. I ended up loathing Guy Fawkes Night and any other firework displays too, and had to tell my mother I didn't like the noise. "I wish you'd told me sooner, child," she said. "I've never liked it either. Your father only takes us for your benefit, so that's one less task on his plate."

Every time he finished displaying his firework he reminded me it was our secret and how we were saving my mother from having to make some kind of effort that he never specified, and I convinced myself that if it stopped her crying out because of him I was doing some good, however much I didn't like it. He told me how letting her into the secret would only make her feel guilty for needing my help, though she never seemed to feel that way about the other chores I had to do, and then he would hurry to the bathroom to flush a wad of paper. I kept hoping my mother would wonder why he needed to, but the nearest she came to asking was the time I overheard her say "You were up there a long time with her."

"Just seeing she said all her prayers, my pet."

"There must have been a lot of them."

"That's how good a girl she is."

Was I committing a sin of omission by concealing from my mother what actually happened? He did make me say prayers, but not the ones he heard. They were inside my head, and I hid in them while I waited for the firework to blow up in my hands. While I couldn't tell my mother any of this, I thought the complaint she'd made was my excuse to mention something Mr Randal hadn't warned me to keep secret. The next time we were alone I said "Mummy, I don't like it when he comes in the bathroom."

"And who's he supposed to be when he's at home?"

"Mr Randal." When her face let me know this was unacceptable I said "Dad."

"That's who he is, and don't you ever forget how much we owe to him. Now what are you trying to make out is a problem?"

"He keeps coming in when I'm in the bath."

"This is his house, child. He's bought it, and we couldn't have afforded to before."

I thought she was belittling my real father again. "It was ours, though."

"When you're older maybe you'll understand. It's secure at last. Our family is. Our life."

This sounded like a gibe at my real father too. With a frown that made not just her forehead but her entire face look old my mother said "Now what are you trying to say about your dad?"

I wanted to say far more than I could. "I don't like him seeing me in the bath."

"What do you mean by having such ideas at your age? You shouldn't even know about such things. He'll just be seeing you're clean. You should be grateful he cares."

I tried to edge closer to the truth. "He doesn't just look."

"If he gives you a scrub I'm sure you need it. Maybe you'll remember Mr Batchelor did."

Presumably the name was meant to distinguish him from Mr Randal, but it felt as if she was denying he had ever been her husband. Before I could protest she said "I'd like to know where you're getting these ideas. Have you fallen in with someone nasty at school?"

I yearned to tell her the ideas were Mr Randal's doing, but all I could say was "No, mummy."

"Then they must be coming from yourself or else the devil. They're called impure thoughts, and you'll need to confess them to the priest, and then I pray you'll never have them again."

She made a sign of the cross as though she was keeping it for herself, warding off my thoughts and maybe me as well. There was no use telling her that Mr Randal sometimes used the toilet while I was in the bath, another opportunity for him to produce what he liked me to hold in the bedroom. She'd left me feeling these occasions were my fault somehow, and guiltier than I could put into words. My secret was growing harder to keep, but she'd made me unable not to do so. I could only pray that Mr Randal would betray it himself.

One night I thought my prayers had been answered. When he flushed the toilet it wakened my mother, because I heard her say downstairs "Have you been with the child since I fell asleep?"

"How long are you thinking that is, my pet?"

He meant to persuade her she'd made a mistake, but she said "I can see the clock, Malcolm. What took you so long?"

I held my breath, because I thought his hesitation would at least make her suspicious, and then he said "I was instructing her."

"Instructing her in what?"

"In our faith. Helping her get ready for her confirmation."

"I'm sorry for doubting you, Malcolm. I didn't have my wits about me for a moment, that's all."

His answer must have inspired him, because he made it into the truth. He started questioning me about the catechism in my room, loud enough to be heard downstairs. No doubt she thought I got some questions wrong and needed him to coach me, since he had some favourites he kept asking. "If you have injured your neighbour by speaking ill of him, what are you bound to do?"

"If I've injured my neighbour by speaking ill of him," I mumbled, "I'm bound to make him satisfaction by restoring his good name as far as I can."

The first time he put that question in my room he said "Who do you think neighbour means?"

"Don't know," I said, because I could tell I wouldn't want to.

"It's everyone who isn't you, and don't you think God means you to take the most care what you say about your own family?"

"Spect so," I had to mutter.

"Then what do you think you're doing to my name by talking about me?"

I didn't think I had, or I'd forgotten. "Don't know what you mean."

"You've been complaining to your mother about me bathing you. Did you think I wouldn't find out? I know everything about you, just like God." He stared at me so hard I could imagine his watchfulness lingering even when he wasn't there. "You upset her, so I hope you're satisfied," he said. "You've made her feel she's not doing enough for you. Do you want her breaking her back on the stairs? She's not supposed to be at your beck and call."

"I didn't mean to hurt her," I said and managed to suppress my tears, because I didn't want him ever seeing them.

"This once you're forgiven. Just remember that commandment forbids talebearing and words that injure anybody's character."

After that he frequently reminded me of the eighth commandment when he was in my room, but the catechism question he liked asking most of all was "Does Jesus Christ also command us to love one another?"

He said it so loud he might have been preaching in the street. I imagined the Sheas and the neighbours in the other terraced house that boxed us in could hear him. Sometimes he shouted it because the way he was having me deal with his firework made him. "Jesus Christ also commands us to love one another," I would have to respond, feeling trapped by his words. "That is, all persons without exception for his sake."

He would lower his voice before reminding me "Love means doing what they like. You'll learn more of that as you get older."

All too soon I did. His behaviour and his comments had begun to confuse me so much that I could hardly put my feelings into words. If Jesus wanted what I had to do to Mr Randal in my bedroom, why did it need to be kept secret? I might have asked Mr Randal, except I wasn't sure I would want to hear the answer. I came near to concluding it was one of those mysteries only grownups understood or kept to themselves as if they did – and then Mr Randal gave me another secret to hide from the world.

I was nine, and he'd begun to watch me as if I'd turned the age he most liked. One night he took me through his choice of questions about the commandments and then gazed at me even harder. "You're a big girl now, aren't you?" he told me nowhere near as loud as he'd questioned me. "Just lie on your bed for me. You don't need to do anything else." When I made to slip between the sheets he muttered "I told you on the bed."

I lay on my side with some of my face in the pillow, but he eased me onto my back and reached for the waistband of my pyjamas. He pulled the bow apart as if he was opening a present – that was how his face looked – and began to pull my trousers down. I didn't like that, but when I grabbed the waist he thrust his face at me, squeezing it smaller with a scowl. I thought that was squeezing his voice higher too, and tinier. "You were told not to do anything," he said. "You wouldn't stop a doctor seeing you. I'm your father and I've seen you in the bath."

He frowned at my hands till I let go, and then he hauled my pyjama bottoms down so fast that one leg caught on a toenail, which made me bite my lip. It hadn't stopped stinging by the time he finished gazing at me from the end of the bed and let himself out of his trousers. He climbed on the bed, murmuring "No more babies" as if he meant to reassure at least one of us. I remember thinking his tip looked like an extra eye that was helping him watch me. He pushed my legs apart and planted it between them and started repeating "Love, love," but he'd barely set about bucking up and down – I thought of a horse on the roundabout my father used to take me on, or at any rate I did my best to fill my mind with it – when he erupted more violently than my hands had ever made him. As I cried out with the shock and the cold slimy sensation, I felt as if I was imitating my mother. Mr Randal was still spouting when she called up the stairs "What's wrong with Carla?"

I'd never seen him caught out before. His face clenched as if he was trying to squash it too small to be seen. He twitched the last drop onto me with one hand and shoved himself off the bed. "Stay there," he warned me and stowed himself away, zipping up his trousers while he hurried to the door. "She's perfectly all right, Elaine," he shouted as he opened it. "Just a nightmare she was having. No need to come up."

"I'm more than halfway. I can tell her goodnight in bed for a change."

"Let me help, my pet. I can see you're wearing yourself out," Mr Randal said, having left me a cautionary look on his way out of my room. I heard his headlong footsteps on the stairs, and then both he and my mother cried out. They'd never done that together before, and they sounded more shocked than I had a minute ago. Then came a disorganised series of rapid clatters followed by a heavy thud. "Elaine," Mr Randal shouted loud enough to be sharing it with an audience, and hurried downstairs, though not as fast as his voice had seemed to mean he would. My mother didn't make a sound, and I was afraid how alone I might be. I pulled on my pyjama bottoms and ran out of the room.

My mother lay on her back in the hall. Her face looked as if a hook had dug into one corner of her mouth, dragging it sideways. One leg was trapped beneath her, and the other was stretched out on three stairs. I was sure she couldn't have borne that position if she'd been conscious, though she was breathing. Mr Randal had his back to her, and I thought he was showing how little he cared till I saw he was twirling the dial of the phone on the wall, not as urgently as I would have liked. "Ambulance," he said as though he was giving an order. "My wife has had a fall. I think she may have broken her back."

I must have made a sound at that, because he turned to peer at me. He gave the address and hung up the phone before saying "See what you've done now, Carla." He looked ready to say more, but the doorbell rang. Perhaps that took him off guard, because he opened the front door at once.

Mrs Shea was on the doorstep. "I thought I heard—" she said and then "Oh dear Lord, what's happened?"

"Elaine tripped on the stairs. I've called emergency and they told me not to move her."

Mrs Shea stepped into the hall and saw me. "Oh, you poor poppet," she said the same way she'd greeted the sight of my mother. "Did you see your mummy fall?"

As I shook my head Mr Randal remarked "No, but I'm afraid the child has soiled herself."

He meant the stain on my pyjamas. "Never mind, Carla," Mrs Shea said as if she was offering me a treat. "You go and get cleaned up and we'll get you out of your daddy's way. Shall I send James round to wait with you, Malcolm?"

"No need, but thank you for the thought. I'll be praying over her."

"Your daddy's a good man and a brave one, Carla. You get ready now and we'll give Bridie a surprise."

However dismayed my mother's injury made me, I couldn't help feeling relieved to escape from her husband. I cleaned up in the bathroom and got dressed, and went downstairs to find him and Mrs Shea saying prayers for my mother. As we left him behind Mrs Shea said "God bless you, Malcolm."

Mr Shea didn't act entirely pleased to see me, but rearranged his expression and made his voice sympathetic once Mrs Shea explained why I was going to stay with them, just as the ambulance raced into our road. Bridie wasn't too happy to be woken up, and complained that the bed wasn't big enough for us both any more. "You make room for your guest, Bridie," her mother said, but once we were alone Bridie used her elbows to fend me off the middle of the bed. While I was staying with the Sheas this time I felt less invited than tolerated, and sometimes hardly even that, though Bridie's parents seemed to want to keep their feelings unadmitted. I was glad when my mother came home from hospital, even though she cried "Don't go hugging me, child" when I ran to her. This left me feeling blamed for her condition, which had her walking with a pair of sticks. At least she was home again, but then I saw that she might never climb the stairs without help, which meant Mr Randal could strand her downstairs whenever he wanted me. "Good heavens, child, you look as if you didn't want me home," she said. "Just you thank Almighty God I haven't gone for good."

ALEX

"And now before we take some questions from the audience, will you read to us from your book?"

"One day we stopped at a petrol station for Mr Randal to check the tyre pressures and fill up the tank. 'Come and feel this, Carla,' he said as he pumped the tyres up...."

Alex senses how Kirsty has relaxed beside him. Some writers read their work aloud as if they're struggling to grasp material someone else wrote, but that isn't happening now. The only disconcerting element is Randal's dialogue, which comes out close to falsetto. The nervous laughter this incites dies away as Randal directs Carla to feel the hose throb. Unease spreads through the audience when Randal starts handling her, and perhaps the reaction is exacerbated by the sight of the decidedly masculine victim recounting how the man's hands wandered under his skirt. "I wasn't to know that the nightmare had hardly begun," he reads and shuts the book, and Alex has the odd impression that words he wrote have been plagiarised for a performance.

Carl's partner on the podium in the bookshop – Amelie, a tall close-cropped blonde in denim overalls and a T-shirt of the kind all the Texts employees wear, which turns them into advertisements for the shop – sets off applause and follows it by saying "Who has a question? Yes."

The man she's prompted behind Alex says "You sound like you want to go back to being a girl, Mr Batchelor."

"That's not a question," Amelie objects, but Carl sits forward to demand "How do you mean?"

"The voice you put on when you were being your father."

"I said at the start he was never my father."

"He took the role on, though. I know what that's like." With equal peevishness the man says "You didn't make your mother sound like that."

"I just want everyone to know all about him. He didn't have much more of a dick than me."

As this revives a scattering of nervous mirth the man says "Not such a threat as you made it out to be, then." This provokes a groan and muttered protests. "Just one man's view," he says. "I thought places like this stood up for freedom of speech."

"Like I said, there's different kinds of dicks."

Several listeners reward Carl's response with titters, but Alex wonders whether the event is escaping control. He's about to raise a hand while he thinks how to change the subject when Amelie says "Yes, the lady there."

"I read some of your book, as much as I could stand. Why did you have to go into all those details to sell it?"

"I didn't, did I, Kirsty? I just told you a few." To the audience Carl explains "She's my editor."

"One of them," Lee murmurs on the other side of Alex.

Kirsty is whispering as well. "Carl's making this his own, isn't he? He's a natural."

Once again Alex feels set aside. Though he's only at the reading because this part of Carl's tour is in London, he wouldn't mind the odd acknowledgment. Meanwhile the questioner is saying "I don't mean selling to your publisher. I'm asking you how much you put in to make people buy your book."

"I didn't put anything in. I'm just telling everyone what happened to me."

"If I'd been abused as a child," a man says, "I think I'd be keeping it to myself."

Perhaps he's praising Carl's willingness to expose the truth, but Carl retorts "You would if you'd done the abusing."

A woman joins in without indicating she wants to. "You aren't asking us to believe none of your book was contrived."

This silences Carl, and Kirsty intervenes. "What are you suggesting might have been?"

"The way it starts. You can see that's just there to make people read on. It's like a story, not a biography," the woman says and reads the opening sentence. "My stepfather nearly killed my mother, and I used to wish he'd killed me."

Hearing his prose in yet another voice makes Alex desperate to recapture it. "Carl wanted everyone to know that from the outset," he says. "It wasn't a commercial ploy."

"What do you think you know about it?"

"He's Alex Grand," Carl says. "He wrote my story down."

"He's like my secretary, you mean. You dictated it to him."

"He's a good deal more than that," Lee wants it to be known.

"He's a ghost," Carl says. "That's what they call them."

This leaves Alex feeling less present than ever, even when the woman says "He should be up there with you, then."

"I'm just one of the audience," Alex feels bound to say. "I don't want to muscle in on your show, Carl. I shouldn't even call it a show."

"Alex Grand," a man pronounces. "Don't you write crime fiction? That's how that book sounds to me."

"As Alex says, it's Carl's event," Kirsty says. "Amelie?"

"Yes, the gentleman with your hand up at the back."

"How does it feel to have someone take over your life?"

"Like he's got inside you and you don't matter any more," Carl says. "Like you don't exist any longer."

"You'll be grateful to him, though."

Carl sends a scowl across the room. "Why am I going to be that?"

"For your book."

"There wouldn't be a book without him, is that what you're getting at? Doesn't mean I didn't loathe every inch of him and wish him dead and me as well."

The questioner lets out a laugh almost indistinguishable from a gasp. "You're nothing if not honest."

"That's what my book's supposed to be."

"Particularly when he can hear."

"He can't. I got my wish. Just not soon enough."

"He sounded pretty much alive to me."

"Thanks for that," Carl says and stares at the man who criticised the voice he gave Randal. "See, someone thought he sounded real."

This time the laugh from the back of the audience is ampler. "Who do you think we're discussing?"

"My stepfather," Carl says and brandishes the copy of *When I Was Carla*. "Here's the only way he's going to live."

"Not that kind of ghost. I was asking you about Mr Grand."

"Don't worry, Alex, I haven't been wishing you dead." With less of a grin Carl says "It did feel a bit like you got inside me, though."

"He gave you a voice," says the man at the back.

"I've got one of my own, maybe you noticed."

"More than one, but I'm saying he helped you bear witness. He let you speak."

"I don't need any letting. Kirsty there can tell you I was speaking before he came into it."

"If the book was all yours you wouldn't have needed him."

Alex feels bound to speak up. "Some of the words are mine, but not the memories."

"Whose idea was the business with your stepfather and the petrol pump?"

"His." As Alex makes to deny it Carl adds "Malcolm Randal."

"Only it sounded like the kind of thing a novelist might have made up."

"Well, it wasn't. I remember it like it was yesterday." Fiercely enough to be confronting disagreement Carl says "Once you've been through stuff like that it doesn't go away."

He could almost be speaking for Alex, who feels as if he experienced the memory by shaping the prose. He's tempted to say so, but he would be stealing it from Carl. Amelie is inviting any further questions, though she hardly waits. "Then thank you, Carl, for sharing so much with us."

Neither this nor the applause silences the man at the back. "Will Mr Grand be signing your book?"

"I don't think I should. It's Carl's story and I shouldn't intrude any more."

"I expect Alex will be here again signing books soon," Kirsty says.

Surely this means she'll consider his next novel. He and Lee take the escalator to the ground floor and are emerging into Oxford Street when his phone rings, wakening a man encased in a sleeping-bag from the neck down beneath the bookshop window. As Alex takes out the phone it says "Kirsty Palmer."

Is she calling to rescind her implied promise? "Kirsty," he says without having found a tone of voice.

"I didn't realise Maggie Rotheram was here. She's the presenter of *Literary Natters* on London Calling Radio. She wants to do a show about the book."

"I expect Carl will be just as natural on radio."

"She wants you as well. Can you make tomorrow?" Kirsty gives him the time he'll need to be at London Calling, and as she rings off she says "We must see about getting you on television."

She's talking to Carl. "Good news?" says the man in the sleeping-bag, and Alex feels prompted to drop a pound in the plastic cup beside the supine head. Surely the answer to the question will be yes, though not having been recalled to the shop to meet Maggie Rotheram leaves him feeling like an afterthought rather than a collaborator on the book. "At least I'm being trusted to do publicity again," he says and takes Lee's hand as they make for the Underground.

CARLA

My mother came upstairs at night, but only once I was in bed. She always needed help to climb the stairs. At first I offered, but she just wanted Mr Randal. "Let me alone, child," she said. "You don't want to make me worse." Now I realise she didn't think I would be capable because I was a girl, but then I thought she was blaming me for her fall. I'd already left her weak by praying for her to come home too soon after her miscarriage, and I'd been warned against making her break her back on the stairs, which I had.

Mr Randal followed me upstairs every night and did what he did to me twice a week. It was a ritual like prayers followed by catechism – his face shrinking with a kind of secret concentration as it loomed closer while he propped himself over me, and the tip of him doggedly butting between my legs as if he was hoping this time he would find a way in, and eventually the inevitable result, after which he would wipe us both and flush the wad on his way to joining my mother. I often heard her thank him for doing so much for me, if she wasn't asleep and taking a break from the pain I knew she was in. I felt as if she was taking how he used me for granted, even though she was unaware of it. Whenever I heard the stairs creak as he made his way up to me I had to stop myself praying they'd collapse under his weight, which always felt like a threat of breaking my back as I lay beneath him on the bed, or asking God to make him fall downstairs and be hurt worse than he'd crippled my mother. I couldn't say such prayers, because they would be unforgivably sinful. I felt forbidden to discuss my plight with anyone, even God, and I grew desperate enough to think of telling my grandmother. I wanted to know if any of it was a sin I was bound to mention in confession.

She might as well have been my only grandmother. My father's parents didn't come to see us any longer – Mr Randal hadn't made them anything like welcome – and his parents lived hours south. I didn't see her very often, because my mother found her visits quite a chore, especially since the old lady insisted on helping her daughter. She seemed determined to tidy items away into places my mother never kept them and couldn't find them. "Just leave that, mother," mine would say, but my grandmother would assure her "It's no trouble, Elaine" or insist "You sit there and let me be some use." My mother never managed to persuade her not to bring us dinners she'd made, stews in which she'd somehow overcooked the vegetables till they were hardly recognisable and yet left the meat tough. To make sure they hadn't picked up any germs in transit she would microwave them so fiercely that they came out dry as well.

Her large hands looked scrubbed raw, which I thought was why she smelled harshly of soap. I had a fancy that she'd rubbed her face thin as tissue and crumpled it too, since it was full of wrinkles so whitish I imagined soap had lodged in them. She had a look of constant disappointment, which I was afraid she thought I was, and I'd always found it hard to talk to her. "I hope you're helping your father care for your mother," she kept saying now that my mother was injured, and "Children are supposed to be a blessing, Elaine. You always were."

"She does her best, mother."

"Well," my grandmother said and turned her dissatisfied look on me, "I hope that's better than I've been seeing."

I was scared that nothing I could say to her would find favour, and that included talking about Mr Randal. I tried more than once, but my tongue wouldn't work – it felt as if he'd got into my mouth and cut the connection to my brain. I started hoping he would use me in my room while she was at the house, so that she could catch him at it, though I didn't dare to foresee what would happen then. He never did, and it took me a while to see he was taking care not to be found out, he'd gained so much control over how I thought about him.

One night he gave me a different kind of chance. He had to drive some businessmen to a dinner at the town hall, which meant my grandmother saw me to bed. She watched me wash my face and brush my teeth, and then she waited outside the bathroom while I used the toilet. She crossed herself and shut her eyes when I knelt at the end of my bed. Once I'd finished praying she tucked the sheets in so hard I felt pinned to the mattress. She planted a kiss that felt as light and dry as a communion wafer on my forehead and stood up at once, and I still hadn't managed to speak to her. To keep her there I said the first thing that came into my mind. "I'm glad you're putting me to bed, grandma."

I hoped this might win her over, but her face didn't change. "Why wouldn't you want your mother?"

"I would. I wish she did."

"Then stop wishing and try praying."

This struck me as worse than unfair. "I do. You heard me asking God to make her better."

"So long as you're asking for her and not for yourself." As I wondered if this was just a rebuke, not a warning that prayers didn't work if they were selfish, she said "Pray harder."

My most heartfelt prayers were the ones I did my best to hide from Mr Randal in. As if my thought of him had prompted her, my grandmother said "I should have done what your father does."

At first this left me too dismayed to speak. "What?" I pleaded.

"Your mother says he helps you pray."

He did, but not in a sense anyone but me could know. Some of my feelings must have shown, because my grandmother demanded "And what could be wrong with that?"

"I don't like him being in my room."

"I'm sure I can't imagine why." Before I could let this prompt me to speak she said "For a start he's saving your poor mother the trouble."

As I tried to think she was saying the stairs were the trouble, not me, she said "You should be just as grateful to him."

"What for? He's not my dad."

"He's more. Your birth father didn't choose you, but he did. He's made you his." While I struggled not to think she meant my father hadn't really wanted me, my grandmother said "Just you remember he had no children of his own. Don't make it any harder for him."

"I don't do anything."

"Then it's about time you did, a big girl like you."

I felt more accused than I could define, and my tongue was starting to censor my speech. "He does," I barely managed to pronounce.

"What are you trying to say, child? No use mumbling like that if you want anyone to know what you're talking about."

My tongue obstructed telling her the secret he'd made me feel I had to keep, but I was able to blurt "He comes into the bathroom."

"Nothing wrong with that at your age, and you've no business thinking there is."

"He doesn't just come in, he baths me."

"So your mother doesn't have to." This provoked her to declare "You should be doing it yourself at your age. You don't want your poor mother thinking you can't look after yourself."

My grandmother had left me more confused than ever, not least about the meaning of my own age. In a desperate bid to put across some of the truth I said "He doesn't go out when you do, gran."

"I've not the slightest idea what that's supposed to mean."

"You went out before." In the hope that using words I'd never spoken to her would make her see the help I needed, I said "When I was having a wee."

"If your father thinks there's nothing wrong with that, I'm sure there can't be." In the tone of someone talking to a toddler she said "Don't tell me a big girl like you needs helping with the toilet."

"Never said I did."

"Don't speak to me like that, Carla, and I've not the least idea what you have to complain about. Try feeling thankful instead for everything you've got, and that includes your mother and your father."

All that I was frantic to tell someone seemed to be receding deep into my brain, out of reach of being spoken. "Won't I have to tell the priest?" I pleaded.

"Tell him what, child?"

"What I said."

"You certainly should if you're having grubby thoughts about it, and I'm afraid I see you are. Just don't tell any of your friends or they'll think you're a nasty little girl nobody wants to play with, and their parents won't want them being friends with you." She turned as she took hold of the doorknob. "And don't you dare tell your mother," she said, "or your father either."

I felt she'd left me nobody to tell. I thought of the teachers at school, but wouldn't anything I said about my home life be bound to get back to my mother or Mr Randal? There was Bridie, but I was afraid she would stop being my friend, and in any case what could she do when she was only my age? I was feeling as though lockjaw had trapped the secret in my head when the police came to our school.

The policeman who talked to our class was about as old as Mr Randal. He reminded me of an uncle at a children's party, where he wasn't quite at ease. When he warned us to remember that parts of our bodies were private I thought he was talking to me and about me, and watching my reaction. I pressed my legs together so hard my thighs grew sore, and stared at the blackboard behind him and the teacher, as if not meeting anybody's eyes would let me hide. The letters that hadn't quite been rubbed out on the board looked like a message I needed to read. The policeman explained that a man had been showing his private parts to children in school playgrounds, and I thought he could be Mr Randal – in fact, I prayed he was so that he would be caught without involving me. But the man the policeman described was too tall, and Mr Randal would never wear an anorak. "If you see anyone doing anything like that," the policeman said, "tell a grownup as soon as you can."

The soonest was that moment, and before I knew it I'd put up my hand. "Yes, Carla," the teacher said.

Not just Mr Randal's warnings but my grandmother's clamped my mouth shut, and then I had a different but equally urgent reason to speak. "Please may I go to the toilet?"

"You should have gone before we came in," the teacher said as she always did to anyone who asked. "Go on if the gentleman's talk has upset you, but remember what he said you have to do."

Being urged to tell didn't help. It simply made my mouth feel more unworkable. For the rest of the school day I kept putting up my hand so that I'd be made to answer questions, in the hope this would dislodge the things I had to say. Did I honestly believe I could have done that while the entire class would have heard? I hadn't by the time the final bell rang, but I might have lingered in case I could speak to the teacher alone if Bridie hadn't told me to hurry up, because her mother needed to go out once we were home. As we walked three abreast along the road, her mother asked how the day had been. "A policeman came to talk to us," Bridie said.

Her mother made it sound as if every child was suspect. "What's somebody done now?"

"A man's been showing kids what he shouldn't show them, and the policeman says we have to tell if we see him."

"Just make sure you do, then."

Before my mouth could stop me I blurted "I think I know someone like the man."

"Did you tell the police?"

This sounded even more accusing than her previous question had. "I couldn't," I confessed.

"Then don't go trying to tell me, or Bridie either."

I felt as if she was reinforcing Mr Randal's prohibitions and my grandmother's. "Why not?" I pleaded.

"If you can't say it to the police there must be something wrong with it, and I don't mean wrong the way you mean. It wouldn't be the first time you nearly damaged someone's reputation."

"Whose, mummy?" Bridie said.

"Your father's, if you must know. Your friend's a bit too ready to start rumours and not care about the consequences."

"I never," I protested, but the accusation wouldn't go away. "When?"

"The very first day you were at school. When Bridie's father picked you both up and you had people thinking he was up to no good."

"I didn't mean to. I was little then."

"I know it was the day your father died. We'll say no more about it." I thought she'd given way till she said "And don't you about anyone."

"If you're going to say mean things about my dad," Bridie said, "I won't play with you any more."

"There you are, Carla. That's what will happen if you keep on spreading rumours."

Nobody said anything more as we tramped rapidly home. I ran into my house and would have taken refuge in my room while Mr Randal was at work if my mother hadn't said "There you are at last, Carla" as if I was hours late. "Put the oven on so your father's dinner's ready and just run the hoover for me," she went on, and I felt as though my only hiding place was in my head, where there was nothing except emptiness. If only I could think how to do what the policeman said we should – and then I wondered if he'd told me after all. If we let anybody see the parts of us they shouldn't, wasn't that a sin we were bound to tell the priest? I'd given in to letting Mr Randal see, and it was past time I confessed. While I was doing that, surely God would help me tell Father Brendan the rest too.

ALEX

London Calling is an elongated single-storey concrete block on Bethnal Green Road. Above a pair of glass doors a metal statue of a woman as grey as indecision cups a hand beside her mouth and extends the other, upturned. A young black woman sits in a wheelchair behind the whitish horseshoe of the reception desk, and raises a face like the rest of the question her eyebrows are posing. "Alex Grand," she says.

"Are you here for someone?"

"Maggie Rotheram."

"She's with some people just now."

"I'm meant to be one of them."

Without relinquishing her expression, the receptionist depresses a key and speaks to a microphone like an undernourished snake. "I've got a Mr Grand for Maggie," she says as though it's rather less than a statement of belief.

Alex hears no response by the time she releases the key and lifts her face, though not her eyes, towards him. "There'll be somebody out in a minute."

A speaker lodged in one corner of the ceiling brings Alex the present transmission, a review of a production of The Magic Flute that deals with the Queen of the Night's problems as a single mother. A table on stumpy legs in front of a drooping white plastic couch is scattered with brochures about the radio station. As Alex sees its slogan is **INSPIRED BY INCLUSIVENESS**, a tall woman with metallically grey eyes and a shock of red hair inches high appears from behind the scenes. Her skin is as pale as her ankle-length kaftan is black, and the defiant lump of an Adam's apple betrays her original gender. "Alex Grand," she says as if he needs to be informed, and thrusts out a large hand. "Maggie Rotheram."

Her handshake feels like a contest for strength, and he hopes the firmness of his grip communicates enthusiasm for the discussion that's ahead. She steers him towards the corridor beyond the lobby before relinquishing his hand. He's following her when the receptionist jumps out of the wheelchair to add a new brochure to the array on the table. Once he's well along the corridor he can't help asking "Isn't that girl disabled?"

"Nobody's disabled if they don't let themselves be told they are."

"She looks as fit as I am."

"We want everyone to feel welcomed as soon as they look in the door."

As Alex refrains from saying how he was made to feel, Maggie Rotheram leads him to a room at the far end of the corridor. "We're all here now," she says. "I believe you know one another."

"I think we should by now," Alex says, having caught sight of Carl crouched forward on a nominally upholstered straight chair. They exchange terse token grins as Alex steps into the room, and then he sees that a similar chair is thoroughly occupied by ToM from TransMission. "I don't think that," ToM wants it to be known.

"I meant Carl and me."

"Shouldn't that be Carl and I? You're supposed to be a writer."

"Someone must have thought I am or I wouldn't be here."

"That's me as well," Carl says.

"Shall we keep the disagreements for the studio?" Maggie intervenes. "As lively as you like. If everybody's ready we'll go in."

ToM pulls the lowest plastic cup off a stack dangling beside a watercooler and fills it to the brim before taking an unexpectedly dainty sip. When Alex takes a cup he finds ToM's tug has dislodged half a dozen of them, all of which come away in his hand. "Leave some for the rest of us," ToM says with not much of a laugh.

Alex attempts to return all the cups except one to the stack, only to displace several more. He piles cups on top of the cooler and fills his while Maggie and the men watch his performance as if they're barely tolerating an incompetent entertainer. His first gulp of water turns into a cough he has to swallow, which leaves him needing more than three syllables to pronounce "Ready now."

The studio is next door. Maggie takes a seat at a control desk while ToM sits opposite, in front of the first of a trio of microphones, and Carl manoeuvres Alex into sitting in the middle. "Hope you aren't feeling too outnumbered," ToM hardly bothers to sound as though he means.

"I imagine you must do," Alex says, "most of the time."

"I don't let myself."

"I get it sometimes," Carl admits.

"Then you should examine who's responsible," ToM says and stares at him or Alex if not both.

"Thank you all for that," Maggie says, and as Alex wonders why she's grateful "I've taken everybody's levels and we're ready to record. I'm sure I don't need to tell any of you, but just the standard warning – no racist language, no misgendering, no transgender slurs."

"Are we allowed to criticise religion?" Alex finds it relevant to ask.

"I can't see why you'd think otherwise when you go after it in your book. You weren't attacking Islam."

"Whose book are you saying it is?" ToM wants to hear.

"That's one of the issues I want to discuss," Maggie says and finds a file on her computer screen, which produces a Bach prelude played on an instrument not much like a harpsichord. After a few bars she fades the electronic clangour down and out. "Welcome to *Literary Natters*," she says. "Tonight we'll be looking at *When I Was Carla*, the new memoir of surviving child abuse. With Carl Batchelor we have Alex Grand. How would you like to be styled, Alex?"

"Writer, do you think, Carl?"

"You can't claim it's your book," ToM objects. "You haven't had the experience."

"That's our third guest," Maggie tells her microphone. "ToM Lincoln, spokesperson for TransMission."

"I wonder how much it's Carl's book either." ToM barely waits for her to finish before he addresses Carl. "Don't you feel your memories were stolen?"

"There's some I don't mind someone else having."

"To what extent do you feel," Maggie says, "that your memories aren't yours any longer?"

"I don't. They're still mine, all of them."

"Then I'd like to explore how they were composed for the book. Can you choose one you're comfortable with discussing?"

"I don't mind talking about any of them now I have." As Maggie starts to speak he says "When he made me feel what the hoses felt like."

Alex thinks this sounds disconcertingly like the child whose voice he tried intermittently to capture in the book, but Maggie says "Can you talk us through that?"

"When he was checking the tyre pressures he got me to hold the air hose so I'd feel it throbbing. And then he said if I thought that was exciting I should try the petrol pump. So I held that hose while he filled up, and I felt the petrol pumping through it. My mother was in the car, but she acted as if there couldn't be anything wrong."

"Did you think there was?"

"Didn't then. I do now I remember."

ToM tilts his head towards Carl, which puts Alex in mind of a joker being eased into sight from a hand of cards. "What do you think he was doing?" ToM says.

"Getting me ready to feel something worse."

"You're talking about your stepfather."

Carl jerks his head away from ToM. "Who else am I going to be?"

"You could just as well have meant Mr Grand." Before Alex can deal with this, since it appears to have confounded Carl, ToM says "That memory sounded just like your book. Whose words were you using?"

"Mine. You heard me."

"But when did they become yours?" Maggie says. "Can you remember the process?"

"Alex helped me get the memories back. He was with me every day for weeks."

"Did he make you live through all those experiences?" ToM is determined to establish.

"He helped bring them back. Some things I'd forgotten till we found the words."

"I wonder how that must have felt. I'd call it a kind of rape."

"I'm sure you'd like to tell us what kind," Alex says.

"The abuser wants to get into his victim, and you have."

"Don't know if he's done that," Carl protests.

"Then what would you say he's done?"

"Like he says, it's a collaboration."

"Listen to yourself. You've just admitted you're using his words."

ToM sits back so triumphantly that Alex feels as though the winning card has been hidden in the hand again. "How did you approach collaborating?" Maggie says.

"Carl told me his story and I turned it into what you've read. I made changes where he didn't think it sounded like him."

"Now it all does," Carl says.

"I'm sure Mr Grand's lady friend had her say as well," ToM comments.

"My partner edits all my books. Carl saw what she did and he approved it. I hope you don't have any problem with her gender."

"No, my problem is a cis man occupying space that could have empowered a transgender person. Mr Grand has colonised your memories even if neither of you will admit it, Carl. He appropriated them to make his book."

"It's both our book." Carl revises his grammar by adding "It's both of ours."

"You've just proved my point. That isn't how you talk in it." Before Carl can argue, unless he's waiting for Alex to object on his behalf, ToM says "Are you sure you aren't using him to separate yourself from your past?"

"It's all mine. It just feels like a story now it's a book."

"You need to embrace the whole of yourself. Remember each of us has to for us all."

"Here's me," Carl says and hugs himself.

ToM plainly finds this flippant, and shuts his mouth as tight as the fists he plants in front of him. "So you're saying the book conveys your authentic experience," Maggie prompts Carl.

"It's all me."

"I'll confirm that," Alex says.

"Thank you, Alex Grand." As he wonders why she has grown so formal she adds "And thank you, Carl Batchelor and ToM Lincoln. We've been talking about ghostwriting with reference to *When I Was Carla*, now available in shops as well as online."

Carl barely waits for her to stop recording before he says "I thought we were the whole show."

"You're the opening segment," Maggie says as if this should placate him more than it does. Having ushered everyone out of the studio, she murmurs to ToM "Stay for a word."

"I'll just have one with our friend here." To Carl he says "Remember there's a community who've had your sort of experience. You don't need to depend on anyone who hasn't. Just be true to yourself and the rest of us you stand for, and that includes taking a name that's yours, not just snipping a bit off your old one."

"I'm keeping as much as I can of it. It's all I've still got that my real dad gave me."

Night has fallen outside the windowless studio. As the exit doors part they admit an eager chill. The receptionist bids Carl and Alex goodnight from her wheelchair, and as the doors glide shut behind them Carl mutters "Sorry if it was my fault."

"I don't know why you should be sorry. What do you think you did?"

"Got us cut short for arguing with him. I'm who I am, and I know who I used to be and everything that happened to them."

"I'm certain everyone who reads your book will see that, Carl."

At the entrance to the nearest Underground station they shake hands. Carl's feels friendlier than the first time they met: softened by acquaintance, almost reverting to a female state. As Carl makes for his hotel, Alex clatters down the chipped stone stairs. He was heartened by Carl's answer to his question, which is why he let the book sound like a solo effort. By the time he reaches the platform ToM's comments have ceased to disturb him, and he can't even remember why one did, or which.

CARLA

"Mummy, I need to go to confession. I haven't been for months."

"You're a good girl, Carla. She's a good girl, isn't she, Malcolm?"

"I don't know a better one. Just make sure your mother never has to think any different, Carla."

I wasn't listening to him. My mother's reaction had left me afraid she might think I'd no reason to go to the church, and grow suspicious if I insisted. Then she said "You ought to go now while there won't be many people. Just wash up the breakfast things first."

I did that as fast as I could for fear of her changing her mind. I was putting on my shoes by the front door – she made us all wear slippers in the house "to keep the muck out" as she used to say – when she said "Could you take her, Malcolm? You know I don't want to impose, but I don't like her walking so far by herself when you don't know what kind of people may be about these days."

"She won't be any trouble, so don't give it another thought. You're never any trouble to me, are you, Carla?"

My mother widened her eyes at me till I mumbled "Don't suppose."

"Just thank your father anyway for putting himself out for you."

I had to choke down an urge to laugh or react some other way to her choice of words. "Thanks," I said to get it over with.

"Don't strain yourself," she said and closed her eyes as if she didn't want to see me. "Sometimes I don't know what to do with her, Malcolm."

"So long as I do," he said and opened the front door. "Come with me and we'll see to your soul, Carla."

He spoke only once on the way to the church. "I shouldn't think you have much to confess at your age," he said, which sounded like a warning to keep quiet about him. People in the street glanced at me as if they'd seen a jailer escorting a criminal to a cell. Perhaps that was how I looked and he did, because I felt as if I would never escape the trap that was Mr Randal.

The church smelled of candles someone had just blown out, which put me in mind of the birthday dinner he'd bought to show my mother how generous he was. Rather than remember that, I tried to recall birthdays with my real father. Every year my mother told him off for being too extravagant, but he always made me feel I deserved it, and eventually she would give in on my behalf. She used to bring out a lopsided cake scattered with tottering candles, and my father would say "The chef's excelled herself again." I'd liked those cakes better than the one Mr Randal must have paid a lot for at the restaurant, and now the waxy smell of the church was making me feel a little sick.

"You pray while we're waiting," he said and stayed seated on the pew while I went down on my knees. Though the kneeler was padded with leather, before long they began to ache. I prayed that he wouldn't be able to overhear my confession and that I would be able to say all the things I'd rehearsed in my head. I pressed my lips together as hard as I was clasping my hands, because I was afraid that if my lips moved he would read them. I kept my eyes open just enough to watch people going to confess. Every time someone came out of the booth and knelt to pray, my hands grew sweatier, and my armpits were prickling as well. The last person before me reappeared, and I crouched lower, hoping whoever was next in line would take my turn while I tried to be ready to talk to the priest. "Hurry up, Carla," Mr Randal said so close that I felt his wet breath in my ear. "Your mother needs you at home."

I stumbled to my feet and almost ran to the confession box to get away from him, though I felt as if I was leaving my ability to speak behind as well. I let myself into the sinner's half of the box and bruised my knees on the unyielding kneeler. Ahead of me was a mesh with gaps so small that I could barely see the outline of a head. I supposed that was meant to make you feel you were talking to God, but it put me in mind of a cage you might keep insects in. "Bless me, father, for I have sinned," I said. "It is about mumble months since my last confession."

"Speak clearly, my child. How long has it been?"

Recognising Father Brendan's voice didn't help me speak. I'd been hoping whoever was there wouldn't know me. "Four months, father," I said.

"Why has it been so long?"

This could have been my cue to reveal how Mr Randal had silenced me, but I failed to seize it. "Don't know, father."

"In future you must not leave it so long. Now make a full confession of your sins."

"I have sworn twice." I felt hindered by the formal language we'd been taught to use in confession, but I struggled on towards the words I had to speak. "I have lost my temper three times," I said. "I have fought at school. I have answered my mother back twice...."

"Ask Our Lord Jesus Christ to help you control your emotions," Father Brendan said as I trailed off. "Remember He has set your parents in authority over you, so you must always respect them and never resent them. For your penance say three Our Fathers and—"

He was dismissing me, which made me desperate enough to blurt "Wait, father."

"Had you not finished?" As I prayed I hadn't wearied him he said "Go on, my child."

I was sure this was my last and only chance to speak, but knowing how close Mr Randal was obstructed my tongue. I clasped my hands so tight that every finger felt like a separate set of aches, which only made my mouth feel clenched as well. I couldn't utter so much as a word about Mr Randal – the years of staying secretive had grown into a gag that was jammed into my mouth – and then I managed to remember that confession was supposed to be about myself. "I let someone see me when they shouldn't," I mumbled.

"Speak up, my child. Only God can hear."

I was terrified that Mr Randal might. "Letting someone see me when they oughtn't to," I said not much louder.

"What occasion is that? You must tell me all the truth."

"When I've got nothing on."

"Are you saying you flaunt yourself? That is a very grave sin. It's provocation and may lead others into evil."

My sense that this was painfully unfair let me liberate a few words. "He makes me."

"Who does?"

I couldn't say the name, not least because I was afraid it would bring him to listen outside the booth. "He lives in our house."

"Is he related to you?"

"No." This felt like an obstacle I couldn't struggle past, but somehow I succeeded in adding "He married my mum."

"You must be very careful about making accusations, my child. Is he of our faith?"

I didn't see how this could be relevant. "You married them."

"Then God has made him your father. What are you trying to tell me about him? Remember that bearing false witness is a very serious sin."

I seemed to have almost no words left. "What I said."

"My child, we are all of us born naked. It was the sin of Eve that took away our innocence. I believe I hear how she has stolen yours. Would you have made this accusation about the father who sired you?"

"He was my dad."

"And now God has blessed you with a new one. Pray to Him for guidance and examine your conscience. Consider very carefully whether your new father has really done anything wrong in the eyes of God before you accuse him."

My mouth felt so clogged I was afraid of spitting out more than words, but I succeeded in dislodging a lump of them. "He touches me."

"How does he do so?"

Every word felt like a blockage I had to eject. "With himself."

"You need to be clearer, my child."

"With his, with his—" It felt like a hurdle too high for me to clamber over, and the eventual product of my efforts was "With his man piece."

"That is the gravest charge you could make." Father Brendan leaned towards the mesh, and I saw his frowning face within his silhouette. "Have you told anyone else about this?"

"He said I mustn't. He stopped me."

"You understand I am bound by the seal of confession." He translated this by adding "I can't tell anybody anything I'm told."

I had an awful sense that he was as muzzled as I'd been till I overcame it – that I'd fought to speak for no purpose at all – and then I had an inspiration. "You can say to him."

"My child, you haven't understood."

"You can talk to him about it when he comes to confession," I said and was overtaken by another thought that needed to be spoken. "Hasn't he been saying what he does to me?"

"I have just told you I cannot discuss anyone's confession."

"But it's about me and I don't mind."

"You're confessing you were complicit."

"No," I whispered, close to panic. "I mean you can tell me what he said about me. Hasn't he got to confess?"

"I have made the situation absolutely clear to you. I am not prepared to discuss it any further."

"You could tell him he has to." More desperately still I said "He's here now. He's waiting for me."

I heard the door creak as Father Brendan peered out of the box. I was afraid that would alert Mr Randal, and was holding my breath by the time the priest said "I shall ask God how I must proceed. Now for your penance say three Our Fathers and three Hail Marys, and I shall hear your act of contrition."

"Oh my God, I am heartily sorry for having offended Thee, and I detest all my sins...." I detested Mr Randal more, and felt he ought to be bruising his knees where I was. Father Brendan absolved me, and I stumbled out of the booth. He had time to watch me trudge to Mr Randal before the next sinner went into the box. I knelt more than an arm's length from Mr Randal, but all the way through praying I sensed his nearness like the threat of a soft hot intrusion. When I'd finished I risked asking "Are you going to confession too?"

"I don't believe I've any need just now," he said and stood up. "Let's get home to your mother."

He said nothing on the way there. His silence felt like waiting to reveal he'd overheard me in the box or to let my mother know what I'd accused him of. If he did, wouldn't she have to intervene at last? As soon as I was home she beckoned me into the front room from her armchair. "Did you tell the priest everything you had to?"

I couldn't look at Mr Randal while I said "Yes."

"We knew she was a good girl who wouldn't let her parents down," Mr Randal said and looked like all the innocence he'd robbed me of.

I could hardly keep my mind on my household tasks that day for wondering what Father Brendan might do. I could only pray he would help me somehow, and I was so intent on praying that I knocked a leg of the Scandinavian dresser with the vacuum cleaner and nearly toppled all the china plates my mother had propped up on metal stands. "Don't smash the happy home up, child," she cried.

I couldn't eat much dinner. Every time I heard a car in the road I thought it might be Father Brendan. The longer I waited for him, the more I didn't know what I wanted him to do or what he could. He hadn't shown up by the time I had to go to bed, and I was on my knees beseeching God to send him when the bedroom door opened. But if my prayers had brought anyone because I hadn't kept them quiet enough, it was only Mr Randal.

As he came into my room the doorknob chafed against the headboard of the bed. Months of him bumping against me on the bed had shifted it towards the door, and by now every time he visited me at night the headboard and the handle scraped together. I felt as if each of his visits rubbed me a little smaller, just as he was damaging the doorknob. I thought the noise might bring my mother upstairs, however painful an effort she would have to make, but it never did – she didn't even call out to him. He waited till he thought I'd finished praying and said "Usual place, Carla," which meant I had to lie on the bed. I prayed harder than ever while he thrust at me and wiped up, and I remember thinking in between my prayers that this was just about the only cleaning I saw him do, his token household chore. I prayed that Father Brendan might arrive and catch him in the act, but there was no sign of help, just a police siren mocking my plight. I was still praying when Mr Randal left me alone and I crawled into bed, and when at last I fell asleep.

I wondered if the priest might come to find me at school, where Mr Randal would be out of the way, but praying all day for Father Brendan to show up didn't bring him. When Bridie's mother took us home he wasn't there, and Mr Randal wasn't. He'd rung my mother to say he was dealing with a client, apparently too prestigious to be named. His absence gave me back my appetite, but when I asked for a second helping of Irish stew my mother said "Leave it for your father, child. He's the one who does all the hard work." I could have argued, but I felt sinful enough without offending God that way. I'd begun to feel the priest had abandoned me because everything was my fault after all.

He hadn't appeared by the time my mother sent me up to bed, but at least Mr Randal hadn't either. "You can recite your catechism," she said, "even if your father isn't there to help." Instead I spent time feeling safe in the bathroom and then in my room. Once I'd prayed on my knees I crept into bed to continue praying, and I was whispering to God when I heard the front door open. It let in Mr Randal's voice and another man's. It was Father Brendan.

I wriggled out of bed and tried to make no noise as I padded to the door. The carpet felt rough as concrete under my bare feet. "Father," I heard my mother say as if she didn't know how to sound.

"Father Brendan came to see me at the office, Elaine. He'd like a private word with Carla."

I wondered if there had been any client after all. If not, Mr Randal had told her a lie. "What about, father?" she pleaded. "What's the child done, for pity's sake?"

"I believe she may be spiritually troubled, Mrs Randal. Let me reassure you I can put her mind at rest and do what needs to be done."

I thought I was hearing two promises – to save me while managing not to upset my mother. I couldn't have prayed for better, and I retreated into bed to pretend I hadn't been listening. I heard measured footsteps mount the stairs, less ponderously ominous than Mr Randal's, and then knuckles rapped on the door. "Carla, it's Father Brendan. May I come in?"

"Yes, father," I said and had to raise my voice. "Yes, father."

I felt pleased he'd asked permission. When he eased the door open he didn't push it far enough to nudge the bed with the doorknob. He closed it without a sound and paced over to me. He smelled of dry black cloth and a hint of the spicy aftershave he must recently have dabbed on his long smooth grey-cheeked face. "We must be very quiet now, Carla," he murmured.

"I will, father." I did my best while asking "What did Mr Randal say?"

"You know full well you must not ask me that."

I hadn't realised that confessions had to be kept secret wherever they were made, unless he'd taken Mr Randal to the church for it. "I'm sorry, father."

"You are forgiven, my child. All is going to be well. Now let me see you."

I thought he could, since my head was above the bedclothes. When he beckoned them away from me with a hand, I folded them back. "Show me what he does to you," he said.

I assumed he needed to be sure what I'd meant in confession, and I inched my pyjama bottoms down, but only as far as my navel. "Show me properly," the priest said. "You would for the doctor, wouldn't you? No need to be coy. Only God can see you, and He always can."

I told myself I mustn't hesitate when the priest was going to protect me from Mr Randal. I heard Mr Randal talking to my mother downstairs, far enough away that he was no threat to me. I pulled my pyjamas all the way down and kicked them off. "That's the spirit, my child," Father Brendan said. "Now just move yourself over and keep in mind how quiet we have to be." When I made space he lay down beside me, and I thought this might be his way of praying. Then he groped under his cassock and reached for me, and all I could do was find a prayer to hide in.

ALEXANDER

"You can make it, Alex," Lee says, glancing back with a wry but sympathetic grin.

"I'm right behind you," Alex tells her, though he isn't quite. He's toiling up yet another street in Hilly Fields, the London district determined to earn the name, though most of the fields are buried under roads and houses now. Several screeching fox cubs chase one another through back gardens as if they're searching for the vanished countryside, and a piping flock of parakeets like the vanguard of an altered landscape perch among the squat suburban chimneys and vintage television aerials. Above the park at the summit of the slopes, planes leaving Heathrow or bound for the airport over the horizon have chalked the pale blue sky with the lopsided grid of an obscure game. The scurries of a sitar and a tabla in an upstairs room urge Alex to tramp faster, fading behind him as Lee leads the way into the lofty street where his parents have their house.

It's one half of a linked pair, and painted brick red to set it apart from its pallid pebbledashed twin. An obese bay window bulges under a flattened version of itself. Much of the concrete that has covered the front garden is occupied by a gleaming silver Volvo estate. Potted plants like tokens of the suppressed garden are ranked on shelves within the shallow porch. A March chill penetrates his fingertip as Alex pokes the impeccably polished brass button next to the austerely panelled pine door. The bell trills not unlike a bird restricted to a solitary note, and he hears a voice. "Ring ring," his father is pronouncing. "Ring ring."

Alex assumes this is a species of joke, which the petulant tone is meant to render funnier – at least, he hopes all this. A sound of footsteps falls some way short of eagerness, and then his father opens the door an inch and by stages several. "Alexander," he calls, more an announcement than a celebration, and a frown together with a grimace appear resolved to concentrate his already compact features as he peers at Lee. "You've escaped me for the moment."

She sounds forgiving. "It's Lee, Gordon."

"Ah, I knew it could be anyone." He steps back to welcome them, unless he's regaining his balance. "Accompanied by Lee," he calls towards the kitchen.

"I'm not sure what you mean," Lee says.

"Aren't you my son's partner in crime?"

"If you like to put it that way." With a laugh she plainly hopes he sought to prompt Lee says "I meant about being anyone."

"It could be a man's name or a woman's. Would that have been your aim?"

"No, my parents gave it to me."

"It's refreshing to meet someone who respects their parents."

Alex's mother appears from the kitchen, which saves Alex from responding to his father. Her diminutive front is largely covered by a plastic apron printed with a stream of words out of the midst of a sentence by Joyce. It goes with the decorations in the hall, a framed terse play autographed by Beckett, a series of prints depicting writers – Austen, Forster, Woolf – asleep at their desks. Her face, which looks cramped by her small head, does its best to widen with a smile. "Alexander, Lee," she says, and somewhat less heartily "Is everything as it should be?"

"We're discussing the significance of names," Alex's father says, "and how little they appear to mean to some."

Despite keeping up her smile she looks as wary as Alex has begun to feel. "Come and have a drink before dinner," she suggests.

"Just aid my memory. Is it wine for both?"

"White is fine," Lee says, and Alex feels no need except to nod.

"Are we still allowed to say that?" his father says, which Alex wouldn't have expected him to ask even as the joke it has to be.

While his father fetches a bottle from the kitchen, Alex joins Lee on the podgy white leather couch, the arms of which resemble rolls of paper. On the floor between a pair of armchairs he sees a copy of *When I Was Carla*. The dust jacket is crumpled and torn, as if the book has been flung down if not thrown across the room. When his mother meets his eyes he says "So somebody's reading Carla."

"We both have been, Alexander."

His father reappears so precipitately that he might be anxious to involve himself in the conversation, but devotes himself to opening a bottle of pinot gris, stuffing a wad of foil into his trousers pocket and muttering over his efforts to crank forth the cork. He hands out glasses and takes a swig from his before planting it on top of the book while he gazes at Alex. "You were never who you said you were."

The rebuke reaches deeper into Alex than he understands or likes. However he has disappointed his father, he can only say "I did my best."

"Then I should very much prefer not to see your worst, unless we already have."

With more politeness than Alex senses she feels, Lee says "What are you saying Alex did?"

"I'm surprised you need to ask, since presumably you were involved."

"I'm with Lee," Alex says and takes her hand, which stirs uncertainly. "We've no idea what you mean."

His father's stare contains enough disfavour for them both. "I'm saying you were never Carla."

"Nobody said he was," Lee says on the way to a laugh.

The old man gropes for the book beside him, toppling the glass of wine. Only his wife's swift grab saves it from spilling across the carpet, and he glowers at her. "What are you doing with my drink?"

"You were going to upset it, Gordon."

"I doubt I'm quite so incompetent yet, and I'm not the author of the upset." He wrenches the book wide at the title page. "Read that," he says.

"We have," Lee reminds him.

"More than once," Alex adds.

Like a tutor wearied almost beyond bearing his father says "Aloud."

"When I was Carla. Agreed, I never was."

"And the rest of it."

"Carl Batchelor with Alex Grand. Dad, you surely can't think—"

"It scarcely matters what I think. It certainly seems not to matter to you. What in the name of anything that's holy did you have in your head?"

"You've lost me again."

"I fear we lost you when you started putting out these books of yours, but this one is a different matter and a worse one. You've lent your name to all this filth that has not the slightest thing to do with you."

"I think it has, you know. With all of us."

His father's grimace draws his lips inwards as though he has been punched in the mouth. "Precisely what do you want to be thought about me?"

"It's not about you, dad. How could it be? I'm saying we all need to be concerned about Carla's kind of situation, because it still goes on."

"I'm not concerned with that. I'm referring to the situation you've brought into our home."

"Which is that, Gordon?" Lee says with an attempt at gentleness.

"This house and all it represents. The life Amy and I thought we'd earned. If you don't know what a home is, young lady, something is very amiss with your life."

"No," Lee says forcefully enough to be denying a good deal. "Which situation?"

Alex's father slams the book shut and brandishes it so furiously he looks close to hurling it at Alex. "Claiming this past for his own."

"You can't seriously think he's done that. You'll know what a ghostwriter does."

"Stays a damn sight more invisible than he has, I should hope, and it isn't a question of what I think." He drops the book and thrusts out a hand for his glass, taking a gulp that sets off a cough. Before he has finished spluttering and waving away his wife's attempts to help, he struggles to pronounce "How many of his readers will he have led to believe his childhood was like that?"

"None at all, I'm sure."

"They'd have no reason," Alex says.

"Meet someone who was made to feel it was," his father says, thumping his heart so hard his wife winces. "This deplorable appalling parent."

"Honestly, you shouldn't. People can't miss the fact that the book's about Carl."

"If I did, the innocent reader assuredly could. You've soiled your memory and mine, and I don't doubt your mother's too."

"Mine hasn't altered, Gordon."

"I'm touched there's someone here who's staying loyal."

"It was never your story," Lee is provoked to retort, "and it needed to be told."

"It bears our name, which means our name is associated with that, that—" His search for a satisfactorily hostile word entails waving the wineglass over the book, spattering the cover. "That," he says with sufficient rage to be deploring the inadequacy of the word as well.

"Maybe you should make a statement that it isn't about you," Lee suggests. "You could online."

"I won't be undermining my mind with any electronics, I'm afraid, and I shouldn't have to defend our name."

"Perhaps Alex might put it out," Alex's mother says.

"I've no wish to have even more attention drawn to me, thank you."

She turns to Lee and Alex, not quite concealing desperation. "Have the people in your book been brought to justice?"

"Carl's stepfather died years ago," Alex tells her.

"What about that awful priest?"

"He'll be in jail for a long time."

"There you are, Gordon. The book has done some good."

"No further discussion ought to be permitted, then. Let it be forbidden."

"Gordon, really," Alex's mother says, but Alex feels bound to add "He was convicted before the book came out."

"A little honesty at last," his father says, using the wineglass on top of the book to lever himself to his feet while Alex's mother makes to intervene. "What's troubling you, Amy?"

"You'll break that if you're not careful."

"I believe I know my own strength," he says, leaning harder on the glass, which fails to splinter. "Please bring your drinks to the table while I serve."

As he makes for the kitchen his wife stays the guests with a hand. "He's been having a few lapses lately," she whispers. "You'd know if you saw us more often."

"I expect we will once Alex finishes his first draft," Lee says, and Alex manages a nod.

A small tub of flowers displaced from the porch squats in the middle of a ponderous oak table that occupies much of the dining-room. The floral scent is stronger than the scarcely identifiable aroma from the kitchen. Even when his father plods in with a steaming casserole between his padded fingerless hands, Alex can't make much of a guess at the contents. "Do serve yourselves," his father says as if he has forgotten what he previously said, and Alex wonders if this is an example of a lapse.

His father fetches rice and raita while Alex's mother ladles out helpings, possibly of stew, and the old man returns once more with a bottle of wine apparently so chilled it makes his arms shiver. "I'll have some too," he unnecessarily tells his wife, and mumbles about struggling to extract the cork. Alex might take over except for sensing that the offer wouldn't go down well. Having refilled all the glasses, his father takes a mouthful of the dinner he made and glances at his fellow diners as if searching for the judgment he should make. "Very nice, Gordon," Lee ventures.

This only provokes pedantry. "Precise in what way?"

Lee tries a laugh, which fails to satisfy him. "Flavoursome," she says, which Alex thinks is too close to a fib. "What is it exactly?"

"Lamb curry. Indian. The sort one used to enjoy before it had to be brought up to date."

"Gordon," Alex's mother says and would clearly prefer not to add "I think you may have left out an ingredient or two."

"I can't imagine why I would have been distracted," he says and stares at his son.

Before Alex can decide on a response, having suppressed at least one, his phone rings. "Kirsty," it adds, but his father is louder. "Ring ring," he declares with distaste.

"It's my editor. I should find out what she wants."

"I'm sure she must take precedence," his father says as if his frown may not be enough of a rebuke.

"Kirsty, we're dining with my parents. What's up?"

"Have you seen Carl on YouTube?"

"I didn't even know he was there."

"Watch it as soon as you can, and then we'll need to talk. I should tell you it's quite a long item."

"Can it wait until we're finished here?"

"All right, but not much longer."

Alex meant the question to placate his father, but it has the opposite effect. "Do finish as soon as you choose to," his father says. "We're aware how many better things you have to do."

"I'll watch the video after dinner."

"Not in this house, if you don't mind. We don't welcome enemies of conversation." When his wife opens her mouth he says more loudly "Especially since it relates to that book."

His outburst proves equally inimical to conversation. The curry is succeeded by rice pudding with some ambition to taste Asian, and tepid coffee overwhelmed by milk. When Lee makes to wash up after dinner Alex's father says "I'm sure Alexander is impatient to be gone." He sees them to the front door, and Alex's mother hastens to give them each a hug. The one she accords Alex feels like reluctance to let go. "Don't leave it so long next time," she says, "either of you."

"And whatever your publishers are so eager you should see," his father says, "I hope it will resolve the issue with your book, Carla."

It's impossible to judge how much of a joke the name is meant to be. As Alex looks back from the gate, his father retreats into the house. "I can't even recall when I ever touched the boy," he's complaining to his wife. The front door shuts, and Lee gives Alex a sympathetic look he fails to return. He's too preoccupied with trying to remember the last time his father touched him.

CARLA

The morning after Father Brendan came into my bedroom, Mr Randal and my mother waylaid me in the kitchen. They made it feel like an interrogation room even before my mother said "What did Father Brendan want with you, Carla?"

I'd spent half the night trying to get ready to tell. Whenever I woke from not realising I'd fallen asleep I prayed to be able to speak. I managed to open my mouth and listened to the words that succeeded in escaping. "Don't know."

"Don't be so stupid, child. How can't you know? Just speak up for yourself for a change. I wouldn't be surprised if people think you're dumb or not right upstairs. I won't have the priest come to this house and not know why he did."

Everything she said to force me to talk left me less capable of talking. Her stare and Mr Randal's felt like a contradiction they'd planted in my mind, blocking the part of it that made my mouth work. "Have you ever seen such a stubborn girl, Malcolm?" my mother cried. "That isn't how we brought her up. It's what they used to call dumb insolence."

"Perhaps she has her reasons. No need to upset yourself."

"What reason could a child have not to confide in her own mother and father? You tell me that if you can."

As I sent God a silent prayer that Mr Randal would be forced to tell, he said "She could think it's like confessing and she can't say what she told the priest."

"God help us, Carla. What have you been up to that you can't tell your parents?"

"I don't believe she's done anything wrong, my pet. I think she just needed Father Brendan to sort out some doubts for her."

Far more like a complaint than a question my mother said "What has she got to have doubts about?"

"Carla, you're allowed to tell us. Just remember we're the ones who care for you. We're why you have the life you have, and I know your mother wouldn't want it any different." With a look that warned me not to distress her he said "You weren't sure about me marrying your mother, were you?"

"She's got no right to feel that way after everything you've done for us."

"We can afford to have a little sympathy, can't we? When you're her age the world can be a confusing place, and you need someone to show you what's right."

"She's had someone. There's been you as well as me. The last person she ought to blame for anything she thinks is wrong is you."

"Let's see if we can understand her. After all, I did come into her life."

"And she should be thanking you for it. Thanking you and thanking God you did instead of treating you like an intruder."

"I don't mean she resents me. I think she was troubled for us."

By now I felt I was hardly there at all. Certainly my feelings had been denied and dismissed as if they were no more than fancies I ought to have outgrown. "Troubled about what?" my mother demanded.

"Let me say it for you, Carla. You were afraid in case your mother and I were living in sin, weren't you?"

I had no idea what might come out of my mouth till I heard myself mumble "Yes."

"I don't know how she dares to say such a thing about you, Malcolm. What else is she going to accuse you of, for heaven's sake?"

"We shouldn't condemn her for bring concerned for her family, should we? Some things are new till you get used to them, and I'm sure some of them can be disturbing to start with. Embrace everything God sends you, that should be our motto," he said, and I tried to hear it in the squeaky voice my real father used when he was being him, and not to feel Mr Randal was referring to me. "You don't think we're sinful any longer, do you, Carla?" Mr Randal said.

My mouth felt incapable of producing any answer except "No."

"Then I think we can be grateful Father Brendan took the time to counsel her, don't you, Elaine?"

"I think she's the one who should be grateful you're so

understanding, Malcolm. Just you apologise to your father, Carla, and thank him as well."

"Sorry." Even less distinctly I said "Thanks."

"I'm sorry she's so sullen, Malcolm. She doesn't like to be told off. I just hope she's said enough for you, and I really hope she's happy with our situation even if she doesn't look it. I wouldn't want Father Brendan to have wasted his energy."

"I'm sure he won't mind if you ask him."

"I won't be taking up his time. She's already done too much of that." As though I'd suddenly become present my mother said "Eat up your breakfast before you have Mrs Shea worrying where you've got to."

Despite her declaration, I was afraid my mother might decide to question Father Brendan. She'd changed her mind over more important matters, after all – Mr Randal for one, after laughing at the way my real father had portrayed him. If she approached the priest he might come to the house again – but he never did. Whenever I knelt at the altar rail while he was handing out communion, I had to force myself not to recoil as I spied under my eyelids his fingers reaching for my open mouth. I was remembering how much else that hand had offered me. He was just another man like Mr Randal, except he'd brought a handkerchief smelling of his church into my room instead of a wad of paper.

Mr Randal still came to my room. Now that I'd been confirmed, he couldn't pretend he was helping me with my catechism. He had to wait for my mother to fall asleep after she told me good night and heaved herself halfway up from the armchair to receive a kiss, which made me feel it was a duty she had to perform before she could get any rest. Sometimes she would wake up when Mr Randal went downstairs after he'd finished with me, and I would hear him convincing her that he'd been with me just long enough to watch over my prayers. I was finding it hard to believe in them since Father Brendan had revealed himself, but I felt all the more desperate to hide in them from Mr Randal, especially once I reached my teens and he found more of me to touch.

By now Bridie and I were walking to school by ourselves – St Brendan's College next to the church – though my mother supported the idea less than Bridie's did. "Don't speak to any strangers," she would warn me at least once a week. "If anyone does anything they shouldn't, just you run and tell a grownup," which reminded me how hard I'd tried and how it had only brought me worse.

Bridie was in a higher class than me, which didn't please my mother. "I don't know why you can't do as well as her," she frequently complained, and Mr Randal said "You make sure you develop all your talents, Carla. That's what God wants." I knew he was responsible for making it hard for me to learn or even think, but I couldn't say so, and my mother told me off for being insolently dumb.

Soon Bridie made new friends, and I saw less of her. Other friends I'd had at primary school had ended up elsewhere, and I didn't seem able to make new ones. I felt as if people shouldn't want to know me and wouldn't like me if they did. I stayed inside myself as much as possible, in class as well, where some teachers tried to coax me out and others made me feel I wasn't worth the effort. Walking home with Bridie was one of the few regular events I looked forward to, even though we didn't talk much, because it meant school was over for another day – and then I found out what she'd been saying about me and my mother.

I confronted her over it on the way home. "What have you been saying about when I stayed at yours?"

Bridie tried to look as if I shouldn't even have asked. "Don't know what you mean."

"You've been telling everyone I took up all the room."

"Well, you pretty nearly did. You kept acting like it was your house."

"That's what Mr Randal does, not me."

"My dad says you wouldn't even have it any more if it wasn't for Mr Randal."

"Don't care. I wish my mum had never married him."

"You're not meant to say things like that. My mam says he's a saint for looking after her."

I could have tried to say he made her need to be looked after, but I was busy saying "Don't you tell anyone my mum takes advantage."

"She never walked us to school for years when my mam did."

"She did till Mr Randal made her fall downstairs."

This felt like a step towards telling Bridie more, but she robbed me of the chance. "She said he never, and anyway if she's that bad she ought to be in a wheelchair."

I might have conceded the last part if Bridie hadn't said "My dad says she'd better not pretend she's any worse, cos you can't stay with us any more."

"Don't you want me to?" I pleaded.

"You're too big to go in my bed now. You used to nearly kick me out when you were staying. Anyway, I don't want anybody coming in my bed."

She'd brought me to the edge of telling the truth again. "I don't either."

"I won't be, so you're safe, aren't you?"

"No," I blurted and found more words I could just about eject. "Didn't mean you."

"Don't start that again, Carly."

I was almost too confused to speak. "Start what?"

"That's why my dad says you can't stay. He says you go round making people think someone's interfered with you."

I made a last effort, which felt like vomiting and tasted like it too. "They do."

Bridie picked up speed and didn't look back till she was yards ahead. "He says I can't hang round with you if you do that. I remember when you did it about him."

"Bridie, wait. Just listen," I begged, though I wasn't sure I could go on.

"I'm not listening," she called, pressing her hands over her ears as she began to run.

I dashed after her and dragged her hands away. "Bridie—"

"Get off me. Get off." When I tried to speak she started to sing at the top of her voice as if she hadn't time to find a tune, and I let go of one of her hands so as to cover her mouth. She bit my hand and pulled my hair, and we fell on the grass verge, wrestling close to the traffic. "Girls, girls," a woman cried, and another one helped her separate us. "We know which school you go to," one said. "We'll be telling your headmaster, Bridie Shea."

Bridie stumped home and I trudged after her. I thought that when my mother saw me she would ask what was wrong, but she either didn't notice or was used to my being morose. When Mr Randal came home for dinner he only said "Liven yourself up, ladies. God likes a cheery house," which sounded like one of his phrases my real father would have imitated, and gave my mother her cue to blame me for acting sullen. I was wondering what the headmaster would do, though I didn't even care much. I seemed to have almost no feelings left at all.

The next day he called me to his office. Bridie was already there and had told him who the other girl was. He put his hands together as though he was praying for us and lowered his head to frown at us over them. "You have let yourselves and St Brendan's down," he said. "Your parents will have to be informed." He gave us letters in brown envelopes that reminded me of the ones that used to make my real father sigh before he even opened them. Mine said *For the attention of Mr and Mrs Randal*, which made me want to tear it up, because that oughtn't to have been my mother's name. I would have except for knowing Bridie meant to take hers home, so that my mother and her husband would know I hadn't brought them mine.

"What have you been up to now?" my mother cried before she'd even opened the envelope. She shook her head as if she had to move it slowly back and forth to read the letter, and then carried on the shake without bothering to look at me. "God alone knows what your father's going to think of you now," she said as if Mr Randal's view of me meant more than hers, and I almost retorted that my father wouldn't be thinking about me, because he was in heaven. I still wanted to believe that, though Father Brendan had started to make me lose faith in the church.

I was vacuuming the stairs when Mr Randal let himself in. "What's this I hear about you fighting in the street?" he said, and I thought everybody must be talking about my crime till I saw Bridie's mother behind him. She must have caught him on his way home. "Come in, Mrs Shea," he said and to me "And you come to your mother."

My mother looked bewildered by having a visitor. "You know you're always welcome, Maddy, but what's bringing you just now?"

"Your Carla started a fight with our Bridie and it got back to their school."

"She brought a letter home, but she never said the other girl was Bridie. What have you got to say for yourself, Carla?"

"I just wanted her to listen to me."

"From what I hear," Mrs Shea said, "it wasn't anything we'd want her hearing, and I'm saying no more except bless her for not wanting to either."

"God help you, child," my mother said, but not like a prayer. "What were you trying to put into her head?"

I was further than ever from revealing what I'd struggled to tell Bridie. The best I could manage was "She said I said things about her dad when I never."

"Speak properly, Carla," my mother said as if she didn't want to acknowledge my meaning.

"I expect that's how girls of their age can be," Mr Randal said, "squabbling over nothing much."

"I hope you aren't saying my James's reputation is nothing."

"Not for a minute, Mrs Shea. I'm sure it's as spotless as mine."

"I'm glad you know, but I'm afraid we won't want Bridie seeing Carla any more."

"See what you've brought on yourself, child," my mother cried. "Just you apologise to Mrs Shea."

"Sorry," I mumbled, as I'd been made to think I should feel all the time.

Mr Randal showed Mrs Shea out, and my mother stared at me till he came back. "I hope you're satisfied now you've lost your best friend," she told me. "I wonder who you'll go about with now. I wouldn't like to think what kind of company you'll end up keeping."

I felt as if she'd doomed me to become the worst she thought of me, or how Mr Randal wanted me to be, supposing there was any difference. Next day as I walked to school I saw Bridie ahead. She glanced over her shoulder and doubled her speed, and I didn't try to catch up. When she saw me later in the schoolyard she said something to her friends, who looked at me and sniggered till I retreated to the far side of the yard. Even there I felt as if the entire school was gossiping about me, and I didn't want to hear what anybody said, because I was afraid it might be the truth.

Soon it was. One day I was coming out of the girls' toilets when a boy from Bridie's class accosted me. He had pimples all over his pale rubbery face, even in between the hairs of a moustache like a faint shadow of his piggish snout. Though there was nobody in sight, he kept his voice down. "Want something good?"

Despite feeling that my life contained nothing of the kind, I muttered "Don't know."

"What do you smoke?"

"Don't."

He stared at me as if I'd told him I didn't believe in God. "Haven't you done weed? It takes you somewhere else."

It wasn't in the list of sins I'd learned for my confirmation. "Sounds good."

"I'll give you some if you show me what you've got. I know you do."

I felt less wary than exhausted, but I lied "Don't know what you mean."

"What you've got down there." He glanced about and dodged into the boys' toilet block, where he flourished a fat cigarette at me. "You can have half," he said. "Come on, quick."

When I ventured through the doorless entrance he darted into the nearest cubicle and bolted the door as soon as I joined him. A smell of disinfectant caught in my throat, and I coughed till he said "Shut up, for Christ's sake." I managed to swallow the rest of the coughs, and he lit the joint with a transparent orange plastic lighter. "Let's see it, then," he urged.

I reminded myself he'd promised to send me somewhere else, which felt like a chance of escape. As I yanked up my skirt and slipped my knickers down around my knees, he took a drag and planted the joint between my lips. "Take the biggest one you can and hold it," he said, all of which was wreathed in smoke.

I sucked hard on the joint, and by the time I had to exhale my head felt as if it was lifting off like a rocket starting a flight. Or perhaps it was more like a cloud sailing into the sky. The boy reclaimed the joint and gave the gap between my legs a final look. "Go away now," he said more urgently than he'd asked to see it. "We can do it again if you want some more." He bolted the door the instant I was past it, and I heard him snatching paper off the roll on the wall. When I edged out of the toilet block, having checked that nobody was in sight, I'd forgotten about him. I went to the schoolyard wall and gazed across the playing field at the gestures trees were shaping out of the wind, and that was how I spent the rest of lunchtime, which felt as if the trees were caressing the seconds to slow them down, turning each one into at least a minute. My tormentors – Mr Randal, Bridie and her cronies – were so distant they no longer mattered. I didn't need prayers, because I'd found somewhere much better to hide.

ALEX

"Tell us how you felt the first time you got stoned again."

"Like I said, like a rocket taking off."

"You said your head felt like that."

"That's right, my head."

"Like what exactly? You don't say."

"Like it's taking forever to lift off and all of a sudden it goes whoosh."

"Whoosh."

"That's how it felt. I don't mean sounded."

"I shouldn't think it sounds like anything unless you're stoned out of your head. You said you felt like a cloud as well."

"Right, sailing in the sky...."

"Can you see what Kirsty thinks we ought to look at?" Alex says, having paused the video. "I think he's handling questions well enough."

"You should have asked her what it was."

"I was having enough trouble with my father, and we mightn't have wanted him to hear."

They're on the train to Brighton. The edge of London races backwards, reversing the afternoon's journey. Now that night has fallen, the streets resemble an imperfect memory conjured up by lamps. Recalling the confrontation with his father makes Alex uneasier than he understands, unless that's an effect of waiting to see how Carl went wrong at the readers' group in Norwich, and he restarts the video. "So you're saying," says the woman who's questioning Carl, "you felt like that the first time you smoked cannabis."

Carl's eyelids flicker, and his eyes do. "Right, that's how."

"Does it usually have that much of an effect so soon?"

"I wouldn't know. It did on me. I was just a kid."

"No doubt this is of vital interest to some," a man objects, "but the rest of us are here to discuss books."

"I was simply wondering how it may have affected Mr Batchelor in the long term."

"Mr Batchelor, you've a line about trees shaping gestures from the wind."

"That's mine."

"It wasn't yours," Alex protests as the man says "That isn't how you talk."

"It isn't how I do," Alex says while Carl replies "No, it's how I write."

"Aren't they supposed to be the same?"

"Real writers don't need them to be."

"You're claiming you're one of those."

"That's because I am." Carl flourishes a copy of *When I Was Carla* and jabs his name on the cover with a fingertip, which looks as if he means to score a goal in the central letter of his surname. "That's me," he says.

"Then who is Alex Grand?"

"Another one."

Lee laughs, but Alex sees no reason. He feels as if his thoughts are being voiced as the man says "Surely he's the author."

"It's all my story. Except for me he'd have none. I told him it and he helped me remember bits I forgot. They're my words and he polished them a bit to make it more like a book."

As Alex stares at Lee without the need for speech, the woman says "How much do you actually remember?"

"All of it. I just said."

"Shall we see?"

Carl rubs his cheeks and chin as though to reassure himself they're masculine, a gesture suggestive of feeling for his mouth. "See what?"

"What did you say to your friend that made her fall out with you?"

"Bridie? She said I was spreading rumours when I never did."

"How did you start the argument?"

"I didn't. She did when she said."

"What you accused her of saying, you mean. You'll remember what that was."

"She said I'd been taking up all the room when I stayed at theirs."

"That's approximately it. Well, you pretty nearly did. You kept acting like it was your house."

"I never." Much in the same tone of a reversion to childhood Carl says "What are you trying to do?"

"Just quoting what you say your friend said. What do you say to her now?" As Carl picks up *When I Was Carla* from the table he's behind, the woman says "Don't read it from your book."

His protest sounds more childish than ever. "You are."

"They aren't supposed to be my memories." As inexpressively as she might read a sign aloud the woman says "Well, you pretty nearly did."

"I never, so—"

"You kept acting like it was your house. Your line now, Mr Batchelor."

Carl glares at the unseen woman and clenches a fist on top of the book. "That's what Malcolm Randal did."

"You said Mr Randal, but not too far off the mark. My dad says you wouldn't even have it any more if it wasn't for Mr Randal."

"Don't care." Alex thinks Carl has retrieved the memory until he says "He was a shit who abused me for years."

"That's what you couldn't tell your friend. Don't you know what you actually said?"

Carl slits his eyes to twin glints. "I wish my mother hadn't married him."

"Close. My mam says he's a saint for looking after her."

"No, he was a devil, the only kind there is. Him and Father Brendan."

"You couldn't say that either. My mam says he's a saint for looking after her."

"Maybe she took advantage sometimes, but that's because he made her like that. Lady, I'm talking to you now, what are you trying to get at?"

"You didn't say much of that to your friend. I'm raising an issue about your kind of book."

"I don't read any. I just know about mine."

"That's what we're testing. My mam says he's a saint for looking after her."

"I said he wasn't. If you make me I'll say worse."

"Let's not have our ears offended. Very well, she never walked us to school for years when my mam did."

"She did till he shoved her down the stairs and crippled her back."

"No, your exact words if you can put your mind to them."

"They're all you're getting," Carl declares, and a man speaks offscreen. "Who says he did?"

"Crippled my mother? I do."

"You didn't see it happen, did you? And you never say she said he did."

"I know he did. He'd do anything he thought he could get away with."

"You must be glad he's out of your life."

"Shows prayers maybe sometimes work. Just not quick enough." As Alex hears murmurs that may express agreement or mild shock, Carl turns his gaze towards the woman beyond the camera. "Finished?" he scarcely asks.

"I believe I've made my point, so let someone else speak."

His gaze hardens. "Which point's that?"

"That you couldn't possibly remember what was said in so much detail."

"It's how memoirs are written," Alex protests as Carl retorts "I don't have to now. I did for my book."

"I wonder if you may have exaggerated your powers of recollection."

"Didn't exaggerate a thing. That's how my life was."

"Claimed to have a better memory than the rest of us possess, then. I suppose you have to seem to in the interests of your book."

"Don't know why you'd call it better. Nothing good about remembering Randal."

"Lydia's saying," a man calls out, "you've faked some of the details."

"No, I'm not a fake. Some of you lot are. Telling me I'm not a writer when I bet none of you have written books, and making out I fucked my mind up when Randal did if anybody did, except he never managed. And your friend Lydia if that's her name, trying to make me sound like I can't remember my own life. Can you remember everything you said last week? Know what, I can't either. I just remember all the stuff that left its mark in here." He thumps his brow so hard with several fingertips that the impacts can be heard across the room. "Thanks for having me," he says but then "And I was nearly had. Gave you more than you deserve."

The camera pans with him as he stalks past the small audience and vanishes beyond a library bookshelf. The spectators have started rather more than murmuring when the video ends. "Well," Lee says with an attempt at humour, "now we know."

Alex is already reverting his mobile to its phone mode. "Let's hear what Kirsty wants."

Kirsty's response abbreviates the ringtone before it has a chance to double itself. "Alex," she says like a flattened question.

"I've been looking at our wild child."

"I guess we could call him that, only not to his face."

"Better that than calling him an author."

"I think it'll be wisest to call him what he likes."

"Other than that," Alex says as unironically as he can manage, "what do you think we should do?"

"Have you any ideas? We do seem to be having trouble with your books."

"I thought you were saying Carl was the author."

"We'll deal with who is when we meet. Can you make tomorrow?"

"Any time the train will get me there."

"He'll be with me by twelve, so let's say then."

"You don't want to sort out any kind of plan before we see him."

"We need to get everybody who's responsible together as soon as possible."

"I don't think I can be held responsible for anything Carl does," Alex says and is glad Lee appears to concur. "I wonder if he cares as much about his customers as he wanted me to think."

"I'm not getting that, Alex."

"When I interviewed him he gave me the impression he was concerned about his passengers, but he seems pretty ready to leave the job behind."

"So long as we're all concerned about our customers."

This feels unreasonably close to a rebuke. "The plan is just to educate him in handling our public, is it?"

"If you think you can. We'll see how the meeting develops tomorrow."

The train is drawing into Brighton. As the lights of the station fend off the night, Alex pockets his phone. "I don't know where all that leaves me," he admits.

"With me," Lee says, but even her squeezing his arm seems not to change the situation.

Ten minutes' walk through winding streets redolent of restaurants brings them to their flat, where the sea can be heard but not seen. Alex senses Lee might like to make love, perhaps to enliven his mood, but he's too exhausted to produce enthusiasm. In bed he hugs her close, hoping this feels like appreciation. She's asleep before he is, but at last the faint sound of waves washes away his awareness.

"Just be yourself," Lee tells him over breakfast, and he wonders why she feels the need, of that phrase at any rate. On the London train he watches the YouTube video once more. Would Carl have behaved differently if he'd realised he was being filmed? There's no sign of him on Euston Road, but Alex hurries through the crowd in the hope of reaching Kirsty first for a discussion. Below the glass lift pedestrians shrink towards their phones as though the devices are battening on them. On the floor that won't own up to being thirteenth, Rod says "They're in Kirsty's office. I'll tell her you're here."

"Who is?"

"You." With a smile that looks poised to be puzzled Rod says "Alex Grand, if I'm not mistaken."

"Of course you aren't." Alex has no time to add whatever kind of laugh this might deserve. "I was asking who's in her office."

Rod unfolds a hand towards copies of *When I Was Carla* on the low tables. "Our latest celebrity," he says and meets a phone halfway with his face. "Your other author's here."

Alex can't help recalling that the reception area displayed just a solitary copy of his last novel. As he remembers how Carl reacted to it, Kirsty comes to find him. Her habitually expectant look seems determined to be satisfied. "Here I am," Alex murmurs while she escorts him along the corridor. "Your other author."

"I'm sure Rod didn't mean it that way."

Carl is sprawled on a starved leather chair in front of her desk, the present centrepiece of which is a copy of *When I Was Carla*. As Alex sits next to him while Kirsty returns to her chair, which is fatter than the others put together, Carl lifts his head as if a thought has lightened it. "Glad you could make it, Alex."

"I thought the meeting mightn't be complete without me."

Having conveyed that he's considering the possibility, Carl says "Don't suppose it would."

"So what has anyone been saying in my absence?"

"Don't worry, we haven't been talking about you."

"I'm asking whether there was anything I ought to know."

"She was saying I should stop remembering things I remember."

"No, Carl, I said maybe don't make so much of some of it when you're talking to an audience."

"I call that remembering, talking to my readers," Carl says and twists to face Alex. "You can tell me more than her."

"That might sound sexist to some people," Alex says.

"Don't see why. I was a girl as well. I meant you're a writer like me and she isn't."

"I wouldn't be the writer I am without Kirsty. Kirsty, did I miss anything I should have heard?"

"She said I oughtn't to tell anyone I smoked weed."

"I didn't say that, Carl. You mustn't deny anything that's in your book, but maybe don't remind your public you used cannabis."

"I don't any more." Even more defensively Carl says "Anyway, Alex said he did."

"Only at university, and it panicked me so much I never went near it again. I wasn't hearing my own voice when I spoke."

"I never went to uni like my dad wanted me to. Randal saw to that," Carl says and faces Kirsty. "Anyway, can we get that video taken off? I didn't say anyone could film me."

"I'm afraid our legal lady Ruth says we wouldn't have much chance."

"I wouldn't have said half what I did if I'd known it was going online."

"So long as you're more careful what you say in future."

"You said we've both pissed the public off."

"When did you do that, Kirsty? It must have been before my time."

"No, she said you did." Before Alex can react Carl says "I won't be keeping quiet if anybody goes for me like that woman in the video. I can't be anyone I'm not."

"I wonder if you could use some support," Kirsty says. "Maybe when you're on television."

"Won't be going there."

"Carl, we've booked you several appearances. They're important for us all."

"Not me. Don't like being watched when I can't see who's watching. It's like that bastard Randal watching me in the bath." As Kirsty parts her lips Carl says "You can't make me and I won't."

"Perhaps I could substitute," Alex says.

"That may have to be the solution if you let it, Carl."

Alex gathers that she's hoping to provoke Carl to change his mind, but Carl tells him "You've got to know the story just like me."

"That's assuming the programmes will accept you, Alex." Perhaps Kirsty realises this leaves him feeling close to redundant, since she says "You did well as a team for Maggie Rotheram. Maybe you should deal with audiences together."

"Don't need him helping me remember any more."

"I'm sure you don't. I'm suggesting Alex could field any questions you'd prefer not to answer."

"There's none of those."

"Let's say questions you might find too provocative."

"If they're about me it should be me that's answering."

"Perhaps Alex can tone them down for you at least. You could rephrase them, couldn't you, Alex?"

"We all know how good I am at changing people's words."

"Will you give it a try, Carl? I'm sure you'll agree that whatever is good for your book will be good for us all."

"If you put it like that," Carl says but pauses, "suppose I can see."

"Just do your best not to say anything you might regret."

"I don't. I tell the truth."

As Alex tries to decide how Carl has contradicted himself, Kirsty says "Your next gig isn't television. See how it goes and maybe Alex will help you change your mind about being watched."

Carl shrugs so ambiguously that it could be taken as a move towards agreement, and says nothing more to Alex until they're in the lift. As the heads of pedestrians swell towards them while the crowd continues hiding its faces, he says "You may have to do what she says, but not me."

"She's looking out for all our interests, Carl."

"I'll just be looking after mine. See you at our next show," Carl says and is speedily lost in the crowd. Presumably he doesn't realise Alex is heading for Euston too. By the time Alex reaches the station Carl may well be on his train home. As the escalator lowers Alex into the depths, his self feels as remote as the commuters all around him seem. He's trying to grasp what Carl said today that has left him indefinably vulnerable, but it's so far out of reach that it might as well be someone else's memory, and the screech of an approaching train cuts it out of his mind.

CARLA

I left school when I was sixteen. I'd done too badly to stay on, never mind trying for university. I passed English Language and just managed with Religious Knowledge, and failed every other exam. I thought it showed how useless praying was, because I knew my mother had prayed for my success. I'd prayed at least as hard, thinking university would take me out of Mr Randal's reach. Now the solitary prayer I said was for him to go away somehow. It felt like a dull ache behind my eyes, if that wasn't a hangover from smoking weed. The only thing I missed about school was how easy it had been to score whenever I needed some. All it took was letting boys feel me in the toilets, which at least was my choice, not like Mr Randal.

My mother made it clear she didn't think that God had let her down, just that I had. "I hope you're happy with yourself," she said when Mr Randal opened the envelope with my results in and read them to us. "You should have had plenty of time to study when you've got no friends to distract you. What were you up to instead?"

I could have told her I'd made quite a few friends – the boys who gave me weed. Instead I retorted "I'd have had more time for homework if I didn't have to do so much round the house."

"There you are, Malcolm. It's your fault for going out to work to keep us and mine for being such a useless crock."

"You mustn't blame yourself, Elaine. You've done everything you could for her and more."

"Everyone's to blame but you, Carla. Don't you dare let anybody think we are. What are we going to do with her, Malcolm?"

"I think I may have something for her, my pet."

"Just you hear that, Carla. Even now your father hasn't given up on you. Tell her what she has to do, Malcolm."

"I believe I can find a position for her."

"With your firm, do you mean?"

"What else do you think I could have in mind?"

"You haven't forgotten she can't drive, not that I'd want her to. I wouldn't feel safe, not like we are with you."

"Of course I wouldn't think of hiring her to drive, but I'm just about to lose one of my receptionists. She's leaving to have a child."

"God bless her and her little one. And just you thank God for your father, Carla. And right now, thank your father for finding something you can do for him."

I didn't want to be grateful to him, but she stared at me till I mumbled "Thanks."

"No wonder you didn't do better if that's how you spoke up at school. You'll need to get yourself more of a voice if she's going to be on your switchboard, won't she, Malcolm?"

"Don't fret, I'll see our girl makes herself heard. You have a little rest now while we put out the dinner." He followed me into the kitchen, where he murmured "You make enough noise when you want to. Try making it so your mother can be proud of you."

I thought she might never be, especially when she threw down her knife and fork at dinner as if she'd just been struck by an awful realisation. "She's got nothing decent to wear for your office, Malcolm."

"We can take her shopping tomorrow and I'll let the other girl go at the weekend."

The next day we drove into Liverpool, where my mother insisted on choosing me a suit with trousers. "We want her looking businesslike," she told the salesman, "not provocative." When I came out of the changing room she made me walk up and down in front of her and Mr Randal, and I felt like a model who was trying to look like a man. I remember feeling I'd be safer if I were one, maybe wishing I could be. "If you're happy with her I am," she told Mr Randal. "You can stop the price out of her salary."

"No need for that, my pet. I'm dressing her up on behalf of the business."

"Just you make sure you appreciate that," my mother said so fiercely she might have been telling the salesman as well. "See you're as good as you look."

On my first day at work she made me a cooked breakfast instead of the cereal I usually served myself. I suspected she wouldn't have gone to the trouble if I hadn't been working for her husband, and perhaps she meant to impress him with her commitment too. She gave him that kind of breakfast every day, of course. "Let's get you fit for your father," she said. "Don't let him down when he's putting his trust in you."

"No need to worry your head over her, my pet. So long as I'm her father she'll have a job," Mr Randal said, and I felt weighed down not just by the breakfast she insisted I had to finish but by their words as well.

The taxi firm was half a mile away, on the edge of a shopping precinct. As Mr Randal drove me there I felt as if he was taking me to prison. At least there would be other people, and I thought I might be able to make better friends than I'd made in the toilets at school. He called everyone into the reception area, which had bare boards and folding canvas chairs for waiting customers to sit on and a boxy counter in front of a switchboard. "Welcome the new addition to the team," he said. "She's replacing Emma. Say hello to Carla. She's my girl."

"Hello, Carla," the six drivers said, and Doris, who occupied the bigger of the two chairs at the switchboard, just about joined in. "Bit young for you, isn't she, Malcolm?" a driver said.

As I thought how little they must know about their boss, Mr Randal gave him a disgusted look. "No place for smutty talk in front of ladies, Barry. You know perfectly well I'm saying she's my daughter."

"Only making her welcome, Malcolm," Barry said with a grin at how this nearly rhymed. "Only having a bit of a laugh."

"Less laughs mean more work," Mr Randal said as he lifted the flap in the counter to let himself through, and I heard my father say it like him. "Doris will show you what's expected of you," he told me and strolled into his office.

"So you're taking Emma's job," Doris said.

"I thought she was having a baby."

"Yes, and then she'd have come back. She'll be needing her pay more than ever."

More hopefully than thoughtfully I said "Can't we each work some days?"

"We wanted that, but your daddy wasn't having it. He just wants you and we're stuck with you, so you'd better be some use."

She thrust a pair of headphones at me and showed me how the switchboard worked while I tried to find a comfortable way to sit on the rickety swivel chair, which felt as if it was acting hostile on behalf of the girl I'd replaced. "You take some calls now," Doris said, and soon she was saying "Not like that" and "Oh, let me fix it" sounding like a weary sigh and "I told you not that way" and more of the same. That was most of my first day at work.

I told myself I'd survived worse at home. I put up with her attitude so that I could learn the job and not let my mother down. Before long I was more skilful at the switchboard than Doris, which gave her an excuse to leave most of the work to me. "You get that," she would say while she combed her curls that were always grey at the parting no matter what colour she'd turned the rest, or while she touched up her round jowly face with rouge and lipstick, or lit another of the cigarettes her fat cardigans smelled of along with too much cheap perfume, or read a tabloid and complained about every story, a performance that she made last all day. Soon I didn't see much of her, because she persuaded me to take the night shift on the switchboard. She may have fancied she was getting the better of me, but it meant I wasn't in my bedroom at Mr Randal's mercy. I thought he would keep his hands off me at work, but I quickly learned to put the desk between us when I took in the mug of tea Doris had more important things to do than bring him. Maybe she'd had to fend him off when she was younger, though now she was at least as old as my mother.

The way my mother started treating me left me more confused about myself than ever. Mr Randal paid my salary to her every month, and she thanked him for it and never failed to remind me I should, but when he wasn't there she was likely to complain "Is that all you've earned?" and leave me feeling I wasn't worth the allowance she doled out. "When are you going to find yourself a boy?" was another favourite question, and I mumbled nothing much instead of telling her that most of the men I met were drunks who reeled in to lean on the counter and talk at me till the cab they'd ordered came. "Dress nicely or the boys won't want you" was one more thing she often said, and I could have retorted she'd selected my outfit for work, but I was tired of arguing. Since I was incapable of telling her about Mr Randal, I hardly talked to her at all, which meant she never missed an opportunity to tell me what a sullen girl I was. No doubt she thought that was keeping boys away from me as well.

Since I'd left school I didn't know where to get weed. I didn't need it so much now that Mr Randal stayed out of my room. I thought he was afraid I might be old enough to disobey all his warnings and let my mother hear, but maybe I'd just grown too old for his taste. I was still afraid he would trap me in his office or come to the switchboard while nobody was about, but he never did. Sometimes when I emptied the bin next to his desk I found wads of toilet paper that I looked away from when I binned them in the alley behind Reliablest. You always had to knock and wait before you went into his office, and sometimes I heard him switch off his computer.

I felt breathless with nerves whenever I was alone at night with him, and only concentrating on the switchboard helped. For a while I thought all the weed I'd used had caught up with me, when I started hearing words in my head and feeling I was close to seeing them. "Scar stable liar," I kept hearing, and then it turned into gibberish – "Srac tsel bailer." I was afraid I'd have to own up to smoking weed till I saw the words. They were the back of the neon name in the window, and I laughed so much that Mr Randal came out of his office to see what the joke was. When I couldn't tell him he frowned but said "I'm glad you're happy in your work."

I wasn't, not with him or Doris. My only refuge from them seemed to be some night shifts and working Sundays, when they both had a day off. "We hardly ever see you any more," my mother complained more than once on the way to early mass before I started work. "You'll have us thinking you want to avoid us." I still took communion, though it tasted as meaningless as my prayers felt now, and seeing Father Brendan loom up like Mr Randal used to left me feeling sick. After church Mr Randal drove me to the taxi firm, a gesture my mother always treated as a major favour, and then took her touring the countryside. "You missed another lovely drive," she would tell me like a rebuke, but I was just relieved to have eluded him and Father Brendan for a while. Whenever I went to confess a few token offences – envying the drivers for being paid more than me, swearing back at a drunken customer – I made sure he wasn't the priest in the box.

Working for Mr Randal didn't seem too different from all the times he'd come into my bedroom. I was resigned to my new situation, which left me feeling dull and shrunken inside myself, too small for anyone to see or reach. I'd begun to think this was all my life would ever be till the night Barry made a proposal.

Mr Randal was out with the limousine. "Only the best for the best," he'd said, and I heard my father say it in an even shriller voice, and wondered if Mr Randal meant the car or himself, more likely both. Barry had parked his taxi outside and was sitting in the canvas chair nearest to the smallest electrical heater Mr Randal had found to buy, which he often reminded the drivers was only meant for customers. I had my coat on and could see Barry's November breath. He finished rubbing his hands and gazed at me, and I saw him make his mind up. "Don't tell Malcolm I pinched any of his warmth," he said with a wink, and ambled over to the counter. "Can you keep another secret, Carla?"

I thought I didn't do much else, which made me even warier. "Who from?"

"Everyone but us for now." He leaned across the counter, and I flinched inside myself, having been reminded of Father Brendan at the altar rail. He glanced around to make sure we were going to stay alone and said "Are you happy with Malcolm?"

I thought Mr Randal must have boasted to him, the way I supposed he had to Father Brendan, and now Barry planned to use me like they had. "What are you asking for?"

"I'll keep your secret if you keep ours." When I kept my mouth shut he must have taken this for a promise. "I just get the feeling," he said, "working for him doesn't make you any happier than the rest of us."

"He gave me a job."

"We know, your first one, and you're his girl as well." I couldn't suppress a grimace at that, and Barry looked encouraged. "You're not planning to spend the rest of your life here, are you?" he said.

"Don't know."

"This tells me not," he said and thumped his chest like a sinner miming an act of contrition. "We'll be telling Malcolm soon, so don't go saying, but me and a couple of the lads are going to start our own operation."

"A taxi firm, you mean?"

"Cheerful Cabs, we're calling it. Sound good to you?"

I liked him the best of the drivers, and felt I had to trust him. "Better than here."

"We hoped you'd say that. All we need now is a receptionist, and that old misery you work with won't fit our image."

"Don't suppose she would," I said, adding a silent prayer that he meant what I wished he did.

"But me and the lads think you could."

"Some people say I'm miserable too."

I regretted saying that, but I was so used to thinking I was worthless that I couldn't find any other response. "Do you reckon that's how being around Malcolm makes you?" Barry said.

My answer felt like the start of an escape. "Yes."

"Me and the lads were saying you'd be a different person if you got away from him."

This released more words I hadn't been able to utter. "I'd like to find out."

"Then do you want to make the move when we do?"

At once I was back in prison. "I'd have to tell Mr Randal."

"We can tell him together, or we'll do it for you if you'd rather."

The thought of standing up to Mr Randal with Barry's support and his team's filled me with excitement, or was it nervousness? "Let's wait and I'll see," I said.

"Just keep it quiet till the day," Barry said as the switchboard buzzed with a call that sent him out to his car.

I was all too used to hiding situations, but I did my best to feel this one was different. Certainly the effort I had to make to keep it secret was. In the weeks that followed I avoided meeting Barry's eyes in case that might betray us. Since I didn't know who else would be leaving with us, I was nervous of looking too long at any of the drivers. All this left me afraid that Mr Randal might ask me what was wrong with me, and Doris didn't help. "I don't like people who can't look you in the eye," she said one day. "If you ask me, it means they're up to no good." She was talking about a customer who'd just gone out, but I couldn't look at her in case she meant me as well. I felt as if she was waiting to draw Mr Randal's attention to my behaviour, and I shrank inside myself whenever he came near us.

When the builders started work on the premises across the road, my secret became even harder to keep. "What are they making us over there?" Mr Randal said. "My vote's a takeaway. I'd even put up with an Indian if they keep their smells to themselves." Before long he went to investigate, strolling across the road as if the traffic ought to stop for him, and I couldn't breathe as I watched him tramping back in a rage that squeezed his features smaller. "Some swine's starting up another cab rank. I'd like to know who they think they are," he said, and I nearly couldn't hear the call I was answering, my heart was thumping so loud.

After that he kept coming out of his office to spy on the progress opposite. He stood close to me with his hands on his hips, drumming his thumbs as if he was secretly excited, though I suppose he was miming rage. When the builders started putting up the Cheerful Cabs sign he gave us a furious commentary. "Think they're revolutionary, do they?" he said once the first three letters were in place. "Ungodly lot of swine." The next two letters went up, and he stared at everyone around him. "I hope nobody's cheering here," he said, and I only just stopped myself biting my lip to hold my mouth shut and expressionlessly straight. Three more letters provoked him to declare "They won't be so cheerful when I'm done with them." He watched the rest of the name go up, and then he marched across the road, shaking his fist at a car that failed to slow down for him. I saw him talking to a builder and wished I could hear what they were saying, but I didn't have to wonder long. He stalked back through the traffic as if he thought he should be blessed against danger, and leaned on the door he'd shut behind him. "Call everyone off the road, Doris," he said, though his mouth looked as if it could hardly get the words out. "I want the lot of them in here."

I didn't know how much he'd learned, but I might have called Barry to warn him if I wouldn't have been overheard. He was the first driver to return. "Everything good, Malcolm?" he said, and Mr Randal told him "It will be." They didn't say any more while they waited for the other drivers, and I felt Mr Randal had gagged me all over again, particularly since he wouldn't let me or Doris answer calls. Once the last of the men arrived Mr Randal locked the door. "Carla," he said, "how well do you remember your religious studies?"

I remembered how he'd taught me the catechism and then what he'd done while he was pretending to. Barry laughed and looked round for the others to join in. "You've never brought us in for a Bible class, boss."

"You could do worse than learn from it. Can you finish the psalm for us, Carla? Even my close friend in whom I trusted, who ate my bread...."

"You've pinched a few sandwiches yourself," Barry reminded him, but Mr Randal kept his eyes on me. "I don't think they taught us it," I said.

"Has lifted up his heel against me," Mr Randal said with enough disgust to be turning some of it on my ignorance. "I expect that's why the Yanks used to call people like that heels. Do any of you know your Luke?"

I didn't know what he might have in mind, and in any case I was as wary of speaking up as I had been at school. "Be content with your wages," he said. "That's what Luke tells us."

"Some of us are, Malcolm," Doris said.

"God bless you then, Doris. You're a good soul. I can't imagine you knew there were traitors amongst us."

"That's a bit strong, isn't it?" Barry objected. "What are you saying anybody's done?"

"Went behind my back to try and ruin my business with this outfit over the road after they'd pretended I could trust them."

"Nobody wants to ruin your business, Malcolm. I reckon there's room for both."

"We'll be finding out, won't we? So you're confessing you're the ringleader."

"It'll be a team. We'll all be equal."

"Sounds communist to me, which explains why you're so godless."

"At least we don't tell the priest what we've been up to and then go off to do it all again."

"If you're aware of any sinfulness on my part, please do point it out."

Their argument had made me nervous, not least because I felt it was delaying my escape, and Mr Randal's challenge disturbed me even more. "I wouldn't know where to start," Barry said.

"You'll know where to finish, and that's right here and now. Who's leaving with him?"

Daz and Bill moved to stand with Barry while the other three stayed on the far side of the room. "May you enjoy just as much success as you deserve," Mr Randal said and unlocked the door. As he flung it wide, Barry and his colleagues turned their eyes to me. I was starting to get to my feet – the rickety chair felt determined not to let me up – when Mr Randal said "Not you, Carla. Stay where you've been put."

"She wants to be part of the team," Barry said.

"She's that already. Part of mine."

"I reckon she knows her own mind. You haven't got a contract with her any more than you gave us."

I found I was shaking, and the chair was. As I tried to stand up once more I said "Mr Randal—"

"That's father to you, Carla, or daddy if you like," Mr Randal said, still facing Barry. "She's my daughter and she's under my protection. She's underage."

"Doesn't look it."

"Then it's a good job you didn't act on your misapprehension, isn't it? Try anything like that again and you'll be seeing the police," Mr Randal said and stood away from the door. "Now be off where you may be wanted and take your cronies with you."

The three of them trooped out, and Mr Randal shut the door as if only the glass pane stopped him slamming it. "God bless you for your loyalty," he told the staff who'd stayed, who looked almost as awkward as I felt, though they weren't as trapped as I was. The switchboard buzzed, and he said "You can answer that now, Doris. Carla, come with me."

I watched Barry and Daz and Bill stride across the road and out of my life while the other drivers looked away from whatever Mr Randal meant to do to me. "Close the door," he said and didn't speak again till he was seated behind his desk. He propped his elbows on it and folded his hands as if he was about to pray or lead me in praying, though his fingers wagged so much they looked eager to grab me. "I'll forgive you this once because you're so easily led," he said and poked his face over his fingers. "But it's well past time you got used to being with me. You and your mother are mine until death do us part, and God send us all a long life."

ALEXANDER AND ALEX

"Dad."

The phone says that, and then Alex does. "I believe that's the case," his father tells him. "I understand I'm still your father."

"I don't know anyone who'd say you weren't."

"No doubt you don't know them. I'm sure they're too numerous."

"I'm sorry, who are?"

"It's something that you're sorry, I suppose, or are you denying all responsibility for them?"

"I meant I don't know what you're talking about."

"I'm referring to everyone you've led to believe I'm someone other than I am."

With growing unease Alex wonders "How are you saying I've done that?"

"You assured your mother and myself that this book of yours had no bearing on us."

"That's because it hadn't," Alex says, feeling as confused as he's afraid his father has become. "Hasn't still."

The train has nearly reached Leeds, passing between fields that glimmer with frost in the dark as if they yearn for light. The young businessman who is tapping at his laptop on the table hasn't glanced at Alex, but he's listening. "Did you hope we wouldn't notice you had put me in the book?" Alex's father says. "What kind of joke are you making of me?"

"We've had this conversation once, dad. Remember, I told you—"

"Kindly don't attempt to undermine my certainty. I remember what was said."

Alex can't help recalling how Carl's memories of dialogue were questioned. "Then you'll remember we established it was Carla's stepfather."

"Indeed." For as long as it lasts this poses as agreement. "He wanted to be taken for her father, did he not?" Alex's father says. "Her father, his father, whichever's dictated. There was a time when I should have been proud to be identified as yours."

The businessman ducks towards the laptop as if this may persuade Alex he can't hear. Though Alex wishes he could end the conversation, he can only ask "What are you saying has changed?"

"Do you genuinely not know what you're about? I think it's you your mother ought to be concerned for, not me."

Alex can't see how to follow up the last remark. "I apparently don't know, so tell me."

"You dismay me, Alexander. Are you taking drugs, by any chance?"

"No," Alex says but feels too close to hearing someone else's voice emerge from his suddenly dry mouth – his cannabis experience from decades back. "Would you mind explaining if you're going to? I'm nearly where I have to be tonight."

"Is that a train? I thought I was hearing you type while we spoke. You're about to be public, are you?"

"I already am."

"Then whoever you're with can hear you explain what you wrote," his father says and expels such a furious breath that the rest of it almost falls short of the last of his words. "For my father, who'd have liked me to be what I am."

At last Alex understands. As the businessman dons a set of headphones Alex says "That was Carl, dad. It's his life and that's his dedication to his real father."

"You're fond of that phrase, aren't you?" Before Alex can decide on a response his father says "If those are his words, why isn't that made clear?"

"I'm sure it will be to most people. Just his name is on the cover, if you notice."

"I'm perfectly capable of observing that without help. I very much doubt most people are as perceptive as you would like to believe."

"Look," Alex says in some desperation, "Carl will be at this event tonight. Would you like to talk to him about the dedication? He's heard from readers who've been touched by it. They obviously knew it was him."

"There are few encounters I should relish less. I'm afraid I see the fellow as a further stage in your decline. I'm coming directly, Amy," he calls but returns his voice to the phone. "Let me just advise you not to confuse me any further, Alexander."

"I didn't try," Alex says, but he's talking to himself, or perhaps inadvertently to the businessman, who has removed the headphones. It's clear that he donned them to avoid overhearing the last of the conversation. As the train dawdles into the station he packs the headphones and the laptop into their compartments in a bag, and then widens his eyes to aim sympathy at Alex. "Families," he murmurs.

"We might be worse off without them," Alex says, only to reflect that he can't say so on Carl's behalf.

"You're a generous fellow." This contains more emphasis than Alex can interpret. "I hope you don't mind that I heard," the businessman says, "but are you giving a talk at the bookshop by the station?"

"I'll be there, yes."

"I've been seeing the poster all week." He remains seated while all around them passengers stand up. "Do realise you've got plenty of support," he says.

Alex wonders if this means "You'll be going to the talk."

"I wish I could. Work to finish," the businessman says and strokes the bag as if this might grant his wish. "Break a leg."

"I think that's just for when you're putting on a show."

"That's the opposite of you," the businessman says and thrusts out a hand. "Here's hoping you give other people the courage to be whoever they really are."

His handshake is even more emphatic than his declaration. He grasps Alex's hand while he stands up and then delivers a vigorous farewell squeeze. Before Alex can follow him, a woman pushing a wheeled suitcase and dragging its doppelganger blocks the aisle. As he steps onto the platform, where the man is already lost in the crowd, he realises what the conversation was assuming. The man took him for Carl.

Several commuters glance at his laugh. He supposes he can accept the encouragement on Carl's behalf and pass it on to him at the bookshop. He's making for the ticket barrier when his phone rings and identifies Carl Batchelor. Have the passengers who stare at Alex recognised the name? "I'm on my way," Alex says. "I'll be there in a couple of minutes."

"I'm not." Perhaps to highlight his regret, Carl pauses before adding "Sorry about that."

"What's the hindrance?"

"Migraine." For some moments Carl appears to think this is sufficient explanation, but then he says "Started getting them when I smoked a lot of weed."

Alex recalls his own migraines, which cannabis precipitated in his student days. He feels close to reliving the experience – the way his perceptions would contract to a glittering point as a prelude to exploding slowly into blindness – until he takes a prolonged breath. "Where are you?" he says. "Maybe it won't last long."

"On the train home. Don't ask me where."

Since Alex is surrounded by train noises and announcements, he can't tell which are on the phone. "Have you told the bookshop?"

"Can't see to call them. Nearly didn't find your number. Can you tell them for me?"

"I'll have to."

"You'll do fine, Alex." Presumably Carl has moved on to talking about the event. "You can do my book if you want," he says. "You must remember it as well as me by now."

"Not quite, I should think."

"Remember the first thing I said. That's where we started." As Alex thinks of their initial conversation in Carl's office – his misapprehension that Father Brendan was a saint – Carl says "Just talk to everybody like I would."

The barrier sticks out Alex's ticket like a mocking tongue as Carl rings off. Should Alex be concerned about some comment Carl made? The bookshop is too close to give him time to identify the issue, even though the homebound crowd slows him down. In the window of the branch of Texts he sees a poster for tonight's event, *When I was Carla: Carl Batchelor in conversation with Alex Grand*. The young woman behind the nearest counter in the shop greets him with a smile of unspecific welcome. "I'm your speaker for tonight," he says. "Alex Grand."

She picks up a phone, and her message resounds from speakers on both floors of the shop. "Alex Grand for Samira. Just Alex Grand."

The tall slim woman this summons has mahogany skin and a long elegant face beneath a black scarf that conceals her hair. "Your other half isn't here yet," she tells Alex.

Her usage disconcerts him so much that he retorts "My better half, you mean."

She blinks and looks poised to smile. "I didn't realise you were married."

"It just feels that way sometimes." When her smile doesn't surface Alex says "Better was a joke."

"More real, maybe."

Alex feels defensive if not undermined. "How would that work?"

"It's his story, isn't it, not yours. It's his life."

"Thanks for reminding me," Alex says, not altogether ironically. "It's not far from feeling like mine."

She leads the way along a boxy corridor narrowed on both sides by metal shelves full of books, and ushers Alex into a small office strewn and piled with paper, some of it in volume form. "What will you drink while we're waiting?" she says.

"White wine is always welcome, but I should tell you we aren't waiting for Carl Batchelor. I'll be the lone voice tonight."

"Who made that decision? We've created interest in you both."

"It was made for him. He got a migraine on the way here."

"Surely that wouldn't rob him of his voice."

"I remember how mine used to feel. You just want to go home and lie down in the dark."

"You'll have to remember for two, then. We've got double our usual audience." As she fills a plastic cup from a wine box in a dwarfish refrigerator she says "Might you be able to bring him up on video? We could share your phone to a screen."

"I can't imagine he would thank me for asking. Being on a train in his state is bad enough."

"It's your decision." Samira grips the cup hard enough to make it creak while she passes it to him, conveying a sense of performing a duty not entirely to her taste. "Can you start by reading from the book?" she says. "It'll help people understand why you're here."

"Of course, but I should think they'd know."

"That depends on who they've come to hear," she says and escorts him through the shop. Between Psychology and Wellbeing a stage a few inches high is occupied by a pair of scrawny armchairs facing an audience perhaps sixty strong. Each chair is provided with a wireless microphone, one of which Samira picks up as Alex takes the other seat. "Thank you all for supporting our latest author event," she says, "but I'm afraid Carl who was Carla can't be with us. He's too ill to travel."

The sighs this inspires sound sympathetic, as do several tuts and shakes of heads. "Can we welcome Alex Grand," she says, which he tries not to hear as a question. "Carl Batchelor's chronicler."

As this prompts polite applause, she retrieves a copy of *When I Was Carla* from beside the empty chair and passes it to him. "Can you start by reading from the book?"

He feels as if she's repeating the suggestion in case his memory has played a trick. She takes a seat on the front row, leaving the microphone on the armchair, a reminder that he's only half the presence that the audience expected. By the time he finishes leafing through the book in search of a passage that conveys Carla's plight without growing too explicit, he's hearing hints of restlessness. "One day we stopped at a petrol station for Mr Randal to check the tyre pressures and fill up the tank...."

By now Alex has read the book so often that he feels as if he's remembering the incidents aloud. The club of a microphone in his fist could almost be recalling how the hoses felt at the petrol station. A man with curls like grey foam bursting from his fat-cheeked big-nosed purplish head sidles into the back row as Alex reads about Randal's hands wandering under the child's dress. His stare makes Alex as uncomfortable as the anecdote does, and referring to hands on his bottom aggravates Alex's discomfort. "I wasn't to know that the nightmare had hardly begun," he reads at last and shuts the book.

This time the applause sounds more uncertain, as though it shouldn't be for him or perhaps even for the book. He's about to discuss his relationship to the material when the latecomer calls out "Are you going to tell us the rest?"

"I think it might be better if people read it for themselves."

"Better for who?" a woman says, not especially to Alex.

"Better for selling his book," a man says just loud enough for everyone to hear.

"It's not the same as being told," says the latecomer.

"We've sold quite a few," Samira informs Alex.

It's clear that she wants him to grant the request, and he asks the latecomer "What would you like to hear?"

"About the nightmare."

"Carl, that's to say Carla, she was abused by her stepfather for most of her childhood."

"Abused how?"

"We don't need to hear the dirty details," a man objects.

"There's all sorts of ways he could have been," the latecomer says. "Her, I mean."

"Sexually," Alex says. "Just no penetration."

His restraint feels like suppressing a memory – being untrue to it, even – particularly when the latecomer remarks "Small mercies."

"I don't associate mercy with Randal."

"That's your stepfather." When Alex nods the man says "Didn't anybody notice what was going on?"

"It was always in her bedroom when her mother was out of the way. Carla tried to alert her, but I don't think she would have believed her, and that was how it was with everyone she tried to tell."

"It wouldn't happen like that now."

"You'd hope not." Once again Alex feels as if he's fending off memories, and then he realises he almost did. "One person believed her," he says. "The priest she tried to tell about it in confession."

"That's awful," a woman says. "The priest wouldn't have been able to do anything, would he?"

"I'm afraid he took the chance to abuse her as well."

The woman looks outraged, not necessarily by the crime. "I hope you aren't making that up."

"I assure you I'm not," Alex says forcefully enough to be confirming his own experience.

"Was your priest ever dealt with?" the latecomer asks.

"He's in jail for child abuse."

"And this Randal character, what about him?"

"Carla got away from him eventually."

Saying so feels unexpectedly like a liberation, even when his questioner says "How?"

"By transitioning, I'd say."

"Had the op, you mean."

"Just hormone therapy." Seeing the man hesitate, Alex says "Did you want to say something else?"

"It's brave of you to tell us all that. I can see why you had to talk about it how you did." Before Alex can wonder what he means, the man adds "I was only wondering, and you mustn't take this wrong because I'm simply asking, if you ever feel disloyal to your sex at all."

"Why would I need to feel that?"

"Becoming a man so you could leave your past behind."

For a moment Alex feels as if he's done that without changing gender. "Who do you think I am?"

"Whatever your name is now. The fellow who used to be Carla."

Alex doesn't know how much of a laugh to produce or what kind. "I'm glad I was so convincing," he says, which fails to leave him any surer of himself, "but I'm just the man who brought the story into shape."

"Then where's he?"

"Home by now for all I know. He was taken ill or he'd be up here with me. I'll just say there's no reason to call him disloyal."

"I didn't know there were meant to be two of you. I heard you reading and came to listen." More defiantly than Alex welcomes he says "I still think you could have been him."

Did the audience realise he was making that assumption? Alex feels as if they've been sharing a joke at his expense. "Let me tell you how the book came to be written," he says and makes sure of establishing that the story belongs to Carl, not even remotely to him. The audience seems interested enough, or else polite. Afterwards he autographs copies of the book, and when the latecomer brings one Alex almost signs Carl's name as a prank – indeed, he has to turn the initial C into an A, which doesn't resemble the rest of his signature much. He signs copies for the shop and a few of his novels as well, and then hurries to catch the last train that's any use.

He needs to be home tonight to work on his novel tomorrow. The outermost streets of Leeds are reeling their lights backwards into the dark, and he's pocketing his phone after telling Lee he's on his way, when it emits a ping to signify a Twitter message. It's from @hilwls, and it says *Mr Grand, you need to call me on this number.*

If it weren't for his name in the message, Alex would be sure it was a scam. It still could be, since he recognises neither the Twitter identity nor the mobile number. The woman's tweets seem innocuous, even banal – baby pictures, dessert recipes, complaints about the local school. Best to find out what she wants, and then perhaps he can snooze until he reaches London. He rings the number, and as a car at a level crossing finds him for a moment with its headlights a woman says "Hello."

It's less a greeting than a statement. "You wanted me to call you," Alex says.

"When did I say that?"

He sees no excuse for her to act as warily as him. "Just now," he says as flatly as she greeted him.

"Is this Mr Grand?"

"The very same. Alex Grand and no other."

"I had to be sure."

"Well, now you are," Alex says vigorously enough to be assuring them both. "What can I do for you?"

"Mr Grand, we need to meet. I'm Hilary Wilson."

"I saw you were, but I'm afraid that means nothing to me."

"It's going to." She gives him a moment to prepare if not to grow nervous before she says "I was Hilary Randal. I'm Malcolm Randal's daughter."

CARLA

One Sunday at breakfast Mr Randal said "I'm afraid I may have some bad news for you, Elaine."

"Don't say it's anything serious, Malcolm."

"Let's hope not. I pray it's just a misunderstanding, but I wonder if there's someone who's not happy where she is."

"Malcolm, I couldn't be happier. You've seen to that in every way you could."

"We aren't talking about you, my pet."

"Does your father mean you, Carla? What have you been up to now?"

They were at the kitchen table while I cooked breakfast, one of my Sunday tasks, and I didn't turn round. "Don't know," I said like the child she made me feel like.

"You don't know if it's you or you don't know what you did?"

"Neither." In an effort to show them why I'd passed my English Language exam I corrected this to "Either."

"Make up your mind what you're saying, child. Malcolm, will you tell her what you think she's done? And Carla, just you look at your father while he's talking to you."

"He isn't yet."

"Don't be so clever. We don't like clever girls in our house. You let him see your face."

As I turned round, the bacon in the pan spat on my hand. It felt like a red-hot needle, the start of a torture to make me confess. When I grimaced my mother said "Will you look at it, Malcolm. I've never seen such defiance."

"I hurt myself," I protested.

"Then for pity's sake be more careful. We can do without another invalid in the house."

"You're never any trouble, my pet."

"I know you're the soul of kindness, Malcolm, but you shouldn't have to prove it all the time. Now what do you need to say about the child?"

"I'm sorry to have to tell you this, my pet, but I think we may have a rebel in our household."

"You can see that just by looking. Watch you don't spoil that breakfast, girl. Let's hope she grows out of it, Malcolm."

As I moved the pan onto a cold part of the stove Mr Randal said "I'm afraid it may go beyond teenage misbehaviour."

"God help us, what, then?"

"I'd call it fraternising with the enemy, Elaine."

"You don't mean the devil."

"Perhaps not quite that dangerous. The people who betrayed us. The firm that wants to undermine my livelihood."

"What has she got to do with them?"

"I think you should ask your daughter that."

"Carla," my mother said like a warning or worse.

"You didn't ask," I said, because defiance was all I seemed to have left of myself, "and I don't know."

"God hears every word you say," Mr Randal said. "You've been caught talking to the opposition."

For a moment I fancied he could mean God had spotted me. "I just say hello on the way home."

"And how do you suppose that looks to our clientele?"

"They weren't there."

"You've absolutely no idea who may have seen you supporting our rivals. If you had I can't imagine you would dare to do it. Better keep in mind you never know who's watching."

I felt as stupid as my mother seemed to want to think I was for repeating "I just say hello."

"Then kindly say nothing in future." As I reflected that he'd made me good at that, Mr Randal said "In my view you've been encouraging our rivals. I won't have them being led to think they're welcome where they are."

I thought this wasn't up to him, but my mother said "You do what your father tells you. Now for heaven's sake get on with breakfast or you'll have us late for church."

That was all she said to me till Mr Randal went to brush his teeth while I washed up after breakfast, and then she turned on me. "What are you trying to do to your father?"

"I haven't done anything to him."

"You're making people think this other firm is as good as his. Do you want to put him out of business?"

I didn't care if God heard me lying, though I no longer believed there was any such creature. "No."

"Do you want to lose the job he gave you out of the kindness of his heart?"

My only answer was the same lie, because I still didn't dare to tell the truth. "No."

"Then just you keep away from that bad lot. You were warned about mixing with the wrong sort at school, and this is just as bad, betraying your poor father. I think that's a sin you'd better tell the priest next time you're in confession."

I promised myself I'd stop confessing once I turned eighteen, which felt like the prospect of some kind of escape. I must have looked repentant, because my mother left it at that till Mr Randal came downstairs. "I'm sure she didn't mean anything by talking to them, Malcolm," she said. "You know how easily led she is."

He knew that better than she did, but I vowed I wouldn't be led for much longer. Once I was eighteen I'd escape somehow. I could put up with Mr Randal watching me from Reliablest when I went home, to remind me not to go anywhere near his rivals. He did that for weeks, standing in the doorway with his thumbs drumming on his hips as if his hands were eager for some activity that would satisfy him better, and then he just watched from his office. That let me wave to the men in Cheerful Cabs without him seeing so long as I stayed on his side of the road, which was a secret I was happy to keep. "Have you been with anyone you shouldn't?" my mother would demand when I went home, and a voice inside me wanted to scream that since I was little I'd been with her husband too often to count, though he'd given me up now because he liked them younger and must be contenting himself with whatever he had on his office computer. Putting it that way in my head sounded too much like feeling cast aside or even jealous, which left me loathing myself more than ever, and convinced

I would never deserve to have a relationship with anyone or want one either.

I was seventeen when Emma, the receptionist I'd replaced, brought her baby to show everyone. My stomach clenched when Mr Randal started tickling the tiny girl under her chin, because I fancied he was wishing he could touch her somewhere else. "Are you making ends meet, Em?" Doris said while she stared at me, and Emma told her "I'll need to find some work soon." The guilt Doris wanted me to suffer just confirmed my feeling I should get another job.

I started passing work to Cheerful Cabs when nobody at Reliablest could hear. If we didn't have a driver free to make a pickup I would tell the caller to phone the other firm. One day Barry caught sight of me at the switchboard, and brandished both his thumbs across the road. Doris saw him do it, and stared at me but didn't speak. I wondered if she would sneak on me to Mr Randal, and that night when I left for home I heard someone hurrying after me. "Carla," he said.

I was still afraid of being caught by Mr Randal, however pathetic my fear made me feel, but the man at my back was Barry. "Just wanted to say thanks for putting fares our way," he said.

"Thought you might need them more than Mr Randal does."

"He's doing all right for himself still, is he? We're doing great, and some of that's down to you." I saw Barry think what else to say before he spoke. "I'll bet he doesn't know it was," he said. "Don't worry, I'm not telling."

"Don't care if you do."

He glanced back at Reliablest and gestured me to keep on walking. "Sounds like you aren't too happy there."

"Never was. Less now you and Bill and Daz have gone."

"The job we offered you might be coming up again. Our girl's wanting to move on."

"I don't know what he'd do to stop me."

"He can't touch you once you hit eighteen. When's that?"

"November. Six months," I said, which felt like at least a lifetime.

"Our Betsy won't be leaving till round then. We could fix it so she goes when you take over."

I would have embraced the proposition and him as well if another hindrance hadn't come to mind. "My mum and him might throw me out, and then I don't know where I'd live."

"Our daughter Donna's flatmate will be moving out by Christmas, and she'll want someone else to share with her. You'd have your own room."

I felt as if Christmas might bring my best present ever and the kind of blessing I could use, but I was still insecure enough to ask "Do you really want me?"

"Just like we did. Betsy's good but she's not that good."

I went home so excited that it hadn't left me by the time I got there, which meant I had to counter it by looking glum. My mother didn't seem to notice, unless she was tired of commenting. After that each day felt like another secret step towards independence, and even Doris remarked how cheerful I'd become, though she didn't seem to approve of it much. At first I was nervous that Mr Randal might wonder why I'd changed, till I realised he assumed I was content to work for him, maybe even that he'd made me happy somehow. As far as I was concerned he could do that only by dying, and he'd do me that favour far too late.

The week before I turned eighteen I answered a call at the switchboard. "Reliablest," I said, which I often had to stop myself pronouncing like the joke my father used to make.

"Hello there, almost birthday girl. Just checking everything's going to be like we agreed."

Doris hadn't gone home yet, and I tried not to say anything she shouldn't overhear. "It'll all be fixed then."

"When are we letting Malcolm know? Would you like me to?"

I wanted the chance to assert myself at last. "No, I will."

"Good for you. Let us know when you have and we'll see you over here."

I risked a glance across the road and saw Barry flourishing the thumb of his free hand. I thought Doris might have seen, but she was staring at me. "Was that a private call?" she said. "You know Malcolm doesn't like us having them."

"Go and tell on me if you want. I don't care."

I almost wished she would, so that I could be done with confronting Mr Randal. I was supposed to be looking forward to my birthday, but its approach had started to tighten my nerves. In bed I tried to rehearse what I would say to him, which only made me feel I was bringing him into my room. I did my best to hide my state, but not enough. "What's wrong with you now, child?" my mother complained as if she would rather not know. "If it's a lady's problem, don't go bothering your father with it. It needn't keep you off work."

When I got up on my birthday the house was so quiet that I thought I'd been left alone for some reason, but as I made for the bathroom I heard someone growing restless downstairs. I felt sure Mr Randal was lying in wait for me. Then my mother called "How much longer are you going to be, Carla?" and I felt a little safer, though my nerves didn't get the message.

As soon as I ventured into the kitchen she and Mr Randal started singing happy birthday to me. I heard the Sheas joining in through the wall, though I hadn't spoken to Bridie for years, but they stopped before the song reached my name. Mr Randal and my mother clapped at the end, though I thought they were applauding themselves more than me. My mother nodded at a parcel sitting on my plate and tied up with a silver bow. "Open it then, Carla," she said as if she was doing her best to control her impatience.

When I tugged at the bow the wrapping fell open, exposing a purple box. Inside was a silver ring etched with tiny letters, *To Carla from Mother and Father on her 18th.* It went best on my middle finger, and I fitted it on my right one and displayed it, though it made me feel shackled. "Thank you very much," I said, and my mother held up her face to be kissed. Once I'd delivered she said "Give your father one as well. I don't know when I've seen you kiss him."

I made myself plant a fast kiss on his cheek. It felt like mouthing perished rubber. As my mother gave my haste a disapproving blink Mr Randal said "Doris will be filling in for you tonight, Carla."

He made it sound like a business arrangement, but my mother said "Your father is taking us out for your birthday dinner."

I had to thank Mr Randal again, though the prospect simply left me struggling to confront him. I didn't want to do it as soon as they'd given me my present, but the longer I delayed, the more my old enforced silence came back to clamp my mouth shut. I wished I'd agreed to let Barry speak for me after all. The Reliablest drivers had bought me a birthday cake from the bakers next to Cheerful Cabs, and Mr Randal sang the song that went with it so loud you could have thought he'd paid the bill. He cut the cake and took the biggest piece, and I saw the drivers weren't too pleased with that, which nearly prompted me to say I was finished at Reliablest. "We'll soon be celebrating yours," he told Doris, and when she protested that she didn't want to be reminded and the drivers set about teasing her, I felt I'd missed another chance.

That evening Mr Randal drove me and my mother to a steakhouse in New Brighton. "That was special, wasn't it?" my mother said as I opened the door of the limousine to let her out, and I wondered how it was supposed to be, if I wasn't simply meant to think it was. The restaurant was called Aye There's The Rib, and all the staff wore historical costumes. The steaks came As You Like It, and the condiments on the barrels used as tables were labelled Measure For Measure, while the dessert menu was headed All's Well That Ends Well. My mother laughed at all this, but I suspected she was trying to incite me to laugh, to show the other diners I was clever enough to get the jokes. At the end of the meal a waiter brought a birthday cake I thought was designed to put the drivers' cake to shame, and Mr Randal and my mother sang the song again, with some diners joining in. "Don't blow your smoke at me," my mother said at once.

As soon as I'd blown all the candles out Mr Randal said through the tendrils of smoke "I hope you made a wish for us."

"Thought you were only supposed to pray."

I no longer believed either worked, but he said "I expect you can be forgiven on this occasion."

"Thank you for the lovely treat, Malcolm," my mother said and gazed at me as if she was directing the words to come out of my mouth.

"Thank you for the lovely treat, Malcolm."

"No need to be rude, child," my mother said, "even if it is your birthday."

"I wasn't being rude, and I'm not a child any more."

"Will you listen to it, Malcolm. She thinks she's grown up all at once."

"No, I've been growing up for years. You both just haven't noticed."

"Well, since you're so mature," Mr Randal said, "why don't you give us the benefit of some of your experience of life."

His attitude and my mother's made me furious enough to speak. "I want to live my own."

"What's wrong with the one your father's given you?"

"And God was responsible too," Mr Randal said. "Never leave out God."

"It was you gave me life, mum, and daddy did."

"You know good and well what I meant, or you should if you're half as clever as you'd like to think you are. He couldn't have given you the one you've got now."

"No, he'd have given me one I'd like."

"Malcolm, I don't know what she's turning into. You apologise to your father this instant and tell him you didn't mean what you said."

"That's all right, my pet. I don't ask for gratitude. Good works are their own reward."

My mother stared about as though she hoped nobody could hear or see me either. "That's even more reason she should say she's sorry."

I'd begun to feel afraid of being driven past what I had to say. "I don't want any favours any more. I want to depend on myself."

"And how do you think you're going to do that?"

Though she didn't call me a child this time, my mother might as well have. I had to take more of a breath than I'd used to blow the candles out before I could say "Emma wants to come back and everybody wants her to. I'll get another job."

"Emma gave up her position for our girl," Mr Randal told my mother.

"Then she ought to be grateful to her as well," my mother said, staring even harder at me. "What kind of job do you think you're going to be able to get?"

"The same kind somewhere else."

I saw Mr Randal's fingers tighten on the glass he was raising to his mouth, and thought it was about to shatter, spewing water everywhere. As he set it down on a coaster, an action so precise it felt like a silent threat, he said "Where?"

Before I could answer, the waiter came over. "Excuse me, are you waiting for me to cut your cake?"

"It will be dealt with when it's appropriate, thank you." Once the waiter retreated Mr Randal said "I asked you where."

I was saving up a breath I'd taken so that I had to let the words out. "They still want me at Cheerful Cabs."

My mother shut her eyes as if her scowl had forced the lids down. "Aren't those the people who did the dirty on you, Malcolm?"

"That's who they are, my pet."

When her eyes opened they looked as if she was hoping not to see me. "I don't believe you care about this other girl at all. What are you trying to do to your father?"

"I'm just trying to do it to me."

"I don't even want to know what that means. I wouldn't blame him for firing you right now, but Malcolm, do remember how easily influenced she is. Can you find it in your heart to give her one last chance?"

"I've got one and I'm taking it," I protested. "I'm going for that job."

"If there's a more ungrateful girl in the world I hope I never meet her. Please try not to listen to her, Malcolm. I'll pray that when she wakes up in the morning she'll see the error of her ways and ask you for forgiveness."

"I never will. He should be asking me." I was on the edge of saying more, but I had to concentrate on achieving my freedom. "Anyway, it shouldn't matter to him," I said. "Barry's always going to have a receptionist. It'll just be me."

"Do you really not know how disloyal you are?" my mother cried, ignoring the diners who stared at her or pretended they weren't listening. "I thank God the priest can't hear you, but you'll be telling him about your behaviour."

"I won't be going anywhere near him."

"What are we to do with her, Malcolm? She wants to turn her back on God as well as you. I hope you're happy you've ruined the evening, Carla. Have you finished now?"

"It's my birthday and it hasn't been ruined for me."

"I think it's time we all went home, if your father will allow you in his car," my mother said, and then her eyes gleamed with inspiration. "On second thoughts you won't be coming home with us unless you promise your father to give up this evil idea."

"I'm not giving up, and he can't make me."

"Do you not hear how childish you sound? You promise him this instant or you'll be out on the street with nowhere to live."

"I won't. I'll be sharing with Barry's daughter."

"Sweet Jesus, what kind of girl tries to tempt someone away from her family? I wouldn't be surprised if she sells herself."

"Maybe we shouldn't make that kind of allegation in public, my pet. We don't want to be prosecuted for bearing false witness."

"I'm not so sure it's false," my mother said but turned on me. "Won't you be satisfied till your father's in trouble with the police? Just you keep away from that girl, and let's be hearing the other promise as well or you'll have no bed tonight."

"I don't like that one. I won't be sleeping in it any more," I vowed and stood up. "I'll find somewhere till I get the one they've said I'll have."

"Don't you dare go." My mother struggled to rise and sank back onto her chair. "Don't even think of disobeying," she panted. "You tell her, Malcolm."

"See what you're doing to your mother, Carla. Do you want to make her even worse?"

This made me waver. How badly might my behaviour affect my mother? If I didn't act now I was sure to lose all my courage. "You made her like that. You can look after her," I said and snatched my coat from the back of the chair.

I was nearly at the exit when I heard the waiter say "Shall I parcel up your cake for you, sir?"

"Just bring the bill," Mr Randal said, "and make it quick."

I wondered whether I had time to ring Cheerful Cabs to rescue me, but I was afraid he would catch me while I waited to be picked up. I ran along the seafront, where waves were exploding scummily against the wall, and up the nearest hill. I dashed along the first side street and did the same at every junction, glancing back to make sure the limousine wasn't following. After a while I slowed down, and at last the devious route brought me to Cheerful Cabs. Barry was talking to the receptionist, and swung round. "Tell us you've done it," he said.

"They've thrown me out because I said I was coming to work here."

"Let's see what we can fix you up with," he said and picked up a phone from the switchboard. "Donna, Carla Batchelor's looking for a kip. Can she have your couch? Betsy, I'll be back as soon as I've delivered."

He hurried me out the back way to a taxi and drove off as I strapped myself in. The further he drove, the more reassured I grew. We ended up in Birkenhead, several miles from the house Mr Randal had made too much his own. Barry introduced me to his daughter, a small plump redhead with a round freckled jolly face, who shared the top floor of a large Victorian semi with a girl who was out just now. He left us to get acquainted, but I hadn't even finished my coffee when I began to nod, exhausted by the day and happier than I'd been since before my real father died. Donna helped me extend the couch into a bed and make it up, and as soon as I was in it I started falling asleep. I felt safe and eager for tomorrow, two ways I hadn't felt for too much of my life. As I drifted off my last thought was to wish my little sister had been born, so that I could have shared a flat with her.

ALEX

By the time Alex arrives home Lee is fast asleep. He thought of calling her from the train but was afraid of being overheard. Suppose someone realised which book he was talking about and put the information online? He kept his conversation with the woman who's claiming to be Randal's daughter as brief as he could, promising to let her know when they can meet once he has checked his schedule. Before he talks to Carl, he wants to talk to Lee. So many doubts are disputing in his head that he doesn't expect to sleep, though travelling has exhausted him. He climbs into bed beside Lee and slips an arm around her soft warm waist, prompting a sleepy murmur. She still isn't awake, and before he knows it, neither is Alex.

If he dreams, he can't remember. He wakens to find Lee's sunlit face gazing down at him. Mist drifts across it, so that he wonders if he's only dreaming he has come back to himself, or are his eyes behaving unlike his? He's struggling to grasp his consciousness when he realises he's seeing steam from one of the mugs of coffee she's holding, which she plants on the table next to his side of the bed. "What was the matter?" she says.

Perhaps he's insufficiently awake to understand. The question seems disturbingly familiar, often asked but never answered. It may not have been phrased quite like that, and whose name would follow it? Of course he's thinking of the way Carla's mother used to interrogate her, or rather how Carl agreed with him that she would have. He mustn't start taking Carl's memories for his, and he fends them off by asking "Why should anything be?"

"What were you dreaming? You woke me up, you were muttering and mumbling so much. You didn't even sound like you."

"Maybe I wasn't." His response disconcerts him even more than her comment. "Dreaming, I mean," he makes haste to explain.

"Then I don't know what you were doing. It was noisy, whatever it was."

"Thinking would be my guess."

"What came out made no sense, though."

Alex finds he's unexpectedly wary of learning "What did?"

"As far as I could make out you were telling your father to stop something or other."

"I'd say that's understandable. You know how he's been. Yesterday he rang me convinced *When I Was Carla* was dedicated to him." Saying so fails to quell the unease Lee has roused, but he needs to tell her "I heard from someone else, and maybe that's the matter."

Lee sits on her side of the bed, having retrieved her mug. "Who are we talking about?"

He takes a sip of coffee and then a larger mouthful to enliven his thoughts, though both feel like attempts to delay answering. "She says she's Hilary Randal. Malcolm Randal's daughter."

"She can't be. You know that. She was never born."

"According to Carl. I've said I'll meet her."

Lee's doubtful look leaves Alex more so. "Would you like me to come?" she says.

"Maybe not in case it panics her. I want to get as much out of her as I can. Listen when I call her, though, and see what you think." The height of the sun above the rooftops opposite adds to his confusion. "What time is it?"

"Past nine. I didn't want to wake you when you'd had such a bad night."

This feels like a memory beyond recapturing. "Late enough to call her," Alex says and reaches for his phone.

The bell barely repeats itself before the woman speaks. "Mr Grand."

"That's still me." He hasn't listed her among his contacts, since using the name she gave would feel like endorsing her assertion; he simply recalled the last number. "About meeting," he says.

"Free whenever you are. Free now."

"Shall we say tomorrow in London at one?"

"Can't you do any earlier?"

"One's best for me. Shall we meet at Victoria, let's say by the escalators up from the Underground into the concourse?"

"I'll be there." As Alex wonders how to keep her talking for Lee to hear, the woman says "I hope you're ready for the truth."

"Always," Alex says, but she has rung off.

"She's eager, whatever she wants. Maybe Carl Batchelor ought to be there, not with you but where he can watch."

Perhaps calling Carl will help Alex decide, though he's thrown by Carl's greeting. "How was our talk?"

"At the bookshop, you mean."

"Unless you've been talking about me somewhere else."

Could this be a warning? "Someone took me for you," Alex says.

"You can see how they could. You've got my memories now."

"They came in late while I was reading from the book. They must have wondered why I was talking about myself, that's to say you, in the third person."

"Maybe you have to think of yourself like that when you've been through what I have."

Alex wonders whether this describes Carl's own experience, but he needs to learn "Have you heard from anybody unexpected recently?"

A silence suggests Carl has, and so does "Like who?"

"Someone saying they're from your past."

"I still know the ones I want to know." As if the answer has drained his patience Carl demands "What aren't you telling me?"

"I've been approached by a woman who says she was Hilary Randal."

"Tell Mrs Balakrishnan I'll be there on time." After a pause that presumably lets a receptionist leave his office Carl says "You know just like I do she was never born."

"What do we suppose she wants?"

"How should I know?" Just as fiercely Carl says "What does she look like?"

"I'll find out tomorrow. Would you like to?"

"Try and keep me away." With no lessening of fury Carl says "Where?"

"Victoria, where the Underground comes up into the concourse. Might it be best if you stay out of sight, though? We want to find out all we can about her, and if she sees too many people she might change her mind about meeting."

"Out of sight till you've finished. Anyone else know about her?"

Lee puts a finger to her lips and shakes her head. "Kirsty will need to," Alex says.

"We can tell her when we've sorted out this bitch. What time are you going to get there?"

"I've arranged to meet at one."

"I'll be there before that, and you be as well. Christ, I'm looking forward to this. Here's a question and I'll let you go. When they thought you were me at the bookshop, did they believe you if you said you weren't?"

"I can't imagine what you mean by if. Of course they did." Alex has an absurd but disconcerting impression that Carl has doubted his identity. "If you still won't appear by yourself," he says, "I hope you're free for the rest of the events."

"Sorry you were let down. Head's fine now. Look for me tomorrow," Carl says and ends the call.

Lee collects the empty mugs, holding them together by their handles with a stony clink. "Let's hope he won't rush in and scare her off."

"I can imagine how he feels when someone's claiming what she's claiming. I can't want to know what she's up to half as much as he does."

After breakfast they head for their desks. Beyond the wide window the sun has moved on, leaving a sky like unshed rain, permeated with the whisper of slow waves beyond the houses opposite. Lee is editing the first volume of a trilogy while Alex rewrites his new novel, in which the man who has hired the detective proves to be at least as unreliable as the perpetrator of the forgotten crime the client wants investigated. Alex is taking some delight in condensing a chapter to half its length when the phone rings and names Carl Batchelor. "Not another headache," Alex hopes aloud before answering. "Carl."

"Just letting you know I'm sending you some edits to look at for the paperback."

He sounds resolutely professional – unexpectedly so. "What sort of thing?" Alex doesn't want to wait to learn.

"Stuff I've remembered different. You'll see."

"Kirsty will need to as well."

"You look at it first and then we can talk. It's coming now."

When the email arrives Alex downloads the document at once. *My stepfather nearly killed my mother, and I used to wish he'd killed me....*

He can't help searching for Hilary, but none of those references have changed. Carl isn't as professional as he tried to appear, since he has failed to mark whatever alterations he made. Reading the new version will have to wait until Alex comes back from London, and he returns to revising his novel.

In the morning Lee wakens him. "I let you sleep," she says. "You had another restless night. You kept saying you couldn't remember."

"I don't suppose I said what," Alex says, struggling out of bed.

"By the sound of it you didn't want to know."

She's ready with breakfast by the time he emerges from the bathroom. When he leaves she accompanies him to the gate of the small garden, where the ground-floor tenant's potted plants occupy a dilapidated dangling bench like a confused memory of leisure. "Will you be recording this woman?" Lee says. "She doesn't have to know."

"I hope I'm more awake when I meet her. You're right, of course," Alex says and kisses Lee across the gate as though he's reviving a forgotten custom.

He's in London well before one o'clock. An elongated crowd ushers him along the platform at Victoria to the ticket barrier, beyond which several transport police surround a man who's brandishing a crumpled printout and protesting in a voice as blurred as the illegibly smeary computer type. As Alex dodges past a mass of commuters awaiting revelations from the destination boards above the concourse, he sees the escalators for the Underground aren't working. Rather than sailing up into the glass-roofed sunlight or gliding down into the depths, the heads of passengers are jerking into sight or out of it, step by step. He makes to stand beside the escalators, where he can watch both the concourse and the crowd incessantly emerging from below, and then he realises the escalators aren't out of service. Beyond the entrance are flights of tiled stairs, not escalators at all.

Did he tell Carl and the woman he would wait by the escalators? He can't recall. The gap in his memory, together with his mistake about the stairs, leaves him feeling he can't trust his own mind. Now he remembers there are escalators up to the street outside the station. Will the woman think he meant to meet her there? Perhaps if he can locate Carl this will establish what he said, except that he could have told Carl something else. He dashes out onto the street, where he can see no sign of Carl, but how about the woman? He strides fast to the top of the escalators and stares at the crowd, which produces nobody he recognises or anyone who acknowledges him. He returns to the Underground stairs and surveys the crowd inside the station, but this delivers no result either. Back to the escalators, back to the stairs as digits everywhere display the hour with pairs of blind zeroes like eyes pretending not to watch him, and his skin prickles with anxiety and frustration as he heads for the escalators once more. Any number of women have glanced at him, but none of them own up to being who they said. It's time he called the woman to see where she is – why didn't he do so before? Perhaps for fear she mightn't want to be identified so publicly, but as he makes yet again for the stairs he calls her number. His phone brings him the sound of a bell, and then a mobile starts to ring behind him.

Before he can tell whether it has set about announcing his name, both bells are cut off. He swings around to catch the woman, but nobody's raising a phone to her face. If he glimpsed somebody pocketing one as he turned, he can't tell where. In a moment he grasps that the woman has aborted the call. He stares about in search of someone who looks as if she wants to pass unnoticed, but everyone might be pretending, and if the woman is so reluctant to be singled out, will she have fled? "Well done, Alex," he mutters as he shoves the phone into his breast pocket. "As a detective you're pathetic. Stick to writing and hope nobody questions it." He can only trudge back to the escalators, staring all around him on the way, activities that leave him feeling mindless as a puppet. The automatic doors shut an announcement about cancellations behind him, and a voice that sounds tentative by comparison says "Mr Grand."

He turns to find a woman reaching for his arm, a gesture she rescinds at once. She's a head shorter than Alex but makes up for the difference with breadth. Her eyes are set too close for the width of her squarish face, and she has a small mouth and not much of a nose. All this is framed by a helmet of glossy black hair stiff as plastic, and she doesn't look remotely like Carl. "Yes," Alex says with no tone at all.

"I think you're looking for me."

"How long have I been doing that?"

"I was watching you to be sure." Rather than say of whom, if indeed that's what she has in mind, the woman adds "Now we're here let's have a drink."

"Can you just remind me who you are?"

"Who I told you on the phone." With defiance somewhat reminiscent of Carl's she says "Hilary Wilson."

"There are bars in the station," Alex says and leads the way. The least crowded bar appears to be the Puffin Billy, where a couple are vacating a table by a window overlooking the concourse. "Do you mind if we sit here?" Alex says.

"What am I going to mind for?"

Although there are other unoccupied tables, he oughtn't to have asked, in case she suspects she's being spied upon. He avoids glancing through the window while she sits in a chair like an upholstered bucket bereft of its front and printed with repeated images of a steaming engine. "What will you drink?" he says.

"White wine this time of day." As he makes for the bar she calls "Don't like anything sweet."

He might retort that he can tell, though he isn't sure how much of her brusqueness may be a defence. As he waits for the bottle he's ordered he switches his phone to record and hides it in his breast pocket, ensuring that the hangdog bottles behind the bar obscure his reflection in the mirror. At the table he fills two glasses, and the woman lifts hers so abruptly that several drops darken the coaster. "What are we drinking to?" she says.

"Let's try the truth."

She narrows her eyes so hard that a fleshy ridge swells between them. "Sure that's what you want?"

"It's why I'm here."

"So here's to it." She raises her glass higher without bringing it to his and swallows half the contents. "For a kick off," she says, "I never saw my dad touch Carla once."

"Your father was...."

"Don't start playacting. You've got his name. You dirtied it in your book." Glancing around to establish nobody is listening, she mutters "Malcolm Randal."

"You'll understand my asking, but do you have proof?"

"I wondered when you'd get around to that." She unclasps her handbag, which is composed of tapestry depicting unicorns, and takes out her phone. She skims through images too fast for Alex to catch sight of them until she finds one she wants to show him. "Will that do you?" she says more like a challenge than an offer.

It's an image of a birth certificate dated more than thirty years ago, listing Elaine Soubirous Randal and Malcolm Xavier Randal as the parents of Hilary Louise. While the handwriting looks authentically individual, how easy would that be to fake? Alex notes the Wallasey office where the certificate appears to have been issued – he can check its authenticity later – and hands the phone back. "Everyone's a saint," he comments.

The woman – he'll call her Hilary for now, at least inside his head – gives this a less than saintly look. "What do you mean by that?"

"Everyone on there is named for one. There's just a slight mistake."

Her stare grows fiercer but falls short of convincing Alex. "What one?"

"My partner pointed it out to me. She's an editor. I'm sorry to tell you if you don't know, but St Hilary was a man."

"Then my parents didn't realise. They'd never have tried to confuse people like that, not like Carla."

"You were saying Randal never touched her."

"Never like that. Not much at all."

"And how about you?"

Her outrage sounds primed to explode. "What are you asking me?"

"Was he affectionate to you, since you're saying he wasn't to her?"

"No, that's one of the things she'd like everyone to think. My dad looked after us all, and that's the best kind of affection."

"Do you think that could just be how it seemed to Carla's sister?"

"I'm not that stupid." Before Alex can decide whether she resents his careful phrasing, Hilary declares "She hasn't changed."

Has the woman trapped herself? "You mean you've met him."

"Didn't need to. Saw her online putting on her act. That's why I got in touch."

"What are you saying was an act?"

"The one she is. Blaming everyone but her and never telling anyone the truth if a lie would serve her better. And now she can't even make a name for herself without killing people off."

"I suppose her sister might have reasons to resent her."

"Other way round, Mr Grand. She resented me for being born and getting in the way when she thought the house was all hers, and when I wouldn't do everything she told me to."

"Can you say what you refused to do?"

"I remember everything the way it happened, not like some people." Hilary or at any rate the woman drains her glass and refills it. "One thing I'd never do," she says, "is sneak on my dad."

"You don't think there was ever a reason."

"Like crippling my mum, you mean."

"That sounds like one."

"He never did. I did by being born," the woman says in some kind of triumph. "She couldn't even walk for weeks, and she had to sleep in the front room for months because the stairs hurt too much."

"How do you know all that?"

"She told me when I was bigger."

This seems plausible but proves little – perhaps just that the woman has thought about the book. Alex glances out of the window in case he can locate Carl. Might any of the pairs of legs visible under billboards bearing timetables belong to him? Before Alex can decide, he has to meet the woman's eyes for fear she may suspect she's being watched. "So Randal would have bathed you," he says.

"Try saying Mr Randal. You're not Carla, are you? Just because she's a bitch doesn't mean you have to be."

"Mr Randal, then," Alex says, unable to decide how significant it is that she's calling Carl what he called her. "He dealt with you in the bath."

"He must have if mother didn't, and what's wrong if he did? He was my dad."

"Might he have shared the bath with you?"

"I wouldn't know, and what are you trying to get at? Even Carla never said he did that to her. It isn't in your book."

Too late Alex recalls that it was a memory Carl rejected for inclusion, having failed to bring it to life – indeed, he seemed to feel Alex was imposing it on him – and Alex searches for a question that won't let him down. "I ought to be asking why you contacted me."

"Who do you think I should have got in touch with?"

"I was thinking of the publishers."

"Wanted to give you a chance first."

Alex isn't sure he wants to learn "To do what?"

"To see what she really is," the woman says and takes a mouthful before replenishing her glass. "How she took you in."

"Have you spoken to Carl about any of this?"

He finds he's hoping she will claim she has, because surely this would refute her whole tale. Carl has no reason to deny hearing from her, or is Alex too eager to disbelieve her? "I wouldn't go anywhere near her," the woman says.

"Even verbally?" When this prompts a scowl that's presumably meant as confirmation Alex says "How long has that been the case?"

"Since she turned her back on all of us."

"Moved away, you mean."

"That put the lid on it, but I don't remember when she ever had much time for us."

Alex feels as if the facts are more remote than ever, and certainly vaguer still. As he risks another glance in search of Carl, the woman says "Are you wanting to be off? Go on if you can't take the truth."

"I want to hear everything you have to tell me." He sees that the bottle is empty, and so is her glass. "More wine?" he says.

"Don't bother trying to get me drunk." Just the same, she tips up her glass to swallow a last trickle. "I know what I know," she says, "and you better had. Now what are you going to do?"

"I'm still listening."

"You've heard it all now," she says, and Alex can only conclude he has antagonised her. "I want to know what you'll do about it."

"I'll be speaking to my editor."

"Just them."

"The obvious person as well."

"You think it's obvious." Presumably this is a gibe at Carl and his transition. "So why did you write all that stuff like that about him?" she says.

"Because that's his account of his life."

The woman reaches for the bottle, apparently having forgotten it's empty. "What are you on about? Whose?"

"I take it you haven't met Carl since he made the change, but I think you mightn't call him her if you did."

The woman's pause lets Alex realise that she didn't use the female pronoun just before. "We aren't talking about her," she says. "I mean my dad."

"Malcolm Randal." A laugh feels eager to escape, though Alex doesn't know what kind. "How are you suggesting I communicate with him?"

"I don't know if he'd want you to after all the lies you wrote."

"You're asking me to believe he's alive."

"You'd better. It's only the truth."

"I've seen the death certificate."

"Had it in your hands, have you?"

"It was emailed to me."

"And I don't need to guess who by. How easy do you think things like that are to fake?"

"About as easy as a birth certificate, I should think."

She stares at Alex as if she wishes he were someone else. "Since you were offering, I'll have a drink."

Despite not having finished his, Alex feels in some need of another. As he returns to the table with a pair of glasses rather less than full of wine, the woman beckons with her phone. "You need to hear this," she says. "Dad, say who you are."

The peevish voice sounds determined to be vigorous. "You just said."

"I know, but can you settle an argument? Don't fret, it's nothing serious."

As Alex supresses a response to this remark the voice says "Name's Randal. Malcolm Randal."

"And you're very much alive."

"For a few years yet, God willing."

"Thanks, dad. That's all I needed. See you next time we're up."

As Alex opens his mouth she ends the call. "I'd have liked to speak to him," Alex says.

"I'm only bothered what he likes. I haven't even told him about your book."

Alex has begun to wonder if her contradictions are designed to confuse him, unless that's her state of mind. "What do you actually want to happen?" he's provoked to ask.

"It'd better be enough." Her second mouthful drains the glass, and she stands up. "Call me if you've got a proper reason for talking to him," she says, "and call me when you've seen your editor."

She's out of the bar before Alex has time to react. He snatches out his phone to stop recording, and has brought up the camera by the time she appears beyond the window. He pretends to consult the screen while he takes a burst of photographs, but she doesn't even glance in his direction. Two of the eight images show enough of her face for him to save them. He downs a drink, though by no means as large a gulp as any of hers, and phones Carl. "Did you see her?"

"How was I going to do that?"

"She wasn't your sister, you mean."

"I wouldn't know." In a tone Alex finds increasingly hard to place Carl says "You know she couldn't be."

"You'd hope so, but I'm asking you."

By now Carl sounds openly accusing. "You never spotted I wasn't there."

"You weren't supposed to be seen. Where were you, then?" Alex needs to know.

"At the firm. Didn't you hear the trains are off?"

Encountering the woman has left Alex so suspicious that he doesn't immediately grasp the explanation. "Yours don't come into this station, so they wouldn't have announced it here."

"Then they ought. So what did you make of whoever she was?"

"I have to say she didn't look much like you at all."

"Why were you expecting her to?"

Carl's accusing tone is back. "It would have made her more convincing," Alex says. "I'll send you a photograph."

"She let you take her photo? Must be mad."

"She wasn't aware I was taking it. I recorded her as well."

"Give us a look, then. Send it now."

Alex sends the clearest image to Carl's mobile, and while he waits for a response he checks the national railway website. Trains from Manchester to Euston are cancelled because of a signalling problem, and he feels ashamed of his suspicions, which he can't even define. "See what you're getting at," Carl says. "What a bitch."

"You wouldn't recognise her by any chance."

"I just agreed with you. She hasn't got a thing to do with me."

"I was only wondering if she could be somebody you used to know."

"Trying it on to see what she could get for herself, you mean. I don't know anybody like that either."

"I should tell you she showed me her birth certificate."

"A real one? Doubt it."

"On her phone. It said she was born to Elaine and Malcolm Randal."

"Wonder how long it took her to fake that up. Maybe the bitch got hold of my little sister's death certificate."

"It didn't look like that."

"Wish I'd seen it. Wish I'd been with you and not said I'd just watch." As if he finds it hard to leave fierceness behind Carl says "So what was she after?"

"She didn't really say. She's waiting until we've discussed it with Kirsty, I think."

"Will the bitch be there?"

"Not this time, I shouldn't think. Perhaps not at all."

"I'd like to see her. I'd like to do a lot more." Not much less furiously Carl says "So she didn't ask for money or anything."

"Not yet, if she means to. She did do one thing you should know about." Alex hardly knows why he pauses before saying "She put a man on the phone she said was Malcolm Randal."

"Christ, what else will she try on? You've got his death certificate."

"We'd better let Kirsty have a copy, do you think?"

"You can. Like I said, this bitch must be mad. Who wants me?" Having aimed the question away from the phone, Carl returns to say "Got to go, Alex."

"I'll let you know what Kirsty says," Alex promises and calls her at once. Only her voicemail responds. He leaves an unspecific message and finishes his drink before heading for the train. He's halfway to Brighton when his phone announces Kirsty. "You wanted me," she says.

"I've just met someone claiming she's Carl Batchelor's sister, who wants us to believe Randal is alive as well."

"Met how?"

He's disconcerted by her untypical brusqueness. "She sent me a message and I arranged to meet her."

"Where, Alex?"

"At Victoria."

"You should have sent her here and come yourself. What did she want?"

"She hasn't made that clear yet. I said I'd contact you, and I've talked to Carl."

"Who says...."

"She's an imposter, of course."

"We need to get together on this as soon as everybody can. Are you both free tomorrow?"

"I will be. Shall I call him?"

"Please, while I speak to people here."

"Hope she's buying lunch," Carl says by way of agreement, and Alex leaves Kirsty another message, committing Carl and himself to be with her by noon. Now he wants to talk to Lee as soon as he's home, but the only sign of her is a yellow note stuck to the frame of his computer screen, telling him she's on the weekly supermarket expedition. At least he can send Randal's death certificate to Kirsty while he's waiting, and he switches on the computer.

A minute later he begins urging it to ask for his password. The screen stays blank, and all at once his guts feel emptied too. He pokes the button to shut the system down and powers it up again, and eventually switches it off at the mains and back on. All this achieves is to make his palms grow slippery while his dry mouth tastes of metal and his innards seem to struggle to close around a hollow at the core of him. The system stays as silent and inactive as a slab, because the computer is dead.

CARLY

The day after my birthday, Barry drove me to my house. "Want me to come in with you, Carly?" he said.

"Better not in case it upsets my mum." I was there to fetch my clothes and the rest of my possessions while Randal was at work. "I'll be doing that enough," I said.

I was still in the taxi when my mother threw her front door open. She seemed to have regained her strength overnight, and I wondered if not having to put up with me around the house had let her have her health back, confirming it had been my fault all along that she was ill. "Can't you even use your father's cars?" she cried. "Another slap in the face for him."

I got out before answering. "I don't expect he'd want me to."

"You mean you're afraid what he'd say to you, and so you ought to be." She squinted at the name on the side of the taxi and stamped her foot on the doorstep. "Paying his enemies into the bargain," she cried.

"I didn't have to pay. I work there."

"That's right, remind me. Rub it in."

"Mum, I didn't want a scene."

"Then stop causing one in the street. I have to live here even if you've chosen to abandon us," she said and glared at Barry. "What are you waiting for? You take yourself off. We don't want your lot round here."

"I'm picking up her things, Mrs Randal."

"Yes, you know who I am right enough. I can't believe you'd dare to show your face in this street after everything you and this ungrateful wretch have done to my husband." When the taxi didn't move she flailed a hand at it. "Don't you try and bully me," she cried. "You should be ashamed, a big strong man and a girl that thinks she's big against a woman all by herself."

"I'll be here whenever you need me, Carly."

"That's it, when you need protecting from a poor crippled woman on her own." Even more bitterly she said "And that's never been the girl's name."

"Oh, mum," I said, but she looked ready to spit in my face.

I grabbed two of the suitcases Donna had lent me and carried them into the house. As I struggled with them up to my room my mother slammed the front door. I dumped them on the bed that no longer felt like mine, not that it really had since Randal had invaded it, and threw clothes into them as fast as I could. I filled them as full as the zips would take, and was grappling one to the stairs when I saw my mother climbing doggedly towards me. "Watch what you're doing with that," she protested. "Do you want to knock me down the stairs?"

"It wasn't me who hurt you, mum."

"If you truly believe that, you haven't the brains you were born with. You've hurt me and your father with everything you've done."

"I didn't hurt your back."

"That's my cross to bear, and it's not your place to blame anyone. It's nothing to the suffering you've caused me." She plodded up the rest of the stairs and only just stood out of my way. "I'll be seeing you don't take anything that isn't yours," she said.

"I've just got my clothes in here. Go on, check."

"I'll pray you're telling the truth for once." As if she'd decided this wasn't enough of a retort she said "I'll know if anything's gone that shouldn't have."

When I took the case out to the taxi Barry must have sensed I didn't want to talk, because he just sent me a sympathetic grin. As I brought the second case out I saw Mrs Shea watching through her window, but she immediately dodged back. I wondered if my mother had made such a fuss outside the house in the secret hope that some of the neighbours would come to her aid. I went back to load the last case with cosmetics and bathroom items and books, during all of which my mother didn't say a word. "Go on, tear the carpet while you're here," she said as I wheeled the laden case across the landing. "This is the end then, is it, Carla?"

Till then I don't think I realised how final my move might be. She was still my mother, and I said "Won't I be seeing you?"

"Not while you're betraying your poor father in every way you can think of. I'm shocked you even have the gall to ask."

"Will you stop calling him my father? I only ever had one, and he's dead."

"And what do you suppose Bertie thinks of you if he can hear you where he is?"

"If he can he'll have been watching Malcolm Randal, and I know what he'll have thought of him."

"I'm only glad Malcolm can't hear you," my mother said, and my chance to expose him had gone, even if I could have spoken. "Now let's have your keys. You won't be coming back in his house while you're betraying him."

"He's been betraying you with me since I was little." I would have told her if I could have got the words out, but the gag he'd created was crushing my tongue. "Maybe I'll see you somewhere else, then," I said.

She waited till I'd handed my keys over, and then she said "Not if I see you first. You're no child of mine any more."

Barry hauled two cases up to the flat while I carried the other, and I managed not to cry till he'd left me alone. Once I'd finished I vowed never to cry again, because I'd left all the reasons behind. Barry's sister was handling the switchboard that day to give me time to settle into my new home. When I'd unpacked I cooked pasta for Donna and me, and over dinner with a bottle of supermarket red she told me her flatmate was moving out by the end of the week. My life was starting to feel secure, and at first it did when I went to work.

Rachel was the night receptionist, and she hung around for half an hour to see I didn't let the firm down. "You're as good as me," she said, "and maybe better." Barry made everyone coffee before she left, so that she could join in when he raised his Cheerful Cabs mug and said "Here's to the new member of the team." I answered calls while everyone finished their coffee, which made me feel more competent than Randal had ever let me feel. I was alone in the reception area when I saw him watching me across the road.

He was standing next to Doris at the switchboard, and she was watching me too. I told myself they could look all they liked, because there was more than just a road between us. I was tempted to make a face at them, except that would have been childish, which I wasn't any more. Instead I set out to show Doris how much more efficient I could be than her, even if she was too far away to appreciate it. "Cheerful Cabs," I said in a voice that went with the name, and by the time I finished dealing with the call, Randal was back in his office. I didn't want to think what he might be doing there or how much I was in his mind. But when I looked up from sending Bill a job I saw Randal standing outside his firm.

He stared at me and drummed his thumbs on his hipbones, and I thought his hands wanted to be somewhere else. He hadn't shifted when Barry came back from an airport pickup. He frowned at Randal and moved to stand by me. "What's old Randy after? How long's he been there?"

"A bit." I had to answer Barry's first question as well, which was closer to the point than he could know. "I expect he wants me."

"Well, he won't be having you. Like me to go and have a word?"

"You've done enough for me. He can't bother me any longer."

"Don't be shy of saying if he does. I wish we could have put the switchboard in the back, but we need reception where everyone can see it."

Randal hadn't moved. He looked more defiant than I thought I needed to feel. As Barry went into the office a van blocked my view across the road. When it moved off it seemed to have wiped Randal away, because there was no sign of him. I located a taxi to send on a call and glanced up as the street door opened. It was letting Randal in.

He shut it with hardly a sound and strode slowly over to me as if he was trying to act like a policeman. He planted his hands flat on the counter on either side of me and leaned across it. The sight of his face descending towards me brought back my worst memories, and I wondered if the action roused his memory along with him, but I wasn't going to let him crush me into my old self. "What do you want, Malcolm?" I said.

"Just what your mother and I are entitled to. And while we're talking about her, I wonder if you're aware how ill your unannounced visit made her."

"I didn't mean to." He was able to revive some of my guilt after all. "I just had to get my things," I said.

"I hear you got a good few digs at her in as well, and me while I wasn't there."

"I didn't say half I should have."

"How brave you think you are now," Randal said, and I heard the office door open behind me. "Ah, here comes one of your protectors. Was he the fine fellow who helped you intimidate your mother?"

"What are you doing over here, Malcolm?" Barry said.

"Having a private conversation with my daughter."

"You just brought me into it, pal."

"You're admitting you were her strongarm man."

"I'm saying no such crap. I was her transport and that's all."

"Your language tells me all I want to know. God forgive you if you used it to her mother, and God knows how soon the girl will be at home with it if she isn't already." Randal hardly seemed to be talking to either of us. "Now if I may be permitted to speak to my daughter," he said.

"What do you want me to do, Carly?"

"Do you mind staying with me?"

"I'll be going nowhere while he's here."

"I hope you aren't flattering yourself you'll cow me," Randal said. "I'm not her mother."

"You reckon women are easier to handle, do you, Malcolm?" Barry said.

As Randal stared at this I said "Whatever you want to say to me, you can say it for Barry to hear."

"You need an audience for your performance, do you? You want him to see the show you're putting on."

"I've stopped doing any of that."

I hoped this might scare him, but if he heard a threat he didn't admit to it. With a scornful look at the office he said "So this is what you're planning to do with your life."

"She's settled in fine, Malcolm. She's an asset and we're treating her like one."

"I'll tell him, Barry," I said and did. "I'm going to be what I want to be."

"You must be proud of yourself for luring her away," Randal said to Barry, not bothering to glance at me. "You've been working on her since she wasn't even old enough to choose."

Instead of everything this made me yearn to say I told him "I am now, and I have."

"You heard her, Malcolm. Anything else you were after? We've got jobs to do even if you haven't."

"You're as anxious to be rid of me as she is, are you? I wonder if your consciences are troubling you."

"Do us a favour and don't start that crap again. If there's anything else, make it quick."

"I'm here to take what's mine."

I met his stare as forcefully as I could. "I'm nobody's property to do what they like with."

If his eyes flickered, they steadied at once. "Your mother and I chose a special present for a good girl, but now we know how wrong we were."

I felt his gaze crawl down my front before it found my hand. "You want my birthday ring back," I said.

"After everything you've done to us we feel you don't deserve it any longer."

"Jesus Christ, Malcolm," Barry said. "Is that your little pissy victory? You're even more pathetic than I took you for."

"It's all right, Barry," I said. "I never really wanted it. See what it says and you'll see why." I slipped the ring off and told Randal "You've never been my father. You know what you've been to me."

This time there was no doubt his eyes wavered. I wished Barry could have seen, but he was squinting at the ring. When he held it out to me I said "Give it to him."

Barry dropped it on the counter, where it rolled towards Randal and then tottered flat. Randal captured it and shoved it in his trousers pocket, where I imagined his hand groping near his penis. "Perhaps you can spare a thought for your mother," he said. "I wonder how she'll feel when she sees how little her gift meant to you."

"Since you care so much if she's upset, maybe you shouldn't tell her."

"That kind of cleverness comes from the devil, Carla. I wouldn't be so proud of it if I were you."

"You aren't. We're nothing like, however hard you tried."

I was sure his eyes were hiding apprehension. I felt very close to saying much more while Barry could hear, but I hadn't managed when he said "We won't be seeing you again, Malcolm."

"Is that a question?"

"It's a bit of good advice, pal. And as long as you brought intimidation up, if you try it on with our Carly again I'll be having a few words with my chums in the police."

"You don't call that intimidation."

"No, I call it protecting one of the team."

"If that's all my daughter is to you." Perhaps Randal realised the implication endangered him more than Barry, because he made for the door, only to face me once he'd opened it. "God will forgive me for saying this," he said, "but you aren't the daughter we prayed we'd have."

Barry and I watched him stalk through the traffic to his firm. "So that's Malcolm with his mask off," Barry said. "Has he always treated you like that?"

"Worse," I said, and felt on the edge of explaining, but perhaps Barry didn't want to hear too much. "You let us know if he ever does again," he said and went into his office as the switchboard buzzed like an alarm.

ALEX

He's searching on his phone for computer repair firms when it announces Carl. "What is it?" Alex says at speed. "I'm pretty busy just now."

"Don't bother with me if it's more important."

This sounds like pique, and not knowing why he's calling won't help Alex. "It's important, but can you tell me quickly what you want?"

"Just seeing you've got my ideas safe."

Alex abandons examining the website of Terminal Saviour. "Which ideas?"

"The ones I gave you. Don't say something's happened to them too."

The last word aggravates Alex's nervousness. "I'm sorry, I'm not following you."

"The ones I sent you for our book. Have you read them?"

"I looked through what you sent. To be honest, I couldn't see what you'd done, and—"

"You will if you give them a proper look."

"I can't just now. My computer's crashed."

"You're having a joke." Before Alex can make his reaction heard Carl says "It's not one, is it?"

"I don't believe I suggested it was."

"No call to talk to me like that. I'm saying it's not for me either."

"I'm sure that would be the case, but—"

"Mine's gone too. Crashed and can't be fixed and I've got to buy another."

One element of this disturbs Alex most of all. "Who says it can't be fixed?"

"My pal who knows about them." After a pause that lets Alex hope the friend is mistaken, Carl says "Christ, that must be what did it."

Alex strives to find the prospect of an explanation hopeful. "What would that be?"

"My pal said there was a virus. If your computer's down as well it must have been in the email I sent you or it got into the attachment. Did you open it on your phone?"

"I didn't, thankfully. I'll delete it now."

As Alex sends the email and its attachment to the electronic bin and empties that, Carl makes a sound like a thought in search of words. "All right," Alex says, "that's done."

"Any chance of getting it back?"

"It isn't even in a cloud."

"I wish you hadn't been so quick now. I just remembered something else."

"You can note it down for now, can you? Tell me later."

"Not about me. Did you say that bitch you met showed you something on her phone?"

"A birth certificate."

"Did her phone get close to your one?"

"Within inches."

"Maybe she did it to us. My pal said phones can pass viruses like that."

"Wouldn't her phone have been infected too?"

"Maybe not if she knew what she was doing. I'll have to ask my pal."

The notion that disaster may be lying dormant on his phone leaves Alex anxious to diagnose its state. "You'll have noted your revisions somewhere, will you?"

"Just on the computer that's gone. Didn't keep a backup."

"Maybe you can go through the book again and tell me them next time we meet. If there's time you could after we've seen Kirsty."

"After she's taken us for lunch," Carl says. "If I can remember them."

Alex finds the first idea ambitious if not presumptuous, and the second more unwelcome than he cares to define just now. The call has left him feeling vulnerable, so that even searching for a programme to scan his phone for viruses seems to threaten it with further damage. The scanning process takes a good few minutes without revealing any information, which means he doesn't dare to look for anyone who may be able to fix the computer. His mind is as blank as the computer screen by the time Lee comes home, a bag of groceries under each arm. "You get the rest," she says, and at once "Oh, what's wrong?"

"My computer's screwed and my phone may be, and I can't use it until this scan's finished."

"Have you got someone to look at the computer? Let me find somebody while you fetch the shopping."

A car twice the height and size of hers, parked by a supporter of the football team whose stickers cover the rear window, has barely left Lee room in the resident's parking space. As Alex dumps the bags of shopping on the kitchen table, Lee comes to him. "Your phone's clean," she says, "and I've found some people who make home visits. Towering Computers and Desktop Dave want several days' notice, but Terminal Solutions promise next day service."

"I'll call them now."

"I already have." As Alex fends off an absurd unworthy notion that she borrowed his voice or substituted hers she says "I'll be here tomorrow when they come."

In the morning as he boards the train the phone shrills in his breast pocket. The sound and the urgent vibration, which seems to penetrate his heart, feel as if he has set off an alarm. If the news is this swift, he can only hope it's good – but the phone substitutes Kirsty's name for the one he's anxious to hear, and she just wants to establish that he's on his way. For the rest of the journey the phone has no more to say, at least until he's hurrying along Euston Road, where it turns him into yet another member of the crowd speaking to nobody visible. "Mr Terminal's just gone," Lee tells him.

He can't help wishing she would edit her own dialogue to render it more immediately informative. "And?"

"He's taken the computer, but he isn't holding out much hope."

This leaves Alex feeling as hollow as he imagines the computer to be, and isolated from the crowd around him. When the swarm of hasty figures dwindles outside the glass lift, they're beyond seeming any more remote. Rod's face is as flawlessly made up as ever, and Alex can't help feeling the receptionist's impeccable smile is made up in another sense. Rod leans towards the switchboard, reminding Alex of Carla's action even though he has never seen it. "Alex Grand for you," Rod murmurs.

Kirsty comes out of her office at once. "You made it, Alex."

"I said I would."

"Some people don't live up to what they say."

"I'm not some people, am I? I hope I'm only me."

She gives this a look as odd as the exchange has made him feel. "Come and be introduced," she says and hurries him along the corridor.

The solitary person in her office isn't Carl, and why should Alex have imagined he needed to be introduced to his collaborator? The woman is seated behind Kirsty's desk, although not in her chair. Her compact face, which is enclosed by matching curves of cropped relentlessly black hair, looks organised to convey a terse unambiguous statement – that everything she meets is subject to evaluation. "Ruth, this is Alex Grand," Kirsty says. "Alex, Ruth Nyman from Legal."

The woman stands up just enough to give his hand a single shake across the desk. "I'm afraid you're on your own here, Mr Grand."

"Please call me Alex." When she responds with a nod and a comparably slight smile he says "Won't Kirsty be with me?"

"I don't think this is quite the time or place for jokes."

"I didn't know I'd made one."

"Ruth means Carl can't be with us, Alex."

"Again? What's his excuse this time?"

"The same as the other day."

"Another migraine? He's having a lot of those lately." Perhaps this is unreasonable, and Alex adds "I suppose it's all the stress."

"No, the trains have let him down again."

Though it scarcely feels rational, Alex says "Will you have checked they aren't running?"

"You think I should have."

"We may as well in case he can still make it, I should think."

The attempt to sound reasonable feels even less so than his question. Ruth Nyman watches him consult his phone, which confirms no trains have left Manchester for Euston all day. As he makes a gesture somebody confronted with a gun might offer, she says "Did you have a reason to be suspicious?"

"I wouldn't say that. I just feel he should be here."

"You might like to be more careful what you do say, Mr Grand. Will you not feel able to proceed without him?"

"By all means let's get on with whatever we're here for."

"I'd like to start by looking at the evidence."

"Go ahead."

She gazes at him across the desk, and Kirsty joins in. They're making him feel he's the evidence, an impression that the empty chair beside him only aggravates. "So what have you brought me?" Ruth says, though not at once.

"I'm not sure what I should have."

"Any documents you hold that support your book." When he fails to produce anything she says "I assume Kirsty told you they were required."

"I did, Alex, didn't I?"

Perhaps her job may be at risk, and so he doesn't answer. "There's nothing physical," he tells Ruth.

"We'll print them from your phone, of course. Let's begin with the death certificate."

"I'm very much afraid that's gone unless my computer can be fixed."

"You haven't kept it on your phone."

"I always clear as much as I can onto the computer." Her silence and Kirsty's provoke him to add "It isn't only up to me."

"If you sent me the document," Kirsty says, "it never reached here."

"I'm talking about Carl. His computer's down as well, but he should have the image on his phone."

"He thinks that may have the virus too," Kirsty says. "He called from his firm."

"My phone hasn't, so his can't. I'll call him now." Alex finds the site and fingers the number. "And there's no reason he can't stay on while we all talk," he declares.

Nobody speaks until a receptionist says "Carl's Cars."

"May I have a word with Carl? It's Alex Grand."

"Is he going to know who that is?"

"He wouldn't have a story without me."

"You're the feller that's got your name on his book."

Alex hopes Kirsty and Ruth are as amused by the comment as he wants to feel, but they're expressionlessly intent on the conversation. At the end of a pause measured by the women's blinks, which make Alex feel he's fending off infection by the tic, Carl says "Won't be with you today, Alex."

"I know that. I'm in Kirsty's office. I should tell you there oughtn't to be any problem with your phone. I've scanned mine and there's nothing to worry us."

"Oh God. Wish you'd told me sooner. I'll talk to you in a while."

"Hold on," Alex says as Ruth extends a hand towards his phone, having heard Carl over its loudspeaker. "We want to check some things with you."

"Good afternoon, Mr Batchelor. My name's Ruth Nyman. I'm with the legal team."

"You're going to fix the woman who's been trying to spoil things for us, are you?"

"If you like to put it that way. I understand you haven't met her."

"No plans to, either. I might end up giving her a few thumps like she should have got when she was younger."

"That isn't necessary, as I'm sure you must realise. It might very well harm our case, at least in the eyes of the public."

The phone, which Alex has placed on top of a copy of *When I Was Carla*, lies silent for some moments before Carl says "What do you mean, our case?"

"However much of one we need to bring against your sister and your stepfather."

Ruth wags her fingers to denote punctuation, apparently forgetting Carl can't see that she has enclosed two words in quotes. Loud enough to make the microphone vibrate he demands "Who are you saying they are?"

"I'm simply repeating what I heard them say."

The sound Carl makes is some distance from a laugh. "You've gone and met them."

"Not yet, but I suggest I'm present when you do, and Mr Grand may as well be."

"You'll need me all right," Alex is provoked to point out. "They've only spoken to me so far."

Ruth hasn't looked away from the prone mobile. "I want to have the evidence in hand before we proceed. Can you supply me with Randal's death certificate, Mr Batchelor?"

"That's what I was going to tell Alex. It's gone off my phone as well."

Alex feels as if a memory has been snatched away. "How did that happen?"

"I was only going to delete your email we thought had got a virus, but I did all yours by mistake and all the ones I'd sent you as well."

"You'll still have the document somewhere on there, surely."

"Only had it on my computer."

"I'm sure it's easily obtained," Ruth says. "Where was it issued?"

"I forget just now." More resentfully than Alex thinks is called for Carl says "It wasn't me who got it, and the girl's not here."

"Please send me the information as soon as you have it. Ruth Nyman all one word lower case at Tiresias Press all one word lower case dot com," the lawyer says, twirling a forefinger to sketch the preposition symbol. "I'd like no further communication with the claimants until I have the certificate in my hands. For the moment all I need is your commitment to the process."

"Which one's that?"

"However much is necessary to protect the integrity of our property and yours. If needs be, prosecution."

"Prosecuting them, you mean."

Ruth permits herself a smile so faint that Carl might overlook it even if he were in the office. "I doubt it will come to that, but if it must, then yes."

"Can't we just scare them off?"

"I'm here to see the situation permanently resolved. No need to concern yourself further just now." Alex assumes she means to reassure Carl until she says "I should point out that in your contract you've undertaken to support any legal action we find appropriate."

"Alex never told me about that. He's supposed to know about contracts."

"No doubt he does, but I rather think it's your responsibility to scrutinise your contract for yourself. You should realise nobody would have taken on your story if you'd struck out that clause."

"It's your story as well." This could be taken for a warning, and so could "Speak to you later, Alex."

At once the phone is as inert as a paperweight, and Alex breaks the silence. "At least we're old hands at the game."

"It's rather more serious than that, Mr Grand."

"I'm as aware of that as you are. It was just a form of words."

"I'd advise you to be careful with those."

"I rather think I am. It comes with being a writer." Alex sees Kirsty is growing uncomfortable, and regrets having let the lawyer lead him. "Is there anything else I can do to help?" he says.

"I understand from Kirsty you recorded Mr Batchelor's account of his life. You might let me have that before you leave."

"I'm afraid it was another casualty of the crash."

"That's most unfortunate. You didn't think to back it up." She waits for his admission before saying "In that case we need to bring him in as soon as I've had time to look over the book."

"When do we want him?" Kirsty says.

"It won't be tomorrow. Certainly this week. Can you keep yourself free as well, Mr Grand," Ruth says but doesn't ask.

"Count on me. I'll want to hear what's said."

"We may need you to deal with any discrepancies. Either Kirsty or I will be in touch."

Apparently this is a dismissal, since Kirsty says "I'll see you soon, Alex."

He can't help reflecting that Carl would feel denied a lunch, unless Carl's presence would have earned them one. He senses the women are waiting to start a discussion, and feels so out of place that he nearly forgets to retrieve his phone from the desk. In reception Rod gives him a puzzled look to which Alex can find no response. The journey to Victoria surrounds him with the enigmatic backs of heads. At Victoria he's disconcerted by expecting to be borne up to ground level by an escalator, when his last visit showed him that wasn't the case. There mustn't be anything wrong with his memory. He's distracted by problems that are going to be solved, that's all.

He's just a few minutes from Brighton when the phone rings and identifies Hilary Randal, though it can't pronounce the quotes he put around the name when adding it to his contacts. "Ms Randal," it prompts him to comment.

"That was me. I hope you aren't saying it's you."

Alex does his best to summon up a laugh. "Why would I be doing that?"

"You pretend you're her in your book."

He shouldn't even be talking to the woman, but he resents obeying Ruth Nyman. "Nothing of the kind," he says. "I'm just the medium."

"You go in for calling up the dead, do you? She'd like you to think you're talking to one of them." Before Alex can comment the woman says "I expected I'd have heard from you by now."

"I'm having trouble with my computer."

"Nothing to do with me," she says, and Alex can't decide how defensive this is. "Have you been seeing anyone?"

"Can you be specific?"

"My sister for a start."

"Carl says he has no sister."

"I've got no brother, so we're quits." With quite as much contempt she says "Do you truly believe what he tells you, or are you just doing what you're paid to do?"

"I can't discuss the situation at the moment, but I will say the publishers have brought their legal people in."

"Is that supposed to frighten me? You've just made me more determined. I'd better hear from you again damn soon or this'll all be public."

"If you're looking for some form of compensation you should approach the publishers, not me."

"I'm giving you a chance to sort out things in your own head first. If I were you I'd take it, Mr Grand."

Rather than retort that she isn't Alex says "I've still no idea what you want."

"You'll be finding out if you aren't quick. Thought you writers were supposed to be intelligent," she says and ends the call.

What can she do to him? At least he has a lawyer on his side. All the same, he refrains from telling Lee about the conversation. In the morning the owner of Terminal Solutions phones to let him know that nothing on his computer can be salvaged, news that leaves him feeling hollowed out, as if more information than he could have grasped has been stolen from him. Having chosen a new system, he does his best to let the prospect of delivery tomorrow enliven him. Since the external drive onto which he copied his novel in progress isn't infected, he can work on the book whenever Lee isn't using her computer. As he stares at a paragraph he can't remember – he feels so remote from the book that the words might as well be someone else's thoughts – the phone shrills at him and declares "Unknown caller."

Are they cancelling his delivery? His hasty grab sends the phone clattering across the keyboard, printing nonsense on the screen. Once it's recaptured he says "Yes."

"Alex Grand."

Why does he feel he ought to recognise her voice but not her words? The words are his name, after all. "Yes."

"Ruth Nyman, Mr Grand." As he realises he has never previously heard her use his first name, the lawyer says "You're fine tomorrow, I hope."

"If I need to be."

"You do." Not much less like a rebuke she says "Can you be here by eight in the morning?"

His mouth opens well in advance of his reply. "How long is the meeting likely to be?"

"We have to get there first." The grunt she adds may be a bid for humour. "Since Mr Batchelor is so elusive," she says, "we'll go to him. I want to pin him down once and for all."

CARLY

One day Barry came out of his office and over to me. "Carly, how would you like a different job?"

He'd caught me staring at the firm across the road, but he surely couldn't think I had anything like that in mind. "I never want to go back."

"Don't worry, love, we won't be sending you to Malcolm. More like he's sending somebody to us. Remember Emma you filled in for when she had a little one?"

"I wanted to let her have her job back."

"He's told her no. Maybe he's acting like a twat because he's still hoping to get you."

"He never will again."

"He's got to know that if he lets himself. Thing is, she's stacking shelves but she'd like something better, and I'm thinking you could help her out. Want to see if you can drive?"

I felt as if he was asking somebody who wasn't me. "I've never learned."

"I can take you out." When I hesitated Barry added "On the road."

"I didn't think you meant a date." The idea disturbed me just the same, because it reminded me of Randal. "I'd like to try," I said.

"Some of the ladies have been saying they'd rather have a girl pick them up. Let's aim to get you in a cab next year."

That was only months away, but it felt more like a promise than Christmas did. Barry showed me the basics of driving and then had me drive in all kinds of weather, in the rush hour and late at night as well. Once I'd mastered all that he started playing every difficult passenger he'd ever had to deal with, and some of the ones his partners in Cheerful Cabs had. "You'll do fine," he told me, not just once. I passed my test in October, and a few days before Christmas I got my taxi licence. It felt like my best present ever, or at any rate as good as anything I'd had from my real father. I wished we could skip ahead to the New Year, when Emma would take over so that I could start driving for the firm, but first I had to deal with Christmas.

I wasn't planning to do much. Donna kept inviting me to go to clubs with her, but I always felt out of place. I'd had enough of being picked up since I'd sold myself for drugs at school. At the start of Christmas week Barry's wife cooked dinner for the firm, and I felt like part of a new family. We were open over Christmas, and I supposed Randal would be – he always acted as if working at Christmas was a sin he had to suffer committing – and that reminded me I needed to decide what to do about my mother.

I hadn't seen her since I'd collected my things from the house. I'd tried phoning, but she always cut me off as soon as she heard my voice. I might have gone home when I could be certain Randal wasn't there, but I suspected she wouldn't let me in and was liable to make sure the neighbours heard, not that I ought to have cared. I might have told myself I'd done everything anyone could be expected to do, but the nearer Christmas came, the more I felt I hadn't. On Christmas Eve I watched till Randal arrived across the road, and then I phoned the house.

The phone rang till I wondered if Randal had set it to identify callers, letting my mother know it was me. She could be taking time to find it or to limp to it, and at last she said "Hello" like a question she didn't much want to ask.

"Mum, it's me."

"Am I supposed to know who that is?"

"Your daughter."

"Which is that when it's at home?"

I wasn't going to let her make me feel she didn't know me. "It's Carla, mum."

"Well, there's a name we haven't heard for a long time, because nobody uses it in this house."

"So long as you don't mind hearing it now."

"I mind a lot." She gave this time to leave me feeling bad, and then she said "Don't think you're going to get round me just because you think it's Christmas."

"I know it is as much as you do."

"You're so big and clever you can tell your mother how to talk now, are you?"

"I don't care how you talk so long as we're talking."

"You've said one true thing, and that's you don't care." My mother gave a gasp that told me she'd sat down. "What do you want?" she said. "It's tiring me out just having to listen to you."

"Like you said, it's Christmas, so I wondered—"

"Your father isn't here, but I know he wouldn't want you in the house after everything you've done to him."

"I wasn't going to ask that." Instead of retorting that he would never be my father, I glared at his firm across the road. "I thought I could buy you dinner somewhere," I said.

"Buy who dinner?"

The idea of inviting Randal made me feel as if I'd swallowed something nobody should, but I couldn't let it stop me reaching out to her. "Whoever wants to come."

"You really believe your father would."

I managed not to tell her I hoped the opposite. "I can't say how he'd feel."

"You're owning up to that at least. I'll tell him what you said, and that's all I'm saying to you just now, Carla." She contradicted herself by adding "I want you to know I pray for you every night. I just hope it does some good."

I knew I wouldn't like whatever she was praying for, and so I didn't ask. In any case she rang off before I could speak. The switchboard buzzed, and for a moment I was so confused I thought it was my mother calling back. I took the call and sent a taxi, and I'd dealt with several more customers when I saw Randal march out of his office.

He met my eyes and kept his gaze on me while he opened the door onto the pavement. When he didn't look away as he crossed the road I expected to see him run down by the traffic he was refusing to acknowledge. As his face approached it reminded me of all the times I'd had to watch it swelling closer to me in my room. He let himself into Cheerful Cabs and leaned over the counter, and I vowed I wouldn't be made to feel small, the way I used to shrink. "So you've been trying to win your mother over," he said.

"I shouldn't have to. She's my mother."

I heard Barry come out of his office behind me. "Do you want reminding to leave her alone, Malcolm?"

"I'm all right, Barry. I'm handling it," I told him.

"You let me know if you need me," Barry said and didn't quite shut his door.

Randal hadn't glanced away from me, and I hadn't stopped giving him his stare back. "If your poor mother could see you now," he said. "The face of defiance."

"I'm only looking like you, Malcolm."

"And the voice of it into the bargain." He sighed and clasped his hands together on the counter as if he intended to lead me in prayer. "Just what exactly was the purpose of your call?" he said. "Were you hoping for the fatted calf?"

"I told mum I'd buy dinner."

"As clever as the devil," he said, though I hadn't meant my answer that way. "You expect her to welcome your charity."

"Isn't it supposed to begin at home?"

"In your case it should have years ago."

"It did as soon as you moved in."

The skin around his eyes twitched, and I was sure he'd just refrained from glancing towards Barry's office. "I take it you expect to be forgiven," he said.

"Do you think some things can't be?"

"We aren't talking about me, and I won't presume to speak for the Almighty." He seemed to need another twitch around the eyes to let him say "Your mother's a good woman, more Christian than you've any right to expect. She wants to accept your invitation."

Though I resented sharing any pleasure with him, I had to say "That's good."

"I've booked the restaurant where you were taken for your eighteenth birthday. I hope you appreciate how difficult it was to find a table anywhere. It's reserved on Boxing Day at seven in the evening. No doubt you can make your own way."

He was crossing the road by the time Barry came to the door of his office. "Well, happy bloody Christmas to you, Malcolm."

"So long as I'm seeing my mum," I said.

"Donna wants you to have Christmas dinner at ours if you're free."

I was embarrassed that so many people knew about my situation, but I said "That's really kind, and it looks like I am."

I bought them presents – boxes of chocolates – and some earrings for my mother. I loathed the idea of buying Randal any gifts, but I knew she would cause a scene if I didn't, and the cufflinks didn't cost much. They were shaped like a pair of cannons with their barrels sticking up between the wheels, which I hoped would remind him of what he used to do to me – make him feel guilty, even. Once I finished work on Christmas Day I had dinner at Barry and Lottie's, a few hours that reminded me of Christmases with my father. I worked Boxing Day as well, and then it was time for another kind of dinner.

Barry insisted on driving me down to the seafront. Maybe he just didn't want me walking all that way in my best shoes, but I thought he was ready to back me up with Randal if I asked. When I saw the limousine was parked outside Aye There's The Rib I didn't say anything. "Give me a bell whenever you need me," Barry said.

I thanked him and headed for the restaurant, and nearly walked straight out again once I saw Randal and my mother. They were facing the entrance to the dining area as if to make sure of seeing me the moment I came in. They didn't look much like a welcoming family, more like a probation board. Of course half of it wasn't my family at all. Randal stuck out a hand as though he was offering it to shake, but he was only indicating me. "Here's the Christmas treat," he said.

I didn't know whether he meant me or the occasion, but I saw my mother thinking it couldn't apply to me. When I made to kiss her forehead she ducked, which might have been designed to show me how dustily grey her hair had grown. Certainly the gesture felt like a reprimand. "Sit down, child, don't draw attention," she muttered, and then the instant I was seated "Hasn't your father earned any affection?"

"That's perfectly all right, Elaine," Randal said. "We shouldn't force it on her."

I could have retorted it was far too late for him to decide that, but the prospect of saying so made my mouth feel as unworkably clogged as ever. A waiter in a doublet and hose and a pink paper hat came to take our order. "We'll have the festive dinner," Randal told him.

"I will as well," I said.

Randal gave me a look that didn't bother having an expression. "I already said we, Carla."

The waiter put so much concentration into uncorking a bottle of merlot Randal ordered that I thought he was trying to cover his embarrassment at the exchange he'd overheard. "How many glasses for the wine?" he said.

"She can have a small one," my mother said, "since it's Christmas."

"The smallest you provide," Randal said. "We don't want anybody's tongue running away with them."

I wondered if he was afraid I might say too much about him. He couldn't know how just the thought of trying paralysed my tongue, but I hoped the threat of exposure made him nervous if not worse. The waiter poured him a sip of wine, which he swirled round the glass and then tossed back. "That's quite satisfactory, thank you," he said.

The waiter swapped my glass for a smaller one from the nearest table, which was occupied by a Reserved plaque. "That's enough now," my mother cried well before he'd filled my glass.

"I thought you didn't want to draw attention," I couldn't help remarking.

"I hope we won't be hearing any other comments that aren't called for," Randal said and raised his glass. "Here's to the birth of Our Lord."

My mother clinked her glass against his. "And all the good it brought the world."

They gazed at me as if they were comparing my birth and its effects unfavourably with that one, unless they were simply waiting for me to join in. I tapped my mother's glass with mine, which I let rebound onto Randal's, producing a shrill note. "Happy Christmas," I said and took a mouthful.

"To every Christian in the world," Randal said.

"That's right," my mother said, "to all of them."

Were they purposely leaving me out? I couldn't tell, and so I tried to lose myself in the carol that was playing overhead, only to find I was hearing the real words for the first time. "Good tidings we bring..." My father had made it rhyme, and I'd thought he must be the king in it, with my mother as his queen and me for a princess. I preferred the memory to the proper word, and was trying to recapture how my father used to sound when Randal said "Is anything the matter, Carla?"

Quite a lot was, but I said "Just remembering."

"Pleasant memories, I hope."

"I wish we had more that were," my mother said.

"Let's make sure this is one," Randal said.

If that was a rebuke, I knew it wasn't aimed at her. The waiter brought us all prawn cocktails, which the restaurant made more festive by topping each one with a plastic snowman on a stick. As Randal laid his snowman on his side plate, having looked round for someone to take it away, my mother said "What did you do yesterday, Carla?"

"Had Christmas dinner."

"Never by yourself."

"At Donna's.'"

Her surge of sympathy was ebbing fast. "The flat you share, you mean."

"No, with her and some people."

My mother narrowed her eyes. "Don't you dare to tell us who?"

"Her family."

"They're the one you've chosen, are they? The man who lured you away from your father and his family that helped him do it."

"I'd have come to you if I'd been invited."

"That's your way, isn't it. Blaming everybody but yourself for your situation and your behaviour."

Her voice and mine were growing lower, which made me feel she was dropping me into some kind of depth. "I wouldn't have said if you hadn't kept on asking."

"There you are, Malcolm. She's just proved exactly what I said."

"Shall we forgive her this once, since it's Christmas? She's chosen her own path. Don't let it spoil our meal."

"Just you make sure you appreciate your father for once, Carla." When I didn't answer she said "And I wasn't even asking what you did for dinner. We didn't see you at mass."

"Which one were you at?"

"The one we always go to. Father Brendan's morning mass."

"I like midnight mass best. I used to like seeing all the stars on the way home."

Perhaps my mother realised this needn't mean I'd gone to mass. "When was the last time you went to Father Brendan?"

I felt my stomach writhe like a baby inside you might feel. "What would I go to him for?"

"You know good and well." My mother had lowered her voice again. "To tell him your sins," she said.

"Why him specially?"

"Why wouldn't you want to confess to somebody who's known you since you were little?"

"That isn't how it's meant to work. They aren't supposed to know you." I was thinking he'd known me far too well in a way she would never believe, which provoked me to ask Randal "Do you think I ought to go back to him?"

I was gratified to see the skin round his eyes wince for an instant as if he didn't know where to look, but he'd steadied it and them by the time he faced my mother. "So long as she confesses all her sins," he said, "I shouldn't think it matters too much who hears them."

"Which one is he then, Carla?"

"I haven't got to tell you that." She was making me feel childish, which turned me crafty in a way I didn't especially relish. "You wouldn't know anyway," I said. "I don't go to that church any more."

If she saw this meant I didn't go to any, I no longer cared. The waiter took away the remains of the first course, including the snowmen lying on their backs as if they'd been spiked to death, and I hoped the interruption had brought the questions to an end. My mother stayed quiet till the waiter retreated, and then she said "So what sort of mischief have you been up to, Carla?"

"None I'd call any. I don't even know what you mean."

"What have you been doing now we aren't there to see?"

"Working." It wasn't just her stare that goaded me to add "He knows that. He's forever watching me."

"Your father has a name if you don't mind."

"You don't like me using it, do you? You don't like me saying Malcolm." Feeling nauseous, I took more than a sip of wine. "Maybe Malcolm does," I said.

"He doesn't care for disrespect any more than I do, and I think you've had quite enough to drink." My mother patted Randal's hand and stayed well clear of mine. "What do you expect him to do," she said, "put up shutters so he can't be seen? I'm sure he has better things to do than watch you betraying him. Maybe you think he's watching because you feel guilty, if you could bear to admit it to yourself."

"Shall we put it to bed for the duration, my pet? You don't want to upset yourself and not enjoy your dinner."

I thought he was more concerned about convincing her he didn't watch me. I hoped he was at least as nervous as all the talk had made me feel. The waiter returned with a costumed colleague, and everyone fell silent while they served us turkey and accompaniments. When the first waiter set about topping up our glasses my mother said "No more for her."

"I'll have some," I told him. "I'm paying, and we'll have another bottle."

My mother barely managed not to speak again till the waiters left us alone. "You think treating your parents like that makes you into some kind of grownup."

"If I'm being childish I'm not the only one."

"Listen to her, saying that to her own mother. This isn't how we did our best to make her, Malcolm."

"Perhaps we can allow her another small glass if it keeps the peace. It's not as if she could be driving."

I nearly retorted that I would be soon. The only peace I thought he'd want to keep was silence about how he used to abuse me, and I suspected he was wary of provoking me in case I said too much. The waiter returned with a bottle he opened, and my mother glared so fiercely at it that he didn't try to pour. As soon as he'd gone she resumed her attack. "Is it this Donna of yours who's made you this way?"

"She didn't have to, mum. This is who I am."

"I won't have that. You weren't like it when we had you in our care. She belongs to that traitor Barry, so no wonder she's a bad influence."

She was no longer keeping her voice down, and Randal glanced 'round. "Maybe we shouldn't call people too many names in public."

"You aren't usually so shy of saying what you think about him." My mother took a gulp of wine and turned on me again. "Has she been taking you to all these clubs that are open half the night? God knows what you get up to in there."

"Nothing, because I don't go."

"You keep your mischief at home, do you? Has she been giving you drugs and that's why you've changed so much?"

"I've already said I haven't. You never noticed who I was, that's all."

"Listen to it, Malcolm. It's my fault again, and she hasn't said she isn't taking drugs."

"Except I'm not."

"God forgive you if you're lying. You still haven't said when you last went to confession. I just pray you do it soon, because I'm certain you've got plenty to confess."

"Eat up now, my pet. You don't want it going cold."

My mother gave in to his urging, but I could tell she was holding accusations in reserve. I topped up her glass and so as not to invite another attack Randal's too, and ignored her glare as I refilled mine. I was trying to enjoy my dinner despite the tightness of my guts when I grew aware of the song the overhead speakers were playing. My father used to sing it to me, and I murmured along with some of the words. When the couple in the song asked the snowman to marry them, my mother made her gaze felt. "Are you trying to tell us something, Carla?"

"It's just a song I liked, if you remember."

"I don't remember anything of the kind. I'd like to know who got you singing about people living in sin." I was about to remind her of my father – I thought she was too eager to wipe him from my mind – when she said "You won't ask us to believe you aren't carrying on with boys."

"I think Malcolm might believe it."

"What are you trying to blame him for now? Tell me what he could have to do with it if you can." As my throat grew as tight as my stomach she said "If you've got a boyfriend you should have brought him, or are you ashamed to show him to us?"

"I've got none and I don't want one."

"Well, I'm sure I can't imagine what's made you like that. So we can say goodbye to any grandchildren."

"After all you went through having kids I shouldn't think you'd want me to."

"It's God's plan for us, Carla. It's what we're for, and if we have to suffer, just remember who had to suffer worse for us."

"We shouldn't try to force her, my pet. I'm sure nature will take its way when it's God's way as well."

I only just managed to swallow the food I'd put in my mouth. I felt capable of spewing it onto the table. I pretended to eat while my mother and Randal cleared their plates, and the waiter risked refilling all the glasses, though he looked braced for a protest. As he took my plate, which was still half full, he said "Too much clubbing last night?"

My mother looked dismally triumphant. "Just had enough," I said, by no means only about the meal.

The waiter cleared the table and brought us individual Christmas puddings not much bigger than tennis balls. If my father had been there he would have laughed till we had to join in, but Randal only commented "No excuse for waste." I supposed he was rebuking me for not finishing my main course, but I had more reason to feel tense. I hadn't given them their presents yet because I'd expected to find mine on the table, and what would happen if they hadn't brought me one? I told myself it would simply show them up, but I delayed till the waiter served coffee, and then I took the presents out of my bag. "Happy Christmas," I said.

My mother opened hers first. "Thank you, Carla. Very nice," she said but didn't put the earrings on.

Randal showed her the cufflinks with the cannons poking up. "Very manly, thank you. I'll wear them next time I have need of any, so you can think of me then."

I was waiting for an apology in lieu of a present, and trying to decide how to react, when my mother produced a parcel from her bag. "This is from both of us, Carla."

From its size and the smell of leather I thought it was a purse. The tag taped to it said just CARLA in Randal's pinched handwriting, which always looked as if he was trying to economise on ink. When I undid the bow and took off the wrapping, which was printed with a duplicated bunch of carol singers – the kind my father used to say came to your house when he was little – I found a book with no name on the cover. My guts began to squirm before I saw it was a bound catechism, and I had no idea what I was going to say when I opened my mouth. "Who chose this?"

"I thought it might remind you how we cared for you when you were growing up," my mother said. "All those nights your father devoted to you."

I wondered if Randal might think better of speaking, but he said "And we hope it may help to bring you back to the right path."

My guts writhed again, and I felt as if I was squatting on a bomb that was close to exploding. "Thank you," I said to be done with that. "I'll get the bill."

Randal lifted a hand high and curled his fingers in a single wave. When the waiter arrived Randal said "I'm paying for us. The girl will just pay for herself."

He must have been saving this up throughout the meal, and I sensed how much he relished it. The nearest to a revenge I could find was to make sure he heard me on my phone. "Barry, I'm ready whenever you are," I said.

"Won't you be satisfied," my mother said, "till you've insulted your father in every way you can think of?"

"Just paying him back." I threw notes on the table to pay for my meal and stood up. "And I'm only starting," I said.

She jerked her head away from me when I stooped to kiss her. I didn't go anywhere near Randal. I was tempted to leave the catechism, but instead I grabbed it to remind me what it would always mean to me. My innards had settled down as if my call to Barry had lent them strength. I left the restaurant without looking back, and after that I hardly saw my mother, not even at Randal's funeral.

ALEX

As soon as the glass lift brings Alex into sight, Ruth stands up and shows him the palm of one hand. "Stay there, Alex."

"I'd quite like to use the men's before we hit the road."

Rather too much like a frustrated parent she says "Please be quick."

"I will, but I thought I was early."

When Kirsty nods, Ruth gives her a sharp glance. "I'd have preferred to be through the traffic by now," she informs them both.

After using the urinal Alex almost scalds his hands at a tap beneath a warning notice and leaves the hand dryer to roar to itself. Ruth has recalled the lift he let go and is holding it open with one glossy black shoe. The instant she sees Alex she urges Kirsty inside and follows, barely waiting for him to join them. "I hope that will hold you for the journey," she tells him.

"Can you just remind me why I'm needed?"

"I want you and Kirsty there in case any points about the book need to be raised with Mr Batchelor."

The heads of the crowd on Euston Road produce faces as the lift sinks to ground level, and then the glass box darkens like an omen of a storm as it continues downwards. In the extensive subterranean car park she hurries to a diminutive black Fiat, which Alex concludes would be blue except for the amber lighting overhead. "You take the back, Alex," she says.

"Girls to the fore," Kirsty says like a possibly apologetic joke.

Ruth spares him a terse look in the mirror as he clips his safety belt. "Make yourself comfortable, Alex. We won't be stopping once I'm on the move."

At least she's calling him by his first name, though it makes him feel more patronised than befriended. She speeds up the ramp to the street and barely waits for the mechanical barrier to defer to her. Despite how heavy the traffic is, she veers to overtake whenever she sees a gap. Every trample on the brake vibrates through Alex's groin, and every forward lurch sends him sprawling backwards if he doesn't brace himself. When he plants his legs wide to stay braced she sends him a reflected glance not far short of a rebuke, and he can only hope the route to Manchester won't take much time to become as clear as she plainly feels it should.

As soon as the traffic starts to thin out she inserts an item in the dashboard player, and a vaguely northern voice says "My stepfather nearly killed my mother, and I used to wish he'd killed me...." It's the audiobook of *When I Was Carla*, and Alex finds it disconcerting to hear words he's written read aloud in an unfamiliar voice. Along with the accent, which the performer may have assumed for the task, the voice is light but perceptibly male, which renders Carla's experiences oddly ambiguous. Gathering that Ruth plans to listen to the entire book, Alex says "Are we supposed to be taking notes?"

"I shouldn't think you of all people need to familiarise yourself with this."

"Of all people," Alex says and adds a laugh, "I'd think Carl."

"The people in this car," Ruth says as if he's making her waste breath. "If you hear anything you feel should be brought up with him, by all means note it down."

She sets the reading off again, having paused it while they spoke. Soon they're on the motorway, and there are no distractions from the book. Why should hearing the reminiscences read in someone else's voice disturb Alex? Audiobooks of his novels don't affect him like that, but this feels like a kind of theft even though he should be more remote from material that belongs to someone else. It doesn't help that his crotch persists in aching whichever way he sits in the cramped space. He's close to fancying this is reminiscent of how Carl may have felt while he was changing gender, a notion that's not just absurd but presumptuous.

Carla has been Carl for quite a few minutes by the time they arrive on the outskirts of Manchester, and the book ends while Ruth drives through Salford. Carl's Cars is on a main road, where it's flanked by Virtuous Vapes and Finest Fones, as if it has infected its neighbours with alliteration. Several taxis stand outside, and Ruth adds the Fiat to the line. As Alex clambers stiffly forth, stifling a groan at a vicious twinge in his crotch, he sees that the car is black after all. His mistake leaves him feeling nervous that his mind may let him down.

The receptionist is a middle-aged woman with a black fringe cut so straight it renders her squarish face even more angular. "Ruth Nyman and party for Carl Batchelor," Ruth says.

"Sure there's enough of you? There's only one of him."

"We're just as involved in the book as he is."

The woman bends a microphone on a metal stalk towards her. "Carl, the bunch about your book are here."

Carl speaks in two voices, through the switchboard and a door beyond it. "Send them in, Meryl."

He stands up to greet the visitors but stays behind his desk as if to establish his authority. "Didn't know you'd all come."

"Who wouldn't you have wanted?" Ruth says.

"Just saying we need another chair."

Did he mean that? While Meryl fetches one from the rank of folding chairs in front of the counter, he says "Anybody for a drink?"

"Water for me," Ruth says. "I'm alert enough."

Kirsty and Alex opt for coffee, and Carl starts a percolator perched on a small refrigerator, from which he produces a bottle of water for Ruth. When Alex sits on the chair Meryl brings, it sways as though it's threatening a pratfall, and he can't help wondering whether she chose it for that reason. Once she shuts the door Carl says "So why's everybody here?"

"Perhaps they needn't be," Ruth says. "I may just require your signature."

Recalling the drive and anticipating the return provokes Alex to demand "Couldn't you have got it online?"

"No, I want the actual signature. I shouldn't like there to be any arguments later."

"About what?"

She turns her eyes away from him to Carl. "Denials of any kind."

The percolator hisses like a greeting for a villain as Carl says "What are you after me to sign?"

Ruth plants her briefcase on her knees and snaps it open. "Just your confirmation that the contents of your book are nothing but the truth."

"My story's true all right, and don't go listening to anyone that tells you different." As Ruth reaches in the briefcase Carl says "What do you mean, the contents?"

"I'm not clear what distinction you feel you ought to make."

"Some of the stuff in there, me and Alex made it up together."

She shuts the briefcase, having left all the documents where they are, and drops it on the carpet. "I thought there might be some issue of the kind."

Alex doesn't quite know who he's speaking for as he asks "Why would you think that?"

"To start with, the business on Twitter."

At least Alex wasn't involved, and he waits for Carl to respond. When they both behave as if guilt has silenced them Ruth says "What exactly are you saying isn't true?"

He can't answer that, and he mutely urges Carl to do so. "You have to let us know," Kirsty says. "You owe that to us."

"Didn't say anything wasn't," Carl says and turns his back while heading for the percolator. "Just ways to make my story more like one of his."

"Which were those, Alex?" Ruth says at once.

"I can't recall saying anything like that to you, Carl." Nothing comes to mind but scenes unnecessarily reminiscent of memories although they're from the book, and he can only insist "I honestly don't know."

"Then I'm sure you must, Carl."

"Let me have a think." Carl pours coffee into two mugs ringed with repetitions of **CARL'S CARS** and adds milk from a refrigerated carton that looks beaded with sweat. As he concentrates on carrying the mugs across the room he says "I've got one."

Kirsty takes her mug. "Aren't you having a coffee?"

"Gets on my nerves too much."

The delay is having that effect on Alex. As he accepts a mug, only to stand it on the edge of the desk before his fingers flinching from the heat can spill it, he says "So what have you remembered?"

"The bit about the petrol pump. It's like a memory, but it didn't really happen like that."

"Of course it did." Alex is so disconcerted that he feels as if he's laying claim to a memory of his own. "I mean," he says not much less urgently, "you said it did."

"No, you did."

"I hardly think I could have when it didn't happen to me."

"Nor me either."

As Alex struggles to recollect their conversation, Ruth says "So what are you saying is the truth?"

Alex is sufficiently confused to start responding until Carl speaks. "That bastard, I mean Randal, he made me hold the air hose. Alex thought it'd be better if I felt the petrol one as well."

"No, that isn't how it went." Recapturing the memory makes Alex feel as though he has fended off a darkness capable of swallowing his consciousness. "You brought up both the hoses," he says, "and I asked you how it felt to hold them and what it felt like to remember."

"You wouldn't let a kid of that age near petrol. That bastard might have, but the staff never would."

"Presumably they didn't notice. I'm simply saying what you told me. Maybe I encouraged you to make it vivid, but you passed it when you read the proofs."

"I'm telling you what happened," Carl assures Kirsty and Ruth. "You can hear what he said if you play it back."

"I'm very much afraid Mr Grand has lost the files."

"And I never had them," Kirsty says.

"I'd say the discrepancy is negligible and needn't be referred to," Ruth says. "It shouldn't hinder your signing, Mr Batchelor. Is there anything else we ought to be informed about?"

"There's quite a lot of stuff like that," Carl says. "Things he made me say."

Alex is overtaken by the notion that the loss of the recordings has left Carl feeling safe to deny his own words. "How could I do that?" he protests.

"Please let Mr Batchelor speak."

"I was trying to make him," Alex retorts, only for his language to catch up with him.

"All the bits where I'm talking," Carl says. "I'd tell Alex what happened and we'd talk like we thought me and the other people would."

"Presumably yours has to be authentic if it came from you yourself," Ruth says. "Or are you proposing to take it back?"

"It doesn't matter if I can't remember some of it, does it?"

"So long as you can guarantee it tells the truth."

"No point else. We left out bits that weren't true enough."

Alex makes to ask, but Kirsty does. "Which were those?"

"Like Alex wanting him to get in the bath with me. Not him, I don't mean. Randal."

For a moment Alex is convinced that the incident is in the book – that he heard it during the journey to Manchester. He must have dreamed it when he succeeded in dozing despite the ache in his groin. "You can't say I wanted that," he objects.

"All right then, asked me if he did. I wouldn't put it past the bastard, but he never."

Ruth lifts a finger as if she's pointing at a thought. "Did you omit anything about the priest?"

"Like what?"

"I felt you could have given us more details of the encounter."

"We put in all I wanted to. I wasn't writing porn."

"I'll agree this ought to be about what's there. What you left out doesn't matter. So you're assuring us the book is basically the truth."

"You know it is, and these two do as well." When nobody denies it Carl says "You believe me, not that bitch and whoever she's got with her. Have you figured out what they're up to yet?"

"That's one of the questions that concern me."

"Then I'll tell you. They hate anyone like me that's made the change. I thought I'd seen her somewhere, and now I'm sure I did. She was at a bookshop. Can't remember which."

"If you should," Kirsty says, "be sure and let us know."

"What are you assuming their motives are?" says Ruth.

"Spoiling my chances because they don't like my book."

"Why do you think they would target you?"

"Must've seen it advertised. That's got to be why she was there at the shop."

Ruth nods and turns to Kirsty. "Until the situation is resolved, best cancel any further events. No need to stir these people up before we've dealt with them."

"I don't mind any more," Carl says.

"Avoid antagonising them even so. We don't want them going public until we've formulated our response."

"I mean I can do shops and stuff when you want. Now I've done the book it's just like telling stories. It's like they happened to somebody else, not that I'm saying they did."

"I'm almost finished here. I'd like to head back to discuss resolving the situation," Ruth says and removes a printout from her briefcase. "If you'll just sign this."

Carl flanks it with his elbows on the desk and clamps his brows with both hands. Once his eyes finish sidling back and forth he says "I'll sign it if he does."

Ruth glances at Alex. "That would seem appropriate."

Carl slides the page towards him. *The author undertakes that all events described or referred to in* When I Was Carla *are true and factually accurate to the best of his knowledge.* Though the final words reassure him, Alex says "I can't sign this."

Everybody stares at him. "Why not?" Ruth says.

"It has his name on it, not mine."

"That's readily amended." She brings up the document on her phone and, having added his name, makes the authors plural. "Can we print this out?" she asks Carl.

He does, and plants the page in front of Alex. "You go first."

As Alex signs he has an uneasy sense of venturing over an edge. Before he can grasp the feeling, Ruth passes the page to Carl. Why is Carl hesitating? Alex is about to urge him to sign, unless someone else tells him to, when Carl finds a marker in a drawer of his desk and scribbles his name in crimson characters at least twice as thick as Alex's. Ruth stands up to retrieve the agreement and notices the photograph on the desk. "Was this your family, Mr Batchelor?"

"It's my only dad and the woman he married."

"Is your mother still alive?"

"I already told Alex."

Apparently he and his gaze are waiting for Alex to speak. "No," Alex says with a shrug that's meant to dislodge the responsibility.

Ruth shuts the document in the briefcase, which she clasps under her arm as though protecting it from theft. "Presumably she would have been in touch if she were still with us."

"You'd think."

"If the book weren't true," Alex contributes.

Ruth makes it clear she's waiting for him and Kirsty to stand up. "I'll be in touch again shortly," she tells Carl. "Please do your best to keep yourself free in case we need another meeting."

Alex wonders what she'll say about the encounter once they're in the car, but she doesn't speak. Instead she plays the entire audiobook a second time, and he finds himself trying to identify which words are Carl's and which his own. Far too often he can't tell. Sometimes he dozes, and when his aching groin jerks him awake he feels as if a memory has eluded him. At last they reach London, and as soon as he sees an Underground station he leaves the car. "The same as I said to Mr Batchelor," Ruth says in place of a farewell.

The journey home takes almost two more hours. The overground train is crawling into Brighton when his phone rings and names Carl, reviving the unease Alex experienced while he signed the agreement. "What is it now, Carl?"

"Can I hear you're on a train?"

"Not for much longer."

"You'll be by yourself."

"I am," Alex says, though the carriage is only largely empty. "Why?"

"This is just between us. You'll have to swear."

Partly to amuse himself with a sally at a joke, but mostly to express his confused feelings, Alex says "Fuck."

As nobody who overhears him in the carriage bothers to react Carl says "Not that kind of swear. Swear you won't tell."

With a sense of crossing a further edge Alex says "All right, I've sworn."

"Can you meet tomorrow? Make it somewhere in between. Stoke's about halfway. I'll be on the station at one." Presumably Carl takes the silence for assent, because he adds "I want to tell you all the truth."

CARLY AND CARL

"Does your feller know you're out, love?"

The fare was a stocky man who'd almost outgrown his suit and shirt and lopsided bow tie. "Anyone who needs to does," I told him.

"You tell him, girl," his wife said. "Score one for us."

I drove them under the river, and when I dropped them off at an expensive Italian in Liverpool the man planted just the right amount on my tray beneath the glass partition. "Looking for a tip?" he said.

"If you and the lady are happy with the service."

"Here's one for you. Don't cheek the customers and you'll earn more for yourself."

He wasn't the worst I had to deal with, not even in the top ten. Some of the female parties I picked up bothered me more. Most of them acted glad, saying things like "Let's hear it for the girls," but too many seemed to think I mightn't be as competent as my male colleagues, unless they had some other reason for wanting a man. Some male fares were so courteous it felt patronising, and others asked how much extra I'd charge to pleasure them. Those ones reminded me of Randal, and while I faced them down and even joked about it if they meant to be funny, they made me feel I was trying to impress him by proxy in his absence. As for the men who tried to advise me how to drive, most of them weren't joking at all.

I was determined not to let any of this put me off. I even insisted on picking up late at night, though Barry said I needn't and let me know he was concerned for me. I didn't mind drunks so long as they didn't throw up in the taxi, when we always locked them in till they paid for the cleaning. There was just one party of four men that left me feeling vulnerable. They were so noisy and restless I suspected they were coked as well as drunk, and when I delivered them to a street with no working lights in Birkenhead they tried to convince me they'd paid in advance. I kept the doors locked and said I'd call the police unless they paid up, and when they told me to do it and started suggesting what I could do to myself I made the call. They began trying to smash the partition and the windows, and one of them phoned someone to help. I heard a front door slam somewhere up the road – at least I wasn't parked outside the house they would be visiting – and more men than I'd got in my taxi appeared in the headlights, brandishing baseball bats. I was getting ready to drive at them till I saw red and blue flashes in my mirror. They were lights on a police car, and they felt as joyous as fireworks used to before Randal came into my life. The men with bats vanished back into the dark, and the police made my passengers pay up, and would have arrested them if I'd pressed charges. Because I was afraid of making trouble for the firm, I let the men go. I drove some way to keep the police in sight, and then I parked while my legs stopped shaking and the rest of me did.

Barry said I'd done all the right things and told me I was brave. I wanted to believe him, but I couldn't help thinking the party wouldn't have tried to steal from any of the other drivers. Some of my confrontations with passengers made me feel I was playing a role that wasn't quite me yet – that wouldn't be till I grasped what it was. I think I was well on the way to figuring that out by the time I picked up Lucy Hunter.

The call Emma sent me sounded ordinary – just to collect a woman from Hoylake, where a train had broken down. When I arrived at the station she waved as if she was greeting a friend. She was tall and lanky and about my age, with mousy hair sprawling over her broad level shoulders. She gave me her address in New Brighton, and I was driving past the fields outside Hoylake when I noticed she was staring at my name badge on the partition. "Carla Batchelor," she said.

"That's me. Always has been."

"You've always gone by it."

Though I had no idea why she was asking, I said "Someone tried to call me something else, but they've got no chance. I've always known who I really am."

"Like me, only different."

"Sorry," I said, "how?"

"I'm the one that should be. Sorry, Carla."

We were on a straight stretch of road with very little traffic, which let me stare at her in the mirror. "Do I know you?"

"I was Phil at school."

"I don't remember any girl called that if you're saying you went to St Brendan's."

"I was there. Closer to you than I am now."

She might have been trying to distort my memories. "I remember who I sat next to, and you weren't any of them."

"Carla, I'm really sorry if you'd rather not remember. I was the Phil who made you show yourself for weed."

I felt as if the taxi was about to veer onto the verge if not all the way across the road. I steadied the wheel before staring hard at her reflection. "You're saying you were a boy back then."

"I never really was, no. I tried to make out I was, and I'm afraid part of that was what I did to you. Deep down I knew who I ought to be, but I couldn't have come out at that school. I know that's no excuse, Carla."

"Don't get yourself bothered about me." I had a sense that more than just her situation was falling into place at last, becoming clear. "You never forced me," I said. "It was my choice."

"I hope it didn't stop you making the right one for yourself like I have."

"I'm happy doing what I do." I felt as if I hadn't dealt fully with her question. "What's it been like for you?" I said.

"Like trying to convince a bunch of medics for a year I was serious."

I wasn't sure I'd been asking about that, but I was glad she'd taken it that way – gladder than I understood. "You did, though."

"I wish I'd had that year, that's all. It felt like knowing who I was and nobody would believe me, or they tried to find reasons not to. If I was doing it now I'd skip all that stuff and buy the hormones online."

I felt as if she was speaking thoughts I'd had or could have had. "Anyway, you're where you want to be now."

"Hundreds of per cent I am," Lucy said but looked guilty again. "Listen, I know you wanted it, but I hope all that weed didn't mess with your head."

"Not that I've noticed. How about yours?"

"I think it may have screwed up my memory a bit. Some things can't have happened the way I remember."

I didn't need to hear this. Except for my memories of my real father, there weren't many I wanted to keep. I drove Lucy to her flat in New Brighton, and she gave me a tip so big I thought at first she'd made a mistake, but she insisted. "Shall I ask for you when I need another ride?" she said.

"They'll know who you mean."

I was driving away when my remark caught up with me. It felt like committing myself to a thought that was waiting to be noticed, maybe having waited for most of my life – ever since Malcolm Randal had invaded my childhood and my room, or was it even earlier? Maybe he'd stopped me realising who I actually wanted to be, because he made me hide from myself so much. Realising felt like the opposite of prayers and cannabis. They'd been refuges I took, but this growing sense of my real identity felt like emerging from hiding at last. As soon as I got home that night I read up on changing your gender. Everything I read excited me and left me eager to experience the results for myself, not to mention frustrated I'd delayed so long. I knew with my soul that the change was right for me, and I ordered my first batch of testosterone from an online supplier.

For too long it seemed to have no effect at all. I went through weeks of thinking it was never going to work for me. I had fits of weeping and had to make sure I was alone when they hit me. I didn't realise that was a change in itself. So was feeling randy, though that disgusted me whenever I did, because it brought back memories of randy Randal. My throat began to feel as though I had a cold, but I couldn't hear it affecting my voice. Every morning I'd go to the bathroom mirror to search for signs of change, but my face stayed as unattractively smooth as ever. Then my periods began tailing off, and after a couple of those I knew I was on the way to myself.

The day the mirror showed me the start of a beard I let out a whoop and heard how hoarse my voice seemed to have grown all at once. In a week it was unmistakably deeper, and I decided to tell Barry what was happening before it was any more obvious. Once we were alone in his office I said "I don't know if you've spotted I'm making a change."

"Don't say we'll be losing our only lady driver."

"I don't want to leave unless you're getting rid of me," I said, and then I had to laugh. "You mean you've noticed."

"Everybody has, Carly," Barry said and put a finger to his lips as if to hush the name. "Is that what you want to be called still?"

"I was thinking Carl."

"Carl's fine with us, and so is how you'll be. We'll just have to hire another driver." In case this sounded ominous he said "As well."

Not all my fares were as happy with my state as he and Donna and the drivers were. As the months brought me more beard and a lower voice, some passengers stared at me or muttered comments, though nobody made any to my face. "Hey, you're on your way," Lucy said next time I picked her up. "You won't regret it, I promise." And I never did, even when I had to confront Randal and my mother.

When I arrived at Cheerful Cabs one winter morning I saw Randal on the frosty pavement opposite. He turned from letting himself into Reliablest to watch me. I gave him his stare back and didn't retreat when he started to cross the road. He looked as if his frown was bringing him, increasing as it came and squeezing his face even smaller. His fingers started squirming as he reached me, and I was getting ready to fend them off when he made a sign of the cross that thumped his frown with a fingertip. "What in the name of all that's holy have you been doing to yourself?"

"Which name's that?"

"We shouldn't have expected you to know, should we, Carla."

"If we're talking about names, mine's Carl."

His forehead tried to writhe as much as his lips managed. "You're distorting the name you were baptised with. Your Christian name."

"That's nothing to do with you, Malcolm."

"And abusing the body God gave you."

"No, someone else did that, Malcolm."

I pushed the door open behind me and felt even more in control when he retreated a step. He must have been afraid we'd be overheard, and I said near the top of my voice "What's my body got to do with you?"

"It has plenty to do with your poor mother. Perhaps you might care to imagine how she's going to feel when she learns how you've mistreated it."

"Never mind my mother. We're talking about you."

"Yes, we know how little you care about her. I'm not looking forward to telling her your latest outrage. No doubt you're proud of excelling yourself."

"I'm just being true to myself at last. If there's a liar here, it isn't me."

"I won't dignify that with an answer," he said, which only confirmed how eager he was to tell tales to my mother. He stalked across the road, breathing out dragon smoke in the frosty air, though I thought it looked as if he was puffing like an old train. I'd forgotten about him by the time I picked up my first fare of the day, and I saw no further sign of him.

The next afternoon I'd just dropped off a party of pensioners who seemed to have no doubt I was a man when Emma called me from the office. "Carl?"

"She's making you call her that, is she, God help us?"

The disgusted question meant Emma didn't need to say "Your mother's here."

"I'm on my way," I said and told myself that only ice beneath the wheels had made the taxi lurch.

I parked it in the yard behind the firm and let myself in the back way. My mother was sitting opposite the switchboard, watching the street with her head twisted round so far it looked painful. "Mum, I'm here," I said.

She swung her head round and winced at however her neck felt. "Trying to sneak in so I wouldn't see you?" she said and peered at me. "Oh, dear sweet Jesus."

Before I could react, Barry opened his door. "Carl, do you want to use my office while you talk?"

"She's got you calling her that too, has she? Has she corrupted you all, or maybe it's the other way round." Without giving him a chance to speak my mother said "I'll say my piece out here, thank you, where everyone can hear. I'm sure you'd like it kept quiet, though I don't know why with her flaunting what she's done."

"I hope you aren't going to cause a scene, Mrs Randal."

"Don't you want a spectacle? You shouldn't be employing one, then," my mother said and transferred her glare to me. "Have you done your worst yet? I shouldn't think even you can beat robbing your father of his daughter."

"I wasn't his."

"I'm talking about Bertie. The man you never stop calling your real one."

"If he knew I'm sure he'd want me to be who I really am."

"Don't you dare to try and tell me what he'd want. I knew him a lot better than you did."

"Not like someone else. There are things my dad wouldn't have wanted as well."

"If that's meant to be Malcolm it just shows how little you knew Bertie. He'd have thanked him for everything he's done for us, even for an ungrateful godless brat."

Barry cleared his throat. "Mrs Randal—"

"I've nearly finished, and then you can go back to pretending everything is how it ought to be. I just wanted to see for myself. I was hoping Malcolm was exaggerating, but he was being just as kind as ever." Her glare at me had turned into weary resignation. "We've seen the last of our daughter," she said.

"Mum, that doesn't have to mean you've seen the last of me."

"When you're turning yourself into one of those creatures it does."

I wasn't going to let her hurt me. As she used the chair to help her to her feet I said "You aren't walking all that way home, are you? I'll give you a ride."

"You'll do nothing of the kind. I wouldn't trust you to take care of me. I'll be going with the man who does." She limped to the door and faced me again. "I don't suppose he let you see how much this latest escapade of yours has upset him," she said.

"I'm sure he doesn't like me not being a girl any more."

"No, Carla, he's upset for me, and I hope all your cronies can hear how little you care about either of us. Do you want to see off both my men?"

"I didn't see my dad off. I never even saw him when he'd gone." I might have stopped there, but she'd provoked me too much. "I wish that had been Malcolm," I said, "and I had my real dad back."

"God forgive you, Carla. I won't even pray for you any more." As she yanked the door open she said "I thank God every night I still have Malcolm."

I watched her limp across the road as if she hardly cared whether she was run over, halting several cars and setting off more than one horn. "That was a bit strong," Barry said.

"I am. I have to be," I told him. "It's either that or let the memories take over."

ALEX

Alex reaches London in time to catch an early train, which brings him to Stoke-on-Trent an hour before he's meeting Carl. The grid of the glass roof casts a net of shadows over the station platforms, so that he feels as if he's venturing into a web. There's no sign of Carl, and Alex uses up most of the hour by wandering the back streets. Very few appear to lead to anything resembling a main road, unless his thoughts are confusing his sense of direction. He's as anxious to hear what Carl has to say as he's nervous of it, and makes sure of returning to the station well before one o'clock. He's looking around for Carl – surely the man won't hide until they're due to meet – when a female voice beneath the roof announces that the train Alex should have been on will be twenty minutes late.

When clocks all around him turn thirteen he still hasn't located Carl. No doubt Carl assumes Alex won't be there yet, which leaves Alex feeling less than present. He phones Carl and thinks he hears a mobile ringing somewhere in the distance. By no means immediately, although before Alex can locate the other phone, Carl says "I know."

Alex feels as if Carl has started as he plans to carry on, by bewildering him. "What are you saying you know?"

"You aren't here yet. You'll be late."

"No, I'm there now. I was on the earlier train."

Carl's silence leaves room on the phone for the sounds of the station – the elongated squeal of an approaching train, a warning to be wary of anything suspicious. A man's voice delivers this alert, as if the announcements have changed gender, and finishes before Carl says "Why were you?"

"Why wouldn't I be? To make sure I was on time."

"Where've you been since you got here, then?"

"I really couldn't tell you. Nowhere I remember."

"You weren't figuring you'd catch me out."

"Of course not, Carl. Anyway, how could I?"

"I was going to be straight with you, but I won't if you aren't straight with me."

Alex has no idea what he's being accused of, but if he fails to vindicate himself, may Carl abort their meeting? "I looked for you and couldn't see you," he protests. "That's why I went for a walk."

"I'm watching you, you know." As Alex stares about more desperately Carl says "Right, I've seen enough."

He's gone at once, and Alex is about to call again in the hope of locating Carl's ringtone when he sees him on the far side of a stationary train. As Carl makes for the exit from the station he lends the windows of the carriages the look of frames in a strip of film. Alex hurries to the platform in time to head him off, and Carl greets him with half a grin that the rest of his mouth contradicts. "Think you've caught me?"

"I didn't want to lose you when you've got something to tell me."

"I was coming to you, Alex."

Alex has no idea whether this is true, but suppose Carl won't trust him unless he feels trusted? "Where do you want to go now?" he says.

"Didn't you find any pubs when you were having your walk?"

At first Alex can't recall, which feels as if his mind has grown not merely unreliable but unfamiliar. "I believe there's one across the road," he has to say.

When he leads the way out of the station he's relieved to see a pub not far away, although not opposite. It's called the Puffer. Above the entrance a giant tobacco pipe may once have emitted smoke, and several men with vapes have gathered under it like a stubborn reminiscence. Pipes of various shapes and materials dangle over the bar, while framed prints of smokers throughout history decorate the walls. The whole place, including diners lunching on varieties of pies, feels like a bid to conjure up a past, however imperfectly represented. Alex finds an empty upholstered booth, patterned like its neighbours with a flock of clouds, and Carl sits down at once. Presumably this is a cue for Alex to enquire "What will you have to drink?"

"Make mine a juice. Orange, I'll have that. I want to keep my head clear like your lawyer."

When Alex returns with an orange juice and a generous glass of merlot, Carl is watching him more narrowly than he finds appropriate. "So what do you have to tell me?" Alex says.

"It isn't much." Carl takes a mouthful of his drink and shakes his head. "It doesn't change much," he says, and even less like an apology "You won't be recording me this time."

Too late Alex realises he could have done so surreptitiously. "If you prefer."

"I need to see you aren't." When Alex shows him the phone Carl says "Put it on the table so I can."

Alex lays the phone on the glass surface, through which he sees Carl's impatient right leg jerking up and down. "This has got to be just between us," Carl says.

"I'm guessing it's about the book."

"It's about me."

"Are you saying it won't affect the book?"

"Don't see why it has to."

Alex hears nothing but defensiveness. "If it does, surely the Tiresias people need to know."

"You swore. If you're going back on it I'm off home."

"Can we at least discuss it when I've heard what you have to say?"

"You swore."

Carl's dogged objection sounds childish, and Alex is afraid that's how he may behave. "All right," he says, "you heard me do it."

"Just make sure you remember." Carl stares at the phone, and his eyes grow defiant as he raises them to Alex. "That woman," he says. "The one who told you she's my sister."

"Yes." For some reason Alex finds it hard to add "What about her?"

"She's not really."

"I rather think you've already told me that, so—"

"Just half."

"Then what's the half you haven't told me?"

"I'm not saying that." Carl takes time to laugh, though it sounds manufactured. "You've got to have a father and a mother, haven't you?"

"I believe that's generally the situation. Mind you, these days—"

"So she can't say she's my sister."

Alex finds it takes quite an effort to ask "Then what are you saying she is?"

"I told you once. Just half."

Alex grasps his glass and makes himself relax his grip for fear of snapping the stem. "You're telling me she's Hilary Randal."

"See, she hasn't even got my name." Carl watches Alex strive not to gulp too much wine and says "Anyway, she can't do anything to us. Your lawyer said what we left out doesn't count."

"Ruth's no more my lawyer than she's yours," Alex says, only to realise he has no idea how much that may be. "You didn't just leave your sister out. You told me she was never born."

"Don't call her my sister or we won't be talking."

"Hilary, then. You said she was a miscarriage."

"I'd call her worse than that, except I didn't, did I? She can't sue us for saying she wasn't born."

"It isn't just a question of the law. What do you think will happen to the book if this gets out?"

"Better see it doesn't, right? That's why I'm telling you now. You'll want to make sure our book's safe."

"And exactly how do you imagine I'll be able to do that?"

"You can think up something, can't you? You've been in the business longer than me."

"Yes, and it's my reputation that's been put at stake."

"There's another reason to come up with the answer."

Even if this isn't as dismayingly innocent as it sounds, it leaves Alex feeling vulnerable. "Why did you lie about her?"

"You try being brought up to hide all the stuff that's happening to you and see how much of the truth you can tell."

"I thought the point of the book was to tell it."

"Think it was easy for me?"

"I'd never presume to say that, but I don't understand why you couldn't about her."

"It was hard enough talking about her father. You've no idea what that felt like."

For a hopelessly confused moment Alex seems to share the sense of a secret struggling for revelation. "I'm nothing but sympathetic, but even so—"

"Didn't want her in my book, that's all."

Alex feels as if his question is protesting on her behalf as he says "Why not?"

"She never did anything for me."

"I'm not sure how you mean that."

"She ought to have known what Randal was up to with me. Don't tell me she never did."

"I've no way of knowing, have I?" When Carl gives him a look hostile enough to have done for his stepfather, Alex says "Would you have shared a room?"

"She made sure we didn't. When she was little she had a cot in their room so my mother could watch out for her. She always cared more about Hilary than me."

Alex wonders how much Carl's resentment may be distorting his account. "That wouldn't be Hilary's fault, do you think?"

"She took advantage of it every way she could. That's how she got her own room. When they moved her into mine she started saying I kept her awake and scared her. I wish I'd scared her more."

"You were getting your own back, you mean." For fear of antagonising him into silence Alex adds "I shouldn't think most people would blame you at that age with everything you were going through."

"No, I wasn't getting my own back." At first rage seems to have left Carl no more words, and then he says "I was having nightmares, and no wonder."

"I'm sorry, I should have realised."

"My mother should have tried to find out why, but she made me feel it was my fault for upsetting her precious little daughter."

Alex considers not asking a question but does. "Don't you think Hilary might not have realised what her father was doing to you?"

"More like she was just glad he never touched her."

"You're certain he didn't."

"She'd have made too much of a row if he had. If she even stubbed her toe the whole street got to hear."

Alex isn't sure this resolves the issue. Before he can pursue it Carl says "That isn't all the bitch did. When she got married she wouldn't have me at the wedding."

"Her parents would have objected, I suppose."

"Wasn't them. She got me barred because I'd made the change."

Alex remembers how Hilary spoke about Carl. "So you won't have seen her since," he says. "She hasn't been in touch."

"Just with you for trying to be me."

Alex finds this description of their relationship disconcerting, not to say unwelcome. "You've told me everything you have to tell me, then."

"Her dad was just as big a shit as I said. He did all those things to me I told you." Carl takes a gulp of orange juice and stares at the dormant phone. As he sets down his glass beside it he opens his mouth, and Alex sees his remarks were simply a preamble, not the end of his confession after all.

CARL

The day I heard about Randal I knew something was wrong as soon as I arrived at work. He always parked the limousine outside Reliablest like an advertisement – he'd started doing that as soon as Barry opened Cheerful Cabs, as if to demonstrate how superior he and his firm were – but now it wasn't there. Before I picked up my first fare some of his drivers and Doris showed up, but not him. When I came back to the office I saw Reliablest was closed – the sign on the door was as clear to me as the number plate you have to read in driving tests – and the limousine was still missing. Randal's drivers were gathered round Doris at the switchboard, and Emma was watching them. "Any idea what's up?" I said.

"They've been talking maybe half an hour."

Doris pointed at me, and the drivers turned to look. Some of them made comments I could tell weren't favourable, which provoked me or at any rate gave me an excuse to make a move. "I'll find out," I told Emma.

I crossed the road once the lights held up the traffic. I didn't mean to act as if I were as invulnerable as Randal always seemed to think he was. Everyone at Reliablest was still staring at me by the time I reached their side of the road. The door was locked, and I was about to rap on it when a driver I didn't know came to peer at me over the CLOSED sign. "What?" he said.

"Has anything happened to Malcolm?"

"Who wants to know?"

Presumably they hadn't been talking about me after all but just about the rival firm. "Carl does," I said.

"She was his," Doris said loud enough that I heard her through the glass.

"Don't see any she," the driver said but opened the door a few grudging inches. "Someone make their mind up."

"Have they sent you to see if we're carrying on?" Doris said.

"Nobody's sent me."

"Just come over to gloat, have you?"

"I don't know why I'd be doing that."

"You aren't telling us you haven't heard the news."

"I haven't, and can you let me in if we're talking?"

"Don't you want too many people hearing you? Malcolm always said you'd never tell the truth if a lie would suit you better." She scowled at people passing, and I saw her decide not to be so public. "Let her come, Norm," she said.

He stepped back without bothering to touch the door. As I shut it behind me I said "So is anyone going to tell me?"

Doris opened her mouth, but it was Norm who said "They've killed Malcolm."

I was shaken by such a wave of relief that I had to grab the counter. "Who has?"

"Whoever did."

He must have taken my response for shock if not grief, because he looked on the way to sympathetic. "How?" I said.

"Robbed the limo up by Bidston Hill. The police have got it now for fingerprints."

"And whoever did it," Doris said as though she was determined to confront me with the details, "they didn't just take all his money, they stamped on his head till Elaine said you wouldn't know who he was any more."

My instant thought was that perhaps the attackers hadn't just been thieves. Suppose he'd abused one child too many to keep secret? I don't know what my face showed, but all I said was "How's my mother taking it?"

"She says it's her latest cross," Doris said and stared at me as if to let me know I was another.

"We're going to tell her we'll keep the business going for her if that's what she wants," Norm said.

"Good luck."

Doris's stare grew fiercer. She must have thought I was being sarcastic, but I meant it now Randal was gone. "Honestly, the best of luck," I said. "There's room for us and you as well."

When I went back to Cheerful Cabs Barry was waiting by the switchboard. "Did you find out much?"

I had to think of words that didn't make it too plain how I felt. "Someone robbed Malcolm while he was out on the road and stomped him to death."

"Christ," Barry said. "You wouldn't wish that on anyone."

Just then Emma took a call I said I'd deal with. Once I dropped the customer off I phoned my mother, but she put the phone down the moment she heard my name. Later in the week Reliablest reopened, and when I ventured over Norm told me the funeral would be at St Brendan's, and the date.

I wanted to be there. Whatever my mother had allowed to happen to me, she was still my mother. She couldn't have suspected Randal, however much I felt she should have. Perhaps she would admit she needed me at last, and we'd rediscover our old relationship. I would never stop loathing Randal, but that needn't stop me offering sympathy for her loss. On top of all this I was determined to prove I could face the occasion, especially if Father Brendan was conducting the funeral.

On the day of the funeral I accepted a job that ought to have left me plenty of time, but once I'd dropped the passenger in Liverpool the roads were hit by the worst storm of the year. The tunnel under the river gave me a few minutes' respite, but on the far side the storm was as vicious as ever. Even with the wipers turned up to maximum I could barely see the traffic, never mind the road. A crash where a motorcycle stuck out from under a car delayed me even further, so that by the time I reached St Brendan's everybody had gone in.

At least the rain was trailing away, though the sky stayed as dark as all the glistening taxis lined up outside the church. You might have thought the day was dressed up for a funeral, but it looked to me as if Randal's sins had turned the world as black as he ought to have believed his soul must be. I parked my taxi behind the rest and tried not to feel I was joining his hired parade. As I let myself into the church, everyone started singing a hymn.

"I loved to choose and see my path...." I recognised 'Lead Kindly Light' from my childhood, but now I was able to reflect that nobody in the church would approve of Randal's choice of path – nobody except Father Brendan. He was in the pulpit, watching me slip into a pew at the back, but I saw he had no idea who I was. I felt as if the religion he pretended to stand for had kept its hold on me, because I couldn't help staying on my feet like the rest of the congregation and mouthing the hymn. It made me feel too much like a child again – like a child whose mouth could produce no words however much it struggled to speak.

I tried to shake off the influence by identifying people in the church. There was my mother on the front row, under a hat like a bell as black as the rest of her outfit. Behind her Randal's drivers and receptionists were lined up in black. All three Sheas were present and dressed just as dark, and other neighbours too, along with people I couldn't give a name. My outfit was the lightest of anybody's in the congregation, and maybe that was why the priest kept giving me a look.

I wasn't about to be cowed into hiding from him. If he eventually realised who I was I hoped that would rouse his guilt at last, though he must be used to suppressing it. Most of the ceremony seemed to be a lie or a denial, but of course those were the core of his life. The first reading he gave was from the New Testament – "The life and death of each of us has its influence on others; if we live, we live for the Lord" – and I felt like shouting that he hadn't lived that way any more than Randal had and letting everybody hear about their influence on me. Listening to the priest talk about Randal, a family man who devoted his life to caring for those closest to him, a blessing to them and his employees, was worse. The next hymn came as a relief at first – 'How Great Thou Art' – till it reached the line "When through the woods and forest glades I wander, and hear the birds sing sweetly in the trees," and I remembered Randal groping me as he lifted me to see a bird. Father Brendan read some more, and "Come, you whom my father has blessed" made me feel several kinds of sick, but not as much as "Happy are the pure in heart." I thought I could stand 'All Things Bright and Beautiful', and I didn't let out any of the words, but "the purple-headed mountain" brought back awful memories of Randal lowering himself towards me, while "He gave us eyes to see them, and lips that we might tell" reminded me what he'd shown me and how he'd left me unable to speak about it, and my mouth was shaping the words of the hymn so much that I felt like a stranded fish. All at once I realised I was mouthing just to convince Father Brendan I was joining in, and I didn't only shut my lips tight, I sat down as well. He sent me a sharp look, but then the hymn was over and it was time for him to serve communion.

I stayed seated while he did. As I watched him stooping to communicants I had to swallow bile. My mother returned to her pew with her head bent, and so she didn't notice me. The Sheas did, but they didn't recognise me. Only Doris and the drivers knew me. Doris twitched her nose as if she smelled something worse than incense, but none of the men reacted. At last Father Brendan finished murmuring about a body and hid the chalice in its place, and eventually went to stand by the pulpit. "Now Malcolm Randal's wife will share some of her memories with us," he said.

Several of the drivers held their hands out behind her as if they were about to help her up or making sure she didn't fall. If she went to the pulpit she was bound to see me, and I wasn't sure what to do. I hadn't planned on meeting her at a distance like that, and how might seeing me so unexpectedly affect her? As she limped to the pulpit and plodded up the steps I thought of dodging out to wait for her after the funeral, but I needed to hear what she said. She bowed her head as she reached the little stage, and kept it low while she clasped her hands on the lectern. She raised it at last and blinked at the congregation, and then she caught sight of me. Her face writhed, and her hands did. "What's she doing here?" she cried.

Father Brendan held up a hand to her and stared over the coffin, murmuring "Mrs Randal?"

"Her at the back. She never wanted to be Malcolm's daughter, and now look at her. She's made sure she isn't mine."

If she was going to forget she was in a church, I could. "Mum," I said loud enough for an echo to send my voice back.

Anyone who hadn't already turned to look did, and so I was the only one to see Father Brendan's hand make a convulsive movement. He might have been starting a sign of the cross, but I thought it looked as if he wanted to fend off my presence or had barely managed not to grab his crotch. "Don't you dare to call me that," my mother shouted and told the priest "I won't say another word while that's in the church."

Some of the drivers, though not Norm, began to stand up.

Reluctantly or otherwise, they looked as if they were preparing to throw me out of the funeral. "Don't do anything you'll regret," I told them. "I'll leave because I want to."

"Defiant even in God's house," my mother cried as I left the pew. "Always wanting to have the last word even when nobody wants to hear."

"That's right." I had my back to everyone now, but I heard my voice where they were. "You never did want to listen to me."

"No, I've changed my mind. I'll talk while she's listening even if she pretends she's not," my mother declared louder still. "Malcolm took her on and treated her like family and hardly ever got a thank you, and you'd have thought saying it hurt her like having a child. He did his best for her like the saint he always was, but she'd have made you think he was doing her some kind of harm, even when he was trying to get her ready for confession. He put himself out to find her a special present for her eighteenth, and she threw it back in his face. He gave her the best job he could find that she'd have been able to do, and when she'd learned everything he had to teach her she took it to the men who'd done the dirty on him. And to top it all she's turned herself into something that oughtn't to be let into a church."

I'd shut the door behind me by now, but I heard her voice all the way to the taxi. I imagined she went on about me even when I couldn't hear any longer. I was tempted to turn back and confront her, but I'd had more than enough, and I told myself I was leaving Randal behind and everyone connected with him. A tender rain was in the air, and it felt as though it was washing me clean.

ALEX

"You've guessed already, haven't you?"

"Guessed what?"

"The rest of the truth."

"This isn't a game. I need you to tell me, whatever it is."

Carl stares at Alex's phone, which looks as inert as the beer mats it's lying between, and raises his defiant eyes. "Nobody's dead."

Alex lifts his glass to take an urgent drink, only to discover he has previously drained it. The gesture feels like fending off the information Carl has given him, or at the very least delaying its arrival. "You're telling me Randal's alive."

"Him and his daughter. I already said her." Carl glances at the glass Alex is brandishing not unlike a weapon. "Get another drink if you want," he says.

Alex plants the glass on a mat, just gently enough not to snap the stem. "No time for that. It's not like her. It's nothing like."

"Don't know what you're getting at."

"You only left her out of the book, but you told me he was dead. You went into all that detail about how he was murdered."

"Maybe that's what he deserved. You're not going to argue with that, are you?" Perhaps Carl takes Alex's lack of words for assent, since he adds "If the book makes someone do it, that's up to them and not our fault."

Alex is appalled Carl thinks this counts as reassurance. "Are you telling me you gave me all those details of a funeral that never happened?"

"Some of that stuff did, and you made me make some of it up."

Alex finds it hard to keep his voice as low as he's afraid it needs to be. "What do you mean, I made you?"

"Asking me what kind of day it was and how the church smelled and how I felt and what people said, stuff like that. I'm not saying I minded. You were a help."

Faced with such apparent innocence, Alex struggles to speak. "I wouldn't have asked any of that if you hadn't lied about Randal."

"Never mind saying I lied about him. He deserved it after all the things he did to me, or are you saying I lied about that?"

"Not if you didn't."

"I never, so don't go telling anyone I did."

"You don't seem to grasp you made me lie about him."

"Not about anything that matters. He can't sue us for saying he was dead, can he?"

"That's hardly the point. Don't you realise the credibility of the entire book is undermined?"

"Not if you don't tell anyone it's not. And him, maybe he ought to be grateful."

Alex has begun to feel he has no sense whatsoever of Carl's mind. "Grateful."

"If everybody thinks he's dead they aren't going to go looking for him."

Perhaps it isn't Carl's mind Alex has so little hold on but his own, since it's only now that he identifies the worst effect of the deception. "You want him to be free to abuse more children, do you?"

"Don't you ever say that about me. He never made me anything like him."

"You've left him at large to do what he likes."

"Not if he's read my book. That'll stop him. You don't see him suing about what I said, do you?"

Once again Alex can't judge how innocent Carl is. "I don't believe that's enough."

"What do you want, then? Shall I tell everybody here about him right now?"

Alex feels sufficiently confused and desperate to say "Perhaps that would be a start."

"It was hard enough talking about him in the shops and on the radio. Maybe I had to say he was dead to let me talk."

"Then you should have told me that at least."

"I've told you now. Would you have helped me write my book if I'd said?"

"I very much doubt I'd have falsified it."

"There you go, then." More accusingly than Alex can quite believe he's hearing, Carl says "It isn't up to you to tell us what to say or how soon."

"I've no idea what you have in mind."

"I'm saying you don't know what having been abused is like till you have been. People like you don't have the right to tell us when we've got to talk or how much."

"But you did talk. You just didn't tell the truth."

"I did mostly. All that stuff after the funeral about how my life kept getting better, that's all true."

"You can't say after a funeral that never happened. You still don't seem to appreciate how you made me lie."

"And what do you reckon it felt like for me, writing the book?"

Alex sees no reason to feel guilty. "A release, I should think."

"It did at first. It felt like stories when I got the book and read it, like they'd happened to somebody else."

Alex isn't sure why this makes him nervous. "Who?"

"Somebody I wasn't any more except in the bits where my life got good, that you said we ought to put in to show people I'd survived. So it was getting easier to talk about it when that bitch Hilary came along and brought all the bad stuff back. That's why I've only told you now."

Alex doesn't know how close this comes to an explanation. He would replenish the drinks – he feels increasingly in need of one – if it weren't for preferring not to interrupt the discussion. "I appreciate your doing so," he says, "but now—"

"Nobody else has to know, do they? If you think Randal needs fixing we can do it together. It won't be so hard when there's both of us."

Though he's by no means eager to, Alex has to learn "Fixing how?"

"Telling him we'll have the law on him if he ever touches anybody else. He'll do as he's told when he knows you know about him."

"I don't think we can be sure of that. I don't think even you can."

"Then what do you reckon we should do to him?"

"I hope you mean about him." When Carl waves his hands, presumably miming a lack of disagreement, Alex says "I really don't think we can decide by ourselves."

The skin around Carl's eyes tightens. "Who are you wanting to bring in?"

"They're already involved, Carl. You must see that." Since Carl looks determined not to do so, Alex says "Kirsty for one, and the legal people are."

"You can't tell them. You swore."

"I didn't know how serious the situation was then."

"You said you swore. I trusted you or I'd never have told you."

"I'd have found out from Hilary sooner or later. She isn't done with us. Carl, whatever I said, we need to let Kirsty and Ruth know. We have to do what's best, and whatever we do affects them. They may see a better course than we can."

"I can't trust you any more." Carl grabs the edge of the table so hard that the phone clatters across the glass, and shoves himself to his feet. "I'll do what I do on my own," he declares. "Nearly always have."

"Carl, please don't be hasty. We can—"

Alex is wary of raising his voice any further. He's already talking to Carl's back as Carl heads for the exit, and several drinkers glance between him and Carl as if they wonder what kind of tiff they're witnessing. As the door shuts he lurches out of the booth and hurries after Carl, who is already halfway to a platform and walking faster than Alex. A train is poised to leave, and as the last doors slam Carl jumps aboard. The train moves off before Alex is alongside him, but Alex puts on enough speed to overtake him as Carl makes his way along the aisle. Why is Alex doing this at all? He feels as if he's invisibly tethered to Carl. He's still panting beside him when Carl takes a seat and looks through the window. Alex brandishes his phone and points at it, actions that fall short of justifying his pursuit, but Carl shuts his eyes or at least narrows them and barely bothers to shake his head. As Alex stumbles to a halt he sees more than one passenger assume the exchange is a lovers' quarrel. While the train dwindles to a distant glinting point he phones Carl, who aborts the call at once. Alex's train has just arrived at another platform, and he sprints to clamber on board.

He's anxious to talk to Lee, but not while he may be overheard. The train is crowded, and so is the London station, and the Brighton train as well. By the time he arrives in Brighton he's trying to recall something Carl said to him, perhaps not today, that it feels vital to remember. He hasn't identified it when he reaches home, where the unseen sea sounds like a promise – or else an illusion – of peace.

Lee is at her computer, editing a book. As she scrolls through it Alex glimpses sentences and paragraphs she has marked yellow next to her detailed comments in the margin. "That," he says, "looks like a lot of work."

"All the work the author didn't do. Someone couldn't have believed in research."

He plants a kiss on her cheek, a gesture that feels like delaying his response. "I wish you'd done that to the Carla book."

"You told me not to bother, if you remember. You said there was nothing we needed to check." Lee backs up the document on an external drive and swivels to face Alex. "What did he have to say for himself?"

"The woman who called me is Randal's daughter. She was born and she lived, and her father must still be alive as well."

"Alex." There's sympathy in that, and a gentle reprimand. "Did you never feel anything was wrong," she says, "when you were talking through the book?"

"He seemed so fluent I never did." He's sure this must have been the case, however difficult it is to recapture the experience. "Maybe he convinced me," he says, "because he'd managed to convince himself."

"He wasn't just being malicious."

"I can imagine he wanted to get his own back. He still insists Randal did all that to him." Alex has a fleeting sense that Lee's suggestion should mean something other than he assumed. The more he strains to recall collaborating with Carl, the less he can be certain where the impression of fluency lies. How much of the eloquence was his, inspired by Carl's reminiscences? "He blames the daughter too," he says.

"At least you haven't got to sort all this out by yourself. You've told Kirsty and the legal team, yes?"

"I wanted to talk to you first. All this has left me feeling I don't really know anyone, even myself."

"I hope you still know me."

"I thought I just said that. Meant it, anyway."

"I'd have to edit it so you did."

At the moment he doesn't relish their game. "I'm just worried how he's made me look."

"He must have taken Kirsty in first, mustn't he? They can't blame you if he took you in as well. Don't put off calling her. I'll make us coffee while you do."

As she heads for the kitchen Lee squeezes his arm firmly enough for the ghost of her touch to linger. Alex takes out his phone but hesitates, groping in the depths of his mind for the detail he failed to identify on his way home. It feels more recent now, as if he inadvertently referred to it, or Lee did – and then the memory resurfaces, and he shouts several words he very seldom uses, although these days Lee wouldn't have to query them even in teenage fiction. When she runs to him Alex has the distracted thought that she resembles a quotation, flanked by inverted commas on the empty mugs she holds. "For heaven's sake what is it, Alex?"

"Nothing to do with heaven, as Mr Randal might say. Or maybe I made him." Alex is desperate to find some humour in the situation, even at his own expense. "It's been about me all the time," he says.

"What has?"

"When I wasn't Carla. The book."

"I don't know what you can mean."

"You were right and you didn't know. You weren't even there and you told me the truth."

"You're disturbing me, Alex."

"I'm disturbed myself." In a bid to respond to the plea in her eyes he says "You said just now he was malicious. You just didn't realise how much any more than I did."

"You need to be clearer."

"I know. I'm trying." Alex holds a hand up, though he isn't even sure who he wants to silence. "He's been playing a game with me ever since we met," he realises aloud. "Finding out how stupid I am, which is more than I'd like to believe. My God, he even reminded me what he'd said that should have tipped me off."

He hears Lee striving to be gentle as she asks "What did he say?"

"The very first words out of his mouth were he didn't like my kind of book, which is to say books about abused childhoods."

"Maybe he meant fiction, do you think?"

"Why would anybody want to work with a writer they had so little time for?"

"Because Tiresias chose you?" Lee hesitates before adding "You mustn't take this the wrong way, but might he have been thinking he could improve your work? I'm not saying for a moment he improved it."

"No, I'll tell you what I think. He wanted to get his own back on the world, and that didn't only mean his family, it included me." Alex rubs his brows with his fingertips but fails to erase the frown that's tightening his forehead. "He pretended he was letting me into the truth," he says, "but really he was putting on a performance, the way he's learned to do for everyone."

"But it's still true about his stepfather."

"I'm not even sure of that now. That's the state he's left me in." A pause for breath lets another thought erupt. "Good God," Alex says, "do you see what else he did?"

"I'm not sure if I'm seeing everything you've said so far."

"He wrecked my computer."

"Alex, I think you should slow down a little. You're getting carried away." Lee is about to come to him when the percolator emits an offstage hiss. "Let me get that," she says, "and then we can talk some more."

"I need to talk now." Alex follows her into the kitchen. "Don't you think he could do that," he insists, "considering he faked a death certificate?"

Lee plants the mugs together by the percolator, leaving no space between them to contain a quote. "Could do isn't did."

"I bet you'd edit that line in a book." As she concentrates on pouring coffee Alex says "I'm sure he sent the virus in his last email. He must have got it from his friend he said knows all about computers. He was making certain I can't prove anything he said when we were working on the book."

"But you can't prove he did that either."

"You believe me, don't you?"

"I'm doing my best." As Lee hands him the end of an empty quote she says "I think I may need time."

"Here's something to convince you. When he rang me that time to say he couldn't make the bookshop he told me to remember the first thing he'd said."

"Did he have to mean when you first met?"

Alex doesn't want to feel his mind still can't be trusted. "If you knew him you'd know."

Lee seems relieved when he takes out his phone, having regained some calm from talking. "Do you think you'd better just tell Kirsty what he said today?" she says. "You mightn't want to hit her with too much all at once."

"I'll keep that in mind. Just now I'm calling Hilary Randal."

"Alex, I don't think you ought to keep Kirsty in the dark, or the legal people either."

"I want to be sure of my facts first, as many as I can."

He brings up Hilary Randal's number before Lee can argue further, and leaves a print like evidence of a crime on the glass screen. Two pairs of rings are all it takes to bring an answer. "Mr Grand, I hope you're calling with some news."

"There have been developments. I'd like to talk about them face to face."

"I'll see you any time at all." More like a warning she says "Make it soon."

"As soon as it's convenient for everyone involved." When Lee gazes at him, perhaps wondering whether he has her in mind, Alex tells Hilary "I need to meet your father."

MR GRAND

At first Alex can't distinguish the face of the solitary figure outside Northampton Station, because the low sun has turned the glass façade into a sheet of light. As he drives up to the station the face develops like an old photograph – small eyes set close together, token nose, restricted mouth. Recognising Hilary Wilson feels unnecessarily like composing a description of her in the book Carl made him write. When he pulls up alongside she doesn't let herself into the car but simply gazes at him. Perhaps she expects him to climb out and hold the door for her, but he reaches across the passenger seat to ease it open. She produces a grunt as she takes her seat but doesn't speak while yanking several times at the seat belt, eventually releasing it to let the reel yield sufficient length for the buckle to struggle into the slot. "I was starting to think you'd got me here for nothing," she complains.

"Sorry for the delay. I'd have been later if I'd stopped to ring you." He feels more rebuked than ten minutes' wait seems to call for. "Don't you often get to see your parents?" he's provoked to ask.

"Not as often as I'd like or they would, but whenever I can, I'll tell you that." Her resentment continues to mount as she adds "Not like some."

Of course she means Carl, but Alex feels he too has been avoiding his parents. Even given the other events in his life, he's warier of seeing them than he understands. He hasn't time to ponder this. "You'll need to tell me which way to go."

"Carry on like you are."

This sounds too much like a rebuke and no sort of direction. Presumably she's sending him straight ahead, since she doesn't protest when he takes that route. He's driving down a street of shops embedded low in timbered buildings – they look as if the ground floors are tinting the monochrome past, like a partly crayoned picture in a colouring book – when Hilary demands "What are you going to say to my parents?"

Alex only just manages not to lose control of the car and himself. "Parents."

"That's right, two of them. Two more than that bitch liked."

Alex feels as if everything he says sums up his own stupidity. "They're both alive."

"No thanks to you or her either. What are you going to say to them?"

With such an effort to regain control that his head throbs Alex says "Carl's owned up to me about the book. Before I discuss it with my editor I want to hear the truth from them."

"Owned up to what?"

"How much of it he made up."

Alex hopes to prompt her by revealing as little as he can, and is gratified to hear her say "I never said it all was."

"What wasn't?" Alex says and finds he's holding his breath.

"The funeral."

For a moment if not longer Alex loses all sense of how to drive. The wheel and the pedals are somewhere he isn't, and the road ahead might be. He grips the wheel and reduces speed, having tramped on the accelerator as if desperate for something solid underfoot, before he feels safe to speak. "Then who am I going to see now?"

"My father. Malcolm Randal." She adds a sound Alex supposes she might call a laugh. "When I said the funeral," she says, "I meant my wedding."

"It was that bad."

"Don't try and be clever. You're sounding like Carla." Although he's concentrating on the road, Alex feels her glare on the side of his face. "I'm saying she got thrown out of that," she tells him.

"Carl did."

"I'll never call her that, so don't waste your time trying to make me. That's why we chucked her out, for doing that to herself and my parents."

"So how much that happened is in the book?"

"All the things you say my mother said to her, she did."

The idea that he told more truth than he realised after all fails to gratify Alex. Why should it disturb him? He might be trying to leave it behind by asking "What else in the book is real?"

"Stop." He's afraid he has asked too much until Hilary repeats the word. "It's not far to the house now," she says. "I want to hear what you're going to say to them."

Alex keeps quiet while he finds space to halt by a newsagent's, outside which a poster caged by wire mesh says **NORTHAMPTON SAINTS WORK MIRACLE**. It takes him a moment to identify the reference to the local rugby team. Not entirely as an answer to Hilary's question he says "What brought your parents here?"

"They used to have family. What do you want to know for?"

"It just seems a long way to move."

"That's because it was. They could have done with more help, but they only had me and my man."

Alex can't judge how much of her resentment he has attracted, but he's unable to avoid inviting more. "You'll understand if I have to ask you something."

"I understand a lot more than some people would like to think." As if ensuring he's confused she says "And don't you tell me what I will."

"Your father never touched you."

"That's supposed to be a question, is it?"

"I'd like it to be one so that I can tell the publishers."

"Yes, he touched me."

This is so unexpected that for several moments Alex's mouth feels cleared of words. "Would you mind saying how?"

"He touched my heart and soul, and he still does." She waits for Alex to meet her stare before she says "And he's given me hugs all my life. I hope that's still allowed."

"You'll appreciate that wasn't what I had in mind."

"I've a good idea what sort of mind you've got. If you ask me you're a lot like Carla."

Surely Alex ought to let this pass, but he's unsettled enough to retort "What makes you say that?"

"My parents would have loved her if she'd let them, but she wasn't having any. She acted like it was unnatural because there was something wrong with her. Were you like that with yours?"

"I really don't believe so."

"Maybe she couldn't let herself feel any more because she lost her dad so young, but that's no excuse for what she said about mine."

Alex is still anxious to leave behind any similarity to Carla, not to mention Carl. "Shall we move on?" he says, and when Hilary doesn't speak he starts the car.

She directs him through a minor maze of side streets, where he looks out for the limousine he has helped to make famous. Instead he's treated to several distant glimpses of the Catholic cathedral. He's in a street that resembles an outlier of the building – two terraces of fawn stone pierced by tall narrow windows arched to points – when Hilary says "Here" like a summons to a dog. As soon as he halts the car she says with glum triumph "You can't park here."

Once she lets herself out he finds a space that's unreserved for residents. There's no sign of the limousine, and he wonders if the Randals are trying to be inconspicuous. When he walks back he finds two women standing in a doorway in the middle of a terrace. The older woman is as stocky as her daughter but more angular, with large eyes set so wide they look resolved to test the limits of her face. They and her broad mouth shrink at but not from the sight of Alex. "This is the man, is it?" she says.

"At least he's always been one, mother."

"The company you keep rubs off on you," Elaine Randal says and looks disgusted by her choice of words. "You should take care who your friends are if you don't want people thinking you're the same as them."

The echo of Hilary's comparison disconcerts Alex more than he believes it should, and her mother frowns at him. "We won't have a scene in the street," she says. "You've already made a filthy show of us."

When she limps with an effort into the hall, where gilded haloes glint in saintly paintings on both walls, Alex ventures past her daughter. It's evident Elaine was restraining herself outside, and she twists around to confront him, only to find him observing her painful gait. "Yes," she says, "I'm as bad as you made out I was. But how you said it happened, that was all a wicked lie."

"It was me, wasn't it, mother?" Hilary says as she shuts more gloom into the hall.

"If it was you know I always told you not to blame yourself. It's nothing compared to what that creature did to me."

"You made your mother fall, you're saying."

"Nobody fell," Elaine declares. "That's one more of your lies. God help you if you don't know the difference."

"It was me being born," Hilary tells Alex. "That's what left her like this."

As Alex revises the memory Carl gave him, a man leans out of the nearest room. His features are by no means equal to his face, and pouchy skin renders his eyes smaller still. His cheeks and his equally wrinkled throat droop, and his smile is so faint it borders on the secretive, not that his mouth has much scope for one. His voice is thin but not as high as Carl led Alex to expect, so that Alex wonders if the man is trying not to sound like the description in the book. "Will that be Mr Grand?"

"That's what he calls himself," Elaine says. "I don't see anything grand about him."

"Do come in and sit yourself down, Mr Grand. I'd like to hear what you have to say for yourself."

"He's already said far too much, God forgive him."

"I'm sure God will, my pet, and perhaps we can. He may be just as much a victim as the rest of us."

She rests her unconvinced stare on Alex while Randal ushers him into the front room. Multiple Christs inhabit the walls, surrounding a fat drab upholstered suite. A pair of armchairs sprout footrests, poking them at a television screen that's blank except for assorted Christly reflections. As Alex takes one end of the sofa, hugging himself when its arm shifts and rattles under his right elbow, Elaine says "I expect someone's going to want a drink."

"A coffee would be very welcome," Alex says.

She stares as if she hadn't thought of him. "I've made tea."

"That would be fine too."

"I made it for you," she says, but not to him. "Don't anyone say anything till I come back. I want to hear what's said."

"I'll help you bring it, mother."

The women disappear along the hall, and Randal lowers himself into an armchair, having cleared several parish magazines from a low table onto the floor beneath. Clasping his hands on his midriff could signify a silent prayer. Besides his watchful gaze, he might be sending Alex his faint smile, which isn't too far from benign. Alex feigns interest in the pictures on the walls while he listens to the murmurs in the kitchen without distinguishing a word. None too soon Hilary reappears with a tray on which cups and saucers keep up a discreet china chatter next to a matching teapot and a sugar bowl, and her mother follows with a jug of milk. Elaine pours teas that Hilary hands out, and Alex turns down sugar but accepts milk, all of which feels like a polite delay of impoliteness. When Hilary sits down he's aware of how much distance she puts between them on the sofa. As he rouses a clatter from the sofa arm by setting cup and saucer on the faded vaguely patterned carpet, Randal says "I wish we'd known from the outset you were mixed up with Carla."

Alex feels prompted to declare he isn't mixed up, but says "Why would that be?"

"We could have warned you how much of a stranger she is to the truth."

"And to her own family," Elaine cries. "I feel as if we never really knew her."

"I hope you won't blame us for withholding information, Mr Grand. Our daughter only told us about the book this week, and we've just finished reading it."

"He's got no right to blame anyone, Malcolm. However many lies that wretched creature told him, he's responsible for what he wrote."

"You know how persuasive she can be, my pet."

"He still should have done his job properly and checked the facts. If you ask me he's no better than she is."

This provokes Alex to retort "Your daughter here tells me some of it happened."

"She's our only daughter. She's my only one." Without lessening her fierceness Elaine demands "What have you been saying to him, Hilary?"

"He can say."

"What are you trying to make out she told you?"

"That you said some of what you said to Carla in the book." Alex feels as if confronting characters in it has robbed him of his hold on language. "Carl, I should say," he's driven to add.

"You shouldn't say anything of the kind. Nobody says that name in this house." Elaine lends the warning more weight with a stare and says "But you're right for once. I said everything I said in there to her. I didn't say the half of what I ought to have."

Alex thinks she sounds increasingly like his depiction of her. A sense that he's inciting this unsettles him, and he reaches for his teacup to pause the conversation. The arm of the sofa exudes a smell of stale upholstery as it grows restless, and Elaine remonstrates "Don't forget your saucer. We don't want any stains in here."

Alex docks the cup on it and raises both to take a sip, which tastes of the stale smell. As he returns cup and saucer to the carpet, Randal says "We've something you should see. It may help you with the truth."

Some of his mop of grey curls unravel as he leans down to retrieve a book from beside his chair. For a moment Alex expects to see a copy of *When I Was Carla* somehow altered. It's a photograph album tagged with slips of yellow paper. "Take your time looking," Randal says.

Each of the tagged pages includes at least one photograph of Carla. The earliest show her together with Elaine and a man with an extravagantly generous face, the couple in the photograph Carl keeps on his office desk. Later images place Carla with Elaine and Randal and eventually their daughter. In all of these her smile looks fixed, and Alex suspects it was poised to vanish as soon as the shot was done. "Not the kind of thing a monster would keep in his home, do you think?" Randal says. "Her mother wanted me to destroy every one of them, but I persuaded her we shouldn't. We should always leave the prodigal a chance to redeem herself, and I think keeping those is the next best thing to a prayer."

Alex finds the evidence suspiciously contrived. If Randal tagged the pages for his benefit, the gesture had to be at the very least premeditated. As he considers asking whether Randal did it for him, Elaine says "Can't you see the truth yet? I think you're hellbent on not seeing. You're as wilful as her you took the name from."

Alex feels trapped by bewilderment. "I took what how?"

"Are you even speaking English any more? You said you were Carla. You never were, and nobody is now."

"I don't think he quite said he was, my pet. Just the book."

"That's just as bad. He stuck his name on it, didn't he? Helped

people believe it was true and never bothered finding out what was."
Randal's intervention has inflamed her rage. "Didn't even try to get
the name right," she declares. "I'd almost thank him for that if it didn't
come so close."

Alex is afraid that another assumption he has lived with is about to
collapse. "Which name?"

"Can't you bear to admit whose house you're in? His name."

Alex glances at Randal, whose faint smile stays reticent. "You're
saying he isn't called Malcolm."

"Are you having a laugh? You aren't entitled after everything
you've helped that creature do to us." Elaine wags her teacup at her
husband, spattering the carpet, and cries "The name he gave us all."

"It isn't Randal."

"It most definitely is, and I'm proud to have it for my own. I know
Hilary was too."

"I was, mother. I only changed it because—"

"You changed it in the Christian way, not like someone I won't
name." Nevertheless she appears to resent the interruption, and turns
her displeasure on Alex. "But nobody with any sense spells it that way.
It's Randall," she says, vibrating her tongue on the final pair of letters
like a child imitating a guitar. "Randall. Randall."

"With a double ell, you mean."

"That's what they call it, isn't it? Double like you were trying to
be in your book. Carla's double." The reflection aggravates her rage.
"Don't bother telling us you thought that was how to spell it, Mr
Writer. More like you were scared to put his real name, and so you
ought to be."

"Perhaps he needn't be afraid, my pet, so long as he's seen the truth."

Alex shuts the album on a picture of a teenage Carla with a
resolutely manufactured smile and passes the volume to Randall. The
image has lodged in his mind, feeling more like a recollection of his
own than it should. He's about to make himself speak when Hilary
says "Better ask what you want to ask."

"What do you think I want?"

"If my father ever did Carla any harm."

"I think you've just asked on my behalf."

"Can't you speak up for yourself?" Elaine cries. "I'm not

surprised. I don't know how you even dare to think such a thing in our house."

"It's perfectly all right, my pet. He ought to ask." Before Alex has time to take this as an invitation Randall says "Yes, I harmed her."

Elaine's cup chatters like teeth on the saucer in her other hand, and Hilary lowers her voice as though it's for only him to hear. "Dad, what are you saying?"

"I must have for her to end up as she has. You couldn't have been responsible, and certainly your mother couldn't."

"Malcolm, you've got to know what turned her that way, and it wasn't any of the family. It's one of the things she couldn't help telling the truth about, though she didn't dare tell us."

"Remind me if you will."

"All those drugs she took when she was at school. No wonder I felt I didn't know her by the time she grew up, but you mustn't start blaming yourself. If anyone should have suspected what she was up to I should. You did more than most men would who'd taken on someone else's child."

"I did give her a job. I thought it would keep us close."

"Which she flung in your face." Elaine's anger doesn't flag as she says "You cared for her in every way you could. You even took her through her catechism."

"You never did that for me," Hilary says.

"That's because you were my good girl and there was no need."

Alex feels as if the answer he sought is receding into memories he has no use for. "So just to be clear...."

"Are you daring to ask now?" Elaine cries. "He's told you how he thinks he harmed Carla, and I'm here to tell you he never did. Now you answer me something, since you seem to think you know her better than we do. Why has she told all these lies about us?"

"I wonder if he might believe them."

"He." Randall's pause has left the word behind by the time he says "Is that how she managed to convince a professional such as yourself?"

"I don't know if taking drugs that young needs to be taken into account."

"You know how they affect you," Elaine says, "do you, Mr Grand?"

"No, I'm starting to think I was mistaken." Her question feels like an indefinable threat. "I think," he says, "Carl meant to get his own back."

"Her own what?"

"His revenge is what I'm saying."

"Who's she got any right to think deserves that?"

"I'm not saying it was deserved." Having said so much, Alex can only go on. "I think he was trying to get even with me."

"Why, what did you do to her?" Hilary says quite like a hope.

The constant switching of pronouns leaves Alex desperate to cling to Carl's identity. It feels too much as though his own is being undermined. "Nothing I meant to," he says. "Perhaps that's true of more than me."

"What are you suggesting now?" Elaine demands.

"I expect Mr Grand has me in mind, my pet. I've admitted it may be the case."

"Then let him say what he didn't mean to do."

"Offend Carl or anyone with my last novel. He complained to my publishers about it."

"Why would she want to make trouble for you?" Elaine says as if she's accusing him as well.

"Maybe the drugs made her think the book was about her," Hilary says.

"I never thought of that." Alex finds it disturbing to consider. "It involves child abuse and gender transition," he says, "if that helps."

"Neither of them ever helped anyone," Elaine retorts. "They're both as bad. They're two kinds of abuse."

"Abusing the body God gave you," Hilary says. "I've just thought why she could have gone for him. Her sort won't let normal people write about their kind."

Alex is disconcerted to be offered understanding, perhaps even sympathy. Before he can react Randall says "May we hope you've learned everything you'd like to, Mr Grand?"

"My husband's asking whose side you're on now."

Alex has heard nothing to revive his faith in Carl. "I," he says and no more, because someone is ringing the doorbell.

While Hilary trots out of the room her parents watch Alex as if they expect him to complete his answer, but he's listening to sounds along the hall. He hears Hilary open the front door, and a man asks for someone named Randall. That's all Alex can distinguish except for one word, and he's straining to hear more when Hilary calls "Dad."

"What are they saying?" Randall says as he takes hold of an arm of the chair.

"Some mumble," Elaine complains, and Alex feels he may as well do better. "Something about a computer," he says.

Randall twists around to stare out of the window and shoves himself to his feet at once. Alex wouldn't have expected him to move so fast at his age, but Randall's reaction confirms the thought he's just had – that Carl has destroyed the man's computer the same way he infected Alex's. He sees Randall stride into the hall, only to falter. "Malcolm Randall?" a man wants to know.

"That's myself. What seems to be the trouble?"

"We have a warrant to search these premises and seize certain items as evidence."

"Evidence of what, for pity's sake? I can't imagine what you could have in mind."

"We're acting on information received, Mr Randall."

"Received from whom, I wonder."

"I'm afraid we can't give out that information."

"I believe I can guess. Did she say her name was Carl and try to sound like a man?"

"As I've said, we aren't at liberty—"

"And I'm sure she'd like me not to be. Did I hear you mention a computer?"

"Any that are here will have to be impounded, I'm afraid."

"I see you have your job to do." Randall peers along the hall, presumably at the warrant. "I just need to finish something on it," he says. "The tax people never leave you alone, even at my age. Elaine, my pet, give these gentlemen whatever they'd like to drink while I see to this."

His voice has grown rapid, and Alex has a sense that it's holding shrillness back. Randall's last phrase trails behind him as he dodges fast across the hall into the room opposite, a ground-floor bedroom. A laptop lies open on the bed, and he dashes to it as three policemen appear in the hall. They're a wiry trio with less hair between them than most men might want for themselves alone. The youngest follows Randall and stands behind him unnoticed as the old man types. "See eight eye ell dee ar five en," the policeman says aloud.

Randall swings around, struggling to maintain his smile, and almost topples off the bed. "All right, you have my password, clever fellow. You'll find I've nothing to hide. Just let me shut this down."

"That won't be necessary, Mr Randall." The policeman who announced the warrant crosses the bedroom swiftly enough to snatch the laptop out of Randall's reach. "It will be returned to you if nothing's found," he says.

"Nothing will be, as God is my witness."

Alex thinks Randall sounds more defiant than innocent, especially since his voice has strayed higher. "I hope you won't try to obstruct us any further," the policeman says, and to his colleagues "Continue the search."

"You knew this was coming, Mr Grand," Elaine cries. "That's why you're here."

"You mustn't think that," Alex protests. "Don't let them hear you say."

He's so intent on Randall, who is perched on the edge of the bed and gripping the edge of the mattress as if he's resisting arrest, that he doesn't realise Elaine has flown across the room until she grabs handfuls of his hair. His scalp blazes with pain, and he tries to pry her hands loose. She lets go with one and starts clawing at his face, and he's clutching at her wrists when the policeman with the laptop crosses the hall. "Enough of that, please, Mrs Randall," he says. "I'm asking you to stop."

No doubt he doesn't want to put the laptop down, which is why he stays clear of physical involvement, though either of his colleagues could intervene. Elaine deals Alex's scalp a parting wrench and steps back, breathing fiercely. Hilary has watched the attack from the hall and looks as if she would have relished joining in. "Now get out of this house while you're still in one piece," Elaine tells Alex. "Get off home where you belong, if anyone will have you," and he hears her talking to him as if she thinks he's Carl.

"He won't be doing that just yet. We've a few questions he'll need to answer," the policeman says and shuts the laptop like a trap, pinning it under one arm. "Mr Grand, is it? You'll be coming with us."

MR GRAND

"I believe we've heard about you, Mr Grand."

"Fine if you've heard the truth." When the policeman's broad smooth apparently placid face displays no expression Alex says "What have you heard?"

"Perhaps you can tell me."

"About my books. This one, at any rate." The absence of any response prompts Alex to add "The one about Malcolm Randall."

"Please be more specific."

They're in Fanshawe's office. He's the officer who led the search of the Randalls' apartment. His room is so uncluttered that it might have been cleared of any items that could hinder observation of whoever's in front of his desk. This bears little except a computer and a telephone and an upright photograph with its back to Alex. Fanshawe sits behind it, with Alex seated opposite on a thinner chair. Both men have coffee in white mugs as blank as the walls, and the conversation could be taken for informal if it weren't for the recorder on the desk. Alex feels the small machine is lying low as he says "About him and his family."

"What about them?"

"If you believe it, how he abused his stepdaughter and they ignored it. No, wait," Alex says, which the policeman already appears to be doing. "His daughter isn't in the book, just the mother."

"But you say it shouldn't be believed."

"I didn't when I wrote it. Say that, I mean." The recorder has made Alex wary of his words, but now he's stumbling over them. "I believed in it completely when I wrote it," he says.

"You don't want people believing it now."

"If I'm being honest, I don't know."

"It's in your interest to be that, Mr Grand."

"I'm saying I am being. I've never been otherwise so far as I'm aware."

"Then please go on." As Alex tries to retrieve his place in the dialogue Fanshawe says "What stopped you believing what you wrote?"

"I should tell you first of all my publishers commissioned the project. They introduced me to the stepdaughter, well, she's not one any more, and suggested I should write her story."

"Do you often play someone else?"

"More like never. Certainly not now." Having said this, Alex has to add "It's the first time I've done it and very much the last."

"Just for the record, why would that be?"

"I'd rather work with my own mind. That way I know what I'm imagining."

A pause feels like a suppressed question before Fanshawe says "Can you say why they chose you?"

"That depends on who you mean."

"Your publishers, you told me."

"There'd been some trouble over my last novel and they were looking for a way to remedy the situation."

"What sort of trouble?"

"Isn't that one of the things you've heard about me?" When Fanshawe offers only patient waiting Alex says "Some people thought I oughtn't to be writing what I didn't know."

"Specifically, Mr Grand."

"Child abuse and gender change. I've never experienced either, but I've written about any number of things I haven't experienced. That's what fiction writers do."

"This book you were commissioned to produce was meant as restitution."

"Call it that if you like." Alex thinks he senses disapproval, which prompts him to add "It would have been."

"But now you're saying it wasn't."

"Because I don't know if Carl was abused. He was the stepdaughter, except he obviously isn't any longer, and after what happened today I'm not sure of anything much. What can you tell me?"

"I'm not here to do that, Mr Grand." Although Fanshawe's tone remains neutral, his quiescence seems to gain weight. "What made you doubt the victim?"

"For a start, he made me say Randall was dead."

"How do you mean you were compelled?"

"I'm saying he told me the man was murdered."

"That doesn't sound too compelling. You didn't think to check."

"I'd no reason to disbelieve him. I assumed the publishers were vouching for him. I thought they'd have looked into whatever needed it. Anyway, if I'd tried to find out about Randall I wouldn't have got anywhere."

"Why not?"

"Carl chopped one of his ells off." In case this seems unduly humorous Alex says "He told me that was how the name was spelled. He doesn't use it himself."

Fanshawe's lack of an expression leaves Alex desperate to reach him. "And he faked a death certificate to show me," he says. "Isn't that against the law?"

"That needn't concern us here." Before Alex can convey disagreement Fanshawe says "You say that when you wrote the book you believed the alleged victim."

"I'd say I had no basis not to."

"In that case why didn't you report the situation to the police?"

"Surely Carl would have if as you say he was a victim. It would have happened to him, not me."

"That's an attitude we're determined to change. Too many people think it isn't their responsibility when they're told about abuse, or that's what they would rather think. Did you suggest it to him?"

"I helped him develop some of his memories, at least that's what I thought they were, but it was all about what he told me. I didn't suggest any of them."

Patience weighs the policeman's voice down. "Did you suggest reporting it to us."

"I'm afraid I didn't, and I don't believe the publishers did."

"Was that meant to help the book sell?"

"I can't speak for the publishers. You'd need to ask them."

"I'm asking you to speak for yourself, Mr Grand."

"Then of course it wasn't. How was it going to help?"

"I'm not an expert on your business. I'm suggesting to you how it might look."

This feels like an undefined threat, which provokes Alex to respond "The book reported it. Why wasn't that picked up?"

"You've only just brought it to my notice, Mr Grand. In any case you don't appear to realise you delayed identification of the alleged perpetrator by however long it took you to publish the book and left potential victims at risk."

"Hold on." Alex wonders how much Fanshawe has managed to undermine his memories, jumbling them until he has almost lost his grasp on them. "I told you before," he says, "Carl convinced me Randall was dead."

"If you thought he was dead, how did you come to be at his house?"

"Because Carl admitted he wasn't dead just this week."

"Why was that, Mr Grand?"

"As you say, I'm Alex Grand, not him. You'd have to ask him why." When the question lingers Alex tries saying "Guilt, I should think."

"You think the victim should feel guilty rather than the perpetrator."

"They often do, don't they? You'd know more about that than me, and anyway I didn't say they should. And according to you he ought to feel guilty for saying Randall was dead."

"Why do you think he would have said that?"

"He told me it let him talk about the man at last."

Fanshawe seems to find this possible, but the pause leaves Alex anxious to establish more of the truth – and then an inconsistency catches up with him. "Hang on," he says. "You've been telling me you didn't know about the book."

"I do now."

"But you said at the start you'd heard about me."

"That had nothing to do with the book." Fanshawe reaches towards the recorder but withdraws his hand. "We were expecting you," he says.

"Expecting me to do what?"

"We were advised you might try to forewarn Mr Randall before we could impound potential evidence."

"Why would I want to do that? For a start, if he's arrested it'll help the book." Alex says this to convince the policeman but senses it offends him. "I needn't ask who told you I was going to tip him off," he declares.

"We can't divulge the identity of an informant, as I'm sure you must know."

"Then I'll say it for your record. Carl Batchelor who used to be Carla Randall, and whichever they are, they're a liar."

This or Alex earns a sharp look. "Are you saying the alleged victim was a girl?"

"At the time he was, and then he switched."

The policeman doesn't seem fond of this either. "Why would anybody lie about the reason you were there?"

"To get his own back because I wrote something he disliked. Or just maybe he thought my being there might tip off Randall by itself."

"And why exactly were you there?"

"To try and establish the truth at last."

"Did you succeed?"

"I thought I had until you showed up." Since this sounds accusing, Alex adds "I'd begun to think Randall was innocent, but now I don't know."

He's hoping Fanshawe will at least hint at the truth, but somebody knocks on the door. One of the men who took part in the raid beckons to Fanshawe, who switches the recorder off and slips it into a pocket. Retrieving the device tips over the solitary photograph, which shows two men with an arm around each other's shoulders while they appear to dangle by their feet. As Fanshawe sees Alex gazing at them he says not quite neutrally "Is there an issue?"

"None I can see. You're upside down, that's all."

Perhaps this sounds too sly, because Fanshawe's look sharpens again. "That's my husband."

He stands the photograph up with its back to Alex as though to protect it from unwelcome attention and strides out of the room, closing the door. Whatever the discussion concerns, Alex can't make out a word. He straightens up, having leaned towards the door as far as he can without toppling the chair, as Fanshawe returns. Presuming the recorder is still off, Alex risks asking "Was that about Randall?"

"I can't discuss it, I'm afraid," Fanshawe says, which Alex takes to mean yes. "I believe we've heard enough from you for the moment, Mr Grand. I just need your details and then you may go."

He copies the address on Alex's driving licence and ascertains his mobile number, and plants his fists on either side of the photograph while rising to his feet. "You may be hearing from us."

"I hope it'll be what I think." When Fanshawe's face stays resolutely neutral Alex says "Any chance of a lift to my car?"

"I think you'd better make your own way," Fanshawe says, and Alex feels the man's gaze burdening his back as he leaves the office.

While he knows which street he left the car in, he can't recall the route. A blue worm contorts itself across his phone to lead him through the streets. He's hurrying past the Randall house, having turned his face away, when somebody appears at one pinched downstairs window. "Is that him?" Elaine Randall cries.

"It's me and nobody else," Alex mutters, making for the car at speed. As he turns it to head back to the motorway, both women emerge from the house. Elaine limps across the pavement while Hilary steps off the kerb, and he's afraid the daughter means to lurch into his path. When he swerves the car Elaine screams "Go on, you coward. Run away from two defenceless women." Presumably she has suspended her own prohibition of making scenes in public.

She and her daughter are barely out of sight when his phone begins to shrill. "Hilary Randal, maybe," it says, and he halts the car just long enough to kill the call. He glances in the mirror in case she's pursuing him personally, but there's no sign of her. Before he reaches the motorway the phone names her again. He mutes it, wishing he could do that to the confused clamour of his thoughts, and recommences the long drive home.

ALEX

"You need to wake up, Alex."

The whole of him disagrees – his burdened eyelids, his skull that too much wine with dinner has left brittle with a threat of pain, his limbs that resent any proposal of motion. It has been the first night he has slept through since he can recall, and Lee's gentle urgency falls short of reviving him. "Who's going to make me?" he mumbles.

"Won't I do? There's just me here."

He could imagine she's saying he isn't. At the moment he wouldn't need much convincing. His mind is cluttered with scraps of dreams like someone's memories, if they aren't recollections he'd forgotten he had. "What time is it?" he's less than eager to learn.

"It's actually quite late. I tried to let you sleep."

While he anticipates the task of opening his eyes he mutters "How late?"

"Almost noon." Beyond the blankness that's all he can distinguish Lee says "I think you'll want to talk to Ruth Nyman."

His eyes struggle open, and sunlight blazes in. He feels as if his blinks leave no room between them for long words. "Is she here?"

"Not even on her way. I mean you'll have something to tell her. When you're ready I'll show you."

Alex flings the duvet aside and sits on the edge of the bed, where the increasingly less faint pain in his skull takes a moment to follow him. "I'm as ready as I'll ever be."

Lee hands him her phone without speaking. The screen shows an item from a newspaper reporting from Northampton. Retired limousine driver Malcolm Randall has been charged with making and possessing indecent images of children. Making means downloading, Alex is sufficiently awake to grasp. Several hundred of the most serious kind have been found on his computer, and many videos as well. "So," Alex says, "we've got to the truth at last."

It leaves him feeling oddly hollow, as if the memories to which he clung on Carl's behalf have deserted him. Or have they all departed? He has a sense that at least one has lingered for some reason, though it's out of reach. He gives Lee her phone and grabs his from the bedside table. "You're right, I should call Ruth."

Lee lets him have a wryly slanted smile. "Don't you think you ought to get dressed first?"

"I've nothing to hide. I'll just be a voice. I want to tell her the truth as soon as I can now I can."

"I'll leave the two of you alone and put some coffee on."

Why should he mean her not to hear the conversation? As Ruth's number rings he switches to loudspeaker and plants both pillows at his back so as to stretch his legs along the bed. He has only just sat against the headboard when Ruth says "I was hoping to hear from you, Mr Grand."

"Before we start, please do call me Alex."

"If that's your preference." Like a denial of the name she says "As I said—"

"You know why I'm calling."

"I should prefer to be told."

Hasn't she heard about Randall, or is this professional caution? Alex can be indirect too. "Will Carl have sent you the death certificate?"

"I've had nothing from him, and he isn't answering my calls."

"I'd better tell you I don't think you'll be seeing that certificate."

"Why not?"

This sounds like an accusation that reaches no further than Alex. "If you haven't heard the news," he says, "it's all good. Malcolm Randall is alive, but he's been arrested for child porn."

She's silent long enough for Alex to wonder if she heard, and then she says "Have you any idea how much of the book is inaccurate?"

"Obviously all the passages about his death. And the woman who claimed she was Hilary, yes, she's his daughter."

This time Ruth's silence is shorter, but it feels close to physical. "We need to discuss this here as soon as possible."

"When would you like me?"

"This afternoon would be ideal."

"Carl could never make that."

"I don't want him involved at this stage. Please don't communicate with him until we've spoken further. Are you able to accommodate this afternoon?"

"I'll be on my way," Alex says and heads for the kitchen, bearing his headache. "Did you hear all that, Lee?"

"I thought you didn't want me to. You'd have brought it in here if you had."

"Of course I did. Who else is there I'd want to hear?" When she only hands him a mug that begins an invisible quotation he says "I've been summoned. I'll take this in the shower and grab something at the station to have on the train."

Lee drives him to the station, where she gives him a token kiss and scrutinises his face. "Maybe be careful what you say."

"You'd like to be there to edit me, would you?"

"I heard some of you on the phone before." As he thinks of asking her to be specific Lee says "And you were talking in your sleep again."

"Any sense this time?"

"Something about somebody behind you and not wanting them to get in."

"Is that really what I said, the actual words?"

"I'm sorry if I'm not doing my job properly. That's how I remember it, but I wasn't too awake myself."

Alex leaves her with another kiss to compensate for the tiff and runs to buy a ticket for the train. There's more of a queue than the time of day led him to expect, and it's led by a slowly loquacious fellow in search of a considerable amount of information. When Alex dodges to the adjoining queue, this proves more sluggish still. By the time he has the ticket the train is about to depart, and a sprint only just takes him aboard. In any case the senseless stuff Lee said he released in his sleep has left him feeling cut off from any appetite.

As the glass lift at Tiresias raises him to the fourteenth floor – at least, that's what it calls itself – pedestrians withdraw their tortoise heads into their dwindling bodies. Rod greets him with his standard smile and ducks towards the microphone to murmur "Alex Grand is here." Alex has scarcely taken a seat by a table still laid with a copy of *When I Was Carla*, its cover somewhat tattered now, when Ruth strides along the corridor. "That's best elsewhere, I think," she says, seizing the book. "We're in my office."

The room might have been organised to demonstrate precision. Identical bookcases laden with bound sets of legal tomes face each other across a white desk so slim it resembles a sketch of one. It bears a computer and a phone and a thin stack of papers. All these items are aligned with the edges of the desk. Ruth's chair stands at the exact midpoint of the far side, and two equally austere white chairs are placed opposite, separated by the width of hers. Kirsty is sitting on the left one, and sends Alex a quick smile that seems somehow out of place, perhaps less welcoming than usual because she isn't in her own office. "Do we need that?" she asks Ruth.

"No need to draw attention to it just now."

"I think Alex will have noticed you've got it."

"The attention of visitors," Ruth says with a look that has scant time for patience. "I'd like it kept out of their sight until all issues are resolved."

Alex can't help asking Kirsty "Are you in detention as well?"

Ruth sits hard on her chair and squares the book with the corners of the desk as though to demonstrate she's ignoring misbehaviour. "I trust we're here as a team."

"I'm sure we are," Kirsty says. "So you've sorted out what's really what, Alex."

"I'll conduct the interview." Ruth is already looking at Alex. "Have you read the reports about Malcolm Randall?"

"That's why I got in touch with you. Lee found one."

"She's your line editor. I assume you noticed her mistake."

"I can't imagine her making any. Accuracy's her middle name."

"Somewhat ironic when the name was the error."

"I don't know what you mean, and she's not here to defend herself."

"Randall, Alex," Kirsty says. "You spelled it wrong in the book."

"That was how it's spelt on the certificate Carl faked. Another way to stop us finding Randall."

"Wouldn't he have wanted Randall to be caught?"

It's Kirsty who asks, and Alex feels he has lost his only supporter. "Maybe he didn't want him arrested until the book was out and people knew about him. Or maybe he thought Randall might try to stop us publishing."

"How likely do you think that would have been?" Ruth may not even want to know.

"It doesn't matter what I think. I don't have Carl's thoughts," Alex says with all the conviction he can find, "so you should ask him."

"I intend to speak to him, but I've been unable to make contact since our visit. I take it you've had none."

"He got in touch. That's how I knew about Randall."

Ruth lifts her head, confronting Alex with more of her blank face while she keeps her gaze on him. "You knew he was alive in advance of the reports. Why wasn't I informed?"

"Carl may feel closer to Alex than us, do you think? Since they've shared so many memories, I mean."

"Not so close it sets you against Tiresias, I trust. I very much hope we're on the same page." Before Alex has a chance to answer Ruth says "I was asking why you failed to keep me posted."

"I wanted to make sure of the truth first. I thought we'd all been taken in enough."

"Establishing the truth is my job, particularly in this kind of situation. May I ask exactly what you did?"

"I had Hilary take me to visit her parents."

"You must certainly have realised I wouldn't have wanted you to act by yourself. It could easily have prejudiced the situation. At the very least you should have contacted me beforehand."

"Look, I'm the one who told lies I didn't realise I was telling. I was desperate to get the truth straight in my head."

"This has never been just about you, Alex." Ruth makes his name sound like an afterthought she has to remember to have. "And are you sure you're able to identify the truth? You've shown yourself to be rather the reverse."

"It wasn't only me. Carl deceived Kirsty as well."

Too late Alex hears himself undermining her reputation. Perhaps she means to distract Ruth from this by saying "Can you tell us about Randall? What was he like?"

"As plausible as you'd expect. He had me pretty well convinced he'd behaved himself until the police showed up. Carl wouldn't thank me for saying so, but I think he takes after the man."

Kirsty turns to him so vigorously it twists her chair out of alignment with Ruth's desk. "You were there when they arrested him."

"Just when they seized his computer."

"That would do, Ruth, wouldn't it? We can say Alex was there when Randall was brought to justice. Did you do anything to help that, Alex?"

"To be truthful, it was Carl."

"What was?" Ruth is impatient to hear.

"He told the police to search the computer."

"You knew that in advance."

"I'm guessing it was him. Somebody told them, and who else could it have been?"

"You, Alex."

Kirsty's answer disconcerts him more than he's prepared for. "I just said it wasn't."

"It could have been, couldn't it, if you're saying it was anonymous?"

"I don't imagine Carl told the police his name, but I think he'd object if we put mine in. I suspect he's had enough of me pretending to be him."

"Maybe you should ask him. If he agrees it wouldn't do our book any harm, or your rep either."

"I think you'll be best advised," Ruth says, "to stay well clear of anything except the truth."

"I wouldn't have felt comfortable claiming I made the call, Kirsty."

"Is there anything else I should know about Randall?" Ruth says.

"Just that I wouldn't be surprised if he carries on insisting he never touched Carla."

"We'll need to keep a close eye on developments." Her gaze makes him feel these may include him. "We must have a plan of action," she says, "by the time the inaccuracies in the book become public. We'll present them in terms of Randall's arrest, since that will instigate the coverage."

She rises to her feet, propping her fingertips on the desk, and Kirsty stands up like a bid for imitation. "Please make certain you don't issue any statements without consulting me first," Ruth says, and after a distinct pause "Alex."

He's provoked to retort "Is that all I travelled here for?"

"I trust you agree that the book and everybody's credibility is worth at least that much of your time." She continues not to blink as she says "Or have you anything else I ought to hear?"

"I wouldn't say so."

"Please let me know if you remember something. Will you see yourself out? Your editor and I have matters to discuss."

If Rod looks at him, he has ceased doing so by the time Alex leaves the corridor. As the lift descends, heads swell like hirsute balloons on Euston Road. The matrix display has just rearranged its fiery crimson sticks into a single digit when Alex's mobile jerks in his pocket. "Lee," it mutters.

Before Alex has time to speak Lee says "Are you at Tiresias?"

"On my way out. Of the building, I mean."

"You may want to go back, Alex."

"I'm hoping I'll be doing that," he says, only to realise "You mean now?"

"There's something else you'll have to tell them. I'm sorry, I should have noticed it was wrong." As Alex makes to reassure her, which feels like trying to reassure himself in advance, Lee says "I'm afraid there's another fabrication in the book."

ALEX

"Why didn't you tell them, Alex?"

"I wanted to be sure before I did. It has to be the truth this time or I won't be giving it to them."

"How can you be any surer?"

"I'd like to see the evidence you said you found."

"I could have sent you that while you were there."

"And I want to hear what Carl has to say for himself."

"That can't change anything, can it? They'll still have to know."

"No doubt, but let's listen to him first." In fact Alex hopes Lee is mistaken; the book and his sense of it have been undermined more than enough. "Just remind me how you came to your conclusion," he says.

"You know how you can feel there's something wrong at the back of your mind. You can't tell what, but it won't leave you alone."

Alex doesn't want to feel that way, especially since he does. "Go on."

"While you were in town I was going through the book to see how much we'll have to change. I've made a lot of notes."

"I'll look at them, but just stay with what you rang about."

"I read that part and at first I couldn't see what was wrong with it, but I kept going back because I felt something was."

"No need to go into all this detail." Once again Alex is disturbed by the resemblance to how his own mind works. "Say what made you realise," he urges.

"You did ask me to tell you the process." Almost as reproachfully Lee says "I think to begin with it was how Carl stops short of describing what the priest did to him."

"Ruth brought that up. He said he didn't want to put his name to porn."

"But he tells us all about how Randall abused him, and not just once in the book. That got me wondering, and I looked up the reports about this Father Brendan."

"He was convicted of abusing several children."

"Not children, Alex. I mean, yes, children, but all boys."

Alex's immediate response is to think Carl was male as well. He wasn't at the time, and Alex fends off the mistake once more, which feels like dislodging a false memory. "He might still have taken advantage of girls," he protests, "if he had the chance."

"Except there's evidence he didn't when he had."

"You never mentioned that." A suspicion that his memory may have let him down makes Alex add "Did you?"

"I only found it while you were on your way home," Lee says and searches on her phone before handing it to him.

It shows an item from a Merseyside newspaper. After the priest was convicted, several women who thought they should have been called as character witnesses came forward to testify on his behalf. Although he'd taken them for catechism and confirmation classes, they declared that they had always felt safe and had never even been touched, except – one said – "in my soul." Alex feels compelled to search for disagreements, but finds none. "I wouldn't call this evidence," he says. "It's like insisting just because something didn't happen to you it couldn't have happened to anyone."

"How much more do you need, Alex? Nobody contradicted them that I can find. Are you determined to think he abused Carla? It isn't as if he did it to you."

"Doesn't it matter if he did to her?"

"You've already said he did. You've told everyone who read the book. Don't you want to know whether you're telling the truth?"

"Lee, if you feel you're implicated—"

"It's you I'm concerned about, Alex."

This leaves him feeling vulnerable rather than supported. "What do you need to be concerned about?"

"Your image, if you like. Accusing someone falsely isn't going to look too good. It's partly my fault whatever you say. I should have wondered why the police haven't prosecuted the man for what Carl said he did."

"Maybe they're putting the case together. We don't even know if they've spoken to Carl."

"Then you're right, it's time you spoke to him."

Alex thrusts the phone at her and takes out his. Well after Carl's must have announced him, the ringtone continues to repeat itself. He's no longer expecting an answer by the time Carl says "All right, Alex. Meant to ring you when I got the chance."

Since Lee looks poised to comment, Alex puts a finger to her lips. "What about?"

"I don't know if you saw we fixed Randall."

"I did see, yes."

"You don't sound too pleased about it."

"I've no reason not to be, have I? I'm just wondering how it was done."

"Someone must have told the law about him."

"Who would that have been?"

"Shouldn't think they said."

"Kirsty wanted me to say it was me."

"Been talking to her, have you?"

"Yes, and Ruth."

A silence suggests Carl is about to terminate the call, but then he says "So do it. I don't care."

"About what?"

"Talk to them all you want and say you phoned the police too if you like. All I care about is they've got Randall."

"You think that's fixed the book as well."

"We'll need to change the bits about him being dead, won't we? And the funeral. And then the publishers will have to bring it out again, so that won't do us any harm."

"Something else might, though."

"She'd better keep it shut or she won't like what we write about her."

"Not Hilary, but we'll need to discuss how to include her."

"Don't want her in."

"We'll have to talk to Ruth and Kirsty about that."

"Don't see what it's got to do with them." Before Alex can respond Carl says "If you didn't mean her, who?"

"Your priest. Father Brendan."

Another silence sounds like Carl's only answer until he says "What about that sod?"

"We've been looking at the media reports. I imagine you'd have seen them at the time."

"I saw he was put away, and I hope he's still getting what he deserves."

"Because of what exactly, Carl?"

"Told you once. You don't need it again."

Lee points at the phone and then twirls her finger. Why is she indicating that Alex should cut the call short? No, she means Carl may be wary of being recorded. Just the same Alex says "I wonder if you read what several women said about him."

"What would they know? He'd never have gone after them."

Alex tries not to sound surprised. "You're admitting that."

"Admitting what? He only went for kids."

"That's what these women were when they were with him, and they said they felt absolutely safe around him."

"So they were lucky bitches. Even if he never touched them doesn't let them say he didn't touch anyone else."

Alex has a disconcerting sense that a paraphrase of his own words has been returned to him. "No other girls said he did either."

"What are you trying to get at?"

"Are you saying you were the only one?"

"Maybe he could tell I didn't want to be a girl. And maybe you want to remember the rest that you put in my book."

Alex feels exposed, since he has no idea how he's being attacked. "Which was that?"

"He knew what Randall did to me and never told a soul."

"Isn't that how confession is supposed to work, though?"

"Then it bloody oughtn't when it protects swines like him. And I'll tell you something else, those bitches aren't the only ones who'd say he never touched girls."

"I don't think they quite said that. Who do you have in mind?"

"Who do you think? Him," Carl says with enough disgust to be aiming some at Alex. "If he owns up he'll only get himself more time in jail."

"I understood he pleaded guilty when he was taken to court."

"Maybe now he's wishing he didn't. It never saved him from going inside."

"It would have lessened his sentence. That's how it works, and so surely—"

Alex hears a mumble near Carl's phone, so muffled that he can't distinguish a word or even the gender. "Waiting now, is she?" Carl says. "Got to hit the road, Alex. Fare wants me. Speak to you again."

As Alex stares at the vacated phone Lee says "Who do you think that was?"

He isn't sure why the question disconcerts him so much. "Carl, of course."

"Both of them."

"Him and his receptionist."

"You don't think it was just him. That's what it sounded like to me."

"What would be the point of that?"

"To avoid dealing with the issues you were raising. All he did was confirm he'd been lying."

"I'm not sure we know that."

"You could hear it in his voice. I think he's so used to not telling the truth that it takes more effort not to lie. Maybe he'd rather have the memories you invented for him than his actual experiences."

Alex doesn't care for the suggestion. "I didn't put them in his head. That's where they came from."

"More like he put them in yours."

He finds this equally unappealing. "If anyone's confusing me just now it's you."

"It shouldn't be." She keeps up a reproachful look while she says "Carl as good as admitted he accused the priest because the man kept Randall's secret."

"As good as isn't evidence."

"And we aren't in court, so we don't need that. Can you honestly tell me you still believe Carl?"

Alex tries not to feel she wants to rob him of a memory whose removal might uncover what it hid. It's Carl's if it's anyone's, and no part of him. "About some things we have to," he says.

"There's just no reason to believe Carl was the only girl the priest abused."

"Unless you think Carl was right and the man could sense he didn't care for who he was."

"I don't. Carl never said he felt that way at the time."

"He did say he felt he always had when he came to the decision."

"Did he? You remember more than me." This sounds unnecessarily accusing. "Besides," Lee says, "that's nothing like the same."

"Let's agree we can't be certain what actually happened."

"I don't agree, Alex. I think you're risking your reputation. Suppose someone else spots the discrepancy?"

"Not many people read as closely as you do." When she looks rebuffed he says "And I don't know why we'd want to risk helping a paedophile get out of jail."

"Now you're sounding just like Carl."

"That's not true and you know it, or don't you care for accuracy any more? I thought that was your job."

"No need to be so fierce about it. I'm not at work all the time, you know. Why don't you call Ruth and let her decide what should be done."

"I don't think Carl would be too happy if I did, and we still have to collaborate on the rewrite."

"You can rewrite by yourself if you have to, can't you? Ask Ruth about that too."

"It's Carl's tale. It's none of mine."

As he searches for a way to end the discussion, which is disturbing him more than he understands, his phone rings and names Kirsty. "There's your chance," Lee urges.

"Alex, have you been in touch with Carl? I've just had an email from him."

Despite how Lee's gaze advises him to respond, he says only "Concerning what?"

"What we were discussing. That's why I wondered if you'd been in touch."

Now his memory feels undependable. "What were we discussing?" he's anxious to recall.

"Who called the police about Randall. Carl says he's happy if we say you did."

"I don't know if I am." He's reassured by adding "I'm sure Ruth won't be."

"She's going to decide once the book's revised and we've worked out a press release."

Alex feels let down by the lawyer. In a bid to cling to professionalism he says "When will you need the rewrite?"

"End of the month at the latest. I should get together with Carl while he's in the mood he seems to be in."

For a moment Alex fancies she's proposing to work with Carl, which leaves him with no sense of himself. "Let me know how you get on," Kirsty says. "That was all unless you've anything."

"I'll be in touch when there's reason," Alex says and ends the call. He braces himself for Lee's protest, knowing that he'll have no answer, but when she simply gazes sadly at him he feels as if he has silenced a voice.

CARLY AND ALEX

"What's she doing here?"

Father Brendan held up a hand and stared at her between the bridal couple. "Mrs Randall?"

"Her at the back. She never wanted to be your daughter, Malcolm, and now look at her. She's made sure she isn't mine."

If she was going to forget she was in a church, I could. "Mum," I said loud enough for an echo to send my voice back.

Anyone who hadn't already turned to look did. Hilary put on an expression like a smile turned upside down, and the podgy red-haired bridegroom's pale face looked as if it was searching for a reaction she'd approve of. I was the only one to see Father Brendan's hand

"We know she said all that, but do we need to keep the other business in?"

"She did if you say, only why are you saying we know? Maybe I don't remember all of it."

"Because she told me she did when I met her."

"Fair enough. So what do you mean, the other business?"

"The gesture you say the priest made."

"Don't remember saying. You asked what he did when I shouted out, and you thought it was the kind of thing he might have done."

"In that case I think it's best omitted."

"Don't care about that bit so long as everybody knows about him."

I was the only one to see Father Brendan thrust out a hand as if to ward me off. "Don't you dare to call me that," my mother shouted. "I won't say another word while that's in the church."

Some of the drivers, though not Norm, began to stand up.

Reluctantly or otherwise, they looked as if they were preparing to throw me out of the wedding. "Don't do anything you'll regret," I told them. "I'll leave because I want to."

"Defiant even in God's house," my mother cried as I left the pew. "Always wanting to have the last word even when nobody wants to hear."

"That's right." I had my back to everyone now, but I heard my voice where they were. "You never did want to listen to me."

"We don't want you," Hilary declared. "You never were my sister and now you're even less of one. You shouldn't even be in a church."

"Now now, dear," her man murmured as what she'd said made me turn round. He reached for her arm but didn't touch it, as if he thought he shouldn't till they were married. "We mustn't speak for God."

"Well said, Herbert," Randall told him. "Even the worst of us can find their way back to God, can't they, father?"

"She won't be finding her way back to us," my mother declared. "I'll talk while she's listening even if she pretends she's not. Malcolm took her on and treated her like family and hardly ever got a thank you, and you'd have thought saying it hurt her like having a child. You know that's true, Malcolm, so don't try to hush me. I want the truth to be heard at last, and God's known it all along. Malcolm did his best for her like the saint he always was, but she'd have made you think he was doing her some kind of harm, even when he was trying to get her ready for confession. No, Malcolm, I'm having all my say. He put himself out to find her a special present for her eighteenth, and she threw it back in his face. He gave her the best job he could find that she'd have been able to do, and when she'd learned everything he had to teach her she took it to the men who'd done the dirty on him...."

I'd shut the door behind me by now, but I heard her voice all the way to the taxi. I imagined she went on about me even when I couldn't hear any longer. The limousine and all the black cabs looked to me as if the occasion ought to be a funeral. I was tempted to turn back and confront my mother, but I'd had more than enough, and I told myself I was leaving Randall behind and everyone connected with him. A tender rain was in the air, and it felt as though it was washing me clean.

"So it was Hilary who said you oughtn't to be in a church, not your mother."

"Right, her. I want everyone to know what both those bitches said."

"And what was the priest doing while your mother had her rant?"

"You didn't ask last time. Why are you now?"

"I suppose I thought it was dramatic as it stood."

"So why don't you still?"

"Because we need to make the book as accurate as possible in all the circumstances. Didn't Father Brendan try to intervene?"

"Expect he didn't care when she wasn't talking about him."

"You're saying he let her carry on like that in his church."

"Maybe he tried to shut her up. How would I know?" Before Alex can interrogate this – it makes him feel he can't trust his own mind either – Carl says "I'd gone out, remember? You know as much about it as me."

"That's a point." Alex is anxious to regain control of every aspect of the book. "Since you weren't there—"

"Who says I wasn't? You're not going to believe those bitches or that swine over me."

"They've said nothing about it to me. I'm suggesting we shouldn't speculate about what happened once you left the church."

"We know what they were all like and the kind of crap they'd get up to."

"I just think it's inadvisable to mention you imagined anything."

"Listen, pal, I didn't. You did."

At once Alex's mind feels vulnerable if not unfamiliar. "What did I imagine?"

Carl leans back in his chair behind the desk, dislodging a mirthful grunt. "You said I imagined how my mother would go on shooting her mouth off about me."

Alex is disturbed to find he can't recall who suggested it. "If it was my idea you won't mind if I remove it."

"Why don't you say I heard her going on but I couldn't make out what she said."

"Is that what happened?"

"It's what I'm telling you," Carl says and stares at him.

Alex notes it on his phone despite feeling it will render the book doubtful. "Do you reckon you've thought of everything now?" Carl says. "I need to ask you about some stuff." Apparently in case Alex proposes to leave, though Alex is only pocketing his phone, Carl adds "I've helped you, now you help me."

"I rather thought it was mutual. It's your book as well."

"Nearly all mine, you mean."

"What are you saying isn't yours?"

"That's what I want you to help me with. I need to know for when I go to court."

Alex feels he may not want to know "About what?"

"Who's it always been about, for Christ's sake? Malcolm scummy Randall. I'll have to be a witness."

"When?"

"They haven't said yet, but it sounds like soon." Any respite this may offer vanishes when Carl adds "I need to be sure what happened. Him and those bitches, they'll all be saying I'm a liar."

With mounting reluctance Alex says "What aren't you sure of?"

"Your friend the lawyer got me started with her stuff about the petrol pump."

"I think it was you that brought up the issue, not Ruth."

"I notice you don't say she's not your friend." Before Alex can do so Carl insists "Doesn't matter who started it. I've talked about Randall making me hold it till it feels like remembering it, but I reckon that's just you."

"I don't remember it." The suggestion leaves Alex determined to fix his sense of his own mind. "I remember how you described it to me," he says, "and that's what's in the book."

"Anyway, your friend said that bit didn't matter. People might spot some other stuff that's wrong, though. Someone did."

"What?" Alex feels reduced to monosyllables. "Who?"

"Some of my drivers don't think the police were using their sirens that much then."

This seems to refer to a memory Alex can't reach. "As much as what when?"

"As you made out they did when Randall used to come in my room. That was definitely your idea, them reminding me how my real dad died and me wanting them to rescue me but they never did."

"I'm quite certain some of that came from you, Carl."

"Yeah, well, it's your word against mine."

"It's not a contest. It shouldn't be." When Carl's expression stays combative Alex retorts "I could check the evidence if somebody hadn't destroyed my computer."

"Maybe that's another thing the bitch was after, getting us at each other's throats."

Could Hilary have sent the virus after all? While Alex isn't so sure any longer that Carl did, the uncertainty is far from reassuring, and his doubts won't even let him accuse the man. "Got to tell you," Carl says, "some of the stuff you made up feels more like memories than my real ones. Must mean you're a good writer."

Just now Alex can't think of any compliment he would welcome less. "So you'll want me to take the sirens out," he says.

"Don't know yet. We'll have to think. We don't want Randall's lawyer seeing it and trying to make out I'm a liar. Depends which comes first, court or the book."

"If it's the court they couldn't reopen the case for anything as trivial as that."

"They might for the other thing."

Alex resents how this is designed to make him ask "Which?"

"What you tried to say Randall did in the bathroom."

"You said all of that. It came from you."

"Him getting in the bath with me never did."

"I thought he might have, but don't bother about it. It isn't in the book."

"Forget it, then." As Alex hopes he can Carl says "I know what you can do for me."

Alex is by no means eager to discover "What?"

"Question me like they do in court, like they do to the detective in your book."

This has to be the novel he dismissed when they first met. Might he indeed have thought he could improve Alex's work, as Lee suggested? Carl's remark leaves Alex more unsure than ever, and he tries to lose himself in his latest role. "Very well, Mr Batchelor," he says. "You've told the court that Malcolm Randall used to bathe you when you were a child."

"That's what he did all right," Carl says, sniggering at their performance. "Except I wasn't just a child, I was a girl."

"What difference are you suggesting that made?"

"Men oughtn't to be handling a little girl like that, specially when they're not even her real dad."

"What do you mean by handling, Mr Batchelor?"

"Touching. What do you think?"

"Please be more specific. Touching how?"

"How he shouldn't. You know good and well."

"I'm sorry, but I must insist on the precise details. Where exactly were you touched?"

"Even if he didn't touch me there you could tell he wanted to. I never said he did in my book."

"If he simply bathed you, what are you saying was the problem? Mrs Randall has testified that her husband took over the task because bearing her second child had left her infirm."

"That's what the bitch would say for sure. It's my fault I had that swine all over me, nothing to do with her precious daughter."

"Mr Batchelor, I'm the judge. Please confine yourself to answering counsel's questions."

"You're a whole lot of people, aren't you? Wonder sometimes if you know who you really are." Carl's version of a laugh has no time for mirth. "Maybe he just bathed me, but I knew what the dirty shit was thinking," he declares. "And he didn't just do that, he watched me piss."

"Was that before or after the bath?"

"Who the fuck's going to say it matters?" When Alex remains ominously solemn Carl says "Must have been before. I wouldn't have pissed in it even if it would have turned that bastard on."

"Please refrain from speculating, Mr Batchelor. Who would run the bath?"

"Him. Mr Daddy. Saint Malcolm."

"You're referring to the defendant. So having run the bath or while he did, Mr Randall would wait for you to use the toilet before he bathed you."

"What are you trying to make me sound like, Alex? Better remember it was you that wrote it all down, not me. If I get done by the court they'll do you as well."

"I'm simply doing as you asked. You may have to deal with a lot worse when you're cross-examined."

"And maybe they won't ask about it. Maybe they're not as clever as you think you are." As Alex hears the echo of an accusation Carl's mother used to aim at him Carl demands "Did your dad ever do that to you?"

"I hardly think so, but—"

"Then just leave it in the book the way it is. And I want to put in Hilary never helped me when she should."

"So long as Ruth and Kirsty approve it. Is there anything else you should tell me?"

"Not that I know of right now. If anything comes in my head I'll give you a bell."

Alex has to hope Carl isn't withholding any information out of pique. The man's face stays sullenly uncommunicative as Alex takes his leave. When Alex joins the first of the motorways home he recalls the discussion as vividly as if he's playing it back. Headlights glare at him out of the dark, and they might almost be searching his mind for a memory – a remark Carl made that has left him nervous of grasping what it means to himself. He hasn't identified it by the time he starts nodding over the wheel and pulls into the next service area for a nap.

He wakens two hours later in a taxi, dismayed to have let down whichever customer he should have collected by now, and has to struggle to remind himself who he is and where. It feels too much like telling himself a story, except that he's seeking wakefulness rather than sleep. Eventually he decides he's alert enough to drive, and reaches home long after midnight. Lee is fast asleep, and soon he is, which means it's almost noon before he sees what Hilary Wilson has said about him on Twitter.

ALEX AND ALEXANDER

Cking ppl 2 b charactr witnesses 4 Malcolm Randall. Ran Reliablest Cars in Wallasey. Adoptd daughter says he abusd her. She got man she trickd in2 writing book about her arrestd 4 trying 2 warn him. Pls contact @hilwls if u can help my fathr Malcolm Randall.

"Is that Ruth on the phone, Alex?"

"I'm just looking at Hilary's post again. I still can't tell if it was malicious."

"Ruth hasn't been in touch yet."

"Maybe she's still in her meeting."

"You're sure she knows you tried to contact her."

"Her mobile's off, but Rod put me through to her desk and I left a message."

"You don't think you should have gone to see her while we're in London."

"Perhaps we can later. Imagine how my father would react if we'd cancelled lunch on the day."

"I know, but we shouldn't put off things we'd rather avoid doing. You didn't confront Carl about making trouble for you either."

"He's quite a lot of that, but any in particular?"

"What Hilary Randall said he did," Lee says, halting on the uphill pavement to turn her concerned face to Alex. "Telling the police you were there to help her father."

"I was waiting to see if Carl would own up. I was there to sort the book out, and starting an argument wouldn't have helped." When Lee withholds her answer Alex says "Besides, he might have been afraid Randall would destroy the evidence when I showed up. He could just have been making sure the police arrived in time."

"You sound as if you're thinking for him, maybe like him."

"I'm just trying to think how he thinks," Alex says, though it feels more compulsive than he cares for. "It comes with the job."

"Then let's hope it goes away soon."

Rather than respond, Alex heads uphill. They haven't reached his parents' house when several sirens begin howling in the distance. Even if they're speeding in the same direction, it feels as if they're receding towards various points of the compass, tugging his mind with them. He could fancy it's about to part, revealing some buried material. Surely he's remembering *When I Was Carla*, and he says "Some of Carl's men don't think he would have heard so many sirens as a child."

"That's nothing to do with me, Alex. You didn't want it to be."

They're in the front porch now, but his finger falters short of the doorbell. "I don't recall saying anything about it."

"You hardly let me touch the book because you said it was Carl's voice and the way he remembered his life."

"Are you certain I called it his voice? I wrote the thing, after all."

"You used exactly those words. I haven't edited that either."

The front door is hauled open, and Alex realises one reason he hesitated was a dread of hearing his father pronounce the sound of the doorbell. His mother produces the hope of a smile as she says "Dear me, are we having our first tiff?"

"Not the first," Lee tells her.

"Then I trust it and its like can be left outside," Alex's father says as he appears in the doorway of the front room. "Will the guests have a drink before dining? The meal is as it should be. Amy advises me I omitted some element last time, and so she's today's chef."

Is it concentration that contracts his face? As he leans all his weight on a corkscrew in the front room his features, already compact, look determined to draw closer together. When the cork loses its hold at last, his wife snatches the latest issue of *Continuity* from beside the bottle on the low table. "When are you going to raise your sights again, Alexander?"

"I think he keeps them pretty high," Lee says.

"Full marks for loyalty," Alex's father says, "but you must see his reputation would be helped by an appearance in our journal."

Alex doesn't speak until he and Lee have taken a glass of falanghina each to the colourless leather couch. "I won't be submitting just now, I'm afraid. I've nearly finished a new novel, and I'm still dealing with the Carla book."

His father lowers himself into an armchair, supporting himself with both hands despite gripping his full glass with one. "Has that not been laid to rest yet?" he complains.

"I'm revising it for a new edition."

"How much longer are we likely to be required to live with it?"

"I think Alex is having to do that," Lee says, "not us."

Perhaps his mother means to intervene by asking "What revisions are those?"

"Not much else you could have checked," Alex tells Lee. "Even Carl isn't sure of some of it. We couldn't agree what Randall may have used to do to him in the bathroom."

"If you start giving us the details," his mother protests, "I for one won't feel like eating."

"I suggest we go through before it becomes too disgusting," says his father.

As he thrusts himself to his feet his glass trembles on the arm of the chair, threatening to spatter wine even if the stem doesn't snap. "I'm perfectly fine," he insists when his wife makes to steady the glass. Though he's the slowest of the party, he insists on preceding everyone into the dining-room, and Alex thinks his determined back view suggests some kind of denial. As Alex follows his mother Lee murmurs "Are you hoping they won't hear about Randall?"

"I'll get to it," he says lower still, and his mother turns her head an alert inch.

He senses she's waiting for him to speak while he helps her carry the lunch from the kitchen. No doubt she refrains from prompting him because she wants his father to hear. Once Alex and Lee have finished enthusing over the meal – poached seabass, boiled potatoes, salad just about sprinkled with dressing, a repast Alex gathers is designed to quieten his father's stomach – he says to his parents "You aren't on Twitter, are you?"

"That's the home of all the fashionable neologisms and abbreviations, is it not?" In case this has failed to make his aversion sufficiently plain his father says "We prefer to have recourse to the whole of the language."

"I should tell you what it's saying about me, but I have to explain something first." With a laugh that he doesn't intend to be nervous Alex says "Malcolm Randall's still alive."

"Then he shouldn't be," his mother says. "How can he be?"

"Are you saying the fellow who hired you to write his book told you a lie?"

"Several." Rather than argue about hiring, Alex says "The daughter is alive as well."

"In that case," his father says more enthusiastically than Alex appreciates, "perhaps his entire tale is an invention."

"I started thinking that myself, but we're both wrong. Randall was guilty all right. As he would put it, as guilty as sin."

"Perhaps you should take care what you say, Alexander. You might be risking libel."

"He's hardly doing that," Lee says. "Certainly not here."

"Ever the editor and alert for errors. May we hear the basis of your accusation, Alexander?"

"The police found child porn on his computer."

As the old man digs his fork so deep into a potato that the tines scrape the plate, Alex's mother says "Please leave that to our imagination."

"I didn't see it, though I was there."

His father projects some of a mouthful onto the plate and wipes his lips with the back of a hand before Alex's mother can reach for his napkin. "You were where?"

"At the Randall house when the police searched it."

"And are we to be told what took you there? Were you establishing whether you'd killed the father?"

"That's an odd way to put it, Gordon," Lee says.

"Indeed, it's mine. Unfashionable, no doubt, but honest. Are you telling us your presence was coincidental, Alexander?"

"As a matter of fact it was, but the daughter doesn't think so. She's as good as saying on Twitter I tried to warn her father."

"You'd never have done that," his mother says.

"Of course not, and I didn't inform the police either, but the publishers may claim I did."

"You would have, wouldn't you?"

"If I'd known what was on his computer? You needn't ask."

His father nods and shuts his eyes as well, which appears to mean he's found a reason to agree with Alex, though it looks like a loss of awareness until he lifts his head again. He blinks at his food and lays down his knife and fork beside the glistening half-exposed skeleton on the plate. "Excuse me, er," he says to Lee.

"It's Lee, Gordon," his wife murmurs.

"I'm conscious of that, thank you. Quite clued up, as I believe they put it. Lee and Amy and Alexander, pray excuse me while I adjourn to the bathroom. Yes, the bathroom."

"Have you finished?" Until she continues it isn't plain that his wife means "Your lunch."

"I believe I am," he says and sends a distracted look back from the hall. "Do proceed without me. It's cold enough."

"He means the food," Alex's mother assures the guests if not herself. They hear the bathroom door shut, and then the only sounds are on the plates, perhaps to cover any noises Alex's father makes. Alex hasn't heard the door reopen when his mother glances past him. "Where are you going, Gordon?"

"For a newspaper in case Alex is in the news."

Alex twists around too late to catch sight of his father. "Don't go now," his mother protests. "I've made your favourite dessert."

"I'm sure I won't be in the paper, dad."

They're apparently too late, since the only answer is the slam of the front door. "Your father's being odd again," Alex's mother says with determined steadiness. "He hasn't been this bad before. Could you go after him? We don't want him getting lost."

"I'll call you if I need to," Alex says, already striding along the hall.

His father is well on the way downhill, walking so precipitately that the slope appears to have robbed him of some control over his progress. Alex is confused to see that he's gripping a large black book under his right arm. "Dad," he calls louder than he thinks the suburb may tolerate.

The old man spins around, and Alex sees the item he's carrying isn't a book. It's a laptop. Turning has unbalanced him, and he staggers backwards several yards before managing to face downhill. As he rushes towards a junction he looks little better than helpless. Alex sprints after him and is about to call to him to wait – to catch hold of the nearest garden wall – when his phone rings and says "Ruth Nyman."

He snatches out the phone without slowing down. "Not now, Ruth."

"It's really quite important. If—"

His father is nearly at the crossroads. Alex shoves the phone into his breast pocket as he shouts "Dad, stop." This only sends his father onwards at a rapid uncontrollable stagger. Alex puts on so much speed that his ears have no room for any sound except his pulse, and he doesn't know where an approaching vehicle may be. He's at least a hundred yards short of his father when the old man reaches the junction. As a van appears beside him, he stumbles off the kerb.

Perhaps the driver doesn't see him or assumes that he's able to halt, because the van speeds across the junction. Grotesquely, Alex finds his brain attempting to decide how relevant or otherwise the logo on the vehicle – **COMPUTERS & ROUTERS** – may be to the situation. He could almost imagine the name has inspired his father to fling the laptop under the wheels as he lurches diagonally across the junction, in front of the van. The laptop splinters, a shrill brittle sound that's followed by a muffled crunch and a gasp like the exhalation of a set of bellows someone's trodden on. These noises are made by an object that flails all its limbs around the right front wheel and then subsides into twitching and stillness. Disbelief or dull incomprehension try to intervene before Alex fully grasps that it's his father.

The van screeches to a stop in the middle of the junction, having dragged its victim by his broken spine. Alex hears a cry behind him up the hill. The plea, if it isn't expressing hopeless despair, resembles his father's name, and it's followed by running footsteps. The pulse in his ears is fiercer than ever, but he has to call an ambulance. He pulls out the phone, only to realise he neglected to switch it off. "Are you able to talk yet?" says Ruth.

ALEXANDER AND ALEX

"Won't you come and sit down somewhere, Mrs Grand?"

Several members of the hushed audience that has emerged from nearby houses murmur in agreement or make gestures signifying offers, but she says "I'm sitting. I'm where I want to be."

She's seated in the middle of the junction with her shoulders pressed against the van, which the driver has backed up just enough to free her husband's corpse. She's holding one dead hand in both of hers and gazing straight ahead at the empty slope of the road. Alex is sure her behaviour is postponing the onset of shock. Perhaps she feels as he does, as brittle as the shattered laptop, which the van only just avoided running over twice. His dry mouth tastes metallic, and the repetitive tic of a pulse has settled into his neck. He's barely aware that Lee is gripping his hand, more tightly as his mother speaks again. "I want to get everything clear while it's fresh in our minds," she says. "I want that for Gordon's sake."

The police have arrived, but not the ambulance. Most of them are closing off the roads with tape while the officer who tried to coax Alex's mother stays with her. He's a broad fellow, not least his deceptively youthful face, where the network of lines incised on his forehead betray his age and no doubt his experience. "Won't you question us?" she urges him.

Alex finds her resolve not to let this sound like a plea makes it more painful to hear. Lee squeezes his hand and releases it so as to crouch beside his mother. She keeps her eyes on his mother's face, and he can't blame her for avoiding the sight of his father, flattened virtually in two by the dent that crosses his body in the region of his heart. "What do you want to hear, Amy?" she murmurs.

"What everybody saw, but this gentleman should ask."

"Ask whom?"

Alex's mother gives her a weak but determined smile that Alex takes to express approval of Lee's grammar. He feels as though the approbation has come too late and in the worst of circumstances. "All of us," she says, "and the gentleman who drove the van."

Alex wonders how much longer she can maintain so much control. He's afraid what its collapse may release. The driver, a tall loose-limbed man whose face has resembled a rounded mask of distress ever since he climbed out of his vehicle, turns towards her and then instead to the policeman. "He threw himself in front of me," he says as though he would rather the widow didn't hear. "I couldn't have stopped in time."

The policeman produces a notebook and copies down the driver's details from his licence. Having noted the man's comments, he considers the remains of the laptop. "At what point did you run over this?"

"He chucked it at me. If it hadn't distracted me I could have stopped sooner."

"You're saying it was thrown directly at you."

"Not at me, at the van. Or more like under it. Looked like he was making sure it was smashed."

Alex's mother lifts her head to him and her hands as well. Perhaps she's unaware of using her husband's lifeless fingers to indicate the driver. "I don't believe it happened in that way," she says with no tone at all.

"Pardon me," the driver says. "You'll excuse me for saying, and I really don't want to upset you, but you did want to know what we saw, and you weren't there."

"I was close enough to see." Perhaps she doesn't realise how fiercely she's grasping her husband's hand, which has turned white. "You were speeding," she insists. "You came out of that road with no thought for anybody but yourself."

The policeman looks poised to ask a question once he has finished scribbling, but it's Lee who speaks. "I don't think he was actually speeding, Amy. Maybe he didn't halt at the junction as long as he might have."

Alex's mother takes some time to switch her gaze to Lee. In a voice as dull as her eyes she says "What else do you not think?"

Lee turns to the policeman and the driver. "It didn't look to me as though Gordon meant to throw the laptop. He tripped over the kerb and it flew out of his hands, I think."

Alex hears more than one of her words grow unsteady, and senses she's confining her emotions for his mother's sake. "He most definitely tripped," his mother says, "and he was going too fast to stop himself. He lost hold of the laptop when he tried."

Alex sees that the policeman prefers to question him and Lee. "Where was he going in such a hurry, do you know?"

"He wasn't in a hurry," Alex's mother protests. "The hill made him seem to be."

"Was he taking the computer to Mr Dodge for repair?"

"Who?" Alex's mother says as if the name is weighing down her brain.

"That's me," the driver says. "Not me. I mean, not to me."

"My mistake," the policeman says, though with a lingering look at the van. "But Mr Grand was taking it to be repaired, is that correct?"

Alex senses that, like him, Lee wants his mother to respond. "He must have been," his mother says.

This doesn't quite satisfy the policeman. "Can I ask what was wrong with it?"

"He didn't tell us." While she has relaxed her grip, Alex wonders if this means she's beginning to lose her grasp of the situation. "He took it away," she says, "the moment he finished his lunch."

"So in fact you're saying he was in a hurry, Mrs Grand."

"To do what?"

"To take it wherever he was going."

"He did that, didn't he?" For a moment her eyes look as if the situation is about to flood them, and then they fasten on Alex, who seems to be the most solid item they can find. "You haven't said anything, Alexander," she complains. "You were closest. Speak up for yourself."

"Alex Grand," he tells the policeman. "I'm, I was their son."

"Which name are you using?"

Alex can only return the man's frown. "Both of them."

"We've always called him Alexander. His father did."

The rebuke is so wistful that Alex finds it hard to speak. "Put my full name. Put Alexander Grand."

"That's Alexander Evelyn Grand," his mother says, "because your father loved Waugh so much."

Alex has begun to feel he may never progress past the obstacle of his identity. The tic in the side of his neck has grown so energetic he thinks it must be visible to the entire silent audience. "All right," he says, "Alexander Evelyn," only to wonder if the policeman may make this the whole of his name. Once the rest of Alex's details are in the book the man says "Please tell me what you saw in your own words."

Who else would they belong to? "It happened as my mother said," Alex hears himself say. "The hill made him go too fast to stop."

He's hoping that he won't be asked about his father's haste. Instead the policeman says "And Mr Dodge?"

"I'm sorry, mother, but I didn't see him speeding, and he did halt at the junction. It looked to me as if he thought dad had managed to as well, and so he started across."

"He shouldn't just have thought," his mother says so bitterly it twists her lips, and strokes his father's hand. "He should have waited to see."

"Maybe I should have at that," the driver admits. "These hills aren't made for anyone like him."

"Like whom?" With a dogged correctness Alex finds as difficult to behold as her fondling his father's limp hand, she says "Such as whom?"

"Don't take it wrong, but like you. Your age."

"You didn't see me stumbling down the hill, did you?" she retorts and grips her husband's hand as though she thinks she has betrayed him.

"We'll need to talk to you again, Mr Dodge," the policeman says and turns to Alex. "What can you tell me about the computer?"

"What do you want to know?"

Alex hopes his hesitation was as unnoticeable as his reluctance has to be. "Did Mr Grand deliberately throw it away?" the policeman says.

"I can't see any reason why he would have."

"I'm asking if you saw him do it."

Alex glances at his father, who might almost be grimacing in heavy-eyed sleep, and hurriedly away again. "I really wouldn't say I did."

Some of the police have returned from taping off the streets, and his interrogator indicates the wreckage of the laptop. "Better bag that," he tells one of them.

She fetches a large transparent bag from her car and collects the remains, down to the last of the fragments that are strewn across the road. Alex's mother watches mutely, caressing her husband's hand, a gesture that reminds Alex of a bid to make a wish. When the policewoman heads for her car with the bag his mother calls "Where are you taking that?"

"Just for examination," the policeman says.

"For what?" she demands and rubs the dead hand harder.

"I'm afraid we need to check there's no illegal content on the disc."

"This is your doing, Alex."

"I don't remember saying there was anything like that."

"You haven't said there couldn't be," she cries and clutches the hand to her breast. "Wasn't getting the Randall man arrested enough for you?"

Alex sees more than one of the police grow alert. "Would somebody like to explain?" his interrogator says.

"Alex was involved in identifying a paedophile," Lee tells him.

"And now he has a taste for it," Alex's mother cries, "he's letting everybody think it's true of his own father."

"Mother, I really didn't say—"

"Then tell everybody there was nothing of the sort on his computer. You know there never could have been. Just you tell them now."

As Alex feels his lips part he can't predict what will emerge, but he has made too many statements that turned out to be false. "I'm certain they'll find nothing, but we can't be absolutely sure until they've searched it, can we? Saying we are won't help now."

"It won't help your father. Never mind about me." She's crushing the limp fingers together, but when Alex stoops to try to disengage her grasp she glares up at him. "Since you won't speak up," she says, "you can go away."

"Mother, won't you let me—"

"Go away from me. Go far away. You aren't our son."

Her voice is rising towards a scream, and Alex is dismayed to think he has made her resemble Carl's mother. As he steps back he gives the policeman a look that may well be imploring. "I have all I need from you for now," the policeman says. "We may be in touch."

Alex's mother shuts her eyes as though to imitate her husband. "Tell me when he's gone. I won't look."

Lee takes Alex's hand as he trudges downhill. While he senses the encouragement she wants to convey, he's distressed by the way the gesture recalls his mother's desperate hold on his father. "Has he gone yet?" he hears his mother wishing aloud. When Lee squeezes his hand he can only respond, though his imitation feels meaninglessly automatic. As a downhill bend takes them out of sight of the fatal scene, she murmurs "I'll call her for you when you think I should if you like."

"I don't know when that's going to be," Alex says, but he's about to thank her – hug her, even – when his phone goes off. "Yes, Ruth," he says with weary resignation.

"I hope it was important, whatever made you cut me off before."

"I think even you might say so."

He waits for her to ask, although confounding her seems unlikely to afford him any pleasure or satisfaction, but she says "Carl Batchelor isn't returning my calls, so I need to speak to you instead."

"I hope I'm an acceptable substitute."

He sees Lee making to counsel him on his response, but plants a finger against her lips. "It isn't a matter of substitution," Ruth says. "You're involved."

Alex halts at the kerb of a junction. "Tell me how."

"The priest Carl said abused him as a child," Ruth says, and Alex feels as if he's teetering on the edge of far more than the kerb. "It has been brought to our attention that he never abused girls. I fear this may leave us in more trouble than you've already caused for us."

ALEX

All the way to the station Alex can't think, and until he does that he can't speak. He feels as though the events of the day have piled up on his brain or occupied its core like a lump of blackness, and his headlong progress downhill seems to be snatching away his ability to catch hold of any thoughts. Lee is just as silent, and he hopes she's simply waiting for him to speak first or concentrating on keeping up with him. Once they reach the station, the closeness of commuters inhibits him. By the time the train arrives at the end of the line it's stuffed with a crowd prefiguring the horde through which he and Lee have to struggle at the mainline station. When Lee grabs his hand he realises she hasn't touched him since he spoke to Ruth. However much her grasp is trying to convey, it only reminds him of his mother's desperate attempts to find or revive life in his father's hand. Just now the contact seems as unable to communicate, whoever may be to blame.

He's resigned to standing on the Brighton train – it hardly seems to matter what he does – but they succeed in finding seats. Lee sidles to a window, past a man who apparently prefers the aisle. Alex sits on the opposite side of the aisle, since the fellow doesn't offer to change seats, lowering his massive sullen bearded head, which he raised briefly and reluctantly while Lee wriggled between him and the table occupied by his laptop. The computer reminds Alex of his father's, a memory that feels like one more hindrance to thinking. The pulse in his neck has subsided, but now the advance of the minutes on a digital display beyond Lee's window feels like a tic that's plucking at his vision, and anticipating the changes tightens his nerves. Why should the time mean anything to him? At the moment nothing seems to – and then, less than a minute before the train is due to leave, he sees why the time ought to concern him. He's on his feet at once. "Ruth should still be at the office," he tells not only Lee. "I'm going to see her."

As the bearded man lifts his head a fraction of an inch – it looks as if he's signifying how little room he will make for her – Lee says "I'm coming."

"Don't. Go home." Alex is disconcerted to hear himself addressing her insufficiently unlike how his mother last spoke to him. "I'll be there as soon as I can," he says, trying to sound gentler.

Several passengers stand between him and the nearest door. He dodges around them in distressingly slow motion and barely makes the platform before the doors are locked. A glance shows him Lee hasn't left the train. Once he has watched it depart he shuts down his phone and hurries along the platform, then breaks into a run.

The underground journey to Euston feels as if his fellow passengers are consuming all the air before it has a chance to reach him. Escalators lift him up at last into the open, but that's at least as crowded, the street too. He's hemmed in by masses of mute introverted flesh intent on phones, and feels squeezed almost out of existence. Below the glass lift at Tiresias the shrinking heads of pedestrians might be portraying the state of his brain. When he looks towards the empty sky, which is being drained of colour, this performs the same trick.

Is Rod's instant smile of greeting a little more studied than usual? "You're late for you," Rod says. "Are you expected?"

"I was called. Ruth." Alex hopes this doesn't sound as though he has assumed the name. "Kirsty," he wishes he'd asked for instead, "if she's here."

Rod ducks to the microphone too fast for Alex to be sure he sees a fleeting frown. When somebody responds Rod murmurs "Alex Grand is here."

Alex hears a door open and recognises Kirsty's, but it's Ruth who comes to find him. "I'm glad you changed your mind about discussing the situation," she says and leads the way to Kirsty's office. A stocky man with a large thick-featured face – small eyes trapped between heavy eyebrows and bruised bags of skin, broad flattish wedge of a nose, prominent almost purple lips – is seated behind Kirsty's desk, where the back of her chair wears his jacket. "You won't know Archer," Ruth tells Alex.

As she sits beside the man he stands up just enough to give Alex a terse but forthright handshake across the desk, along with a waft of deodorant like a scent of tension. "I hope we can work together."

"I don't see why not," Alex says without seeing the opposite. "Is Kirsty joining us?"

Archer gives him a look that rivals the handshake for firmness. "She's moved on."

"That's rather sudden, isn't it?" When Archer's look neither confirms nor denies it Alex says "Where?"

"Elsewhere."

"She's no longer our concern, Alex. We need to focus on the book she mishandled."

Alex finds he needs to take hold of the back of the chair he's about to sit on. "Are you telling me it got her fired?"

"No need to blame yourself so long as you help solve the problem."

"I'm not blaming myself." This sounds as though he agrees it was Kirsty's fault, and he sits down while he tries to grasp his thoughts. So Ruth has reverted to calling him Alex, perhaps to placate if not persuade him, and he has to assume Archer is the man's first name. None of this ought to be important – it's a symptom of how he's struggling to concentrate – and he says "What problem?"

He's only making certain, but she adds her searching stare to Archer's. "The scene you wrote where the priest abuses a child."

"That's what he was convicted for doing."

"Not to her. Not to any girls."

"How do we know that? I don't, because I wasn't there. Perhaps it was the only chance he got and he made the most of it."

Archer wrinkles his nose and shrinks his mouth in visible distaste. "You seem pretty eager to think it."

"No, I'm eager for the truth. I hope you are."

"I believe we have that," Ruth says. "I managed to get through to Mr Batchelor at last."

Alex hears himself protesting more than asking "What's his story?"

"He as good as admitted he wasn't abused."

With a sense that too many assumptions he's relied on are about to collapse Alex says "By the priest, you mean."

"Just that, of course." Ruth's scrutiny grows keener, until Alex could fancy he feels it like a needle between his eyes. "Or," she says, "are you suggesting more?"

"I don't know any more than you do." While her gaze fails to yield Alex says "When you say as good as admitted...."

"He's refusing to confirm that the priest never touched him."

Alex wonders whether Ruth is determined to confuse him further. "That doesn't sound like an admission."

"It would have if you'd heard his tone. I wish I'd thought to record him."

"He wouldn't have let you." When Ruth looks as if she thinks he's taking Carl's part, he says "What does he propose to do about the book?"

"He refuses to alter the scene. You'll be providing the revision without any input from him."

"Tell me one thing first." Alex feels his confused state of mind has thrown the discussion out of order. "Who got in touch with you about the priest?"

"I can't say, I'm afraid."

"Why not? You aren't the police or a priest for that matter. I thought we're meant to be working together." When matching her gaze doesn't bring him an answer he says "I'm guessing I know her."

"I couldn't say that either."

"You would if I didn't, wouldn't you?" He's sure Ruth is resolved not to look trapped, which is all the confirmation he requires. "I suppose," he says, "you wouldn't let me put her name in the book."

"That isn't how these things are generally done."

"You've dealt with a few, have you? I wonder whose fault that would be."

"I hope you aren't intending to be hostile, Alex," Archer says, planting his forearms on the desk as if to signify the territory he's claimed. "We need to be united as a team working towards a shared goal."

"May we expect the rewrite urgently?" Ruth says.

"Expect it as urgently as you like."

"I'm asking how soon I can look for it on my desk."

"If I can't name the source in the book I won't be touching the scene."

"May I remind you of the undertaking you signed? If you need to refresh your memory I have it here."

"Nothing wrong with my memory." Not least in a bid to avoid examining that claim, Alex adds "Carl signed it as well, and I don't see you going after him."

"Alex," Archer says, "we've already explained—"

"Let's just remember exactly what I guaranteed, that the book is accurate to the best of my knowledge. That's how I'll be leaving it."

"I want you to understand you'll be leaving us open to a lawsuit," Ruth says and picks up a folder from beside her chair. "Us, including you, as your contract stipulates."

"A lawsuit from a child molester in jail? I'd like to see that. I should think it's the kind of publicity we could use."

"I have to tell you it won't be," Ruth says, laying the folder on the desk well out of his reach.

"Is that my file? I wouldn't mind seeing what else you have on me."

Archer draws it to him and flanks it with his forearms. "Nothing to worry you if you comply with us."

Alex has to resist an urge to lurch at it. "If we were in a story I'd say that sounds like blackmail."

"But we are, Alex. We're involved in the one you're helping to tell."

"Don't try to confuse me. Today's done enough to my head."

"If there's anything we can help to clarify," Archer says, "just say the word."

"How's this for a start? This cursed book it seems we're never going to be done with, it made me kill my father."

Ruth and Archer stare at him as if they're waiting for someone else to speak. Eventually Archer says "I think you're right, Alex."

"I know I am." He feels he's being forced to contradict himself by asking "Only how do you know?"

"I'm agreeing you're confused."

"You're identifying with the book too much," Ruth says. "You need to stand back."

"It's not about the book. I'm telling you about my father."

"It couldn't be any more about the book than that," Ruth says as she might speak to an invalid. "That's where you killed him."

"Not Randall," Alex says and tries unsuccessfully to laugh. "My actual father."

"We do believe he's dead," Archer says in a tone much like Ruth's, "but he would be without the book."

"So you do know about him." Alex is appalled not to have been offered so much as a hint of sympathy. "But there's something you don't know," he says in bitter triumph.

Ruth sounds untypically wary as she says "Then tell us."

"I think he may have killed himself because he was afraid people would assume he was like Randall."

"Surely you can see that makes no kind of sense, Alex."

"It's a pity you weren't there to tell him, isn't it? I'm saying what I think he thought, not anything he ever did."

"Slow down a little," Archer says. "How could he have thought that when he never had a chance to learn the truth?"

"What truth?"

"That does seem to be your difficulty," Ruth says.

"Let me handle this," Archer says. "The truth about Randall. What else would it be?"

"All right, we know the book isn't all true." Alex is struggling to understand why he needs to say any of this. "We've accepted the parts about Randall's behaviour are," he insists, "and I think reading those may have affected my father."

After several seconds Archer breaks the silence. "You're saying he read the book he was in."

Alex's brain feels like the contents of a vulnerable shell as he tries to grasp the situation. "Who have we been talking about?"

"You said the actual father."

"Yes, mine. Mine." Alex grows aware of thumping his chest like a cartoon caveman. "Not Carl's," he declares. "I'm not saying I was Carla. I don't even think I'm Carl."

"You're suggesting," Ruth says, "the book was somehow responsible for your own father's death."

"Maybe I was too. I said I'd have told the police about Randall." He feels bound to add "You were right, we shouldn't feed that to anyone."

"Given the position Carl has taken about that, it may be worth reconsidering."

"How can't you understand what I've been telling you? I think it pushed my father over the edge."

As this revives the sight of his father straying into the road, Archer extends a finger from his right fist to rest it on Alex's file. "Wasn't your father a professor who worked for a literary magazine?"

"You'd have known if you'd ever met him." A tangle of emotions that threaten to resurrect his confusion makes Alex demand "Why?"

"He doesn't sound as though he'd be easily influenced."

"I'm afraid he'd started losing his mind." When Ruth and Archer withhold any comment Alex protests "I saw it happen. I've just come from it. He ran off with his laptop and fell under a van."

"You're saying you came straight to us," Ruth says.

"I might as well have, yes."

Any thoughts or feelings she may have are too hidden to be guessed. "What made you do that?"

"I'd been planning to in any case." This sounds inadequate even to Alex, and so does "I wanted to sort things out with you as soon as possible, then at least there'd be something clear in my head."

"I hope you'll accept our sympathies for your loss." As Archer nods, adding a manly murmur, Ruth says "But I trust you weren't proposing to hold Tiresias in any way accountable."

"I haven't said so, have I? It was my fault most of all."

When she holds her hands apart as though to frame her silence Archer says "Under the circumstances I wonder if we can extend the deadline for the rewrite."

"Haven't I managed to make myself clear yet? I won't be touching the priest." Alex hears his own words and feels his mouth twist in a grimace. "I won't be changing that scene," he says, "unless Carl lets me have the truth in writing."

"Why don't you take a little time to consider your position, Alex," Archer says, opening his fists. "You shouldn't be expected to decide so soon after your loss."

"But be aware our time is limited."

"I don't need any. I've said what I won't do and nobody's changing my mind."

"You ought to realise," Ruth says, "if someone else makes the change your name will still be on the book."

"Then I'll be letting everybody know it wasn't me. I won't be associated with anything I'm not sure of any more."

"I hope you aren't aiming to make trouble for us, Mr Grand."

"Can't you even decide what my name is? It's you that keeps making trouble for me, Ruth." He's saying too much, carelessly as well, and tries to regain control. "I just want to leave the book behind," he hears himself come close to pleading. "It's brought enough grief into my life."

"Just finish with the priest," Archer says, "and work with Carl on the wedding, and that ought to be enough for anyone."

"I'm going nowhere near it or him either. I don't trust him."

"If we can't reach an agreement I don't see how we can work together."

"Then we're agreed. Get someone else to do the rewrites and put their name on the book as well."

"No, Alex." Archer cups his hands to draw the file closer, a gesture that looks inappropriately protective. "I'm talking about your future with Tiresias."

"You're threatening me with that now, are you? We've gone back to the blackmail narrative."

"You're threatening yourself if you continue to behave like this," Ruth says. "Yourself and your relationship with us."

"You'll excuse me if I'm blunt, but I'm not feeling I have much of one."

Archer lays his hands flat on the file, more proprietorially than protectively. "One thing you don't have yet is a contract for your next book."

"Aren't you at least going to pretend it pains you to say it?"

"Mr Grand, Alex, whichever you like, I'm simply trying to let you know—"

"I know everything I need to. I liked working with Kirsty, she always did her best, but as long as you used me as your excuse to fire her you may as well get rid of me."

"No reason to be quite so hasty. Why don't—"

"How hasty would you recommend I ought to be?" When Archer only lowers his gaze to his hands on the folder Alex says "Have we waited long enough now? If I'd known Kirsty was going I might have gone as well."

"You may find moving elsewhere isn't quite so straightforward," Ruth says.

"There's nothing you can do about it. You heard Mr Archer say he can't work with me as I am."

"It isn't Mr Archer, and you're misrepresenting what he said."

"Don't say it's Ms. I'm never that confused." Alex feels as if he's talking for the sake of talking, to blot out the clamour of his mind. "And my agent tells me several publishers are waiting for me to move on, as you like to put it," he says. "Perhaps I'll end up with Kirsty again."

"I have to say I doubt it," Archer says.

"I don't give a fifth of a shit what you doubt. I'll stay with what I'm sure of, and it isn't you." Was the man suggesting Alex won't be able to place his work elsewhere? Rage lets Alex think so. As he stands up vigorously enough to send his chair backwards, he seems to glimpse Archer taking a firmer hold on the file. "I'm not going to steal that, you bloody fool," Alex says. "Hang on to your bits of paper. They're all of me you'll get to keep."

Is this too large a claim? Tiresias still has his backlist, after all. By the time he thinks of this he's stalking out of the office he still regards as Kirsty's. "I'd make sure you've heard the last of me," he throws back and hopes it sounds like a threat rather than advice directed at himself.

For as long as he takes to reach the lift he feels as if he's striding into a future full of promise, and then he remembers his father and just as dismayingly his mother. On Euston Road a few passing heads discoloured by streetlamps are pumped up to meet him. As he steps onto the pavement his phone returns to life, showing five missed calls from Lee but not a single message. He won't be calling her back. He thought he could at least trust her, but now he knows he can trust nobody except himself.

ALEX

As the co-author of WHEN I WAS CARLA I'm delighted that Malcolm Randall will be prosecuted. I couldn't have wished for any other outcome. I just want to make it public that I didn't inform the police, whatever anybody may say to the contrary, and I certainly didn't inform Randall. I also have no reason to believe that Father Brendan of St Brendan's didn't abuse Carla Batchelor as well. Please don't accept the word of anybody who doesn't show you actual evidence.

Though Alex seldom posts on Twitter, he feels compelled to respond to Hilary Wilson. His inexperience has let his words sprawl well beyond the limits of a post. No doubt Lee would help him edit it, but he won't have her shaping his thoughts. The downpour in the bathroom means she's in the shower, because she surely has no reason to pretend. He's anxious to post before she can interfere, and he sets about condensing his language.

As the co-author of WHEN I WAS CARLA I'm delighted that Malcolm Randall will be prosecuted. I just want to say I didn't inform the police, whatever anyone says to the contrary, and I certainly didn't inform Randall. I've no reason to believe Father Brendan of St Brendan's didn't abuse Carla Batchelor as well. Please don't accept the word of anyone who doesn't show you actual evidence...

It's still too long. The last sentence and part of its predecessor are marked an embarrassing pink. As he crouches over the phone on his desk he hears the shower falter. Lee is still beneath it, since there's a gentle whisper of water. No, that's the unseen sea beyond the houses, and she could be on her way out of the bathroom. His final bid to edit feels far too close to panic.

As the coauthor of WHEN I WAS CARLA I'm glad Malcolm Randall will be prosecuted. I didn't inform the police, and I didn't inform Randall. I've no reason to believe Father Brendan of St Brendan's didn't abuse Carla Batchelor. Don't trust anyone who doesn't show you actual evidence.

It's too long by a solitary character. The final full stop is suffused with pink, but he won't delete it – he hates online usages that dispense with punctuation. He hears the bathroom door open, and searches desperately for a word to abridge. There's a letter nobody needs, and he posts the message, having transformed Carla Batchelor into Carl. Carl did that to himself, after all, and for a moment Alex feels as if Carl prompted him, guiding his mind to the name. He has time to bring his computer to life before Lee comes into the room. "You look busy," she audibly hopes.

"That's because I am." He can think of no reason to mention his tweet, and several for refraining. "I need to send Linder a synopsis of the new novel," he says.

"It'll help if you're really sure you've finished with Tiresias. Are you certain you wouldn't like me to try and find out if they might have had second thoughts?"

"That's right, you're still involved with them."

"I have to be involved with anyone who gives me work, Alex."

"Including me." When she gives him a smile that tries not to look puzzled he says "I'm afraid the separation's permanent. All the trust has gone."

Lee is naked. Just now the sight fails to affect him, and he doesn't think this is only because it's so familiar. It strikes him as a bid to portray innocence, but it can't display whatever may be in her head. She's loitering in the hall as though to ensure nobody else sees her, though Alex doesn't care who does. He thinks she may continue trying to tempt him back to Tiresias, but all she says is "Coffee?"

"If we were in this book of mine I'd want to see what you put in it."

"Only if you thought I was up to no good."

"How could I ever suspect that? Keep me alert by all means. That's what caffeine's good for."

Writing the synopsis feels like summarising someone else's work. His memories of failing to save his father are in the way, but just now

Carl's experiences – even the invented ones – feel more related to him than the novel does. No doubt his post on Twitter has revived them in his mind. He's typing doggedly when Lee brings in the punctuated mugs. She plants one beside his keyboard and strokes the back of his head as she might pet an animal. "Do you mind if I get on with some editing?"

She's dressed now. Did she realise nudity didn't work on him? He needs to establish "Why should I mind?"

"So long as you know I'm here if you need me for anything at all."

Her show of concern has only reminded him of his father's fate. Will his mother ban him from the funeral, as Carl's mother cast him out of Randall's? No, that never happened, however much it feels as though it did. It was his sister's wedding Carl was barred from, except not his sister's either. The clacking of Lee's keyboard seems at least as loud as Alex's, although she's on the far side of the room. Whenever he turns his head her screen shows a book she's marking with comments, but he can't recall any book needing her to type so much. He completes the synopsis at last and emails it to Linder, and twists his chair around to find Lee scrolling through a page she hasn't marked, though he's sure he just heard her typing. "Bad one?" he says.

"Not especially," she says and marks a phrase on which she comments in the margin. "Well, quite bad."

When he squints he can just distinguish that she has suggested changing *don't let them realise* to *don't let him realise*, though he can't make out the context. He brings up Twitter on his computer, and the sound it provokes him to utter brings Lee across the room. "What's wrong, Alex?"

"That was a laugh." He means the sound he made, or perhaps the one he intended to produce. "Wrong?" he says. "Everybody here."

His tweet has provoked screenfuls of responses, though none from Hilary Wilson. A suggestion that Alex should have informed the police about her father brings dozens of posts condemning his inaction. Some commentators don't believe he didn't try to warn Randall, and quite a few grow close to incoherent with rage while they wish a generous selection of horrid fates on Alex. Lee rests her hands on his shoulders and keeps starting to massage him, but he does his best to shrug off the distraction. Even the most rabid posts don't trouble him – they can't undermine his memory of meeting the Randalls or how he behaved when he did, nor the memory of his intentions – but some of the user names lodge in his mind. L. O'Quent remarks that Alex's warning not to trust people sounds too paranoid for words. Lderlylad suggests that anyone so distrustful of others must be equally unreliable, and Ledonnerley goes further, telling Alex he can't know how much he's imagined – just look how he made everyone think Randall was dead. Either Alex was convinced of it or deliberately lied to help the book sell, and whichever is the truth, how can anybody trust him now? Lee's massage has begun to feel like a bid to smooth away his thoughts, and he's about to dislodge her soft grasp when his phone rings, identifying his agent. His lurch to respond is sufficiently vigorous to leave Lee's hands behind. "Linder," he says. "That was quick."

"How's life, Alex?"

"Varied just now."

"I hope that means some of it's good."

"That's the idea."

He's hoping Lee will return to her desk, but her breath invades his ear. "Will you tell her about your father? Or I can if you like."

"You've got your own job over there. The one you told me was so bad. Just sorting Lee out," he's driven to explain.

"Hey there, Lee. Any space for work?"

"We both have our space, me and Alex. Alex and I, you'd expect me to say, and you should."

As Alex wonders whether her mistake betrayed nervousness Linder says "No, I was asking if you could fit in extra work."

"I'll always try. We can't afford to turn it down in our business, any of us."

"I'll be recommending a new house to send you some. Now I'd better speak to Alex before he starts feeling he doesn't exist."

"Nobody's going to make me feel that. I know exactly who I am and who I've always been." He watches Lee return to her computer before he says "Lee was wondering if you'd heard about my father."

"He's a literary type, isn't he? Has he got something new to his name?"

"Just his death."

"Alex, I'm truly sorry. I wouldn't have been talking like that if I'd known." Before Alex can decide whether she means the routine she performed with Lee, Linder says "Should I ask how you lost him?"

"By not running fast enough. He was going faster, straight under a van."

"Truly sorry," Linder repeats as if fewer words may concentrate her sympathy. "Can I ask how long ago?"

"Just stop asking if you can ask. Stop piling words on top of me." Rather than say any of this Alex tells her "End of last week."

"You won't have had the funeral yet."

"Not even the date or an invitation."

"I'm sure you won't need one, Alex." When he keeps his response to himself Linder says "Well, thank you all the more for coming up with the synopsis."

"I needed to find work." This sounds too much like an appeal, and he adds "Something to do with my mind."

"You mean you want to occupy it." Having heard no answer, Linder says "I'm not quite clear what you mean about Tiresias in your email."

"They've fired my editor and I don't care for the substitute."

"Would you like me to try them anyway in case someone else would enjoy working with you?"

"Are you saying they're the only publishers you think are worth a try?"

"Just the opposite. I'll be approaching everyone I think is even slightly possible. I really believe this could be your best book and break you out in the biggest way. We'll want to see all the bids before we decide who's the lucky publisher."

Her speech has left him breathless, as though he was the speaker. "Put Tiresias in. Even if they don't make an offer they'll see what they lost."

"I'll email everyone today and let you know the moment there's news. I hope I've cheered you up a little."

"You've done more than your job, Linder."

The excitement she's communicated lingers until Lee says "I'm glad she changed your mind."

He's immediately wary. "Changed me how?"

"Persuaded you to give Tiresias a chance."

"And they're important to you because...."

"They've been important to you, Alex. They could be again now you've shaken them up." As Alex wonders if he can take this for the truth she says "I don't like to think of you losing control."

"Who says I have? They'd better take care what they're saying about me."

"Alex, you did." She swings her chair around so as to exhibit a concerned look. "You said so."

He won't let her distort his memories. "When am I meant to have done that?"

"You said you went for the lawyer and your new editor."

"That wasn't me losing control. It was exactly the opposite."

She looks unconvinced if not uneasy. "What would you say that was?"

"Them losing control of me and my mind, except they never had it. Nobody has, and they needn't bother trying. I'm the only one who has and I'll be keeping it that way."

"Don't overwork it." Too close to a contradiction she adds "So long as working helps."

She turns to her computer before he can see her face change, and he swivels to confront his screen. No further comments about him have appeared on Twitter. Producing the synopsis has revived the novel in his mind, and he sets about writing a new chapter. The detective needs to realise everyone is suspect, including those closest to him. Composing the scene in which he scrutinises the characters around him feels like living the experience, realising for himself how devious they may be. Of course the process should engage his imagination to the full, though he's disconcerted by how closely it recalls writing *When I Was Carla*. He's occasionally distracted by the discreet clatter of Lee's keyboard, but he's immersed in the chapter when she sneaks up behind him. As soon as she rests her hands on his shoulders he mutters "Not now."

"I'll be making dinner." She retreats, though not so far that he can't hear her intrusive breaths, if they aren't the sea. "You can help," she says, "if you fancy a break."

"I don't." If they were in the novel she would be aiming to convince him that she isn't spiking his food. "I want to deal with this," he says.

By the time he types the final sentence of the chapter – *He felt as if his eyes and ears had been operated on*, exactly how he feels himself – Lee and dinner are waiting. He has a glass of merlot first, and several with the steak, which isn't as rare as he prefers. No doubt that's his fault or would be said to be. "No blood tonight," he confines himself to saying, which earns him a puzzled if not worried look.

After dinner they attempt to choose a film to watch. Alex thinks crime is called for, while Lee is drawn to comedy, and they compromise on Neil Simon. The victim of a murder investigated by several parodic detectives turns out to be alive and criticises their contrived explanations of his death. Having pulled off one mask, he removes another, revealing he's a woman. Long before the end Lee stops even mildly laughing, since Alex stays entirely silent. Whatever the film should mean to him, he won't let it or anything confuse him.

In bed he puts an arm around Lee to feel when she falls asleep. He won't drift off until she does. He's had enough of her overhearing his thoughts while he's unconscious. It's her turn to betray secrets in her sleep. He feels her grow inert, and stares at the dark mass of silence that's her head. For a time he can't hear her breaths, and her stillness starts to lull him until he digs fingernails into his thigh. At last she begins to murmur, but he can't recognise even a syllable. When he cranes so close that their faces virtually touch, he has the impression that her inarticulate noises are retreating from him, trying to hide. He's reminded how someone else did her best to shrink inwards from a similar approach, but he's certainly not Randall, even less Carla. He isn't recapturing a memory, he's just recalling how he wrote the scene. Just the same, the likeness disturbs him, and he sinks onto the mattress. He's still waiting for Lee to stop keeping her thoughts to herself when he falls asleep.

Lee wakens him, or rather a sharp harsh invasion of his nostrils does. It's the aroma of coffee from the mug she has set beside the bed. When she doesn't move away he thinks she's about to tell him he was talking in his sleep again. "Thanks," he mumbles and sits up more unsteadily than he likes. "Something else?"

"Do you want to wake up properly first?"

"It'll wake me. What?"

"We'll have to decide what to do about this," she says and holds her phone in front of his face.

If theres anybody here you dont want to trust its Alex Grand. He lied about Father Brendan of St Brendans. Father Brendan never touched a girl in his life but Alex Grand told everyone he did. This was posted yesterday, and so were dozens of responses, of which the first is the least vituperative. *Hes made it harder for real victims to be believed. Thats what he did with his book that pretends its on their side. Maybe thats what he meant it to do to them.* These posts are followed by a stream of execration, but they're the ones he can't stop seeing. The reply is from L. O'Quent, and the original comment belongs to Ledonnerley, but he's sure fewer people are posting than there are names. "Somebody's been talking to themselves," he mutters.

"You were, Alex."

He won't be made to feel defensive. "When am I meant to have done that?"

"In your sleep again. Something about someone's father being somewhere they shouldn't be."

"You saw it happen to mine." Alex can't grasp why her words disturb him more than the memory does, as if they've been lying in wait for him. "I'm surprised you haven't had nightmares about it," he says.

"I've been having some of those."

"You kept them quiet, then."

"You've got enough to deal with just now. No need for me to make the situation any worse."

"Anyway, you were going to advise me how to deal with her."

Lee hesitates before asking "Who, Alex?"

"My pseudonymous enemy. Don't say you've forgotten the name. Ledonnerley, or L. O'Quent if you prefer. What are you going to tell me to do?"

"Do you think you ought to call someone at Tiresias?"

"I won't be getting involved with anyone who wants to keep that godforsaken book in my head. I've got my own story to write."

"Then just tell the truth. I'm sure that's what they would say as well."

"I always do. I try, at any rate. I don't use any disguises either. No," he says with a ferocity that takes him unawares, "not even Carl or Carla."

"Nobody said you did. I don't know who you're saying is disguised."

"I'd better get on with dealing with them then, hadn't I?"

He gropes for his phone on the bedside table and starts to type once the Twitter thread appears. I've never said anything was true unless I thought it was. *Don't anybody say the title was a lie because I wasn't Carla or even Carl Batchelor. He was the source of the information about the priest and I'd no reason to distrust him. It was his life, not mine, and I couldn't have known what was false...*

The last four words are blushing as if they've been caught out. Lee opens her mouth to suggest a revision, unless she's planning to object to some part of the message, but Alex brandishes the finger he's using to type. *Don't say the title was a lie because I wasn't Carla or even Carl. He was my source of information about the priest and I'd no reason to distrust him.* The pink suffusion has vanished by now, and he flourishes the message. "Approved?" he says and, as soon as if not before Lee has had time to read it, answers himself. "Approved," he says and posts the message.

"You might as well not have bothered asking," Lee says and retreats. "I'm going to have my shower."

"Don't you want to see who responds and what they say?"

"You can show me later. It's your doing, after all."

He has to swallow so as not to say too much. "Just let me go in," he says instead, but is still urinating when she follows him into the bathroom. There's surely no reason this should remind him of Randall, and he goes back to his phone to see a barrage of replies has begun. *He wants us to trust him after what he did.... He's not kidding anyone he never lies.... Ought to be locked up for it.... Right on, locked up with the pedo priest and treated like I hope they're treating Father Brenda up her arse....*

There's no sign of L. O'Quent or Ledonnerley – not even of Lderlylad. Perhaps they, if there's more than one of them, feel the hostility has gained so much momentum that they don't need to contribute, unless they've withdrawn for fear of being recognised. His compulsion to keep checking the thread means Alex writes just a few lifeless paragraphs of his novel. He still can't find the names he's looking for on Twitter, or whenever he checks his phone during dinner. Afterwards he watches *The Big Sleep* with Lee, but Bogart and Bacall can't save the film from feeling like an insoluble labyrinth that has formed in his mind, and the banter of the couple only emphasises how guarded his and Lee's dialogue has grown. At dinner it consisted mostly of silence.

He won't talk in his sleep. In bed he embraces Lee's waist in case he can sense when she's dreaming and may speak. Alertness keeps him uselessly awake for hours, and the gaps it develops feel like invisibly dark memories that are waiting for him to fall in. At last one widens enough to swallow his consciousness, and he wakens to find emptiness beside him, flattened by his arm. As he flounders onto his back he sees Lee standing by the bed, apparently having wakened him. "Phone for you, Alex," she says as if she's repeating herself.

It isn't his. This seems to make no more sense than a dream, even once he realises it's Lee's. She looks determined to withhold any explanation, but he isn't going to take the phone without one, especially while he's hardly awake. "Who is it?" he demands.

"It's Linder."

Are they conspiring to confuse him? At first he can't tell who answered, and then he grasps that they did so in chorus. He gives his bruised thigh a surreptitious pinch, which lets him realise he should ask "Why did she call you?"

He doesn't know which of them may answer until Lee tells him "Your phone's turned off."

"Fair enough. Let me speak."

Does he sense some reluctance to hand over her phone? As soon as he has it he says "This is me now, Linder."

"How are you doing, Alex?"

This can't help reviving the online bids to make him paranoid. "How do you think I should be?" he retorts.

"I'm sure you're still grieving for your father."

Perhaps she genuinely meant that, and Alex tries to let the women think he takes it that way. "I feel as if my life hasn't caught up with me."

"I think sometimes it's best it shouldn't all at once."

"Anyway, you didn't call just to hear how I am." In case this sounds too hostile he adds "Or did you?"

"We care about you, Alex. I do, and I'm more than certain Lee does."

"I think she'd have to edit that. I'm saying that wasn't your only reason for calling."

"It wasn't," Linder says and clears her throat as though to make way for a different voice. "We've heard from some of the editors I sent your synopsis."

"That sounds like enthusiasm." He means the speed of the responses. "Are they talking money yet?"

"No offers just yet, I have to report."

"Making sure we know they're interested, are they? Do you want to tell me who they are?"

"Three of the big ones, but that isn't why they were in touch."

"I see," Alex says on the basis that he will. "What do they want to know?"

"I'm sorry to have to say nothing."

"Then tell me what they did want."

"Alex, just to let us know how much they regret not being able to consider your book."

"Oh." The sound is scarcely a word and hasn't time to find a tone. Lee's concerned look makes it harder still for him to ask "Why not?"

"The general feeling, and you know how sorry I am to be saying this, is that your image just now makes you difficult to market."

"Which image? I'm who I've always been, and that was bloody good enough for Tiresias."

"I was dining with a senior editor last night. You'll excuse me if I don't say who." After a pause she might have left for Alex to put the question she won't answer, Linder says "She feels you shouldn't have responded to those posts on Twitter. If you hadn't the whole thing might have died down pretty well unnoticed. It's too global now for the trade to overlook."

"I should have said what people told me to, should I? I just want all the truth to be known."

"You may want to consider how that can affect marketing you, Alex."

"What am I advised to do?" More bitterly still he says "What's the consensus?"

"Lie as low as you can for now, and we'll hope some of the competitors are more adventurous."

"Lie, right. I'm sure the Randalls would say there are all kinds of ways you can do that. My adopted family, you know. I've taken to hearing them in my head." Alex means this to parody the paranoia he's supposed to suffer, but it doesn't amuse even him. "So you'll let me know when we hear from anybody else," he struggles not to plead.

"The moment I do. And Alex, let me say it shows how much you mean to them, the way the ones who've been in touch were so quick."

Is this meant to hearten him? It merely threatens to confuse him. "Just make sure you use my phone," he says. "I'll leave it on."

Once he's certain that she's gone he hands the phone to Lee, who meets it with a solicitous look. "Only three," she says. "We don't even know who they were."

For a moment he thinks she's talking about his attackers on Twitter, perhaps to distract him from how she hardly looked surprised by Linder's news. "There are too many people like that," he says, "or maybe not that many after all."

"I'm just saying there are plenty more publishers."

"You don't need to tell me that. I'd like to know what you were saying before you woke me up."

"Just wake up, Alex."

He won't be confused, though he doesn't know whether she's saying he isn't awake yet or simply reporting her own words. "Before that," he persists. "To Linder."

"She was asking how you were."

"So why did she ask me as well? Couldn't she believe what you said?"

"She could have thought you were better informed."

"You aren't going to say she was wrong, are you?" When Lee doesn't even shake her head Alex says "What did you tell her?"

"I just reminded her she might have to make allowances."

"For poor distracted Alex, would they be? I imagine you told her that's what you've been doing."

Lee's expression flickers like an unstable onscreen image. "You've no idea."

"You didn't discuss what you should tell me to do."

"That's right, we didn't. If you don't believe me, ask her."

"I'll wait for her to call and let me know who else has turned against me. Who else have you been talking to about me?"

"Nobody at all."

"Not even your parents?"

"Not even them. Would you have talked to yours about me?"

"What about you?"

"I'm just saying if there were a reason."

"You aren't owning up to anything." When Lee doesn't he says "Seems to me you're the one who's confused."

"Do either of us need to be? If you are I'm here."

"I'm simply wondering how you think I'm going to talk to my parents when I've killed my father and might as well have finished off my mother for all the use she has for me now. You'd think I was trying to turn into Carl Batchelor."

"I wouldn't, Alex. Nobody would. Do you think it's time to make your peace with her?"

"I've got none of that to offer, and don't you go trying."

"I won't, but you should. Don't cut yourself off from anyone who cares about you."

As Lee makes a move towards him, perhaps concluding that her touch may be more persuasive than her words, he slips quickly out of the far side of the bed. He's retrieving his mug when she exclaims "What have you been doing to yourself?"

What change is she trying to convince him he's undergone? It takes him several nervous moments to realise she's gazing at the array of purple bruises on his thigh. "Just seeing I'm alert," he says. "No need to call the medics."

Although the explanation plainly fails to satisfy her, he has nothing to add. He wishes the bathroom could feel like a refuge, but a clamour has followed him in, jostling for priority in his skull: his career that's being snatched from him, his mother's rejection of him, the threats and accusations that may be waiting to assail him online…. He takes a shower, which feels as if it's probing for his weaknesses, and locates Lee in the kitchen once he has towelled himself dry, not sparing the bruises however much they sting. "I'm going for a walk," he says.

"Not like that, I hope."

"Not naked, no. I'll need to be a lot more confused before I start behaving like that."

"I was joking, Alex."

"I thought you might be. Just making certain."

"Shall I come with you?"

"No, I want to think."

Before she can try to impede him any further he retreats to the bedroom. "You'll hear when I'm back," he calls on his way to the door. He doesn't switch his phone on until he's in the downstairs hall. Outside the house he brings up Twitter, where more people or at least more names have gathered to condemn him. As he steps off the pavement he glances up at the workroom window. Surely Lee can't have seen what he was examining, but he pockets the phone as he hurries across the road.

Beyond the promenade the pier pretends to reach halfway to the horizon, where the sky is a paler grey than the water. Waves intermittently topped with foam tug at the pier in an insistent bid to draw it out to sea, so that Alex has to keep reminding himself that the land is stable underfoot. The promenade is crowded, and he finds he feels safest among people who don't know him, but how will he feel when nobody does? Even if he can't see anybody watching, that doesn't mean he isn't being watched. Anyone could use a drone to watch and lie in wait – for his detective, he means, or a potential victim. Once the scene is written the idea will be out of his head.

He's hastening back to the house when the phone rings in his pocket, naming Lee. It feels like a bid to prevent him from dealing with the idea that has lodged in his skull, and he doesn't answer. He lets himself into the house and tries to make no more noise while he climbs the stairs. He's inching the apartment door open – perhaps he can start writing before Lee has a chance to hinder him – when he hears voices. Are they on the television? The door is almost shut by the time he's sure that one of them is Lee's, and talking to a man.

Alex closes the door without a sound and gradually releases the latch. The voices are in the living-room, next to the workroom. As he paces along the hall he hears Lee declare that something ought to happen soon – to him? She's speaking to a dauntingly tall man who has folded his limbs on an armchair. His bony smooth-skinned practically colourless face looks reduced to essentials – lips as thin and straight as his nose, token eyebrows not much sparser than his grey hair – with particular emphasis on his keen pale eyes. When he catches sight of Alex he stands up at once as though to intimidate him with his stature. "Alexander Evelyn Grand?"

Alex tramps into the room to confront Lee, who is perched on the edge of her chair. "Christ, have you brought the police in now?"

His dismayed look would be enough to prompt the visitor to retort "Is there any reason why Ms Kinship should?"

It's so long since Alex heard her last name that it revives a memory of thinking her parents had no ear for language. Of course, she told him this was why she'd become concerned with words. All this is a diversion, and he says "Maybe you'd better ask her."

As the man turns to her Lee says "I can't tell you any reason."

If she's being guarded, on whose behalf? "So she didn't call you," Alex says, "since she's no excuse."

"Ms Kinship didn't call. Can you confirm your name is Alexander Evelyn Grand?"

"That's me. The whole of me. That and nobody else, and never likely to be."

The man waits to be sure this is all. "As I was explaining to Ms Kinship, this is in the nature of a courtesy to allow you to prepare."

"You're someone else I've been discussed with, are you?" When the thin face grows officially ominous Alex says "Prepare for what?"

"You have been identified as a key factor in the case of Malcolm Randall."

"I don't think I can be called that. More a glorified stenographer."

"We need you to hold yourself in readiness."

Since Lee plainly knows the answer to the question Alex has to ask, he almost aims it at her. "Readiness for what?"

"To testify in court, Mr Grand." The man's official look renews itself. "It's appreciated that you did a job you were employed to do," he says, "but it will be necessary to establish what actually took place and what came from your own mind."

ALEXANDER AND ALEX

"Lee, I meant to include you. You're welcome, of course." Nevertheless Alex's mother appears to think better of stepping back into the hall. "I hope you know why you're here, Alexander."

He has a sense that she's precariously held together by her neat outfit and coiffure, all of which has reduced her to monochrome – sprayed stiff grey hair, black suit and white blouse, gloomy hose that lend her legs a smoked look. An expression suggestive of bemusement and polite regret is fixed on her small face, as though she's afraid what relaxing her features along with her mind may let in. Her appearance leaves Alex nervous of answering, but he says "You wanted me to come."

"But do you know why I said you should?"

Her voice is as low as the murmur beyond her, muted conversations hidden in the house. Matching it makes his thoughts feel restricted too. "Because dad was my father?"

This sounds like hoping this was their relationship. "That goes without saying," his mother tells him. "Have you really no idea why else?"

He's beginning to feel trapped in the porch, boxed in by potted plants bereft of scents. He might almost be a character in a childhood tale, barred from entry unless he can answer a riddle, but he suspects that his mother's appeal to intelligence is a means of controlling her own mind. "Because he'd have wanted me to be here," he tries offering, "and I hope you do."

Her fixed expression doesn't even hint at a response as she says "Because of the police."

Alex struggles to keep his voice down. "What have they been saying about me? Have they questioned you as well?"

"Yes, they questioned me."

"I won't ask what you said unless you want to say," Alex

immediately regrets promising. "But you can tell me what they said about me."

Although he's aware Lee is trying to attract his attention, he keeps it on his mother as she says "It has very little to do with you, Alexander."

"You mean they were asking about Gordon, Amy."

"Who else would I have meant?" As she scrutinises Alex her face looks in danger of wavering. "Why," she says, "are you in trouble with the police?"

"Not that I'm aware of, but you said I'm here because of them."

"Come in for pity's sake," she says as if Lee and Alex are the hindrance. "Just stay here in the hall. This isn't for anybody else to hear."

Shutting the door darkens the hall. The framed items on the walls – Beckett's autographed playlet, the portraits of writers asleep – look suddenly dusty, bound for erasure. As the indoor dusk settles on his mother's face, Alex thinks he sees her eyes grow dull with suppressed emotion. "They've finished with Gordon's computer," she says.

Alex wills this to mean what he hopes. "Finished how?"

"They found nothing questionable anywhere on it."

This is such a relief that Alex feels as though a barrier is about to give way in his mind. "I never thought there could be."

"Then perhaps you should have made sure he knew."

Alex can't tell which of them this leaves more confused. "Did any of us realise he needed to be told?"

"You saw how your book was affecting his mind. So long as you're here to make amends, that's all I ask."

"I'll do anything I can."

"Then speak up for your father at the funeral and be sure you keep the circumstances to yourself."

Alex wonders if he should have offered quite so comprehensive an undertaking. "Which do we mean?"

"How he left us." Having peered at Alex as if she can't discern why he would ask, she says "There's one thing I can give thanks for."

He's disturbed by how untypically this sounds like Carl Batchelor's mother. Perhaps bereavement affects survivors that way, but he wouldn't have expected it of her. "Which is that?"

"The police never publicised the seizure. Now," she says as if Alex has caused a delay, "just let my colleagues see you're here."

He needs to prepare some sort of eulogy for the funeral, but has to follow her into the front room. Sombre oldsters stand in muted groups as if they think sitting down might be discourteous. "You won't know," Alex's mother says before raising her voice above the rest, "my son Alexander and his partner Lee Kinship."

While the guests nod to them or raise hands or murmur tentative greetings, she heads for the kitchen, where other voices can be heard. As Alex loiters with no sense of anyone he should approach, a couple wanders over. "Erin and Daniel Irvine," the man says for both of them.

His wife's grey hair is as clipped as his. Both are tall but stooped by age, which makes them look as if they're condescending to their new acquaintances, an impression that their loose elevated handshakes fail to counteract. "You've submitted to us, Alexander," Erin Irvine says.

Lee laughs in case she should. "How did Alex do that?"

"Do you prefer Alex?"

He isn't sure which of them she's asking. "It's my name. It's on all my books."

"Alex it shall be, then." To Lee she says "We edit *Continuity*. Alex let us see a piece of his."

"I remember. You weren't in favour."

"We were quite," her husband says. "It was more a matter of advice received."

"Don't assume we never take a stand." Erin Irvine appears to start one by rising an inch from her stoop. "We simply didn't want to be a source of conflict."

"Between whom?" Alex is anxious to learn.

"Are you sure it's appropriate to discuss this just now?"

"Lee will have to hear."

At once he grasps that Erin was referring to the funeral. "We'll just mention," Daniel Irvine says, "the advisor is no longer with us."

"You're talking about my father."

"We'd rather not name names." Inclining his head towards Alex, he adds "Please accept our sympathies upon your loss."

"Perhaps in due time," Erin says, "you might try us again."

"You're asking Alex to give you another look at his essay." When the woman hesitates Lee says "I could see about editing it a little if everybody likes."

"Nobody likes," Alex retorts. "Maybe you've forgotten I don't have it any more."

"Surely our response didn't lead you to destroy it," Daniel Irvine protests.

"I'm not that vulnerable and I never will be. Somebody crashed my computer."

Several nearby guests glance at him. Should he have spoken of a crash when his father died in one? In a bid to leave the memory behind he says "Anything else you'd like me to write?"

"Might you address how you created your latest book?" Daniel says.

"While I'm writing it? I could take a shot."

"Your latest that has seen print," Erin says. "Your memoir."

"If you could involve your other person, so much the better."

"Lee always tells me where I've gone wrong."

"Not this lady. The other author."

"I suppose," Erin says, "we might call him the soul of the book."

"I wouldn't," Alex objects. "How do you expect me to involve him?"

"If you feel proprietary about the book, that's perfectly acceptable," Daniel says. "All we'd want to publish is the truth."

"We'd ask you to discuss the process of experiencing another person's memories."

"Having someone else's thoughts, if you like."

"I don't," Alex protests but suspects nobody hears him, because his mother is calling from the hall "The cars are here."

He can tell her efficiency is designed to hold her emotions in check. As she beckons to him, her face stays fixed. "You come as well, Lee," she says. "You're the rest of the family."

She waits for everyone else to leave, a subdued procession that mostly avoids her eyes but offers a few guarded smiles of encouragement, and then locks the front door. A limousine is parked at the end of the path, and Alex has to remind himself that it's wholly unrelated to Malcolm Randall. The Irvines have left him more doubtful of people, not least himself, than he wants to examine just now. He's troubled that his father tried to silence him, although perhaps he should have realised.

It feels like a memory that was waiting for him to be unable not to notice.

The murmur of wheels as the limousine follows the hearse seems to enjoin silence. On its way downhill and through the suburbs it passes few pedestrians, and they're too intent on their phones to notice the measured parade. Alex has to resist consulting his phone to discover whether he's being freshly condemned. When a taxi gives way to the procession at a crossroads he reminds himself that the black cab has nothing to do with the funeral. It's the junction where his father went under the van, and all the way to the crematorium the memory tries to drag his mind back.

The crematorium is a long low block surmounted by a token tower topped with an aerial resembling the first line of an undecided symbol. A whitish angel is pinned like a lepidopterist's trophy above the shallow porch. Alex loiters with Lee and his mother near the hearse while the congregation disappears into the chapel. Once the undertaker's men have tenderly hoisted the coffin, he and his mother trudge after it with Lee at their heels. "You could have helped, Alexander," his mother murmurs, and he's tempted to overtake the nearest bearer and insist on replacing him. He has to suppress some kind of laugh at the notion of a struggle for that corner of the coffin, and then the idea feels too close to a nightmare he's about to live through.

As the mourners rise the coffin is borne to a plinth at the end of the chapel. The plinth is flanked by a podium and a door under an exit sign that Alex can't help finding wryly symbolic. Perhaps this kind of thought is a bid to fend off a sense that everyone is watching him as he passes them and then behind his back. The impression grows more oppressive as he follows his mother along the front pew, where the women hem him in.

Copies of a pamphlet setting out the order of the ceremony lie on the bench. The covers bear a photograph of Gordon Alexander Grand. Can Alex really have forgotten that he borrowed his first name from his father? What else may he have taken from him that he can't recall? Another photograph shows his father managing to look the age Alex is now and wearing a faint smile that makes his patience evident. Presumably Alex knew him then, but the memory is out of reach. He's straining to recapture it when the celebrant of the funeral heads for the podium.

The pamphlet gives her name as Bronwyn Gale. She's so statuesque – long limbs, face like a practically perfect oval mask of peace, smooth skin not much less pale than marble – that Alex finds it close to comical. She's wearing sandals and a rainbow kaftan, and an equally multicoloured turban hides her hair. She glides past the coffin with a discreet repeated clack of sandals and turns to face the congregation. "We are here to celebrate the life of Gordon Alexander Grand...."

He was a distinguished academic and a loving husband and caring father, Alex hears her start by saying. He's distracted by realising for the first time in his life that his father's initials spell gag, which seems all too appropriate to the man who secretly prevented his son from seeing publication. Now the celebrant is summarising Gordon Alexander Grand's achievements, a speech Alex is relieved to hear bears no resemblance to his eulogy for Malcolm Randall. Of course another difference is that his father's funeral is real, not a false memory – an invented incident, rather, though not invented by Alex. Why is it so warm in the crematorium? His shirt has begun to adhere to his armpits. Perhaps he's simply growing nervous as he waits to address the congregation. Presumably his mother has warned Bronwyn Gale he will.

At least he feels as though the celebrant has drawn everyone's attention away from him, though he can't tell how much Lee is pretending. Bronwyn Gale reads from Donne and then cues a Bach cantata, which begins to fade as soon as it finds words. Alex's mother stretches out her hands and the open pamphlet as if to catch the music in its pages, protesting barely audibly "That wasn't the part he liked." She mustn't want to halt the ceremony, which the celebrant continues by reading from Shakespeare before she invites the congregation to rise and sing one of the lamented's favourite pieces, the chorus of the Hebrew slaves: "Va, pensiero...."

Alex joins in, not least to drown the scrawny notes of an unseen dwarfish organ that's providing the accompaniment, but he's recalling how his father used to bellow the melody in the bathroom when Alex was a child. The acoustic made him sound gigantic, and where does that recollection lead? Apparently to remembering a version that enraged his father. "Is there nothing they won't vandalise these days? Some crooner with a voice you wouldn't even praise a child for has been violating Verdi...." He carried on complaining until Alex found the offender online, a husky performance sung mostly in English. The lyrics replaced the Jewish victims with children, and the destination beyond the river became somewhere children went after hearing the chorus transformed into a lullaby. The place was stocked with heroes to protect their innocence, and Alex wonders how Malcolm Randall would have reacted to the notion. No doubt he would have embraced it, and Alex is glad it angered his father, even if only the distortion of the meaning did.

He has begun to feel inexplicably though tentatively relieved when he notices that Lee has turned her head but not her eyes towards him. What words has he been singing? As his awareness focuses on the lyrics in the pamphlet he hears himself utter syllables something like virtue. It's the last word of the chorus, but he doesn't know what it may have followed out of his mouth. "And now," Bronwyn Gale says, having indicated that the congregation should resume their seats, "I should like to invite to the podium anyone who wishes to remember the lamented."

"Alexander will," his mother calls out no more softly than a bingo winner. "His son."

So she hasn't notified the celebrant in advance. When Alex fails to stand up at once she urges "Do it for his memory. Do it for me."

Does she mean Alex has to speak for her? He's finding it hard enough to think for himself. The chapel feels hotter than ever, so that as he paces past the coffin he's afraid he may be assailed by its smell. Surely there's none, and he advances to the podium, across which he sees the congregation waiting to judge his testimony. It's a chapel, not a courtroom, and he only has to take care not to upset anyone. He mustn't refer to his father's initials, which might prompt him to mention the suppression of his essay. He tries to think what else he shouldn't say as he begins to speak.

He isn't talking about Malcolm Randall, and so there's no need to bring religion in. Randall isn't even dead, however vivid his funeral seems, in fact rather more authentic than this one. Gordon Alexander Grand is Alex's real father, since he has no other, and so Alex needn't say he felt rejected by him as Carla did. They weren't excessively close either, let alone unhealthily; in fact, when did they ever touch? If Alex became someone other than his parents wanted him to be, he shouldn't make it public, since he already wrote about the experience when he was Carl Batchelor – no, Carla Batchelor – no, just half the author of their book. Sweat trickles down his back to the base of his spine and beyond, an intrusion that returns him to himself with a shudder. "I think that's all I have to say just now," he says and lets go of the sides of the podium, to which he has apparently been clinging. His cuff pulls back along his wrist, revealing the watch his parents bought him for his eighteenth birthday. He shouldn't be surprised – it was Carla who lost her present, not him – but then he sees it shows he has been speaking for at least five minutes, and yet he can't recall a word he said apart from his final sentence.

Although the entire congregation is watching him, they appear to be competing to keep their reactions to themselves. Were they bemused or worse by his speech? As he steps down from the podium Bronwyn Gale says "Thank you, Alexander" like an adult praising a child despite their performance. When he sidles along the pew Lee pats his arm, a gesture that could denote sympathy or encouragement, the kind you might offer an invalid. Surely he can trust his mother. "How was I?" he whispers.

"So long as you believed it, Alexander. I can't say any more at present."

Does she mean she was moved by his eulogy or is simply unable to deliver one of her own? Some of his parents' colleagues reminisce about his father, and then Bronwyn Gale announces an interval for silent reflection or prayer. Alex tries to remember his father but feels as if a mental barrier has yet to yield. The harder he strains to capture memories, the further they retreat, until he's reduced to staring at the cover of the pamphlet to remind himself what his father looked like. Far too eventually Bronwyn Gale breaks the silence with a poem by Maya Angelou: "When great souls die...." Alex wonders if the dead man would have thought he fell into that category, though presumably his widow chose the poem. He's distracted by realising that Malcolm Randall would certainly regard the sentiments as godless. He would never have allowed such a reading at his funeral, and Alex has to remind himself again that Randall isn't dead.

Beethoven's thanksgiving melody after the storm is the cue for the coffin to withdraw behind the scenes. The symphony accompanies Bronwyn Gale to the exit, and once the Grands and Lee have sorted out their order in the aisle, Alex's mother leads them. "You stand with us, Lee," she says as if she's tendering a treat or else some form of compensation.

Alex halts Lee inside the chapel to mutter "How did I do up there?"

"I think you made your peace with him, Alex."

She has to mean his father, but she's left him with the fear that he could have been talking about Malcolm Randall. Of course he only thought about the man while he was at the podium, but why couldn't Lee have named his father? He's about to insist that she say who he meant when his mother peers around the doorway. "Don't leave me alone," she pleads.

They stand with her outside the chapel while the mourners pace past. Why is Lee receiving as many expressions of sympathy as Alex? It makes him feel as though he's as unrelated to his father as she is – as though he's an adopted child. He's more concerned that nobody mentions his eulogy, as if he never gave one or they've forgotten what he said, unless they don't want to remember. He's close to begging for opinions when his mobile twitches in his breast pocket. Since it's silenced, he has to take the phone out to identify the caller. "It's my agent," he says mostly to himself.

"Your life must go on, Alexander. Go and speak to them."

He wasn't proposing to answer the call, but since his mother has released him he's anxious to learn what Linder has to offer. He dodges around the nearest corner of the chapel, where a rakish wreath hangs over a headstone like a hoop tossed onto a target in a game. "Linder, I'm at the funeral," he says. "My father's funeral."

Why did he need to clarify that? Whose else would it be? "I won't keep you long, then," Linder says.

"Keep me as long as you need. The ceremony's over. Just the shaking hands now."

"You're suffering a reaction, you mean."

"I'm saying I have to shake everyone's hand," Alex says with a laugh that he hopes can't be heard around the corner. "So what are you bringing me?"

"I wanted to call as soon as I'd heard from everyone I showed your proposal."

"And now you have." When this prompts only silence, presumably signifying confirmation, Alex says "And what do they all think?"

"I'm very sorry to have to report we've had no takers, Alex."

Alex feels as if his mind and guts have been scooped out. "What did they say?"

"Basically they all agree that your Twitter controversy has made you too risky to publish."

"Agree with you, you mean."

"With one another, Alex."

"Can't they make controversy sell?" he pleads. "Isn't that what it's supposed to do?"

"Unfortunately not that kind, especially when it involves child abuse."

A breeze finds the wreath, which slips lower on the stone, covering the name Alex didn't take the chance to read. "So what do you suggest I do?"

"All we can do for now is bide our time and hope the situation may be forgotten. A couple of the houses, I'd rather not say which just yet, asked to be reminded in due course."

"How long?"

"They're both advising several years minimum."

A thought occurs to Alex, who hopes it isn't as desperate as it feels. "My books are still out there, aren't they? Maybe they'll change people's minds about me."

"I'm sorry, Alex. Tiresias told me that most of the shops have been sending them back. Do you think you'd better return to your funeral? You can call me later if there's anything you think we should discuss."

This sounds like dismissing the possibility along with him. Alex shoves the phone into his pocket, where it feels like a cold unhelpful lump weighing on his heart, and trudges around the chapel. Lee and his mother are in conversation with Erin and Daniel Irvine, who turn to him. "All our sympathies, Alexander," Daniel says more forcefully than anyone else has. "I beg your pardon, Alex."

"We can see from your face how much you've lost," Erin says, and Alex can only silence his answer.

ALEX AND MR GRAND

As soon as Carl sees Alex beyond the security gate he calls out "Here's my man."

The security officers glance at him before turning their attention to Alex. "He's my witness," Carl insists. "Alex Grand."

Though he's defiantly unshaven he sports an expensive light grey suit and dark tie and white shirt, the kind of outfit Malcolm Randall might wear while he was driving the limousine. How can Alex know that? It isn't a memory, it's simply a detail he might have deduced for the book, even if he can't recall writing it. The larger officer, who looks as if he would take some persuading to smile, shows Alex the palm of one broad hand. "Please empty your pockets, Mr Grand."

However this feels, he isn't really treating Alex as a criminal. The man knows his name because Carl said it, not because it's universally notorious. Alex plants the considerable contents of his pockets – keys, phone, cash, wallet, comb, handkerchief – in a plastic tray and pats himself in case he has forgotten any items, though he can't recall what they might be. He's about to pass through the security arch when the officer says "Please remove your belt and shoes."

No doubt offenders have to when they enter prison, but here it's surely just another detail of security, and Alex wants to think he has been singled out at random. He consigns the items to the tray and steps through the electronic arch. He can't help holding his breath, and when he doesn't set off an alarm he tries not to gasp too loud. As he retrieves his possessions and shoves his feet into his shoes he sees Lee plant her bag in a tray. Shouldn't she take her phone out of the bag? Why would the guards let it pass unexamined? He's keeping an eye on her when Carl tries to distract him. "I'll show him where we have to wait," he tells the second officer. "Soon as you're ready, Alex."

Alex is threading his belt through the loops of his trousers, and recoils as he feels someone fumbling near his waist. Carl is trying to help him locate a loop. This feels intrusive and unduly urgent, and too close to a memory that surely can't be his. "I can do it myself, thank you," he protests. "I don't need Lee either."

"Why's she here?" Carl says without lowering his voice.

Alex might ask this himself. She insisted on driving him to let him relax before he gives evidence, but he couldn't help wondering if that was why. The Twitter mob has grown more vituperative and numerous, unless just the names are multiplying. The only answer he can find for Carl is "She's with me."

Lee strolls through the arch as if she thinks too great a speed may trigger the alarm. When it stays mute she grabs her bag. "You'll be feeling safer now," she says.

Alex doesn't immediately grasp that she's talking to Carl, who gives the officers a glance. "Why am I going to do that?"

"Now that Alex will be taking some of the blame."

"Randall gets all that for what he did to me." Just the same, he would plainly rather not be overheard. "I told them I'd fetch you, Alex," he says and leads the way along a concrete corridor, only to swing around once the guards are out of earshot. "Blame for what?"

"For telling something other than the truth about your stepfather."

"We told all the truth that ought to matter. Alex is just here so everyone knows which that is." As Alex tries to decide how accurate this is, Carl tells Lee "You won't be saying anything. You weren't there."

"Neither was Alex."

"Who says he wasn't? Don't you go telling anyone."

"I'm saying he only knows what you told him."

"Right, and you weren't there when I did."

"Perhaps if I had been we'd have established the truth before he wrote the book."

"We've done it now, all right? He's done it. Stop trying to confuse him when he's got to tell it for me."

Is Lee indeed trying to bewilder Alex? He's already troubled by the notion that some recent incident should mean more to him than he's ready to acknowledge. He tramps after Carl to a room in a transverse corridor. As Carl makes to open the door, an usher emerges from the adjacent courtroom to frown at Lee and Alex. "Who are you, please?"

"He's Alex Grand that you're going to be calling. She's with him."

"That room is for witnesses only. The lady will need to wait out here or in the public gallery."

"I'll go public." As she follows the usher to the courtroom Lee calls back "Just remember I'm here."

Carl doesn't speak until he and Alex are in the witness room, a bare concrete space furnished with straight chairs and an empty table beneath a small high window reminiscent of a cell. "Who was she telling that?"

"Nobody but me, I should think."

"Sounded like she was warning me as well."

"I wouldn't say it sounded like a warning. She was offering support, that's all."

Alex hopes no more answers are required of him – they've started to fall short of convincing him – but Carl says "What did she mean, go public?"

"She'll be sitting with the rest of them."

"She wasn't saying she'll be telling people about us."

"Have you seen her doing that?"

"Doesn't mean she couldn't."

This isn't the answer Alex sought to prompt. "What do you think she'd have to tell?"

"Maybe stuff you told her I don't know you have. Stuff you've said about me."

"I don't think she's that interested in you, Carl."

"Even less excuse for her to be hanging round here, then. What's she got to do with anything?"

"She edited the book. That's her job." This only reminds Alex that she left him at the mercy of its lies. "She tried to leave its voice alone," he says, "whoever's that was."

"Pity she didn't check if that bastard Randall was alive. We wouldn't be in trouble now."

Alex feels close to a fit of mirthless laughter, but he mustn't lose control. "I rather think you're responsible for that inaccuracy, Carl."

"Sounded more like you were saying she didn't do her job. Maybe you should wonder why."

Instead of doing so Alex says "May I ask what sort of trouble you're anticipating?"

Carl plants his elbows on the table as though it's playing the role of his office desk and stares at Alex over his interleaved fingers. Apparently he's making sure of Alex's attention before he glances askance at the ceiling and jerks his head in that direction. "Think it's wired?"

"I doubt it. Why do you ask?"

"It would be in your kind of book, wouldn't it? So somebody can listen in."

"I don't believe I've ever written that." Alex can do without feeling less than certain. "Listen in to what?" he hardly wants to learn.

"Maybe people fixing their story together."

"I'm sure I've never had that idea." Alex means in fiction, but surely elsewhere too. "Anyway," he says, "they'd hardly do that in here. They'd have agreed it beforehand."

"Don't say stuff like that." Carl's gaze twitches upwards before fastening on Alex's face. "What are you going to say," he mutters, "when they fetch you?"

"That I'm ready, I suppose."

This is more of a hope, but Carl seems to suspect he's being mocked. "When they get you in there," he says low and fiercely.

"That will depend on what I'm asked. I should think what you'll say matters more."

"Don't need reminding. Like you say, depends what they ask."

"Just tell the truth as you told it to me."

Carl is barely audible. "Not sure I remember what I said."

"Then forget that. If you stay with the truth you can't go wrong."

"Maybe they'll ask about bits you made up."

"I assume I'm here to help establish which those are."

"Won't hear you do it, will I? They won't let me in where your lady friend went." Carl ducks his head as if to cheat any microphones before he mumbles "You've got what you were after."

Alex struggles not to feel accused. "Which you're saying was...."

"Christ, can't you hear me?" Almost silently but with a mime's grimaces Carl mouths "I don't know who said which."

"I don't mean to confuse anyone. Too many people are trying to do that to me, or perhaps not so many." As Alex sees he is indeed confusing if not antagonising Carl he says "If you don't remember something happening to you, presumably it was invented."

"Who by?"

"Does it matter? The rest has to be the truth, so just keep hold of that."

"It fucking matters. Some of your stuff feels like I remember."

"I've experienced something of the kind myself. Just concentrate on everything you know is you and nobody else."

The advice feels more ambitious once Alex applies it to himself. When Carl opens his mouth Alex is afraid to hear his doubts expressed aloud, but instead he hears his own name. Still more disconcertingly, it's in a woman's voice. "Alexander Grand," Carl says louder, projecting the summons behind Alex. No, the door has opened, and the usher has come to fetch him. Raising his fists, he gives them a terse shake to convey encouragement to Carl. He hopes some of that will follow him into the courtroom.

The long high concrete space is full of the backs of heads. The judge, a portly red-faced fellow built for jolliness he plainly finds unfitting to the situation, watches Alex trail the usher towards him. The wig perched on the judge's pate makes Alex feel he's being led into a past he needs to recognise. Heads turn to him as he paces past them, and he remembers trudging after his father's coffin. He ended up giving a speech he can't recall, over which he seemed to have no control, but he mustn't let that affect him now. He locates Lee near the back of the courtroom, and she nods at him – nods twice. One nod should mean encouragement, but what's the other for? As he passes the last of the audience he sees Elaine Randall and Hilary Wilson on the front row. They stare at him with such contempt he wouldn't be surprised to hear them hiss, but he's more disturbed when Malcolm Randall gazes at him from the box he's penned in, elevated almost as high as the judge's stage. Randall looks not just saddened by Alex's presence but ready to forgive it, an attitude that comes close to provoking Alex to speak as he's ushered to the witness box. He has no idea what his retort to Randall's silent saintliness would be, and he does his utmost to ignore the watching multitude and concentrate on the clerk who approaches him. "Please take the book in your right hand," she says.

Alex swears to tell the truth three times. "So help me God" – is this an appeal for aid or a way of emphasising his veracity? The phrase isn't on the card he has to read from, but he has heard it so often in films that he utters it before he can suppress the words. If he meets Randall's eyes, will the man see through his pretence of belief? He can imagine Randall condemning him out loud for blasphemy and then assuring him he can be pardoned if he repents. Since Alex is an unbeliever, does this mean he can lie to the court? He can't decide whether the possibility is reassuring or disturbing or somehow both, and he tries to make a mute vow that's more binding than the formula he spoke. He lifts his eyes from the ebony block of the Bible as the prosecution lawyer approaches the witness box.

He's a lanky silver-haired middle-aged man with a lined elongated face that Alex might have used to characterise a permanently disappointed schoolmaster in a novel. His expression looks weighed down by his wig, and his hands are clasped at the base of his spine as if to stop his robe flapping. His light soft voice sounds unexpectedly feminine. "Please state your name for the record."

"Alexander Evelyn Grand."

"And what is your profession?"

"I'm a novelist. I write crime."

"I understand you have a number of successes to your name."

"Coming up to a dozen books."

"Does that include the book you wrote in collaboration with Carl Batchelor?"

"No, that's extra. Separate."

"Did writing it entail a different approach from your usual method?"

"I've never worked with anybody else on a book before, so yes." While he isn't looking at Lee, he's immediately aware how she would suggest editing his statement. "Apart from my partner," he feels she's prompting him to add. "She helps me edit the material before it goes to the agent."

That isn't the truth any more. Recalling the rejections makes the core of him feel hollowed out. "Will you work with an editor at the publisher?" the lawyer says.

"I have, but she's always said I give her hardly any work to do."

This reminds him painfully of how he lost Kirsty her job. As he hopes the lawyer won't pursue the subject the man says "Do your books involve detection?"

"My character goes in for it, yes."

"You wouldn't say you were your character."

"Not the one in my books, no." The lawyer's disappointed look feels like a barrier Alex has to break through. "I just try to make him ring true," he says, "along with everybody else in them."

"And how would you say that applies to your most recent book?"

"Exactly the same, but it isn't finished yet." He's allowed himself to be confused, and doesn't quite manage to head off a laugh. "You wouldn't know about that," he says. "That's another novel. You're asking about *When I Was Carla*."

"The memoir you and Carl Batchelor wrote."

"The one I based on his memories, yes."

"How did that differ from writing your fiction?"

"I didn't have to invent much, as much." In a bid to counteract his stumble Alex adds "It was more a case of building on the truth."

He glimpses restlessness beyond the lawyer, and thinks he hears a hostile mutter from one of the Randall women if not both. Will the judge order silence in the court or even send them out? Apparently they haven't transgressed enough. Alex is disconcerted to feel the prosecution is speaking for them by enquiring "How much did you invent?"

"The whole book is based on Carl Batchelor's account of his life. We developed all the scenes together."

"How much of it did he remember?"

"All of it he told me."

The lawyer's disappointed look has found reason to linger. "Did he remember all the conversations you have in your book word for word?"

"Not every word, no, obviously. That's to say I assumed it would be obvious. It's an accepted convention of that kind of book."

"Please tell the court what kind of book you mean."

"Childhood memoirs. I don't suppose you remember every detail of your childhood any more than I do, but we accept the notion that people like them can."

"People such as whom?"

"Victims of abuse. Well, not just them. Maybe anyone who puts dialogue in their autobiography."

"But this wasn't yours. How did you set about writing the dialogue?"

"Mr Batchelor and I worked on it together until it seemed to ring true."

"But certain sections of the book have been shown to be untrue." With an air of regretting the need for the question the lawyer says "Did those ring true for you as well?"

"Not in the same way, no."

"Is that because now you're aware they were false?"

"Not just in retrospect. I'm remembering how it felt to write them."

"Please explain to the court what you have in mind."

"I had to invent a lot more than I did of Carl Batchelor's actual memories. I worked on those scenes with him until they felt real, but now I see I did most of the work."

"Can you cite an example?"

"The funeral."

"For the sake of clarity, will you say whose funeral that would have been?"

Alex meets the eyes of the supposed deceased. "Malcolm Randall."

Randall looks magnanimous while his wife and daughter provide a pair of contemptuous grunts. "It will be apparent to the court," the lawyer says, "that the defendant Malcolm Randall is alive."

"No thanks to some," Elaine Randall says, not just for Hilary to hear.

The judge clears his throat. "Please maintain order in the court."

Elaine Randall has left Alex struggling not to retort that her husband caused his father's death, and he almost doesn't catch the lawyer's question. "Could you give another instance?"

"When Carla's told her stepfather was murdered."

"Would you have known these events were invented if you hadn't learned the truth?"

"I think I might eventually have."

"But in your professional opinion, the bulk of the book is essentially factual."

"I'd say so." In case this is insufficiently ambiguous Alex adds "To the best of my knowledge, yes."

"Thank you for identifying the differences," the lawyer says and swings around, letting his robe flap at last. "Your witness."

The defence counsel is a short broad woman of about his age with a plump genial face. Whatever hair she has is hidden by a wig. As she approaches the witness box, her robe billows like a miniature sail caught by a breeze. Alex imagines the Randalls urging her to destroy him or at any rate his testimony and only just keeping the demand to themselves, but as she gazes up at him she looks gently encouraging, which is how her quiet precise voice sounds. "Mr Grand, what sort of book are you happiest to write?"

This throws him, though he's not sure how. "All of them once I'm involved."

"How would you say they involve you?"

"Imaginatively." He could imagine he's addressing a book group rather than a courtroom. "Once my imagination is involved," he adds for anyone who mightn't understand.

"In what kind of writing?"

"Crime. As I said before, that's what I write."

"We'll come back to your earlier statements if there's need. Have you written much you wouldn't call fiction?"

"*When I Was Carla*." Alex feels anxious to establish "That's the title of the book I wrote for Carl Batchelor."

"I don't suppose anyone could think your title was more personal. Which of you invented it?"

"Carl didn't have to. It was him."

"You're saying Mr Batchelor thought up the title."

"I think we both may have. I really can't remember." Surely there's no reason why this should trouble Alex, but the courtroom seems to have grown hotter, though presumably only he has. "Is it so important?" he protests.

"We're here to establish what is, Mr Grand." Her tone still sounds like a gentle reminder to cooperate. "Let me ask you again," she says as if she's seeking his permission. "Have you written much that isn't fiction?"

"Just that book."

"Though not all of that."

"Mr Batchelor and I worked up the material together, but I did all the writing."

"No, Mr Grand. As you admitted to my learned friend, some of it is fiction."

"I also said most of it isn't, only the parts that have been proved to be."

He's waiting for someone – the judge or the lawyer – to dismiss this as simply his opinion, but she says "How did you come to write the book?"

"I thought the story was worth telling."

"Won't that have been the case with all your fiction?"

"I mean because this was the truth," Alex says and stares at Randall hard enough to make his eyes sting. "The truth about someone who'd got away with abusing a child."

"I don't doubt the court will agree that's commendable." Having paused as though to let everyone concur, the lawyer says "But I was asking how you came to be selected for the job."

"Mr Batchelor wanted me."

"Was that based on your reputation?"

"Surely you should ask him that."

"I may in due course, but I'd appreciate hearing your answer."

Alex does his best not to lie. "I'd like to think that was his reason."

"Had you previously written about child abuse?"

"My last novel dealt with it." Alex tries not to sound bitter while adding "My last published novel."

"Gender reassignment also, I understand."

"I tried to look at that as well."

"Did you find it necessary to do much research?"

"Perhaps not as much as I should have."

"Have you experienced child abuse yourself?"

"Good God no." As the judge emits a throaty sound heralding intervention Alex says "Forgive me. I mean of course not, definitely not."

He's disconcerted to see Malcolm Randall offer him a nod, pardoning his profanity, perhaps. "Why of course?" the lawyer says.

"Because I'd have said if anything of that nature had been done to me."

"If I understand you correctly, you're telling the court that on the basis of a work of fiction you feel could have been more thoroughly researched, Mr Batchelor chose you to write his testimonial."

"It wasn't just him, not even mostly. My publisher did too."

"I believe they are no longer your publishers." As Alex tries to relax the grip he's taken on the front edge of the witness box – it reminds him too closely of growing unaware of his own words at the crematorium – the lawyer says "Why did they commission you to write the book?"

"Because my editor thought I was the man for the job."

"I gather she has also left them." Before Alex can go further than opening his mouth the lawyer says "Is it not the case that some people had condemned your novel for what they felt was a lack of sensitivity, and the book you wrote with Mr Batchelor was an attempt to regain your name?"

Alex glares across the courtroom. Lee looks concerned about his answer, as she ought to be. "Who told you that?" he demands.

"I'm simply asking whether it was the case."

"I'd say you know it is." When the lawyer only gazes at him Alex has to admit "It was meant to fix things for the publisher."

"What would you say it achieved?"

"If it helped bring somebody to justice," Alex says, shifting his glare from Lee to Malcolm Randall, "it was a success."

"Wasn't there an instance where it failed?"

"You mean the priest," Alex says and looks away from all the Randalls. "Father Brendan."

"Just explain to the court who that is."

"He was Carla's priest and everybody else's there. According to Carl Batchelor, he joined in abusing her as a child."

"According to Mr Batchelor." The lawyer appears to ponder the phrase. "Has it not been shown," she says, "that the priest never abused girls?"

"No, it just hasn't been shown that he did."

"You regard that as sufficient reason to accuse him of further abuse."

"I didn't accuse him. Carl Batchelor did."

"Would he have done that without your support?"

"My job was to help him remember. I'm still not convinced the priest never touched him."

Alex is in control now – he has loosened his grip on the witness box but not on his mind – and yet he feels as if his words have crept up on him unnoticed. The lawyer gives him no time to examine them. "That's your professional judgment," she says.

"I'm saying it felt true to me. All those memories of Carl's did."

"And yet you told my learned friend that you think memories are unreliable, even memories of abuse."

"I didn't say that." He feels as if she's undermining his own ability to remember. The heat has grown as oppressive as the interrogation. Under his prickly armpits his shirt is sodden, and the prospect of sweat coursing down his back makes him shudder. "I didn't, did I?" he appeals to the prosecuting counsel.

The judge deals his desk a single knuckly rap. "Please confine yourself to answering counsel for the defence."

"I'd like to return to your way of writing, Mr Grand," the lawyer says.

He no longer trusts her gentleness. It's a concealment beneath which she plans to sneak up on him. "Ask away," he retorts. "I talk about it all the time."

"Let us say you have an idea for a novel."

"I've had plenty. Still have some."

Alex wishes he believed more in his own defiance, but Lee is there to remind him of the collapse of his career. He manages to withhold an accusing glare as the lawyer says "How does it become a book?"

"You develop it until you have enough material."

"I take it this involves inventing characters and episodes and a plot to hold them all together."

"That's how it works when it does."

"Are you saying you sometimes have ideas which you reject?"

"They're very much part of the job."

"On what basis do you reject them?"

"If they don't convince me."

"Did you reject any Carl Batchelor gave you?"

There's the trap, which Alex ought to have anticipated. "No," he says, "but that isn't the same. He was telling me about his own experience."

"Whereas you know you've imagined your stories."

"That's the point exactly."

"But you thought everything Mr Batchelor told you was the truth."

"It rang true, as I said to your colleague."

"Can you explain how you're able to judge when you say you've had no experience of such abuse?"

"Are you saying social workers need to have before they can deal with it?" Letting out more of a laugh than he planned, Alex says "And how about the police?"

"Mr Grand, we're talking about you. How are you qualified as a fiction writer?"

"Because that's what I am."

"Which is precisely my question." As Alex strives to grasp what this may be the lawyer says "How does that qualify you to make judgments even the police and social workers find it hard to make?"

Alex has no answer. He's hoping the prosecution or the judge may object that he's being asked for his opinion or even some less reasonable answer, but they're as silent as the rest of the watchful mob. He shakes his head, and his body writhes as though in response. It's reacting to the threat of perspiration trickling down his spine and beyond. The prospect recalls his loss of awareness at his father's funeral, but why does it feel like an earlier memory? "One more question," the lawyer says, "if I may."

If this is designed to sound reassuring, Alex is sure it's a trick. "Make it a good one. Give me the best you've got."

Did he say any of that out loud? The mass of impassive faces isn't telling, and Malcolm Randall looks as ready as ever to pardon him, while the Randall women are maintaining their disdain. Alex glances at the judge, but the man isn't looking at him. He's gazing towards Lee, perhaps straight into her eyes, in which case what message is being exchanged? As Alex stares at Lee without managing to establish the direction of her gaze, the lawyer says "How much did you suggest to Mr Batchelor?"

"Not a thing that I remember."

"You put nothing of yourself into the book even though it bears your name."

"I keep saying, it's all about Carl, not me. Carl and Carla too."

"You regard them as separate people."

Where is she trying to lead him? How can this help her defend Randall? "No," Alex says, "I think that's how he tells it, but he was really always Carl."

How did Carl put it, and can that be trusted? As Alex tries to fend off these doubts so as to concentrate on the lawyer she says "So you weren't aware of manufacturing any part of the book."

Alex thinks he senses that the judge is growing restless. She's already had her final question, after all. He's tempted to say so, but instead says "I just tried to bring Carl's memories to life."

"Just his memories."

"Exactly, just his."

Why did Alex say that? It wasn't how she meant the latest of her comments that pretend they aren't questions. He thinks he's about to feel a trickle down his back, and can't help squirming. "Are you unwell?" the lawyer doesn't help by asking.

"Nothing wrong with me. Let's get this done." When the judge's disapproval turns on him Alex says "I mean by all means carry on."

"If I may make absolutely certain, you yourself invented nothing that your book claims the defendant did."

"That's what I said." In case he didn't, Alex adds "That's the truth."

"And nothing that was left out of the book."

He doesn't understand why this puts him on guard. Since she can't know why the question troubles him, it must be random, not founded on any insight into him. Ruth Nyman's observation comes to mind, feeling like a refuge. "Why should it matter," he protests, "when it wasn't in?"

"Please answer the question," the judge warns him.

"It wasn't one. She said she'd finished asking them." When the judge's silence grows ominous Alex blurts "I may have wondered if he ever did something, but Carl said he never did."

"Who are you talking about, Mr Grand?" the lawyer pretends not to know.

"Who do you think? Malcolm Randall and nobody else." To make certain Alex jabs a finger at the man. "I'm saying he didn't," he reminds anyone who needs it. "He just did everything Carl said."

"What are you saying Mr Randall didn't do?"

Alex has begun to wish this were just the courtroom scene he rehearsed with Carl. "How can that possibly matter when it never happened?"

"We're examining the process by which the allegations against Mr Randall came to be published." Is she talking to Alex or the judge or someone else? "If any were rejected," she says, "I think it may be important to establish what they were and why."

"Please continue."

Alex wouldn't say this, but the judge does. Should Alex plead to sit down or request a glass of water? He would only be postponing the interrogation and leaving himself alone with thoughts he can't define but feels desperate to suppress. "Mr Grand," the lawyer says, "who rejected the idea?"

"Carl Batchelor."

"On what basis?"

"I keep telling you, he never did it."

"Did what, Mr Grand?"

"Not Carl. I don't mean him." That wasn't her question, but Alex finds he's more than eager to pretend it was. "He never," he says and has to swallow as a shudder passes through him. "He never got behind anybody when they were in the bath."

"You're talking about getting in the bath with them."

"No, I'm saying the exact opposite. He never did."

"You're being quite specific about an event you say didn't take place. Can you explain why that is?"

"I'm specifically saying it never happened. Never means never and nothing else but. I don't think even you would want to edit that." He's staring at Lee while he wonders why he feels driven to use so many words. "I'll be even more specific if you like," he can't help continuing. "He never—"

He's overwhelmed by a shudder so violent he has to grab the sides of the witness box. The sensation is only a memory, the threat of an intrusive trickle down his spine and lower, but this simply makes it harder to fend off. "Yes," a voice he hardly recognises says, "he did."

"What are you saying, Mr Grand? Please explain."

"He came in the bath, and I mean he came."

"Mr Grand, please remember you're on oath. You have just told the court—"

"Not your client. Not you this time," Alex says while he stares at Malcolm Randall. "My father."

He feels the enormous hairy legs trapping his own from behind, and the mysterious unfamiliar pressure against his back as his father reaches for a bath toy to sail towards the taps, and a sudden protracted convulsive movement that ascends his spine, followed by a descending trickle colder than the shallow water.... "Christ," he says with no sense of how loud. "No wonder I couldn't remember."

Gripping the sides of the witness box makes him feel as if he's addressing the congregation at his father's funeral. Realising that he could have said this then dismays him as much as the resurrected memory. Is Randall looking sympathetic? Perhaps he feels that way on behalf of Alex's father. As the lawyer makes to speak Alex says "No wonder I couldn't remember him touching me. That must have been why he never did again."

He has very little sense of where he is by now. He could be in a courtroom scene in one of his own novels. His words are leaving him as they occur to him, and he no longer cares who hears them. Even the intrusion of another voice only just recalls his situation. "No further questions, your honour."

"The witness is excused."

Did the judge say that? Perhaps Alex did, or did as well. He stumbles out of the witness pen and flees towards the exit, fixing his attention on the aisle so as not to see all the eyes that are intent on him. He especially doesn't want to see how the Randalls may look now. He lurches into the corridor, and as he dashes past the room where Carl is waiting he feels compelled to call out "I'm not you."

Apparently Lee is at his back. "You're still you, Alex."

She says his name again as he stalks along the corridor. "I don't know who I am," he says without turning to her. However fast he tramps, the exhumed memory keeps up with him. Lee's pursuing footsteps seem to urge him faster. When he blunders past the security guards and out of the courthouse, he feels the world is hardly there. It's just a set for scenes he has yet to perform.

ALEX AND ALEXANDER

"I think I know the way, Alex."

"I don't doubt it." Since this lacks the force of the retort he meant to make, Alex demands "To do what?"

"The way home."

"I still have one of those, do I? You'd like to think so."

"You've still got me."

"Whatever that may mean."

"I hope it means enough."

"You've been that for a while."

Her hands shift on the steering wheel, but she doesn't look at him. "Would you like me to stop?"

"Why, have you finished?" When she only gazes at the road they're speeding down he says "Stop what exactly?"

"I'm asking if you'd like me to pull over while you say what you need to say, Alex."

"You think you know what that is."

"No, I'm saying I don't. I'm hoping you may."

"Then that makes two of us at least." Since she doesn't betray any reaction to this Alex says "Carry on. Stopping won't help."

Perhaps he means talking as well as driving. Perhaps he's advising himself to talk too. He feels compelled to let all his words out, if only to distract him from the memories that haven't finished gathering inside him: his father's moist breath on his neck, a whisper of "Here's a game for you, Alexander".... Lee grips the wheel one-handed as she reaches to stroke his arm, but he can't help drawing away. "Alex," she says with a bid for gentleness that reminds him too much of Malcolm Randall's lawyer, "I'm not your father."

"Who are you saying you are?"

"Who would you like me to be?"

If this is designed to resemble a plea, it comes nowhere near convincing him. "Just who I'm seeing," he says. "Nobody anywhere else."

A signboard that indicates the motorway beyond the town distracts him from observing her response. Now he understands her remark that set his words off, and he brandishes the phone. "You thought I was going to look up the route."

He expects her to assume he has regained lucidity, but she seems less than reassured. "What were you going to do instead?"

"I need to speak to my mother."

Lee's foot falters on the accelerator. He can tell she wants to halt the car, but there's no space among the vehicles parked beside the road. "What about, Alex?"

"What in Christ's name do you think? About what her husband did to me."

"Will you put it like that to her? He was still your father, after all."

"It's a bloody sight less than he put to me. Whose side are you on?"

"Yours and your mother's. Who else's would I be?"

Alex might unleash a retort except for realising his question sounded too much like Carl Batchelor. "Do you think you should call her just yet?" Lee says.

"When would you prefer?"

"It isn't about me, Alex. Might you want to wait until you've had time to recover?"

"How long am I being given?"

"As long as it takes, and only you can know that. Just remember I'm here for you and I'll do everything I can."

"I'll remember what you said." Rather than add to this, he says "I need to talk to her before she hears from anybody else."

"Who would she?"

"I'm guessing someone who was at the trial. I'm not saying they would contact her, but they might post about it online."

"Would she be likely to see that?"

Alex hears Lee's pause as much as the words that follow, and it conveys a good deal more to him. "Who knows who might want her to," he says, and as Lee speeds onto the motorway he makes the call.

It's answered sooner than he's ready for, which feels too much like the springing of a trap. "Who is it?" his mother sounds nervous of learning. "Who is this?"

"It's me, mother."

"Alexander. I haven't seen you both in quite a time."

He doesn't realise how much this disturbs him until he hears himself say "Both."

"You and your lady." With more concern than he welcomes his mother says "You're still together, aren't you?"

"She's still here."

"Here I am, Amy," Lee calls without glancing away from the road.

"Lee, it's good to hear your voice. How are you both?"

"Both," Alex finds he's mouthing as Lee says "Life's a little complicated just now."

"I hope I'm not part of it. The complication, I mean, not your life."

Lee apparently has no reply she wants to offer. "Alexander?" his mother prompts.

"I'm it, yes. I'm a lot of them."

"Of course you have your book to write, and you said you may have to go to court. Don't feel compelled to visit me while you're dealing with all that."

"We like to see you, Amy."

"I'm glad to hear that, Lee." Perhaps her pause is inviting Alex to contribute, but when he doesn't speak she says "I meant I could visit you instead. I need to get out of this house more. It's too full of memories just now."

Alex feels as if the women are conspiring to delay what he has to ask. "Memories," he blurts. "I want to talk to you about one."

He wonders how much he's about to distract Lee, who has reached eighty in the outer lane, overtaking two ranks of massive elongated lorries. "As many as you like," his mother says. "I'm sure it will help to share them."

Alex thinks he feels the car start to waver sideways before Lee stiffens her grasp on the wheel. "I just wanted to ask you," he says and has to swallow, "did my father ever get in the bath with me?"

"Good heavens, have you only just remembered that? It does bring back old times. Do you know, I'd forgotten it myself."

"Were you there?"

"I rather think so," she says with a puzzled laugh. "I'd hardly know about it otherwise, would I?"

"I mean were you with us in the bathroom."

"On some occasions." As the car outdistances the lorries she says "I hope you don't think there was ever anything wrong. You were only small, and as your father pointed out, it's accepted all over Japan."

"You never did it yourself."

"I'm sorry if you think I should have. Weren't we close enough in any case?"

The car veers into the inside lane. Not just the threat of the lorries speeding up while Lee was alongside has silenced Alex. Now he knows he was hoping that the memory was spurious, no more than a nightmare he once had rather than one he's living. "I'm afraid," he says and forces himself to continue, "we were too close."

"When were we ever that? I don't see how it's possible."

"Not us." His words are growing harder to expel. "Me," he says, "and my father."

"I shouldn't have said so. What do you think you remember?"

"Once when you couldn't have been with us in the bathroom." At once doubt assails him. "As far as I know," he says, "it was only once."

His mother's voice sharpens while growing remote. Perhaps she's holding the phone away from her face, the better to stare at his name. "What are you trying to say about your father?"

Alex almost wishes Lee would edit his words or even speak for him. "I'm afraid," he says, "he liked being in the bath with me too much."

"What exactly do you mean?"

Alex finds he's digging his nails into his thighs, whether from frustration or to fend off the sensations the memory revives. "He took too much pleasure in it."

"What on earth can you be saying? What sort of pleasure?"

"I'm sorry," Alex says, which merely postpones letting out the word. "Sexual."

The silence this provokes is so total that he wonders if his mother has cut him off. The rubbery rumble of wheels on tarmac obscures any sounds the phone may be keeping low. "I don't need to tell you I wish it weren't true," he says, "but I can still remember feeling—"

"That's enough, Alexander. That's very much more than enough. Don't you dare say another word."

He hasn't by the time she speaks again. "So that's how you comfort me in my loss," she says, "by soiling my memories of him."

"Amy," Lee says without turning her head, "if it's the truth—"

"And you let Lee hear that filth as well. Who else are you going to vilify your father to?"

"It came out at the trial." Alex is desperate enough to add "The defence lawyer trapped me into saying."

"Why didn't you tell everybody at the funeral while you were about it? We could all see your heart wasn't in it when you spoke. So that's what you were holding back. Did you wait until I wasn't there to stop you speaking? God forgive you, Alexander."

She has begun to sound unsettlingly like Elaine Randall. "I hadn't remembered it then," Alex protests.

"You might as well not have remembered anything. That's how you made me feel, but now you've excelled yourself."

"I didn't want you to be more upset by hearing it from someone else."

"Amy," Lee says, "I honestly don't think Alex could stop himself from letting it out at the trial. I think he was too shocked by remembering all of a sudden."

"I appreciate you have to take his part." Quite as tonelessly his mother says "At least I made no date to visit you. It saves all the bother of cancelling."

"Amy, if I can just say—"

"You mayn't, no. I won't look to be visited or contacted further, and I'm very much afraid that includes you as well. I wonder if you were in any way responsible for Alexander's thinking what he said, considering how you involve yourself in what he writes."

"They aren't the same. I never tell him what to think," Lee protests, but the phone has finished listening. She gazes at the empty stretch of motorway ahead and then risks reaching towards Alex, who crouches away from her. As he fingers the screen of his phone she says "What are you doing?"

"Can't I see what anyone is saying about me?"

"You don't need to upset yourself any more just now, Alex."

"Somebody else will be trying to do that," he says and barely succeeds in withholding a laugh.

In court today Alex Grand the fiction writer said his own father abused him when he was a child. Hes safe to say it since his fathers dead. Looks like he loves accusing vulnerable people. Whos he going to say harmed him next, we wonder? L. O'Quent has asked, and this time Alex's laugh is irrepressible, even if it leaves all mirth behind. "Someone's given herself away at last," he says.

"Who's that, Alex?"

"Guess." When Lee shakes her head he thrusts the phone at her, urging "Or look."

She stares ahead as though she's hoping traffic will lend her an excuse not to comply, but they're still on a deserted stretch. She doesn't look at the phone until Alex holds it in front of the windscreen. She blinks and frowns before returning her attention to the road. "Have you taken all that in already?" Alex says. "You must be good at taking in."

"I've read it but I can't see what you mean."

"You wouldn't usually let words slip like that. It must depend whose they are."

"You're going to have to enlighten me, Alex."

"Whoever she'd like me to think she is, how did she know my father's dead? I never mentioned it in court, did I?"

He's protecting the memory of his courtroom outburst from any attempt to confuse him when Lee says "Couldn't she have found out online?"

Alex grins bitterly, since she isn't looking at him. She has divulged she knows the gender of his tormentor. He types Gordon Alexander Grand in the search box and is disconcerted to learn that several reports of his father's death cite him as a son. "Clever," he says, "except some of us might wonder why she'd have looked it up at all."

"Maybe she was thinking of letting him know what you'd said."

"And how would she have done that?" The question is as false as Lee's suggestion, but it rouses a doubt in his mind. How would anyone have posted the message from the courtroom? Phone use is prohibited in there – and then he sees the solution. "I should have known," he mutters. "The perfect place to produce crap."

"What are you saying now, Alex?"

"Just thinking of the toilet."

"Do you want me to stop at the next services? They aren't far."

"That's what you think I'm saying, is it? Or you'd like me to think I am."

"I don't know what you're saying. I'll need a break myself."

"You'll be slipping off behind the scenes again, will you?"

"I'll have to. I know you're distressed, I can't even imagine how much of a turmoil you must be in, but you're making me nervous to drive."

"We can't have that. You need to get me where you can keep your eye on me."

"Alex, I'm really doing my best to make allowances, but do you have to be quite so much like this?"

"What are you telling me you have to make them for?"

"How you must be having to come to terms with what you've only just remembered."

"You honestly believe I'll think that's been my problem."

"That makes sense, doesn't it? It must always have been somewhere in your head. That's why you tried to pass it on to Carl. Your mind was trying to bring it into the open and at the same time deny it was yours."

"You think you know my mind, do you? Sorry, you haven't managed to get in."

"I wasn't trying to. I just want you to be well."

"Which of you wants that?"

This sets off a twitch that jerks at the side of his eye – the left turn indicator on the dashboard. "I don't understand," Lee says.

"Is it Lee or L? Or Eel, it could have been. That's a slippery name."

"Alex...." Lee glances in the mirror rather than at him. "I wonder if you ought to see someone."

"I'm seeing her. I'm seeing all of them."

The car is in the inside lane, and there's no exit for most of half a mile. Does she plan to pull onto the hard shoulder? The side mirror shows Alex a police car gaining on them. "Who are you in touch with now?" he demands.

"I hoped I was with you, Alex."

The pretence of an appeal isn't going to distract him. He glares at the mirror as the pursuing car halves the distance. If he seizes the wheel when the police direct Lee to pull over, what else may he feel compelled to do? As they race alongside he turns his head to watch, and sees Lee glance in their direction. Doesn't she dare betray how she was hoping they would intervene? "They didn't want you to stop," Alex says. "They think you're an upstanding citizen."

"I told you I'm coming off at the services."

That's where the nearest exit leads, which is no reason why she should have indicated prematurely. "For one thing we need petrol," she says as Alex sees the police head up the exit ramp.

He has lost sight of them by the time Lee drives into the car park. When she passes several empty parking spaces he suspects she's searching for the police. No doubt she wants him to think she's making for a space close to the toilets, but she parks in sight of the unoccupied police car. Alex watches her pretend she's unaware of it as she leaves her seat, snatching the keys from the ignition before he has released his safety belt. "I'll see you back here," she says and locks the car. "Will you be long?"

"I'm sure no longer than you'll have to be."

Her face turns so blank it might persuade anyone but him she doesn't understand his comment. He overtakes her once they're in the block of cloned shops and cafés, where fruit machines chatter electronically to themselves in an amusement alcove opposite a hamburger counter. As Alex dodges into the male toilet he sets off a roaring alarm – no, an eager dryer on the tiled wall. The long room is divided by twin ranks of sinks back to back, each pair surmounted by mirrors he could imagine are two-way. Along one wall occupants of cubicles emit an inadvertent fanfare, while the other wall offers the urinals, about twenty manly oval bowls beyond which their little brothers lie low at the far end of the room. Alex stays well clear of the junior section and finds a spot where no immediate neighbours hem him in. He has to relax before he can function, though he's anxious to return to the car ahead of Lee. He deals his penis a terse final shake and is zipping up his trousers when the urinal floods as though to erase any trace of his presence. He hurries to the nearest sink and only just manages not to retreat, because he's next to a uniformed policeman who has glanced at him. If Alex ignores him, will that look suspicious? He mustn't give the man any reason to detain him, and so it seems advisable to speak. "Why do they call them one and two as well?" he says. "You'd wonder which they are."

The policeman turns his heavy squarish head towards Alex, but that's his only response. Of course he can't know what Alex has in mind. "Only thinking aloud," Alex tells him. "The kind of mirror you chaps use to spy on people. One way except they're two. These just reminded me of them."

"You won't find any of that in here."

Does he mean spying? Alex wonders why the man should have assumed he did. He gives his hands a brief though painfully hot rinse and makes for the dryers, only for the officer to follow him, so that Alex feels compelled if not expected to speak again. Above the duet of the dryers he shouts "I've just been in court."

"That so."

"On your side," Alex yells. "Helping you convict someone."

"Good for you."

This could benefit from more enthusiasm. Perhaps he can't be bothered to outshout the dryers. "Paedophile," Alex bellows just as the policeman lowers his hands, quelling half the mechanical roar. Alex twists around, silencing his dryer, to see most of the men at the sinks and even at the urinals staring at him and his companion. "Not him," he calls. "He'll be after them."

The audience turns away, some of them immediately, but the policeman is watching Alex. He's between him and the exit, and when Alex takes a step towards it the man doesn't move. Alex is wondering how to shift him – he must reach the car before Lee does – when the policeman strides ahead to punch a smiling face. It's an icon on the exit wall, denoting satisfaction with the facilities. "Sorry about that," Alex murmurs as he pokes the icon, which bears a large thumbprint. "I hope I haven't harmed your reputation. I know how that works."

The policeman doesn't answer as Alex follows him out of the block. Sunlight coats the windscreen of Lee's car, so that Alex can't tell whether she's inside. Darting around the policeman, he sprints to the vehicle, which is empty after all. He fumbles for his keys and is opening a door when Lee hurries out of the block with a policewoman close behind her. Is she bringing the woman to him? He's in the driver's seat well before she arrives at the car. The policewoman looks as if she's urging Lee to lead her to it, but carries on to join her colleague as Lee climbs in. "Made a friend in the police, did you?" Alex challenges her.

"I didn't even notice her, Alex."

"Then how did you know she was a she?" When Lee doesn't answer he says "I made one myself."

"Are you just driving to fill us up?"

This feels like a bid to ignore his remark. "For a start," he says and drives to the petrol station next to the retail block. Switching off the engine, he springs the petrol cap with the lever by his seat while he keeps the other hand on the key in the ignition. "I'll let you pump us," he says. "I can do without a hose in my hand just now."

Lee seems unconvinced by his reason. "I can drive."

"I'll stay where I am if it's all the same to you. Driving may take my mind off other things. I imagine you'll be in favour of that."

"If you're sure."

"I'm not sure of anything or anyone." When this keeps Lee seated, Alex says "Right now I need to look at something."

Some of that is Lee, but there's also the phone. As soon as she gives in to leaving the car he finds his way to Twitter. Someone posting as Survivved thinks Alex's courtroom revelation was a publicity stunt, a suggestion that attracts a chorus of agreement. One poster claims that Alex was promoting his next book, and another speculates about the theme, which was surely never any Alex thought of. None of the contributors is L. O'Quent or Ledonnerley, which sounds more and more like Lead On Her Lee as he repeats it in his head, or Lderlylad, which is altogether too determined to seem masculine but can't quite hide its real significance – L de Lee'll Add, Elle Duh Lee'll Add. None of the onscreen names even contains an l, which he finds suspicious in itself; his own name does, after all. He's staring at words and urging them to betray their identity when the police car looms up in the mirror.

Does it slow momentarily alongside Lee's car? Is she sending the police a wordless signal? She seems intent on the rapid antics of the digits on the petrol pump. The police car gathers speed towards the motorway, and he feels as if all of them have tricked him into missing what went on between them. While Lee hangs the dripping metal nozzle on the pump and pays for the fuel, he tries to decide how to greet her return. She must have prepared her own speech, because as she resumes her seat she murmurs "Say whenever you want me to take over."

"Why am I meant to want that?"

"If you feel at all tired." Having hesitated as he's increasingly convinced the police car did, she adds "Or even a little bit distracted."

"I won't be that if nobody talks, and I'll rest at home."

Although he can't see the police lying in wait on the motorway, he doesn't let this dull his alertness. He glances so often at the mirror, not to mention at the dashboard to confirm he can't be stopped for speeding, that the action soon feels like a tic. It makes his eyes ache, and so do the headlights that the dusk sets on him as it congeals around the car. Too many of the beams don't sink until they've pasted a lingering glare on his vision. He has to keep squeezing his eyes shut in bids to erase the patches of blindness. It must be too dark for Lee to observe how long his eyes stay closed, but he senses her willing him to recall her offer. She won't be taking him over, and not just on this drive. However much she may have managed to edit his thoughts about her in the past, he's on the lookout now. How many of his memories of her may be as unreliable as his recollections of his childhood? Best to ensure she has no place in his head. When he clenches his fists on the wheel he doesn't know whether he's trying to keep hold of the indisputably real or making certain Lee can't wrest control from him.

The night is well advanced by the time they reach home. As Alex parks outside the house a streetlamp stains the tarmac with the deformed shadow of the car. Several men greet his arrival with a cheer, and he wonders who is mocking him until he realises they're watching football in a pub. Lee lets herself into the apartment and switches on more lights than she usually would. She turns as Alex eases the door shut behind her. "Are you going to rest now?" she plainly hopes. "You said you would."

"I will when you're ready to."

"Do you want to eat first?"

"It'll only keep us awake."

He means this to let her think he'll fall asleep. He shares the bathroom with her, even though recalling how he did so with his father makes him feel as if the entire room is sweating in sympathy with him. At least Lee can't use her phone while he's watching. In bed he makes himself slip an arm around her waist, because it guarantees she can't creep behind him as his father used to or out of bed either, and ought to let him sense when she goes to sleep. Only what about tomorrow? She obviously has plans, since she's pretending not to understand his comments about her. Before he can anticipate what she may do or is even certain she's unconscious, he drifts into thoughtless darkness.

He has no sense of dreaming, and perhaps he doesn't speak. Or are the repetitions of his name a symptom of both? "Alex. Alex. Alex." He does his utmost to struggle awake once he grasps that it isn't his voice. It's Lee's, and she's pointing at him to identify him to someone. His fingers and thumbs prise his sticky eyes wide, but he has to blink hard to comprehend she's holding out her phone. "Here you are, Alex."

"What have you done now? What are you grinning about that you're so eager I should see?"

"Nothing, and I've no idea what you mean. It's Linder."

"She took the chance to call you up again, did she, or did you call her? I notice you always make sure I'm asleep."

Lee's smile disappears, and her expression looks close to collapsing entirely until she jerks the phone out of his reach. "Call her yourself, or don't. I actually have stopped caring." She marches to the door, where she halts without turning. "I'm going for a walk," she says. "I don't know when I'll be back or if I will."

When he hears the outer door of the apartment slam and then the downstairs door, Alex stumbles to the window. Lee is fleeing across the road. He watches her disappear towards the seafront before he retrieves his phone from beside the bed and tells it to call Linder. "Alex," she says, though warily. "I'm sorry if I caused some kind of argument."

"Don't be sorry unless you need to be. What were you going to say to me if you'd been given the chance?"

"I told Lee." Before Alex has time to decide if this is meant to establish whether Lee can overhear, his agent says "I believe there may be news for someone."

EVELYN

"And now who has a question for Evelyn?"

Several hands go up but look poised to give way to one another. "Lady on the front row," Rhoda prompts.

"Are your characters based on people?"

"All the ones inside my head."

"Real people, I mean."

"That's what they are. People I know or I did. I keep them up here until I need them."

"Even your murderer?"

"He has to have been in there too, doesn't he? Perhaps I had to build him up more than the rest of them."

"He doesn't come from anybody in particular."

"Just me."

"I thought he was the most alive of anybody in the book except for his poor partner."

"Well, thank you very much, but let's keep the plot to ourselves for anyone who's going to read my novel."

"Who's next?" Rhoda says. "Gentleman with the cravat."

"Do you rewrite much, Evelyn?"

"Always. More than ever with this one. I even changed the plot."

"How did your publishers feel about that?"

"You're assuming they saw it before. I did let them have a synopsis in advance, but they agree it's improved."

"You weren't afraid you might have let them down."

"I hope I don't do that to anyone who deserves better. That's how I try to be."

"As a writer, is that?"

"In myself. How I do my best to act in life."

"I expect we all do," Rhoda says. "Yes, lady with the scarf, no, behind you."

"Where did you get Dexterity Wright from?"

"She's part of a tradition of detectives I wanted to bring up to date."

"She isn't anyone you know."

"If she comes from life I'd say she came from me."

"She's founded on yourself."

"Let's say she's somebody I played for the duration of the book."

"You'll continue if it becomes a series, will you not?"

"I imagine I'll have to. It's part of the game."

"Will you have gone in for detecting yourself?"

"I don't need to. I know myself inside out."

"That's quite amusing, but my question was were you ever a detective."

"Only an amateur, but it brought results. And of course every book involves research."

"Except the one you didn't do enough for."

The voice comes from the back of the audience. "Excuse me," Rhoda says, "if you'd like to speak to Evelyn—"

"Don't worry, Alexander knows me. Tell them, Alexander."

"It's Mr Alexander," Rhoda protests, "or it's Evelyn."

"No, it's Evelyn Alexander Grand."

"Get it right, Tom." Evelyn has had enough. "It was Alexander Evelyn Grand," he says, "and Alex when you knew him."

"Then try getting mine right," ToM complains, shifting to a seat where he can be seen through a gap in the audience.

Rhoda blinks at Evelyn from her chair beside him on the bookshop podium. "Should I know the name?"

"My old one, you mean? You might well have. My publisher decided this one would give me a new lease of life."

"After you tried to be Carla," ToM says, "and then you found you weren't as much as you thought."

"Is that why he's trying to be Evelyn?" says the man with the cravat. "Some of us were expecting a woman."

"Then my father would say," Evelyn retorts, "you don't know your Waugh."

"Do you want to explain what your friend is talking about?" Rhoda murmurs to Evelyn.

"I helped a fellow called Carl Batchelor write his memoir. He was abused as a child and eventually changed his gender."

"Not by his priest he wasn't," ToM objects.

"By his father who's in prison where I helped to put him."

"Well done to you," Rhoda says as though she hopes the audience will join in.

"The way I saw it," ToM says, "you were more concerned to finger your own father at the trial."

It seems Evelyn has yet to learn how much he has been spied upon. "You were in court, were you?"

"No, it was on Twitter."

"You believe everything you read there."

"I believe her. There's every reason to."

How much was ToM involved with her? What might they have planned together? "What reason's that?" Evelyn demands.

"Who she was." Before Evelyn can respond ToM says "You do seem to get confused about your books."

"Who says so?"

"I think your partner might. She said her name was Lee."

Evelyn suppresses a triumphant laugh. "You've been in contact, then."

"She said it the first time I saw you."

"She won't be telling me about this book. She isn't with me any more."

"Should I say I'm sorry?"

"You can say what you like. She won't hear."

Evelyn senses Rhoda's growing restless, but ToM persists. "Is your other person here?"

"There was never any other person. There's just me."

"I'm not saying you managed to convince anybody you were him. He was the only one who was ever Carla."

"We're back to Carl Batchelor." Evelyn feels as if he's explaining this to himself as well as to the audience. "The last I heard," he says, "Carl was the big man of the district. Celebrated for putting his father away, and it hasn't done his business any harm."

"Are we hearing somebody who wishes they weren't jealous?"

"No," Evelyn says with less force than is gathering inside him, "you're looking at a man who's made a new life for himself."

Rhoda intervenes at last. "I think the gentleman there had a question."

"Just give us a minute." Evelyn feels she wants to silence him. "You haven't said how I'm supposed to be confused," he reminds ToM.

"Maybe you were being polite to your punters. You're here to sell yourself."

"No, just my book, and I'd like to hear how I got it wrong."

"The same as your friend on the front row."

"Tell both of us how incorrect we are."

"The man she talked about isn't the killer. The police think he killed his partner because of all the messages about him he found on her computer, but the detective proves one of the people she was secretly in league with might have, even if nobody can find her. Only the partner says she's still out there and she must have changed her name."

As Evelyn feels his head grow brittle, tightening his mouth so much no words can escape, Rhoda says "I hope nobody's here to spoil the book for others."

"Don't take it so personally, Alex. Try and remember it's only a tale you made up. It can't be healthy to identify so much with whatever you are."

"I'm what you see. That's all I am."

"Whatever you're identifying with in the book," ToM says. "I'd say you could use your editor lady to sort out your language."

"Gentleman in front of you," Rhoda prompts with renewed vigour.

"You must have a lot of ideas in your head to write what you write," the man says, apparently implying a question. Just now Evelyn's skull feels crowded with Lee and his father and Carl, or at any rate with thoughts of them he's anxious to suppress. At least Evelyn is there to deal with questions while he concentrates on keeping order in his head, although who is Evelyn if not him? Eventually Rhoda regains his awareness by saying "And now Evelyn will sign books for anyone who'd like his name in them."

As she ushers him to a table ToM loiters nearby, though without a book. When he doesn't speak, Evelyn says "You could have brought your copy for me to inscribe."

"I wonder what name you'd put in." ToM gives Evelyn no time to answer. "Except you couldn't," he says.

Evelyn resents how uneasy this makes him feel. "Why not?"

"No way you'd have it in your hands." ToM enjoys a pause before explaining "Made of thin air like everybody in it. I got an electronic copy for a good price."

Evelyn almost manages not to ask "How much was that?"

"All I'd ever want to pay for it." As he turns away ToM leaves his answer behind. "Nothing."

Rhoda gives Evelyn a sympathetic look. If it weren't wordless he might be certain the sympathy is meant for him. Presumably she doesn't want to comment within earshot of the queue of customers bearing copies of *Wright She Is*. Why does Evelyn keep hoping to be brought books by Alex Grand? Perhaps it's because the act of signing title pages has grown disconcertingly unfamiliar. However often he writes Evelyn Alexander, he's unable to remember ever having signed either name. Soon enough the queue has gone, and Rhoda brings him a stack of books to autograph for the shop. There are none by Alex Grand, but he sees copies of *When I Was Carla* on a shelf, the edition that someone – probably Kirsty's replacement – revised without credit, leaving it attributed just to Carl and Alex. Evelyn doesn't ask for them, and does his best to ignore them.

"Thanks for your efforts," Rhoda says, which might well refer to compelling his fingers to produce the strange signature.

"So long as people remember my name," Evelyn says.

At first he isn't sure why he's anxious to be alone, and then he thinks he knows. He needs to find out why ToM said he believed L. O'Quent because of who she was. What has she posted now? Perhaps he should wait until he's back at the hotel – his room will be as empty as home – but he wants to know at once. He might as well be by himself, since everyone he passes on the street walled in by display windows is intent on a phone. He finds he can't stop walking as he takes out his. Perhaps he's ensuring nobody else can read the screen.

Kirsty's message is still there. *Good luck with your first date as yourself, Mr Alexander!* He knows he should be grateful to her and the new publisher that has taken them both on, but just now her words are distracting enough to feel like an undefined threat, and he switches hastily to Twitter. He has to slow his headlong progress down as he searches for L. O'Quent, and her latest posting brings him to a stumbling halt and stops his breath. *So Alex Grand and someone I wont name got my husband put in jail, but Ill fight to my death to get him freed for doing something God Almighty knows he never did.*

Whatever sound Evelyn lets out is less than a word. Two young women passing arm in arm stare at him. "That must have been a shock," one says as though she has read the message.

Evelyn hardly knows whether he answers aloud. "I thought it was her."

"Then you'd better tell her you're sorry," the second woman says, and they put their arms around each other as they leave Evelyn behind.

"I can't," he says for just himself to hear. Some things can't be taken back or undone. How did he imagine Lee could have posted recently? He starts walking faster, desperate to outdistance the realisation that none of the names he suspected were Lee. Or could some of them still have been? The thought feels like a refuge, and so does the sight of the hotel beyond yet another street of windows occupied by faceless plastic mimes. He's almost at the doors when he remembers the receptionist may call him by name or ask for it; she did when he checked in. He won't be able to cope with that while he's unsure of himself. In case anyone sees him think better of venturing in he masks his face with a hand as he hastens past the hotel.

In time the shops give way to houses. The streets here are darker, illuminated just by streetlamps and the occasional window extending light across an empty garden. Some gateposts exhibit nameplates too dim for Evelyn to read. Sometimes his presence jerks a housefront alight, reminding him he's being watched. Now and then he thinks he glimpses gaps blinking between curtains as someone hidden spies on him. Soon the gateposts grow unmarked, but the houses stay as large. Doorbells multiply beside front entrances, and the handwritten tags next to the buttons are so smeared by darkness or by weather that Evelyn doubts he would be able to decipher them even if he went close. More than one house beats like a massive heart, and a smell of cannabis reminds him how the drug affected his memories at school or after. No, that was Carla, and Evelyn only encountered it at university. He remembers how it felt as if a barrier was giving way but didn't quite collapse. Since then it has, unless that's his mind.

A streetlamp elevates a broken chalice – the jagged remains of a bulb – towards the lightless sky. Just a solitary lamp ahead is lit, and fails to show him whether the windows of houses are dingily curtained or boarded up. He could imagine that the silence of the buildings has deadened all their lights. The air feels chill and stagnant, as if the district is so dead it has no breath. How long is it since he saw the headlamp beams of a car? The few scattered vehicles parked on the tarmac look derelict, and he can't see whether there's any glass in the windows. He could try touching them, but thrusting a hand through a hole that shouldn't be there would feel like toppling into an abyss, a plunge that's already threatening his mind.

He halts on the illuminated stage beneath the final working streetlamp, where weeds sprout around the foot of the rusty shaft. Beyond it houses recede into darkness and silence. He can't tell whether the street ends there or leads into a section of the district that's darker still. Whose territory might that be? Not Carl Batchelor's, since this isn't even his town – not Malcolm Randall's either, and it can't belong to Evelyn's father. Evelyn concludes that in some way it's his own, but he has to nerve himself to advance, watching his shadow precede him. The shadow fades and grows vague before it's extinguished, and he could fancy the same may befall him. He has to be alone to learn who's here, and once he has established this he may be able to confront what they've done. He's everybody in his head, he tells himself. That's what a writer is. None of these thoughts help him feel less like a child lost by himself in the night as he trudges towards the unknown dark.

ACKNOWLEDGEMENTS

Jenny read it first, as she always does. The eagle-eyed Imogen Howson was the copyeditor, a delight to work with. So was my editor Don D'Auria, as ever. Nick Wells of Flame Tree is a writer's boon, as are all the team – Maria Tissot, Molly Rosevear, Josie Karani, Gillian Whitaker, Jamie-Lee Nardone, Sarah Miniaci....

It had its travels. Sadly, our room at the Potbank Hotel in Stoke-on-Trent offered no area where I could work, and so I lost a day. The first draft fared better at Parque Santiago III in Playa de las Americas on Tenerife, and in the fine Penta Luxury House in Rome. I reread it at the splendid Alma Hotel in Petra on Lesvos preparatory to rewriting.

Reading Robin Wood's novel *Trammel Up The Consequences* let me address some of the more contentious issues, while Steve Mosby's and Alex North's exemplary novels influenced its structure. Sam Cameron established an important London detail.

FLAME TREE PRESS
FICTION WITHOUT FRONTIERS
Award-Winning Authors & Original Voices

Flame Tree Press is the trade fiction imprint of Flame Tree Publishing, focusing on excellent writing in horror and the supernatural, crime and mystery, science fiction and fantasy. Our aim is to explore beyond the boundaries of the everyday, with tales from both award-winning authors and original voices.

•

Other titles available by Ramsey Campbell:
Thirteen Days by Sunset Beach
Think Yourself Lucky
The Hungry Moon
The Influence
The Wise Friend
The Searching Dead

Other horror and suspense titles available include:
Snowball by Gregory Bastianelli
The Haunting of Henderson Close by Catherine Cavendish
The Garden of Bewitchment by Catherine Cavendish
The House by the Cemetery by John Everson
The Devil's Equinox by John Everson
Hellrider by JG Faherty
The Toy Thief by D.W. Gillespie
One By One by D.W. Gillespie
Black Wings by Megan Hart
The Playing Card Killer by Russell James
The Sorrows by Jonathan Janz
The Dark Game by Jonathan Janz
House of Skin by Jonathan Janz
Will Haunt You by Brian Kirk
We Are Monsters by Brian Kirk
Hearthstone Cottage by Frazer Lee
Those Who Came Before by J.H. Moncrieff
Stoker's Wilde by Steven Hopstaken & Melissa Prusi
Ghost Mine by Hunter Shea
Slash by Hunter Shea
The Mouth of the Dark by Tim Waggoner
They Kill by Tim Waggoner

•

Join our mailing list for free short stories, new release details, news about our authors and special promotions:

flametreepress.com